T0022150

When
Things
Get
Dark

ALSO AVAILABLE FROM TITAN BOOKS

A Universe of Wishes: A We Need Diverse Books Anthology
Cursed: An Anthology
Dark Cities: All-New Masterpieces of Urban Terror
Dead Letters: An Anthology of the Undelivered, the Missing, the Returned…
Dead Man's Hand: An Anthology of the Weird West
Exit Wounds
Hex Life
Infinite Stars
Infinite Stars: Dark Frontiers
Invisible Blood
Daggers Drawn
New Fears: New Horror Stories by Masters of the Genre
New Fears 2: Brand New Horror Stories by Masters of the Macabre
Out of the Ruins: The Apocalyptic Anthology
Phantoms: Haunting Tales from the Masters of the Genre
Rogues
Vampires Never Get Old
Wastelands: Stories of the Apocalypse
Wastelands 2: More Stories of the Apocalypse
Wastelands: The New Apocalypse
Wonderland: An Anthology
Escape Pod: The Science Fiction Anthology
Dark Detectives: An Anthology of Supernatural Mysteries

When Things Get Dark

STORIES
INSPIRED BY

Shirley Jackson

Edited by
ELLEN
DATLOW

TITAN BOOKS

When Things Get Dark
Hardback edition ISBN: 9781789097153
Papberback edition ISBN: 9781789097177
E-book edition ISBN: 9781789097160

Published by Titan Books
A division of Titan Publishing Group Ltd
144 Southwark Street, London SE1 0UP
www.titanbooks.com

First edition: September 2022
10 9 8 7 6 5 4 3 2 1

This is a work of fiction. All of the characters, organizations, and events portrayed in this novel are either products of the author's imagination or are used fictitiously. Any resemblance to actual persons, living or dead (except for satirical purposes), is entirely coincidental.

Introduction © Ellen Datlow 2021
Funeral Birds © M. Rickert 2021
For Sale By Owner © Elizabeth Hand 2021
In the Deep Woods; The Light is Different There © Seanan McGuire 2021
A Hundred Miles and a Mile © Carmen Maria Machado 2021
Quiet Dead Things © Cassandra Khaw 2021
Something Like Living Creatures © John Langan 2021
Money of the Dead © Karen Heuler 2021
Hag © Benjamin Percy 2021
Take Me, I Am Free © Joyce Carol Oates 2021
A Trip to Paris © Richard Kadrey 2021
The Party © Paul Tremblay 2021
Refinery Road © Stephen Graham Jones 2021
The Door in the Fence © Jeffrey Ford 2021
Pear of Anguish © Gemma Files 2021
Special Meal © Josh Malerman 2021
Sooner or Later, Your Wife Will Drive Home © Genevieve Valentine 2021
Tiptoe © Laird Barron 2021
Skinder's Veil © Kelly Link 2021

The authors assert the moral right to be identified as the author of their work.

No part of this publication may be reproduced, stored in a retrieval system, or transmitted, in any form or by any means without the prior written permission of the publisher, nor be otherwise circulated in any form of binding or cover other than that in which it is published and without a similar condition being imposed on the subsequent purchaser.

A CIP catalogue record for this title is available from the British Library.

Printed and bound by CPI Group (UK) Ltd, Croydon, CR0 4YY.

Contents

This book is for my mother, Doris Leibowitz Datlow,
who let me read whatever I chose to while growing up.
Thanks, mom.

Introduction

I'VE been a fan of Shirley Jackson's work since I read *We Have Always Lived in the Castle* as a pre-teen. My appreciation of her uncanny fiction perfectly dovetailed with my love of Ray Bradbury, Harlan Ellison, and so many other writers of weird, fantastic, and horrific literature.

July 2019, I attended Readercon, a literary sf/f convention outside of Boston, and got into a discussion about literary influences. Because the Shirley Jackson Awards are given out at Readercon, Jackson's name of course came up, and it occurred to me to edit an anthology of stories influenced by her work—but I never followed through.

Until… a few months later, I met a Titan editor at the World Science Fiction convention in Dublin. Although our initial conversation was about anthologies in general, by November—out of the blue—he and his colleagues suggested I edit an anthology of stories influenced by Jackson. So of course I said yes.

I've come to realize that Jackson's influence has filtered—consciously or subconsciously—into the work of many contemporary fantasy, dark fantasy, and horror writers. Some more obviously than others, so they were the writers I initially approached for submissions. Then other writers, writers I would not have pegged as being influenced by her, surprised me with their interest in contributing to such a book.

What is a Shirley Jackson story? She wrote the charming fictionalized memoir *Life Among the Savage*, a series of collected stories originally published in women's magazines about her family, living in domestic chaos in rural Vermont. But what sticks in most readers' minds today is her uncanny work such as "The Lottery," *The Haunting of Hill House*, and *We Have Always Lived in the Castle*. The brilliant 1963 movie *The Haunting*, based on *The Haunting of Hill House*, brought Jackson a whole new audience.

Her stories, mostly taking place in mid-twentieth-century America, are filled with hauntings, dysfunctional families and domestic pain; simmering rage, loneliness, suspicion of outsiders; sibling rivalry and women trapped psychologically and/or by the supernatural. They explore the dark undercurrent of suburban life during that time period.

For this anthology, I did not want stories riffing on Jackson's own. I did not want stories about her or her life. What I wanted was for the contributors to distill the essence of Jackson's work into their own work, to reflect her sensibility. To embrace the strange and the dark underneath placid exteriors. There's a comfort in ritual and rules, even while those rules may constrict the self so much that those who must follow them can slip into madness.

To, as Jackson said, "use fear, to take it and comprehend it and make it work."

And this is what the contributors have done.

Some of the stories herein take place—or end up—in that most domestic of rooms, the dining room, and they center on meals.

Others feature uncanny encounters with ghosts or the inexplicable: misfits finding comfort in one another despite the inevitable destruction their relationship engenders on themselves and others outside their circle of safety; family members turning on each other; women trapped by expectations; people punished for being outside the norm.

So here for your enjoyment are stories that I believe provide the flavor of some of Shirley Jackson's best fiction. And I would like to think that Jackson, were she still alive, might recognize and appreciate what she birthed.

Funeral Birds

M. Rickert

LENORE had carefully chosen what to wear but felt dissatisfied. She always wanted to be a woman who appeared chic and vaguely kick-ass in black when, in fact, she looked like a half-plucked crow. She reached back to pull down the difficult zipper then drew the dress overhead, momentarily trapped, inhaling the unpleasant scent of her body odor until, with a gasp, she was free, her hair risen in static revolt as she spun on her stockinged feet to the closet. Panic rising, she reached for the hibiscus dress, but what would they think about a woman who arrived late to a funeral in luau attire? She chose the periwinkle instead. The elastic around the waist had grown tight in recent years and the out-of-date Peter Pan collar was much too young for her, but she loved the pattern of demure blue flowers scattered across a cream background. It had been the first thing she bought after her husband died all those years ago. When she wore it she liked to imagine someone had thrown flowers in celebration of her independence, as a counterpoint to the ridiculous rice that had marked the wedding and caused a bird to peck at her head as if trying to drill some sense into her.

Wondering if she would ever like herself again, she fixed her lipstick, brushed her hair, and slipped into the black heels she'd purchased special for the occasion, hoping that, in the right light, they might look dark blue. She dumped the contents from the black purse into her everyday bag. It was beige with brown trim, a gold clasp, and very serviceable. When she finally left, ten minutes later than targeted, she told herself everything would be all right.

"You. Can. Do. This," she said in the car, flicking the radio on and almost ruining everything by arriving with her windows down, Van Halen blaring loud enough for several mourners standing at the church door to turn around and look.

It wasn't until after the long service (why did Lenore always forget how Catholics droned on?) when the priest stepped in front of the altar to relay the family's invitation to the congregation that she remembered the tuna casserole forgotten in her refrigerator. Under other circumstances this mistake might have caused her to feel defeated, but by that point her spirit was quite elevated. Lenore hadn't realized how much she dreaded seeing the casket until she discovered there was none. A simple wooden crate the size of a tissue box rested on a pedestal in the nave. Delores had been cremated.

One of Lenore's favorite things about funerals was the gathering afterward, sometimes spent in church basements but often at a relative's house, eating potato salad and pickles and pastries all off the same plate. She enjoyed finding a quiet place to sit, listening to the murmured voices, pretending it was her house, and her suffering. The usual price of admission for such solace was attendance at the burial, but Delores's daughter had other plans for her mother's ashes, which suited Lenore just fine.

The daughter's house was a brick bungalow with a suspiciously tidy garden, likely managed by a landscaper. Lenore sat in the car for a few minutes, watching, but while an occasional person arrived with a covered dish or casserole, many did not. She used the rearview mirror to examine her lips, which always failed to please under close inspection. What was it Delores had said? "You don't look like someone who could keep a secret," and then Lenore had said, "Well, neither do you."

"I can keep a secret," Lenore whispered to the hot air in the car. She was never sure what happened after death, but suspected it wasn't the end of everything. "I hope you know," she added, just in case, "friendship never dies."

She opened the car door, sucking in the fresh air like a person coming out of sedation. She did not lock it. Anyone could tell it wasn't necessary in that neighborhood; besides, people would be coming and going for a while, though, coincidentally, she walked alone up to the house, the click of her heels like the tap of an insistent woodpecker ricocheting off the trees, picket fence, and stone walls of suburbia.

When she stepped from the dark foyer through the cozy living room populated by mourners into the dining room with its resplendent spread of glistening strawberries and green salad in glass bowls, assorted cheeses and chocolate cake arranged on pretty china atop a lace tablecloth, Delores's daughter (wearing a figure-flattering dress the color of eggplant) stopped in mid-sentence, eyes wide, to gasp Lenore's name, and she was sure she'd made a terrible mistake, misjudged the situation entirely, but the woman walked over to grasp the hands Lenore extended in defensive reflex.

"I'm so glad you came. I want to thank you for everything you did for my mother."

"Jane," Lenore began, embarrassed. Clearly others were listening but pretending they weren't, the conversational hum reduced to a false tenor.

"Jean."

"I'm sorry."

Jean was one of those close talkers, moving in so near to Lenore she worried about her own breath and the onions in her morning omelet.

"I heard you'd been at the church. I hoped you would come."

Lenore glanced away from Jean's earnest blue eyes (quite like her mother's) to survey the room. Who? Who reported her attendance? She didn't know any of these people. Only one stunning woman with severely dark hair and brutal red lips was dressed in black and, judging by how well it suited her, probably owned no other color. No, it wasn't the fact that Lenore hadn't worn the funeral dress that set her apart. It was something else. An aspect she recognized from other occasions but never knew how to remedy. The others looked like they lived in the same country where she was merely a tourist.

"It gives me such comfort to know she had you as a nurse."

"Home health care aid," Lenore said, squeezing Jean's hands slightly, which prompted release.

"Excuse me?"

"I'm not a nurse."

Jean cocked her head slightly.

Like a bird with a worm, Lenore thought. "I'm sorry," she began, interrupted by a large woman who reminded her of Julia Child stepping between them to offer condolences. After a few awkward moments of being ignored, Lenore backed away to pick up a plate from the table she strived to circle with an air of polite engagement. In reality, she felt a holiday level of excitement at all the food before her, pleased she'd forgotten the tuna casserole, which would have looked out of place, like cat food amongst the splendor.

Lenore, paper plate in one hand and wine glass in the other, meandered through the living room, a small TV room, and a very nice kitchen remodeled in silver and white, almost blinding after all the wood. She was just about to perch on the window seat, vacated as she watched, when she noticed another door, down a narrow hallway past the bathroom. The closed door did not suggest invitation but Lenore was not deterred. After all, she was used to breaching private spaces in her work.

An office: desk and chair faced into the room framed by a large window, the kind with glass panes divided by wood as throughout the rest of the house, though this was probably modern. A little addition, Lenore guessed; nicely done.

She set plate and wine glass on a table beside the large upholstered chair in the corner. There were many lovely elements in the room. A lamp with Tiffany-inspired shade, a large rainbow-colored paperweight on the desk (which Lenore intended to investigate once she finished eating), a few baubles on the shelves propped in front of the books: a blue glass bird, a shape carved in wood—vaguely suggestive of the female form—a rock.

The hydrangeas in bloom beyond the window had attracted several butterflies and Lenore found herself torn, while she ate, between staring dreamily at them or studying the cozy furnishings around her when the door suddenly opened and the daughter stepped into the room, her features—in profile—sharp. Lenore made a little clearing-throat noise and Jean turned, hand over her heart.

"My God," she said.

"Sorry," said Lenore. "I just—"

"Oh, no need to apologize." Jean swatted the air. "I didn't realize you were in here. These are such tedious events. I'm sure you attend far too many."

"Well…" Lenore decided not to explain. The truth was she rarely went to the funerals. Delores was special.

"Actually," Jean said, "this might be divine intervention. Do you believe in that sort of thing?"

Lenore shrugged. She'd learned long ago it was best not to engage in theological speculation. Jean, not bothering to wait for an answer, walked over to the only other chair in the room. It was on wheels, yet difficult to maneuver through the tight space between desk and wall. Watching her struggle, Lenore wondered if she should offer to help, annoyed to think of having to do so on her day off. At just that moment, however, Jean managed to free the chair, which she pushed across the carpet to position in front of Lenore, successfully blocking her only avenue of escape.

"I was hoping we could talk."

Lenore, who had the wine glass poised at her lips, took a long last gulp, thereby covering much of her expression, buying a little time to think before she set the glass on the table, then picked it up to place a napkin there as a coaster though she saw a ring had already formed. She hated how easily she ruined everything and, turning to face Jean, fully expected to be confronted with a scowl. But the woman lifted her hands as if to reach across the space between them, though they simply hovered in the air before landing in her lap like baby birds unaccustomed to flight.

"I want to ask you about my mother's last day. Was she at peace? You can tell me the truth. I can take it," she said, her incongruous smile suggesting she could not.

"Delores and I developed a friendship."

"How nice," Jean said, then pursed her lips.

"It was an ordinary day. She went down for her nap and I took out the garbage and when I got back I looked in on her and she was dead."

"Just like that?"

For a brief moment the memory fluttered. Like one of those beetles you think you squashed but didn't. Delores struggling against the pillow, her arms flailing, the noises she made.

"My mother was not an easy woman," Jean said. "You don't have to pretend otherwise. I'm glad she had your company. But I know how difficult she could be."

"No, really. We were friends."

Jean stood up and began pushing the chair across the carpet.

Lenore had not realized she'd been holding her breath until, exhaling in relief, her ribs pressed against the confined elastic of the dress and she felt a button pop at the back.

With a grunt of annoyance, Jean abandoned the uncooperative chair to walk around the desk where she opened a drawer, removing what looked like a checkbook.

"This is just a small token," she said, not looking up while she wrote.

"Oh, no," said Lenore, horrified.

"Nonsense. I know how hard you people work," Jean said, walking briskly back to Lenore. "Take it. Buy yourself something nice."

Her glance might have lingered just a little too long on Lenore's dress. The woman had no way of knowing, of course, but Lenore felt like the exchange was vile, as though she were some kind of hired killer.

Jean bent her knees slightly to place the check in Lenore's lap, amongst the primroses. "I'm so glad we had this time to talk. I wish I could just hide in here with you," she said.

"Yes, of course," said Lenore.

"Stay as long as you like, but close the door tightly when you leave. Guests really aren't supposed to be in here."

Lenore kept her expression placid as she nodded, though she did understand she was being reprimanded. She didn't allow herself to smile until she was alone again, looking at the amount written on the check before tucking it into her purse. She stood up and tossed the paper plate with blobs and smears of food on it into the small trashcan beside the desk, but left the wine glass on the table.

As if her hand worked without any direction from her mind, it plucked the glass bird from the bookshelf as she passed, dropped it into her bag, then closed the gold clasp.

The party had diminished quite a bit during Lenore's little break, making her presence more obvious, yet she passed through the rooms like a ghost, unhindered by anyone. Sometimes when she had that effect on others it bothered her, but this time it made her feel powerful.

Lenore frowned as she parked in front of her place. It was one apartment in a building of four she had been proud to call home for nearly a decade. What difference did it make that there were no hydrangeas outside her window?

She hurried up the walk, in case anyone might be watching and notice how her dress gaped at the back where the button had popped. As soon as she stepped inside she locked the door and kicked off her shoes. They were too tight. It would take a few more wears for them to fit comfortably. She strained to unbutton the dress, and heard it rip before she stepped out of it. She would buy a new one, she thought as she walked down the hall to draw a bath, pouring into the stream a packet of lavender bubble powder one of her clients (not Delores) had given her in a Christmas basket the previous December. While the water ran, she took the tuna casserole out of the refrigerator and put it in the oven. She really hadn't eaten that much, and figured she'd be hungry soon enough.

She opened the purse, reaching inside for the bird made of blue glass, which fit in the palm of her hand. Lovely. One of the nicest things she owned. It deserved a position of honor, not to be stuffed on some shelf. She surveyed her living space from the other side of the breakfast counter she rarely sat at, the stools most often used as dumping grounds. After the daughter's lovely house, the small living room furnished with used pieces Lenore found by the side of the road, or purchased secondhand, seemed bleak.

She placed the bird on the coffee table in front of the sagging couch, then hurried back to the bathroom, arriving in time to turn the water off before causing a flood. She took a long soak until the scent of tuna noodle casserole overpowered the lavender, and her stomach growled.

"Maybe I'll get a new robe," she said, wrapping herself in the old terry cloth one she'd owned for years.

She ate her supper on the couch, only half paying attention to the real housewives on TV, fighting again. The glass bird was so pretty it shamed everything else.

"Maybe I'll buy a new table. And a lamp," she said. "I liked your daughter's lamp."

Lenore fell asleep on the couch, as sometimes happened, awoken by a loud commercial for a frying pan. She shut the TV off but left the light on, as was her practice, to deter any intruder. Once in bed she wondered if she might spend the money on a new mattress, which would be wise if not particularly exciting, debating this until she fell asleep for an indeterminate amount of time before being aroused by the noxious aroma of tuna noodle casserole mingled with lavender. Lenore had always been sensitive to strong odors.

Thinking she would turn the stove fan on, she padded to the kitchen, stopping in her tracks when she saw the back of Delores's head. Dead Delores. Cremated Delores. Sitting on the couch.

Lenore walked slowly, pausing on her way to grab the tea kettle from the stove, only then noticing the casserole on the counter. She could have sworn she put it away, though clearly she hadn't.

"Not sure what you plan to do with that kettle. I'm already dead," said Delores, sitting with a bowl of tuna noodle casserole in her lap.

"What are you doing here?" Lenore asked.

Delores gave her one of her looks. The one that meant "I'm just going to pretend I don't notice you being stupid," as she stabbed chunks of tuna noodle casserole with her fork. "Sit down, Lenore."

Lenore did as she was told, backing into the chair she'd purchased from Goodwill a few years before. It had only been ten dollars, but was so uncomfortable she rarely sat in it.

"Why are you here?"

"I think you know the answer," Delores said, drawing fork to her mouth and chewing, though, after a while, unmasticated tuna and noodles dropped out. "Ah shit," she said.

"Do you need help?"

"You know you're stuck with me now, don't you?" Delores asked, making another stab at the bowl in her lap.

"You should go to the light," said Lenore.

Delores snorted. A noodle flew from her mouth and landed on the coffee table beside the glass bird.

"So, I guess this makes you a serial murderer."

"No it doesn't," Lenore said, insulted.

"Yeah. It does. You killed your husband and then you killed me."

"Twenty years apart," Lenore said. "And I only killed you cause you promised not to tell anyone about it. I thought we were sharing secrets. I thought you were my friend."

"I thought you were my friend!" Delores shouted. "Who did I tell? I told no one. And this is the thanks I get."

"I saw how you looked at me."

"Give me a break. Can't a person be surprised?"

"You were going to tell someone."

"Was not."

"Don't lie, Delores."

"Your tuna noodle casserole tastes like piss."

"Well, that's cause you're dead. You aren't even chewing right."

Delores looked at the bowl in her lap and laughed. It was a quick bark of a sound, slightly feral, quite different from when she was alive.

"Please," Lenore said. "Try to understand my position."

Delores glared at Lenore.

"You should buy that new mattress," she said. "And probably a bigger bed. Cause I'm not going anywhere without you."

Lenore, who would not have believed it possible of herself (because she was not a psychopath), leapt from her chair to swing the tea kettle in a wide arc at the old woman's head. Though she couldn't have felt a thing—she was dead, after all—she looked up at Lenore with horror, raising her bony arms to block the blow. There was no blood, and no impact. In frustration, Lenore slammed the kettle down, shattering the glass bird.

She stared at it and tried not to cry.

"You know what I just remembered?" Dolores asked. "In all the excitement I never got to tell you my best secret."

"Oh. Right," said Lenore. "That's why you're here."

"Yep. I came all the way from heaven to help you."

"To help me?"

"That's right, Lenore. Cause your tuna noodle casserole tastes like shit."

"Oh, for God's sake, Delores—"

"You need to put some crunch into it."

"You mean potato chips? I already know about that, Delores. Everyone knows about that. I just forget to buy them. Okay? You can go now."

"Not potato chips. Broken glass. Like what you got right there. You just try it and see. We learn about this stuff after being dead. I know things now."

"That's ridiculous. Don't be ridiculous," Lenore said, but she carefully swept the shards into an empty pickle jar, which she set in the cupboard beside the salt and pepper shakers, the lid closed tight, turning around to discover that Delores had disappeared; gone back to heaven or hell, or the little box her daughter had put her in. Lenore sealed the aluminum foil over the remains of the casserole, which she placed in the refrigerator, checked that the front door was locked, and went to bed, tossing and turning throughout the night.

In the morning she called the agency to tell them she was sick then drove to the mattress store, where she chose a comfortable queen-sized mattress, and a new bed frame. But, of course, as Lenore was well aware, any solution creates new problems: she needed queen-sized sheets and comforter as well. On the way home from the mall, she stopped at the market for noodles and canned tuna. A woman stared at Lenore as she loaded her cart and said, "Looks like someone has a craving for tuna noodle casserole. Don't forget the chips," and the checkout lady said something snide about how much tuna could one person eat, but Lenore ignored both of them. She wasn't sure what had gotten into her, but she felt free in a way she hadn't since buying the primrose dress all those years ago, no longer interested in accommodating everyone else's preferences or fighting her own unreasonable impulses. If she wanted to eat tuna noodle casserole every night for the rest of her life, she would. Groceries loaded in her car, she paused in the parking lot to stare at a flock of birds circling overhead, so distant she could not identify them.

For Sale by Owner

Elizabeth Hand

I CAN'T remember exactly when I first started entering houses while the owners weren't around. Before my children were born, so that's at least thirty-five years ago. It started in the fall, when I used to walk my old English sheepdog, Winston, down one of the camp roads on Taylor Pond. That road is more built up now with new summer houses and even a few year-round homes, but back then there were only two houses that were occupied all year. The rest, maybe a dozen all together, were camps or cottages, uninsulated and very small, certainly by today's standards. They straggled along the lakefront, some in precarious stages of decay, the others neatly kept up with shingles or board-and-batten siding. These days you couldn't build a structure that close to the waterfront, but eighty or ninety years ago, no one cared about things like that.

Anyway, Winston and I would amble along the dirt road for an hour or two at a time, me kicking at leaves, Winston snuffling at chipmunks and red squirrels. This would be after I got off work at the CPA office where I answered the phone, or on weekends. The pond was beautiful—a lake, really, they just called it a pond—and sometimes I'd watch loons or otters in the water, or a bald eagle overhead. I never saw another living soul except for Winston. No cars ever went by—those two year-round homes were at the head of the road.

I'm not sure why I decided one day just to walk up to one of the camps and see if the door was open. Probably I was looking at the water, and the screened-in porch, and got curious about who lived inside. Although to be honest, I really wasn't interested in who lived there. I just wanted to see what the inside looked like.

I tried the screen door. It opened, of course—who locks their screen door? Then I tried the knob on the inner door and it opened, too. I told Winston to wait for me, and went inside.

It looked pretty much like any camp does, or did. Small rooms, knotty pine walls, exposed beams. One story, with a tiny bathroom and a metal shower stall. Tiny kitchen with a General Electric fridge that must've dated to the early 1960s, its door held open by a dishrag wrapped around the handle. Two small bedrooms with two beds apiece.

The living room was the nicest, with big old mullioned windows, a door that opened onto the screened porch. The kind of furniture you find in camps—secondhand stuff, or chairs and side tables demoted from the primary residence. A big coffee table; shelves holding boxes of games and puzzles, paperbacks that had swollen with damp. Stone fireplace with a small pile of camp wood beside it. On the walls, framed Venus paint-by-numbers paintings of deer or mountains.

Camps had a particular smell in those days. Maybe they still do. Mildew, coffee, cigarette smoke, woodsmoke, Comet. It's a nice smell, even the mildew if it's not too strong. I spent a minute or two gazing at the lake through the windows. Then I left.

The next camp was pretty much the same thing, though with two canoes by the water instead of one, the dock pulled out alongside them. The door was unlocked. There were more games here, also a wrapped-up volleyball net and a plastic Whiffle Ball bat. Children's bathing suits hanging in the bathroom. Nicer furniture, scuffed up but newer-looking, blond wood. The chairs and table and couch looked like they'd been bought as a set. The view here wasn't as open as at the first house, because some tamaracks had grown too close to the windows. But it was still nice, with the children's artwork displayed on the walls, and a framed photograph of Mount Cadillac.

I made sure the door closed securely behind me and continued walking. Winston stopped chasing squirrels and seemed content to stay beside me. I idly plucked leaves and sticks from his tangled fur, making a mental note to give him a thorough brushing when I got home, maybe a bath.

For the next hour or so it was more of the same. Only about half of the camps were unlocked, though all the screened porch doors were open. In those cases, I'd check out the view from the porch, angling among stacked-up wicker or plastic furniture, folded lawn chairs, life preservers and deflated water toys. On one porch, the door to the living room was open, so I got to take a look at that.

There was a pleasant sameness to the decor of all these places, if you could call it decor, and an even more reassuring sense of difference between how people spruced up their little havens. A tiny, handmade camp that consisted of only a single room had fishing gear in the corner, a huge moose rack over the door, and a six-point deer rack on the outhouse. In the neighboring shingle cottage, almost every surface was covered by something crocheted or handwoven or knit or quilted, and the air smelled strongly of cigarettes and potpourri.

I took stock of each place, and considered how I might move around the furniture, or what trees I'd cut down. Once or twice I recognized the name on the door, or a face in a faded family photograph. I never opened any drawers or cabinets or took anything. I wouldn't have dreamed of that. Like I said, I just wanted to see what they looked like inside.

Finally, we reached the end of the camp road. Winston was tired and the sun was getting low, besides which I never walked any farther than this. So we turned round and walked back to the head of the camp road, then onto the paved road, where I'd left my old Volvo parked on the grass. Winston hopped into the back and we went home. I spent about an hour brushing him but didn't bother with the bath. He really hated baths.

For the rest of that autumn, I'd occasionally walk along different camp roads in town and do the same thing. By the time Thanksgiving arrived, my curiosity had been sated. As the days grew darker and colder, I walked Winston close to home. A year later I married Brandon, and a year after that our daughter was born.

By the time I started walking again, a decade had passed. The old dog had died, and we never got another. I walked with other women now, the mothers of my children's classmates. I grew close to one in particular, Rose. We began walking when our boys were nine or ten years old, and continued doing so for almost thirty years. Like me, Rose liked to walk along the camp roads, where there were few cars, though in summer the mosquitoes were terrible, and over the decades we learned to be increasingly mindful of ticks.

Rose was small and cheerful and talked a lot. Local gossip, family news. Sometimes we'd rant about politics. Our friend Helen joined us occasionally. She walked faster than Rose and I, so there'd be less conversation when the three of us were together. Over the years, Rose, like me, had stopped coloring her hair. I went mousy grey but Rose's grew in the color of a new nickel. Helen continued to dye her hair, though it wasn't as blond as it had been. Our husbands were all friendly, and the six of us often got together for dinners or bonfires or the Super Bowl.

So it was odd that I had known Rose for almost a quarter century before I learned that she, too, liked exploring empty houses. We were walking on the dirt road that runs along Lagawala Lake. It was late fall, and the weather had been unseasonably cold for about a week. There were few houses along the camp road, all clustered at the far end, all vacated till the following summer—we knew that because we'd gotten in the habit of peering through the windows. I never mentioned my old habit, though once or twice, when Rose wasn't looking, I'd test the door of a cottage. But everyone kept their houses locked now.

About halfway down the road someone from out of state had bought a huge parcel of the lakefront, where for the last ten years they'd been building a vast compound. We both knew some of the contractors who'd worked there at some point—stonemasons, builders, roofers, electricians, plumbers, heating and cooling experts, carpenters—and they told us what was inside the various Shingle-style mansions and outbuildings that had been erected. An indoor swimming pool, a billiards room, a separate building devoted to a screening room with a bar designed to look like an English pub. A miniature golf course with bronze statues at every hole. The caretaker had his own Craftsman cottage, bigger than my house.

Most extravagant of all was an outdoor carousel housed in its own building. Electronically controlled curtains kept us from ever being able to see what this looked like inside. There was also a hideous, two-story high, blaze-orange cast-resin sculpture of a plastic duck. In nearly a decade, we never saw any sign that someone had occupied the house or property, other than the caretaker.

One winter day early in the construction, when the mansion had been closed in and roofed but none of the interior work had been done, Rose and I halted to stare up at it. Work had stopped for the winter.

"That is a disgusting waste of money," I said.

"You're not kidding. They're heating it, too."

"Heating it? The windows aren't even in."

"I know. But the heat's blasting inside."

"How do you know?"

"Cause I've been in a bunch of times. The doors are all open. Want to see?"

I glanced down the road, toward the caretaker's house. A thick stand of evergreens screened us from it. Besides, if anyone caught us, what would they do? We were two respectable middle-aged ladies who'd served on town committees and contributed to dozens of bake sales.

"Sure," I said, and we went inside.

It was warm as a hotel room in there. Tens of thousands of dollars' worth of tools and materials had been left in the various rooms—electrical wiring, sheetrock, tools, shopvacs, you name it. We wandered around for a while, but I lost interest fairly quickly. There were no furnishings, and the lake view was nice but not spectacular. I also wondered if the owners had installed some kind of security system.

"We better go," I said. "They might have CCTV or something."

Rose shrugged. "Yeah, okay. But it's fun, isn't it?"

"Yeah," I said, and we returned to the road. After few seconds I added, "I used to do that sometimes, on the camp roads. Go into houses when no one was there."

"No!" Rose exclaimed so loudly that at first I thought she was horrified. "Me too! For years."

"Really?"

"Sure. No one ever used to lock their doors. It was fun. I never *did* anything."

"Me neither."

After that, we'd compare notes whenever we passed a house we had entered. Rose knew more about the owners than I did, but then she knew more people in town than me. Sometimes, when Helen walked with us, we'd forget and mention a camp we'd both been inside.

"How do you know these people?" Helen asked me.

"I don't," I said. "I just like looking in their windows."

"Me too," said Rose.

Last October, the three of us took a long afternoon walk, not on one of the camp roads but a sparsely populated paved road that runs from our village center up the neighboring mountainside. We call it Mount Kilden; it's actually a hill. We drove in my car to where there's a pull-out and parked, then started to walk. Helen with her long legs strode a good ten feet in front of Rose and me, and looked over her shoulder to shout her contributions to our conversation.

"If you want to talk you're going to have to slow down," I finally yelled.

Helen halted, shaking her head. "You both should walk with Tim— I have to run to keep up with him."

I said, "If I ran I'd have a heart attack."

Helen laughed. "Good thing I know CPR," she said, and once more started walking like she was in a race.

The paved road up Mount Kilden runs for about four miles, then does a dogleg and turns into an old gravel road that continues for another mile or two before it ends abruptly in a pull-out surrounded by towering pines. A rough trail ran from the pull-out to the top of Mount Kilden, with a spectacular view of the lakes, Agganangatt River, and the real mountains to the north. The trail was used by locals who made a point of not telling people from away about it. It had been a decade since I'd walked that path.

A hundred and fifty years ago, most of this was farmland, including a blueberry barren. Now woodland has overtaken the fields: tall maples and oaks, birch and beech, white pine, hemlock, impassable thorny blackberry vines. The autumn leaves were at their peak, gold and scarlet and yellow against a sky so blue it made my eyes hurt. Goldenrod and aster and Queen Anne's lace bloomed along the side of the road. Somewhere far away a dog barked, but up here you couldn't hear a single car. Our pace had slackened, and even Helen slowed to admire the trees.

"It's so beautiful up here," she said. "We should walk here more often. Why don't we walk here more often?"

I groaned. "Maybe because I'd have a heart attack every time we did?"

"We can go back if you want," said Rose, and patted my arm.

"No, I'm fine. I'll just walk slowly."

Within a few minutes, we all started to walk more slowly. The woods had retreated from the road here: we could see more sky, which gave the impression we were much higher than we really were. Old stone walls snaked among the trees, marking boundaries between farms and homesteads that had long since disappeared. Nothing remained of the houses except for cellar holes, and the trees that had been planted by their front doors—always a pair, one lilac and one apple tree, the lilacs now forming dense stands of grey and withered green, the apple trees still bearing fruit.

I picked one. It tasted sweet and slightly winey—a cider apple. I finished it and tossed the core into the woods, and hurried after the others.

"Look," said Helen, pointing to where the trees thinned out ever more, just past a curve in the dirt road. "Don't you love that house? When Tim and I used to hike up here, we always said we'd buy it and live there someday."

"We did too!" exclaimed Rose in delight. "Hank loved that house. *I* loved that house."

They both glanced at me, and I nodded. "I never came here with Brandon, but oh yes. It's a beautiful house."

Laughing, Rose broke into an almost-run. Helen followed and quickly passed her. After a minute or two, I caught up with them.

A broad lawn swept down to the road. The grass looked like it hadn't been mowed in a few weeks, but it hadn't been neglected to the point where weeds or saplings had taken root. Brilliant crimson leaves carpeted it, from an immense maple tree that towered in the middle of the lawn. Thirty or so feet behind the tree stood a house. Not an old farmhouse or Cape Cod, which you'd expect to find here, and not a Carpenter Gothic, either. This was a Federal-style house, almost square and two stories tall, with lots of big windows, white clapboard siding, and two brick chimneys. You don't see a whole lot of Federal houses in this area, and I'd guess this one was built in the early 1800s. There was no sign of a barn or other outbuildings. No garage, though that's not so unusual. We don't have a garage, either. Blue and purple asters grew along its front walls, and the tall grey stalks of daylilies that had gone by.

The house appeared vacant—no curtains in the windows, no lights—but it had been kept up. The white paint was weathered but not too bad. The granite foundation hadn't settled. The chimneys were intact and didn't seem in need of repointing. I walked up to the front door and tried the knob.

It turned easily in my hand. I looked back to catch Rose's eye, but she was heading around the side of the house. A moment later I heard her cry out.

"Marianne, look!"

I left the door and walked to the side of the house, where Rose pointed at a sign leaning against the wall.

FOR SALE BY OWNER.

"It's for sale," she said, almost reverently.

"It *was* for sale." Helen picked up the sign and hefted it—handmade of plywood painted white and nailed to a stake. "They probably took it off the market after Labor Day."

I stepped closer to examine it. The words *FOR SALE BY OWNER* were neatly painted in black letters. Beneath, someone had scrawled a phone number in Magic Marker. The numbers had blurred together from the rain. I didn't recognize the area code.

"I wonder what they're asking for it," said Helen, and leaned the sign back against the house.

"A lot," I said. Real estate here has gone through the roof in the last ten years.

"Well, I don't know." Rose stepped back and stared up at the roofline, straight as though drawn by a ruler on the sky. "It's kind of far from everything."

"There is no 'far from anything' in this town," I retorted. "And people who move here, they want privacy."

"Then why hasn't it sold?"

"If the owner's selling it, it might not be listed anywhere. Nobody drives up here except locals. And the season's over, it's off the market now anyway. That's why they took down the sign." I gestured to the front of the house. "The door's open. Want to look inside?"

"Of course," said Rose, and grinned.

Helen frowned. "That's trespassing."

"Only if we get caught," I replied.

We headed to the front door. I pushed it open and we went inside, entering a small anteroom that would be a mudroom if anyone lived there, and cluttered with boots and coats and gear. Now it was empty and spotless. We stepped cautiously through another doorway, into what must have been the living room.

"Wow." Rose's eyes widened. "Look at this."

I blinked, shading my eyes. Bright as it had been outside, here it was even brighter. Sunlight streamed through the large windows. The hardwood floors were so highly polished they looked as though someone had spilled maple syrup on them. The ceiling was high, the walls unadorned with moldings or wainscoting, and painted white. I walked to one wall and laid my hand against it, the surface smooth and slightly warm to the touch. I rapped it gently with my knuckles. Plaster, not drywall, and smooth as a piece of glass. Not what I'd expect to find in a house this old, where the plaster should be cracked or pitted. It must have been refinished not long ago.

I turned to Rose and Helen. "Someone's spent a lot of money here."

"It doesn't look like anyone's ever been here," replied Helen. She was crouched in one corner. "Not for ages. Look—this is the only electrical outlet in this room, and it must be almost a hundred years old."

Helen and Rose wandered off. I could hear them laughing and exclaiming in amazement at what they found: an old-fashioned hand pump in the kitchen sink, water closet rather than a modern toilet. I stayed in the living room, enchanted by the light, which had an odd clarity. An empty room in a house this old should be filled with dust motes, but the sun pouring through the windows appeared almost solid. You hear about golden sunlight: this really did look solid, so much so that I took a step into the center of the room and swept my hand through the broad sunbeam that bisected the empty space. I felt nothing except a faint warmth.

"We're going upstairs!" Rose yelled from another room.

I left the living room with reluctance—the days had grown shorter, soon it would be dark and that nice sunlight would be gone—but the hallway was nearly as bright, illuminated by glass sidelights beside the door and a half-moon fanlight above it. A single round window halfway up the steps made it easy to find my way to where Helen and Rose waited on the second-floor landing.

"I'm ready to make an offer," Rose announced, and laughed. "Did you see how big those rooms downstairs are?"

I nodded. "You'd have to modernize everything."

"Oh, I know. I'm just daydreaming. But it's all so beautiful."

"I can't believe what good shape it's in," said Helen, whose husband was a carpenter. "I wonder who's kept it up? I mean, someone can't have been living here—no appliances."

"Big pantry, though," said Rose.

She turned and walked down the hall. Three doors opened onto it, each leading into a bedroom. The largest overlooked the road we'd walked up, with a heart-stopping view of trees in full autumn flame and the distant line of mountains. The other two rooms were smaller but still good-sized, bigger than our master bedroom at home. One looked up the slope of Mount Kilden, to the rocky outcropping up top called the Maidencliff, for a young girl who died there in the 1880s. She'd been picnicking with her family in the blueberry barren when her hat blew off, and she tumbled to her death as she chased after it. In the other bedroom, you had a view of Lagawala Lake, which from here looked much larger than it did when Rose and I walked along the camp roads there.

"This would be my room," I said, though no one was listening. The three of us went from one room to the next then back again, passing each other in the hallway and sharing observations.

"No bathroom—what would that have been like?"

"No heat, either."

"There's a floor register in the main bedroom. I guess the kids would just freeze."

"They would probably have been two or three to a bed, back then," said Helen, who had six grown or nearly-grown children. "That might have helped."

"No lights, though." I looked at the ceiling. "It would have been dark at night."

"Yeah, but they'd have candles and lanterns and things like that. And people went to bed early then, too. Farmers, they have to get up at like three a.m."

"I don't think this was a farm," I said, and peered out the window. "No fields or barns."

Rose shook her head. "They could have owned all this land—it could all have been farms."

"Maybe," I said.

But I doubted it. Every farmhouse I've ever been in was sprawling and slightly ramshackle and comfortably messy—low-beamed ceilings, wood floors scuffed and uneven, walls dinged-up where kids had kicked them and showing evidence of having been painted and wallpapered numerous times over the years. The rooms opened one onto another and tended to be small, with few windows. And once they could afford it, farmers usually adopted new technology—electricity, milking machines, anything that would make their lives easier.

Electric lights and outlets would have marred the clean lines and planes of this house. I've been in plenty of old houses that have been up-to-dated, as the old timers put it, and ruined in the process.

Not this one. The bedrooms seemed to be almost perfectly square. Even the upstairs hallway felt square, though of course that was impossible. This symmetry could have felt restrictive, even claustrophobic. Instead, the plain white walls and warm-toned floors and carefully ordered doorways made me feel not calm, exactly, but quietly exhilarated. Like back when my husband Brandon and I would go to see a movie in the theater and we knew beforehand that it would be good and make us forget about everything else for a few hours. The house made me feel something like that.

"You know what else is weird?" asked Rose. "The way it smells."

"It smells fine." Helen glanced at me. "I don't smell any mildew, do you, Marianne?"

"No," I said. "But she's right, that's what's weird—it doesn't smell like mildew, or mice, or anything like that. And it doesn't smell like paint, either, or polyurethane on the floors."

We all took a final circuit of the three rooms, then trooped downstairs. Rose walked over to the brick fireplace—a Rumford fireplace, its angled sides designed to throw heat back into the living room. The hearth was immaculately clean, and so was the cast-iron bake oven set into the bricks. Rose opened and closed the oven door with a soft *clang*.

"You know what we should do?" she asked, and looked at us expectantly. "We should have a sleepover here."

I said, "I'm in."

Helen hesitated. "Someone would see us. People are still hiking up here."

"They're not hiking at night," said Rose.

"No one would see us," I said. "If we just have flashlights, no one's going to notice."

Helen mulled this over. "It's going to be cold."

"It's cold in the state park lean-tos when we camp there in the fall."

"But there we can have a fire."

"Don't be a wuss," said Rose. "We can tell the boys we're having a girl's night in one of the lean-tos, if there's an emergency or something they'll call us and we can head home."

"It'll be fun," I said, and looked out the window behind us. The sun had edged to the crest of Mount Kilden. The magical squares of gold light had shrunk to the size of a laptop screen. "It'll be an adventure. I've always wanted to do something like this."

"Breaking and entering?" Helen frowned.

"The door was unlocked," said Rose. "Technically it would be civil trespassing—criminal trespassing means you broke in. If we come back here, and it's locked, then we'll just turn around and go home. Even if we did get caught, it's only around a hundred dollar fine."

Helen looked at her in disbelief. "How do you know so much about this?"

"I told you, I've always wanted to do it. Didn't you ever think about it when you were a kid?"

"Yes," Helen said. "But we're all sixty years old."

"That's why it's so important that we do it now," said Rose.

"I'll bring wine," said Helen, and we all cheered.

I lowered my gaze to watch the last slim bars of light slide across the floor. For a few moments no one spoke. At last Helen said, "I've got to go home and get dinner going."

"Me too," said Rose, and they walked to the front door. I stared at the empty room, its white walls greying as twilight fell, the glowing floorboards now charcoal. It still looked beautiful, and my exhilaration became a sort of quiet expectancy. I rested my hand against the wall again, saying goodbye, and followed the others outside.

We decided to have our sleepover the following Saturday night. The weather was supposed to be good, which meant there would be hikers on the summit trail, but we didn't plan to go to the house until sunset, which would be right before six. If we saw any cars parked in either of the pull-outs, we'd just wait till they were gone, then drive up. We told our husbands we'd be camping at a lean-to in the state park, something we'd done many times over the years.

"Don't get eaten by a bear," Brandon warned me as I left. "What time will you be back?"

"Early, maybe ten or so? Helen goes to church, we'll all probably leave when she does."

"You should have gone before now, it's getting dark."

"We'll be fine," I said, and kissed him goodbye.

I went out to the car and put my things in the back. The

day had been warm and sunny, in the sixties, but the air had already grown chilly. I knew it would get colder, so I'd brought my ultralight sleeping bag, good for temps down to the thirties; also my pillow and a backpack with three sandwiches I'd bought at the general store, a big bag of chips, cookies, and a couple of water bottles. I beeped as I pulled away from the house, and drove at a respectable speed. We don't have a police force in our town, only the occasional statie on rotation, but this would be a bad time to run into one of them.

I'd arranged to pick up Rose, then Helen, so we'd only have one car.

"It's going to be cold." I eyed Rose's sleeping bag, one of those flannel-lined camp bags that's really just meant to be used indoors.

"I'm wearing layers. Plus, hot flashes."

"Did you bring the wine?" I asked Helen when we picked her up.

"Of course."

We drove through town, everything quiet as always, and dark except for the streetlight by the general store. The darkness deepened as I pulled onto the winding road up Mount Kilden, my headlights illuminating trees that seemed slightly threatening as their branches moved in the wind. Dead leaves swirled across the road, and a pair of laser-green eyes flashed in the headlights, like bits of glass. Something stirred in the underbrush, too big for a fox or porcupine. A bobcat, maybe.

I slowed the car to a crawl. I don't see well in the dark anymore—I should have let Helen drive, she's a few years younger and has better night vision. I steered carefully between potholes and ruts, keeping an eye out for deer. Rose and Helen chattered in the back seat, laughing at something Helen said. I smiled, even though I wasn't paying attention and hadn't heard the joke.

It took us twice as long to reach the end of the road as it had the last time. There were no cars in the pull-out. I backed in, turned on the dome light, and opened the trunk so we could gather our things, then kept the headlights on so we could see our way to the house.

"No, don't," said Rose. "Turn them off, I want to look at the sky for a minute. It'll be fine."

I nodded, and we stood outside for a few minutes. It was much colder now, and I shivered as I craned my neck to look at the sky above Mount Kilden. The stars looked bright as a string of LED lights, much bigger than they appeared down in the village. I heard wind high up in the trees. In the distance, an owl hooted twice.

"Okay, I'm cold," announced Helen. "Let's go."

We all switched on flashlights and trooped to the door. Rose went first, pausing with her hand on the knob. "What's if it's locked?"

"Then we go home," I replied. I tried not to sound too excited by that prospect, but it really was much colder than I'd expected, and while it was only getting on for seven, I was tired.

But the knob turned easily under Rose's hand. I heard a click, followed by a sweeping sound as she pushed the door open.

"We're home!" she sang out, as Helen and I walked in behind her. I hesitated, then closed the door. Immediately I felt better—safer, even though the three of us were alone in a dark empty house, and trespassing at that.

"Hang on," said Helen, and I heard her rummaging in her backpack. Seconds later, light filled the room as she held up a large brass hurricane lantern. Tim had given it to her as a thirtieth anniversary present. She crossed to the fireplace and set it on the mantle. "Let there be light."

We set down our sleeping bags, pillows, and other gear in the center of the room, a few feet from the fireplace. It felt distinctly warmer in here, or at least less cold. I took out my own lantern, much smaller than Helen's—plastic, not brass, but with a powerful LED light—and set it on the mantle beside hers. Rose did the same with the lamp she'd brought. We each had our own flashlight as well, and our cell phone lights.

I unrolled my sleeping bag, folding it over to make a comfortable place to sit, and dug through my backpack for the food I'd bought at the general store. Three sandwiches, one tuna salad, two Italian. Also the bag of fancy sea salt and vinegar chips, and three ginger-molasses cookies. Those cookies are huge, probably we could have split one between the three of us, and god knows I don't need the extra calories. But it was a special occasion, so I splurged.

I sat on my sleeping bag and lined up the sandwiches, cookies, and bag of chips in front of me. Rose had scooted over to the fireplace and was fiddling with something there. A match flared in her hand, and she began to light a number of little votive candles.

"There!" she said, pleased, and got to her feet. "Now we can actually see."

I was surprised at what a difference those little candles made. Combined with the lanterns on the mantle, they lit up the entire room. I could even read the labels on the different sandwiches

"Everyone warm enough?' asked Helen. "I brought an extra hoodie and a big scarf."

Rose nodded. She wore a bulky sweater under her fleece jacket, also a knit cap. I pointed at the cap.

"That was a good idea."

"Remember that time we froze our butts off at the lean-to? I learned my lesson then." Rose sat cross-legged on her sleeping bag and pulled it up over her legs like a blanket. "I'm starving. Where's the food?"

I handed out the sandwiches, opened the bag of chips, and set it on the floor. I knew that Rose and Helen liked tuna fish, but there had only been one tuna fish sandwich left, so they each took half. Helen produced a screw-top bottle of red wine and three plastic cups. She handed the cups around, then filled each one.

"To us," she said, holding hers up.

"And the house," added Rose, and we clicked our cups together.

We ate the sandwiches by candlelight and lamplight, reminiscing about camping trips, snowstorms, power outages.

"This is *so* much better!" Rose exclaimed. "I'd do this all the time if I could."

"Really?" Helen raised an eyebrow, took a sip of her wine. "I mean, you couldn't—you can't just go breaking into houses. But don't you like being outside? Seeing the stars and a campfire and the trees and everything?"

Rose wrapped her arms around her knees and stared up at the ceiling. "No," she said after a long moment. "I like this. I *prefer* this."

"But we live indoors all the time," countered Helen. "This isn't camping, really."

"I know that. But this is different. It's so… welcoming."

Helen and I looked at each other but didn't say anything. I couldn't think of any reason why Rose would find this empty house more welcoming than her own, which was a perfectly nice house, especially since Hank redid the kitchen a few years ago.

But she did have a point. There was a kind of, maybe you would call it an aura, about this place. It might have been what people mean when they talk about good feng shui. I'd never felt it before, either, but I wouldn't say I preferred it to my own home.

"Maybe I could talk Hank into selling our place and buying it," Rose went on. I couldn't tell from her tone whether she was kidding or not.

"Well, that would make for an interesting conversation," said Helen, and we all laughed.

When the chips were gone, Helen produced a bag of Little Lad's popcorn, and we finished that too. She poured the last of the wine into our cups and placed the bottle on its side on the floor.

"Spin the bottle?" She sent it rolling toward Rose, who put it in the bag we'd designated for trash, then turned to dig into her own backpack.

"It's only half full. But here." She held up another wine bottle, uncorked it, and refilled our cups.

I felt pleasantly buzzed, not drunk but happy. The light from the votive candles made the walls appear washed in yellow paint and cast shimmering circles on the ceiling. I wondered what it would be like to live here. Not seriously, not for myself; but for whoever had lived here, once upon a time.

"They must have had money," I said, thinking aloud. "Whoever lived here—if they weren't farmers, they must have been well off to keep up this place. And who keeps it up now? It must cost a fortune."

Rose yawned. "I don't know. I'm getting tired."

"Don't you think it's mysterious? Even if it's just once a year,"

I continued, "somebody has to do something to maintain it. Otherwise how could it have lasted this long?"

"Me too," said Helen. She stretched and glanced at me. "Tired, I mean. Sorry, Marianne."

I tried not to look annoyed. I'd go to the town office and ask to see the tax maps and determine who the owners were. Someone there would know who kept it up. Regina, the town clerk—she knew everyone. "Yeah, okay."

Helen and Rose took turns going outside to pee while I picked up the rest of the trash. When they returned, Helen walked to the mantle, switched off her brass lantern, and looked expectantly at me and Rose.

"Go for it," I said, and Helen turned off our lanterns as well.

We all snuggled into our sleeping bags. "Are you going to be warm enough?" I asked Rose, thinking of her flannel bag.

She nodded. "I'm wearing thermal long underwear."

I scrunched into my own down-filled bag. Even though I hadn't bothered with a sleeping pad, and I was lying on a hardwood floor, I felt as snug and warm as if I were at home in my own bed. I gazed at the ceiling, where the light from the votive candles danced. I soon heard Rose breathing, deeply and evenly. A little while later, Helen started to snore. Not too loudly, but enough to make me wish I'd thought to bring my earplugs. Brandon snores and I have to wear them every night. I turned onto my side and closed my eyes, grateful for my pillow.

I couldn't fall asleep. My thoughts weren't racing, I wasn't worrying about bills or the kids or anything like that. I just couldn't fall asleep. I looked at the time and it was getting on for ten, my usual bedtime. But sleep wouldn't come. I finally decided I'd go outside to pee, since I hadn't when the others did.

I crawled reluctantly from my sleeping bag and stood. I expected the room to be cold but it was quite comfortable. Most of the votive candles were still burning, so maybe they generated a bit of heat, along with the three of us. I pulled on my sneakers, padded to the back door, and went outside.

Almost immediately, a peculiar unease came over me. The air was still and cold, the stars so brilliant that, after a few moments, I could clearly see the expanse of grass and Queen Anne's lace and goldenrod that swept up to the woods behind the house. I heard nothing except the rustle of leaves. But it still took all my courage to take the first step, and then another, until I reached the trees. I quickly did my business, zipped my pants back up, and started back.

I only took two or three steps before I froze. I've been outside in the middle of the night plenty of times, in places far more isolated and wild than this. I've never felt afraid. Watchful and on alert, in case I came across some wild animal, but I never saw anything more exciting than a skunk, and I smelled him long before I saw him. I'd never been truly frightened.

But now, in the overgrown backyard of a house in my own hometown, surrounded by woods I'd hiked dozens of times over the years, I felt my unease grow into dread, and, after some moments, terror. Gazing at it now, I realized that the house appeared different than it had just a few hours earlier. The neat proportions that had felt so calming now seemed, not exactly askew, but crude. The house no longer appeared three-dimensional: it looked like a drawing someone had made on an enormous sheet of grey paper, four black lines enclosing a grey square.

And as I stared, even that changed. The roof dissolved into the night sky, the windows shrank to black dots. I couldn't see the door, and as I tried frantically to determine where it was, my mind grew sluggish, as though I was waking from a heavy sleep.

Yet I couldn't wake and, as I stared at the looming shape in front of me, I could no longer remember what a door *was*. Something important, I knew that, something I knew and had often used—but for what purpose, and why?

I squeezed my eyes shut, and opened them again to fog, a haze that darkened from grey to charcoal to inky black as it spread across everything around me. The stars were gone, and the ridge of Mount Kilden. My chest grew heavy, as though I was compressed between heavy walls. Was this a heart attack? A stroke? I tried to breathe but the air had been sucked away. I couldn't feel my arms or legs, my face or skin. Everything melted into darkness: I was being snuffed out, like a candle.

A sudden noise jarred me: I lurched forward and felt air rush back into my lungs. As I gasped, the sound came again—an owl hooting not far behind me. I fought to catch my breath, looked up to see the house just a few yards away. I stumbled toward it, sneakers sliding on damp leaves and grass, grabbed the knob and turned it and staggered inside.

I closed the door—too loudly, but I didn't hear a peep—locked it, and walked unsteadily into the living room. Relief flooded me, not just relief but a sudden, overwhelming calm. The stark terror I'd felt only minutes before faded completely, the way a middle-of-the-night dream does when you try to recall it in the morning.

I was safe here. A single votive candle still burned in the fireplace, its flame wavering. I could see Rose and Helen curled up on their sleeping bags on the floor: Helen on her side, arms tucked out of sight and her expression relaxed; Rose face-down, half of her pillow squashed up to cover her head.

I sighed with pleasure, removed my sneakers, and slid back into my own sleeping bag. It was still warm. So was my pillow. I burrowed deeper, gazed through half-shut eyes at a hint of gold on the wall from the tiny candle flame, and felt the house sigh with me as I fell asleep.

I woke early, to Rose and Helen speaking in low tones.

"…going to be so cold," murmured Rose, and she laughed softly. "I don't want to get up."

"I know. But I told Robert I'd be back in time for church."

"You could call him."

"That's not going to make it any warmer in here."

I rolled onto my side and propped my head on my hand. "Good morning."

"Good morning!" Rose said brightly. Her eyes shone beneath her mussed-up hair. "Did you sleep well?"

"I did." I stopped, recalling my trip outside. I felt none of the fear I'd experienced then: I felt detached from it, as though remembering a story someone else had told me. "It was weird—I went out to pee, and… I don't know. I had some kind of sinking spell."

Helen sat up. "Like what?"

"I don't know. I felt dizzy, and then I couldn't breathe. Everything got dark—even darker, I mean."

"Maybe you had a stroke. A mild one," she added.

"Maybe," I said. "It didn't feel like that."

"Have you ever had a stroke?" asked Rose.

"No. But I've read about it, and—I feel fine now." I sat up so I could see them better. "I felt fine as soon as I got back inside. I might have just stood up too quickly or something."

I rubbed my arms. Rose was right—the room was very cold. The light was cold, too, more grey than gold. I remembered the dark haze that had blotted out everything else the night before, and shivered. "We should go get coffee at the general store."

"They don't open till eight on Sunday," Rose said.

"We can go to my house." Helen emerged from her sleeping bag, yawning, and ran a hand through her hair. "I wish there was a mirror here."

"No you don't," said Rose, raising an eyebrow at Helen's disheveled clothing, and we both laughed.

"Well, running water so I could brush my teeth. I'll be right back."

Helen bent to retrieve a cosmetics bag and headed for the front door. I thought of warning her, but against what? I turned to Rose. "You sleep okay?"

"I swear, I slept better than I have for a year." She sat upright, her flannel bag pulled around her shoulders like a comforter. "Hank snores like you wouldn't believe—he has sleep apnea, he should really have one of those machines. I may come back here tonight." She smiled, but sounded half-serious.

I got up and found my own toothbrush and toothpaste and water bottle. When Helen appeared in the doorway and announced "Next," I went outside.

The sun had risen but was hidden by the mountain. Mist streamed up the hillside and clung to the trees at the edge of the woods. Everything looked the way it does through a window screen, dim and a bit out of focus. I stood beside the door, steadying myself with one hand on the wall, waiting to see if I had another bad spell. I felt fine. I started to walk away from the house, pausing to look back.

The FOR SALE BY OWNER sign still leaned against the wall. Overnight, more leaves had drifted around the stake, and the lettering seemed more faded. The plywood had buckled and splintered where it was screwed to the stake, and more of the white paint had flaked off, revealing the bare wood beneath.

Overhead, a crow cawed and another replied. I turned to look up at the mountainside, shreds of mist disappearing as the sun broke over the eastern horizon. The wind picked up, loosing a flutter of yellow leaves from the birches. The brisk air smelled of acorns and dead leaves, the smoke from someone's woodstove in the village below. I brushed my teeth, rinsed with a mouthful of water from my water bottle, and spit onto the yellow grass. I raked my fingers through my hair, felt in my pocket for my cell phone. I walked over to the sign and took a picture of the phone number. I'd call later, just out of curiosity.

Back inside, Helen had rolled up her sleeping bag and was gathering whatever stray bits of stuff remained. A piece of waxed paper, a balled-up tissue, a glasses case. She'd already lined up her backpack, sleeping bag, and pillow beside the wall. The Catholic church was in Gilead, about ten minutes away. She'd have to leave soon to get there in time for nine o'clock Mass.

I started on my own belongings, exchanging my socks for a clean pair. I made a circuit of the room, halting at the fireplace to gather up the spent tea lights. I dropped them into a paper bag and set it with my stuff in the middle of the room. I texted Brandon to let him know I'd be back soon, and asked if he'd like to meet at the general store for coffee and donuts. He replied immediately.

Sure, text me when you're there.

"Brandon's going to meet us at the general store." I glanced at Rose. "You want to tell Hank?"

Rose didn't seem to have moved. She still sat on the floor and stared intently at the empty fireplace, as though trying to will flames to appear in it. Finally, she reached for her handbag, took out a hairbrush, and slowly brushed her hair. When she finished, she replaced the hairbrush and got to her feet. She rolled up her sleeping bag and set it by the wall, along with her handbag and backpack, went outside and returned after a few minutes.

I picked up my own bag. I was ready to go—my back hurt from sleeping on the floor, and I had a slight headache. Too much wine. I knew Helen was growing impatient as well. Rose stood near the door but made no move to leave. Her brow furrowed; she cocked her head, gazing again at the fireplace.

"Do you hear that?" she asked.

Helen and I looked at her, then each other. I shrugged. "Hear what?"

"That noise. Like—I don't know. A radio? Listen."

I held my breath, listening. And yes, after a moment I did hear something, though it was hard to tell if it was an actual sound or something in my head, like tinnitus—it seemed as though I might have been hearing it for a while without noticing it. A nearly inaudible sound, not voices but not quite music either.

Yet it wasn't tinnitus. It sound more like wind chimes, or someone striking random notes on a tiny xylophone. I strained to hear, but it didn't grow any louder.

"It's coming from upstairs," said Rose. She walked to the foot of the steps leading to the second floor, pressed her palm against the wall, and turned to look at me. "If you stand here, you can hear it."

I joined her and gazed up the stairway, saw nothing but the pale morning light brightening the walls.

But Rose was right. The chiming sound was louder here, and slightly more distinct, as if a cellphone set at low volume was ringing in a distant part of the house. I glanced back at Helen. "She's right. Come listen."

Helen stayed where she was. "I think I'm going to just call Tim and ask him to come pick me up."

"Hang on." Rose shook her head and sniffed. "Can you smell that? Someone's baking something. Bread—it smells like baking bread."

I inhaled deeply, and nodded in agreement. "You're right. It smells like bread. Or cookies. That's very strange."

The scent, like the sound, seemed to emanate from upstairs. The faint chiming hadn't grown any louder, yet it now seemed on the verge of being intelligible, though I still couldn't determine exactly what the sound was. It was like listening to an old-fashioned shortwave radio, trying to tune in to a station in some unknown country. Only who was broadcasting, and why?

"I'll be right back," said Rose. Before I could stop her, she ran upstairs.

I gazed after her in alarm, but didn't follow. In a few seconds, I heard her footsteps on the bare wood floor above as she walked down the hallway.

Then the footsteps stilled. The chimes grew louder, as though she'd opened a door onto one of the bedrooms, and whatever produced the sound was inside. At the same time, the scent of bread gusted downstairs, though now it smelled different. Like bread but also loamy, like upturned earth when you're gardening. I wrinkled my nose and looked over at Helen, who'd moved closer to me.

"What's that smell?" she asked, and grimaced. "We should get out of here, it could be a gas leak."

"It doesn't smell like gas," I said. But I agreed with her, we should get out. "Rose!" I yelled. "Let's go!"

No reply. I braced myself, setting one hand on each wall of the stairwell. But I still didn't move to go upstairs. The chimes grew louder and more measured: for the first time, they sounded like music and not aimless tinkling. The earthy smell overpowered me, filling my nostrils, my lungs.

"Rose!" I shouted, coughing. "Get down here!"

From upstairs came the sound of running footsteps, then a thump. Rose appeared at the top of the steps, wild-eyed, one hand clapped over her mouth. She staggered down the stairway, and when she reached bottom, roughly pushed past me. I only had a glimpse of her face, white as a china plate, before she fled outside.

I raced after her and found her kneeling at the edge of the lawn by the road. Her body heaved and I thought she was being sick, but when I crouched beside her and laid my hand on her shoulder, I saw that she was convulsed with sobs.

"Rose! Rose, what happened? Is there somebody up there?"

She said nothing, wouldn't even look at me; just wept uncontrollably with her face in her hands. I took a few deep breaths—the choking smell was gone—glanced back but didn't see Helen. What if someone was inside and had attacked her? I fumbled in my pocket for my phone, started to enter 911 when Helen ran outside.

"There's no one up there," she said. She knelt on Rose's other side and touched her arm. "Rose, what happened? Did you see something?"

Rose shook her head but said nothing.

"I checked all the rooms upstairs," Helen continued, her voice steady. "I didn't see anyone. I didn't hear anything or smell anything, either. I did before, when you first mentioned it, but not just now. If somebody was there, they're gone. Can you tell us what you saw?"

Gently, she grasped Rose's face and turned it toward her. Rose remained silent, her pale face blotched scarlet from weeping. She opened her mouth as though to speak, but seemed to think better of it.

"Come on," I said. "Let's get you in the car." I looked at Helen. "I'll stay with her. Go get everything."

I helped Rose to her feet and walked her down the road to my car. She refused to get into the front seat, so I opened the back and she crawled in and lay face down, covering her head with her hands.

She was afraid to look at the house, I realized. I leaned inside the car and rubbed her back, felt her trembling beneath my hand. I stared out at the second-floor windows, searching for any sign of motion, a glint of light, or the shadow of someone moving.

I saw nothing. If anything, the house seemed even more peaceful and inviting than it had the day before. Morning sunlight set the windows ablaze. The asters along the front glowed amethyst. Above, the bulk of Mount Kilden shone green and scarlet beneath a cloudless blue sky.

After a minute Helen emerged, laden with sleeping bags. She dumped them in the back of the car and returned for our handbags and backpacks, the paper bag containing the remnants from our meal.

"That's everything," she said, and jumped inside the car. "*Go.*"

I stroked Rose's hair and touched her head, closed the back door, and got behind the wheel. I pulled out quickly in a spray of grit and gravel. In the rearview mirror, the house grew smaller and smaller, until we rounded a curve and it disappeared from view.

I dropped Rose off first. Helen and I accompanied her up the walkway, Rose moving between us like a sleepwalker. When Hank opened the door and saw her, his eyebrows shot up. "What the hell were you girls drinking?"

"She doesn't feel well," I said. Rose collapsed against Hank and once again began to cry. His confusion turned to alarm. "What happened?"

"We don't know," said Helen. "She—it seems like she had some kind of episode."

"What kind of episode?" demanded Hank, but he didn't wait for a reply. He shut the door, and through the window I saw him walking Rose to the couch.

Helen and I hurried back to the car. "What do you think happened to her?" I asked as I drove toward town.

"I don't know. I think there might have been a gas leak or something. You said you felt strange last night."

"Yeah, but it wasn't like that—I didn't smell anything. And that noise—what was that noise?"

"A ghost?' She laughed brokenly.

"Ghosts don't act like that."

"Have you ever seen one?'

"Of course not." I tightened my hands on the wheel. "But that's baloney. It's more likely she had some kind of, I don't know, a psychotic break or something."

"Rose?" Helen said in disbelief. "Are you kidding?"

Whatever it was, Rose didn't recover for a long time. She wouldn't see me, or return my phone calls or texts. She did the same with Helen. Whenever I spoke to Hank, he was terse. I could tell he thought Helen and I were somehow responsible for whatever had happened. We hadn't told him the truth—that we spent the night in an empty house up by Mount Kilden, and not at a lean-to at the state park. I still don't know what Rose told him.

"She needs some time, Marianne," he said the last time I talked to him. "When she's ready, she'll give you a call."

Helen and I walked a few times after that, though we stuck to the camp roads by Taylor Lake. For a while we endlessly rehashed the events of that night, but we never came up with a reasonable explanation. Or an unreasonable one, either. Then Helen learned that her daughter was pregnant, and that took up her attention for the rest of the year.

The day after our sleepover, I got out my cell phone, found the picture I'd taken of the FOR SALE BY OWNER sign, and copied down the phone number on it. I had to screw up my courage to punch it into my phone. As I did, my heart began to pound.

The number rolled over to a message saying the call could not be completed. I attempted it again with the same result, then tried varying some of the numbers—the handwriting on the sign was hard to read on the tiny screen, even when I enlarged it. I never got through to anyone.

Later that week I went to the town office. I told Regina, the clerk there, I wanted to look at the tax map for the part of town bordering Mount Kilden. She took me to a room and showed me the oversized books with the information for every piece of land in town, showing property lines and the names of landowners.

"I know the house you mean," Regina said as she pulled one of the heavy volumes from the shelf. "Every year people come in here asking about it."

I wanted to ask her more, but the phone rang in the other room. "Excuse me," she said, and went to answer it.

The house lot was easy to find—the last one on that long road that led to the foot of the mountain. I wrote down the lot number, then went to another book to check it against the landowner's name: J. Jones. I didn't bother to write that down. I closed the tax map and replaced it, waited till I heard Regina get off the phone, and returned to the front office.

"Do you know anything about the property owner for that place?" I asked. "J. Jones? There's a *For Sale* sign there, I tried calling the number on it but I couldn't get any answer."

"No one ever does," she said. "I tried it myself once, out of curiosity. Said it was disconnected."

"But he pays his taxes, right? This J. Jones?"

She nodded. "Every year. By money order, and there's never a return address. I checked that, too. It's been like that for as long as I've been here. The deed goes back to the early 1800s. Same name and initials. Far as I know, it's never left the family."

"But it's for sale. It's a nice house."

"It is, but that's too isolated up there for me. Everyone else must think so, too—that sign's been up for years."

"Who maintains it?" I picked up a pamphlet with information about fishing and hunting licenses and pretended to peruse it. "It always seems in good shape for a place no one lives in."

"That I do not know." Regina shrugged. "Never heard of anyone here doing it. They might hire someone from one of the bigger property managers out of Augusta."

"Okay, thanks."

I set the brochure back on the counter. As I turned to go, Regina's face creased. "How's Rose doing? Hank was in here to register his truck and said she hasn't been feeling well."

"I don't know." I felt my throat tighten. "I think she'll be all right. I hope so."

"Me too," said Regina, and nodded goodbye.

I got in the car and drove up the road to Mount Kilden. A car with out-of-state plates was parked in the first pull-out, and as I continued onto the gravel road I passed a man and a woman, both wielding fancy-looking trekking poles. They waved. I nodded and kept going, past the last turnout until I reached the house. I parked at the edge of the road, and got out.

Someone had mowed the lawn and raked away all the fallen leaves. The purple asters nodded in the wind. By the door, a single tiger lily had opened. The white clapboards appeared newly painted, as did the sign planted in the center of the lawn.

FOR SALE BY OWNER.

I hesitated, then walked warily across the grass. A different phone number had been scrawled on the sign. I held up my cell phone to take a photo, thought better of it, and let my hand drop.

"Oh my god, look at this place!"

I looked back to see the couple I'd passed a few minutes earlier. Trekking poles tucked under their arms, they gazed in delight at the house. The woman smiled and waved and began walking across the lawn.

"Are you the owner?" she asked in excitement. "We've been looking for a place like this for months!"

"A year!" her husband called cheerfully after her.

I opened my mouth and started to say *No*. Instead, I turned, grabbed the sign, and yanked it from the ground. It resisted at first, but I planted my feet more firmly and pulled harder, until it finally came out. Without pausing to catch my breath, I carried it toward my car.

"I'm sorry," I said, as the man and woman stared at me. "I changed my mind."

I got into my car and headed back down the mountainside. Just before the gravel road ended, I stopped and left the car idling while I retrieved the sign from the back seat. I crossed to the far side of the road and clambered over a fallen stone wall into the woods, fighting my way through brush and overhanging branches until I found a cellar hole, deep and filled with decades-worth of moldering dead leaves and fungi. I heaved the sign into the cellar hole and returned to my car, and drove as fast as I could until the mountain fell out of sight behind me.

In the Deep Woods;
The Light is Different There

Seanan McGuire

A CHILD will tell you, if asked, and if they are in the mindset to answer questions as they are posed and not as the child's mind would have them interpreted—for the ears of children seem to work differently than the ears of adults, to be tuned to a different set of sighs and susurrations, not to the clean consonants and simple constructions of the adult vocabulary, and the answers of children are often similarly distorted by the journey they must take in being spoken—that sunlight is the same everywhere it falls. There is only one sun, as so many songs have eagerly told them since the day of their birth; there is only one sun, and its light falls everywhere at the same speed, landing on the just and the unjust alike. Thus it stands to reason that the sun which falls on a quiet suburban street, or a lakeside cabin, must by its very nature be the same as the sun which falls on the trees of the deep and tangled wood beyond the lake.

Those children will already know, of course, that they are wrong, for if they are old enough to venture outside without supervision, even if they have never been farther from their beds than the safe enclosures of their backyards; that they are lying, which is a practice that even the most profoundly honest of children must frequently engage in: for adults have little interest in hearing truth from children, when lies are so much sweeter. The worlds of children are low to the ground, terrifying and confusing, filled with dangers adult minds have forgotten, truths adult hurts have forsaken. So at times, when the worlds of adults collide with others, they must be untrue to be believed. The truth is a rock too big to swallow, especially in adulthood, when years of caustic words and swallowing back inappropriate retorts has left their throats scarred and narrow.

The sunlight is not the same everywhere it falls, as anyone who has been to a desert or a wide urban parking lot, and also to the peak of a mountain or the crest of a hill, can tell you. The sun may be the same, but once the light has left the sun, it is transformed by travel and by time into something new, something as sweet and profound as a secret, sometimes kind and sometimes cruel, but always remaining sunlight. Desert sunlight is unforgiving—not bad, not malicious, but unforgiving, ready to punish any small mistake. Coastal sunlight is diffuse and muddled, unable to warm the frozen, unable to save the lost. And in the very deepest woods, where the trees stand sentinel over ground that has never been free of roots and rot, where the branches block the sky and the birds rule the universe, the sunlight falls like treacle, or like honey from a hive; it is not sweet, but it is slow, ponderous, and intentional. It cannot be called welcoming, cannot be called warm; when it strikes a human face, it offers no succor, extends no hand of welcome. The sun which falls in the deep of the woods does not want us there. It knows who it serves, and that master is not the quick, swift humanity of city and shore, is not the place where civilization meets curiosity, and drives the domesticated descendants of our feral ancestors to seek the woods and waters wild.

It does not want us there.

There are places, liminal places, where the walls grow thin, where the deep heart of the woods can abut upon what has been tamed and tapered down, claimed and collected; places neither civilized nor free, where the sun can shift in an instant, to correspond with the passing of a cloud or the lighting of a match. In these places grow the strange ones, humans who can breathe in both the sweet treacle sunlight of the modern world and the deep, rich, cruel sunlight of the ancient one. They are children of a stranger sun, but they are human still, and their desires matter no less than the desires of their citified cousins. Their needs are no less important or essential.

It is only when those needs collide with the needs of the softer world that trouble can be found.

They walk the deep woods, the places where the light hangs heavy in the trees and the dark hangs heavier still; and what they want and what they dream of is the business of the deep woods and the deep woods alone, and the question they are never asked, and would never answer if they were, is a simple one: if the sunlight is so transformed by its fall into the deep, dark woods, what do they do to the moonlight? What does the night become?

What transformations can such light wreak in its own right, in its own time?

They smile and they know their place and they walk in shadows made of light, and they are perfect and they are profane, and they would not forgive us if they could.

The lake house hadn't been used in some time; that much was clear as soon as the door was opened, sending a puff of stale air and dust billowing out onto the porch. Millie recoiled, unable to quite believe that the place had been allowed to regress into such a state of disrepair. What was the point of the caretakers her grandfather had arranged, the ones whose fee was dutifully deducted from her trust fund three times a year, when the seasons changed and they were meant to air the place out, keeping it ready for human habitation. She fought back the desire to pull out the letter she had already read easily a dozen times, the one that promised this place would be prepared for her arrival.

Well, if this was prepared, she wasn't sure she could understand what had driven her grandparents to spend every summer by this lake, right up until the year they disappeared. Her father always spoke of the lake house as a bucolic paradise, a necessary respite from the speed and stress of city life. Without it, he'd told her once, he would have gone quite mad in the aftermath of his divorce from her mother, when she had seemed to permeate every square inch of the city, turning a wide, clean world into a small and filthy enclosure. Only by getting as far from her concrete cage as he possibly could had he been free of her.

Millie hadn't been able to follow. She'd been too young, and the custody agreement between her parents forbade either one of them to take her out of the state without written permission. She'd hated it as a child, hated being left behind, hated knowing that her mother was forbidding her the lake house out of spite, and that in so doing, had driven her father to forbid her summers at Walt Disney World, winters in Paris, any number of other little luxuries that she, as the child of two well-off New Yorkers, had every reason to feel were her due. Somehow he had always managed to make the lake house seem equal to those grand adventures, to make the punishment fit the crime, even though the crime had never been hers, and the punishment always, inevitably, had.

And now here she is, finally, and her father is gone to the worms and the rot, and her mother is gone to the fire and the wind, one buried, the other cremated, and she stands alone. Her divorce has been finalized, her name sundered from Marcus's forever. She has no family left in the world, and nothing but their combined bank accounts to comfort her through the long, lonely nights. Well, those, and the lake house, which is finally hers to have for her own.

As long as she doesn't mind sharing it with the moths and spiders, it seems.

The gust of foul air has subsided. Picking up her suitcase one-handed, aware that she is, for all intents and purposes, trapped here—the phone line was disconnected years ago for lack of payment, and while she's working to have it reestablished, things here in the country happen at a fraction of the speed the city considers "slow." She'll be lucky if she has a dial tone by August. And apart from that, the driver who brought her here has returned home by now, leaving her alone in what might as well be another century, to say nothing of another country. No. Her mother made the city a cage to keep her, and she has willingly traded it for the cage of her father's design, which may be of a different shape and size, but which has just as many bars on the windows, and just as many walls.

But it doesn't contain any angry ex-husbands who like to settle their arguments with their fists, and it doesn't contain any easy means of tracking her down, and with those thoughts reigning over all others, she squares her shoulders and steps through the open door, into a room full of ghosts.

For a moment, in the hazy sunlight that filters through the windows, filled with dancing motes of dust that seem almost too large to be real, she is absolutely standing in a haunted house. A scream bubbles up in her throat, momentarily trapped behind the cemetery gates of her lips, and she knows that when it breaks loose it will be large enough to shake down the walls. The specks of light catch and hold her gaze, yanking it away from the specters surrounding her. She used to see fairies like this in her childhood, in the days when she bedeviled nannies and lived in what her mother termed "a form-fitting fairyland," a place filled with only peace and magic and no divorce, no warring parents, no miseries at all.

Then she blinks, and the fairies are dust motes again, and the dust motes are fading into the background, and the ghosts are furnishings covered in dusty white sheets, as old and unused as the rest of this place. The money she's been paying for upkeep has been going to line the pockets of her so-called caretakers if it's been doing anything, obviously enough, because they haven't raised so much as a finger to prepare the place for her arrival. She *told* them she was coming, she knows she did. She sent three letters and called twice, and she distinctly remembers receiving at least one reply.

Or she thinks she did. It could be hard to tell, on the long and empty afternoons in her apartment in the city, what was fact and what was supposition. She supposes the afternoons will be just as long here, and just as lonely, with her driver already gone; these walls will be her new cage, one she finds far more pleasant than the dangers of the city.

Her mother warned her, before she died, told her Marcus seemed like the sort of man who might turn cruel if she stopped giving him what he wanted, but since what he wanted was a young, beautiful, independently wealthy wife with which to dazzle his competitors, she had chalked her mother's warnings up to the ramblings of a bitter old woman whose own marriage had collapsed and left her with nothing better to do than torture her only child, since her actual friends had long since died, rendering them unavailable for her lectures.

She hadn't known then—couldn't have known—that one day Marcus's demands would shift to sons and heirs, children born of his seed and her body's labors, to carry on his family name, made great and glorious by her coffers and his business acumen. And she couldn't have known that her body would be opposed to this idea, would refuse to give him any heirs to call his own, but least of all the son he so eagerly demanded. She couldn't have known that after five years of failures, he would turn to making his wishes known with his fists, and with the backs of his hands, and on one dark occasion with his boots, leading to kidney damage, a weekend in the hospital, and finally, at long last, the divorce papers her lawyer had been urging her to file for over a year.

Thankfully, their prenuptial agreement had been drawn up by lawyers far more expensive than he could afford on his own, and she'd been able to walk away with most of her fortune intact, shielded from his grasping hands by restraining orders and legal paperwork. She'd escaped with her money and her reputation, and all it had cost was the city she loved so much.

Well, nothing to be done for it now. This is to be her home, at least for the next six months, and maybe longer than that, depending on the lawyers and the progress of their suits. She turns and grasps the nearest white winding sheet, whipping it away from the antique fainting couch it covers like a dinner theater magician revealing the table during his eight o'clock show. It's a swift, flashy gesture, wasted on the empty room, and she has a moment to feel like she's accomplished something before the cloud of dust that it releases invades her mouth and nose and sends her choking back onto the porch, looking through the open door at the cloudy, sun-streaked room.

"Ms. Ellis?"

Millie turns.

The voice belongs to one of the local youths, a broad, friendly-faced teen of no obvious gender, dressed in overalls and a ruffled plaid shirt. Their hair is short-cropped and very red, with two separate cowlicks at the front. As a child, she would immediately have made them out to be devil's horns, and spun a whole backstory to explain why an imp was walking among the mortal men of this small lakeside town, no doubt granting ill-advised wishes and tempting children into mischief.

"Yes?" she asks, and takes a step down from the porch, onto the second stair, which is rickety and filled with splinters. "Are you the caretaker?"

"No, ma'am, that's my dad," says the teen. "I just go fishing down off your dock sometimes, or I did, anyway, when you weren't here to need the fish…" They duck their head and look at Millie through their lashes, clearly waiting for permission to continue their fish-filching ways.

If they *were* a mischievous imp, what would the correct answer be? Permission to keep stealing fish could be taken as permission to steal whatever they liked, but refusing permission when they weren't hurting anything or taking anything she needed for herself would just be an act of selfishness, and imps, like most fey creatures, didn't care for mortal selfishness. Millie finds her answer and her smile at the same time.

"If you'll teach me how to fish in these waters, you can fish here anytime you'd like," she says.

Her smile is returned, amplified into something bright enough for dust to dance in. "That's awfully kind, Ms. Ellis. Most city folk aren't so accommodating."

"This was my father's place before he died," she says. "I'm sorry I haven't been here before now. I was…" Married? Busy? Trapped by the expectations of a mother who had done her best to create the impression that anything outside the city was filthy and provincial and not worth pursuing? "…otherwise occupied," she finishes awkwardly, and the words are dust and ashes in her mouth. She wants to spit them out, to see them dancing in the sunbeams with the rest of the filth.

The teen doesn't appear to judge her for it, only shrugs and says, "You're here now, start of the summer and everything. We'll be glad to have you for a neighbor, and you'll have plenty of time to learn the way of things before the season changes and you go back to the city."

Millie blinks. Maybe her instructions weren't clear, when she asked them to prepare the property. "I'm sorry," she says. "There seems to have been some confusion. I'm not intending to—"

But the teen has turned toward the lake, chin up and nostrils flaring, like a hunting dog that's caught the scent of a rabbit. "I'm sorry," they say, glancing back to her. "Papa needs me. I'll see you tomorrow, I'm sure, since I'll be helping to bring your groceries in. Sleep well, Ms. Ellis!"

And they're off, loping toward the lakeshore with a curious rollicking gait, reminding her even more intensely of a hunting hound, now returning to its master's side. When they don't so much as look back, she sighs, and turns to the lake house full of dust and sheeted furniture and ghosts and ghosts and ghosts.

So many ghosts, and some of them have names and some of them have faces and some of them only have whispers from her father on dark winter nights, stories with nothing to support them. She moved here for a haunting, and, even if the house refuses to be haunted, she fully intends to be.

Millicent Ellis climbs the porch steps to the door and willfully, intentionally, shuts herself inside.

Cleaning up enough to make the bedroom habitable takes the rest of the daylight hours, culminating in the unwelcome discovery that in addition to everything else that hasn't happened, the power has yet to be restored. If her keys hadn't fit the lock, she'd be wondering whether she was in the wrong house—the money for the caretakers must have been going *somewhere*, and she knows she was very clear about her intentions when she wrote to them. None of this is what she was promised.

But her bedroom has a perfect view of the lake, and the water is beautiful in the moonlight, flat and bright and clean as hammered silver. She could look at it for hours. With no power to read by and no television to watch, she might have to. Laughing a little, she turns back to the small room she's chosen as her own.

The lake house is large enough to host a much larger family than just her—or even just her and her husband, if he was still a welcome part of her world—and despite her grumbling about the lack of housekeeping, the caretakers have clearly been maintaining the structure; the walls are straight, the eaves are sound, and the windows admit no drafts. She wraps herself tight in a roll of blankets that still smell faintly of her grandmother's perfume, and she slides into slumber as smoothly as a seal sliding into the sea, going under without a splash.

She doesn't consciously hear the sound that wakes her some hours later, only opens her eyes on the dark room with the moonlight sleeting through the window. The house is silent around her, and she begins to close her eyes again, to return to sleep, only to freeze as she hears the soft scuff of a boot sole against bare wood. Someone is in the lake house. Someone other than herself, alone. No one here is alone. Not the house, not the intruder, not Millie. They are together, the three of them united by coincidence of place. Not so coincidental: Millie came here entirely on purpose, and this place has sat empty and undisturbed for so long that anyone who walks here now must have come seeking something that hadn't been present the day before.

They must have come looking for her.

She finishes putting the pieces together and slides silently out of bed, bare feet meeting bare wood, to creep toward the antique wooden wardrobe against the far wall. It's still full of her departed grandmother's summer wardrobe, vintage dresses and coats sliding down the steep hill toward antique as they sat, untouched, for year upon year. She inches the door open as she hears the footsteps near, moving down the hall toward the room where she was sleeping.

Into the wardrobe she slips, wrapping herself in the silks and linens of the past, and holds her breath, as much from fear as from the dust. The footsteps grow closer and closer still, until she's sure their owner is in the room, bathed in the thick silver moonlight through the window.

A branch snaps. Something—a dog, most likely, or perhaps a coyote—howls in the woods outside the window. The footsteps draw closer and closer still, and she tenses, wishing she had anything that could serve her as a weapon. But there's nothing, there's nothing, there's nothing here in this tattered world of someone else's discarded fashions. She can't defend herself with a sundress, no matter how daring it may have seemed when it was first worn.

The dog or coyote howls again, closer this time. The footsteps stop, and she hears three things in quick succession.

Hears the window sliding closed, locking the sounds of the night outside, away from her, leaving her trapped in a space that manages to feel even smaller than the wardrobe. Hears the footsteps resume, coming closer and closer, the tread now even and familiar. She knows the man who's coming toward her, and of course she does; of course there was never any real question of who would have followed her here, past the ends of what city people see as the entire world, into this lakeside dream where the sunlight falls like honey and attracts almost as many flies.

And finally, she hears the clacking of claws against the hardwood floor, also coming closer, moving more than twice as quickly as the footsteps. There's an animal in the house with them. Is it running? She suspects it might be.

The man who has followed her here from the city, the man who has broken into her house, the man who used to be her husband before he sacrificed that title on the altar of his fists, stops walking. She hears the scuff of his heel as he turns.

Then she hears him yell. It's not a word—it's a wordless sound of shock and horror. What follows is far more horrible, the wet, visceral sound of tearing meat and breaking bone, occasionally accompanied by the clatter of claws on wood. He screams and screams and screams, but whatever fell beast is tearing him to pieces does so without making a sound beyond those that gravity demands. Eventually, the screaming stops. Millie, who is backed into the corner of the wardrobe, shoulders to the wood and hands clasped over her mouth, is weeping by this point, fat tears forming in the corners of her eyes and breaking free to run down her cheeks and pool at the hollow of her throat. If she makes a sound, she knows, the beast will come for her. If she *doesn't* make a sound, the beast will surely come for her, because beasts can smell their prey at much greater distances than the one between the wardrobe and the room.

The clatter of claws continues, now accompanied by what sounds for all the world like the rasp of a tongue against the wood, and still the beast makes no sound, and still Millie holds her screams inside and cries.

Outside, beyond the closed window, the moon shines on.

Morning finds her stiff and aching from a night spent propped up in the wardrobe. Sometime in the smallest hours of the morning, she slipped into restless sleep, her hands dropping away from her mouth, her tears drying salt-sticky on her cheeks and down the front of her nightgown. She comes out of her curl as silently as she can, but can't suppress a whimper as the motion pulls at her back. She's not an old woman yet, but she's not a young woman anymore, and the events of last night have her wondering whether "old" is even in her future.

Carefully, she eases the wardrobe door open to reveal the room where she went to bed the night before. Everything is precisely as she left it, except for two small things she wouldn't notice under any other circumstances: the window is closed and latched, secured against the outside world, and there is a shoe, one single shoe, under the very edge of the bed. She stumbles forward, too sore to bend, and fishes it out with her own foot. It's far too large for her, sized for a grown man's foot, and far too new to have belonged to her father, or to her grandfather, or to anyone else with good reason to be in this house anytime within the last ten years.

Unlike most of the house, there is no dust on the shoe. What would her careless caretakers have been doing, dusting under the bed and leaving random pieces of footwear behind? It's not like what little she's come to know of them. Which means, logically, that the shoe came from exactly where she supposes the shoe came from. It is a memoir of a man who came, uninvited, into the lakeshore moonlight, and meant to do her harm. A man she loved once, who proved himself a monster in his own cruel way when given the opportunity. She weighs the shoe in her hand and finds it inevitably wanting. As bodies go, it isn't much to bury.

In the end, she dresses in the previous day's clothes, jerkily, trying to compensate for the soreness of the night before, trying not to fall when she lifts her feet off the floor to step into her trousers. In the end, she sits on the bed as she eases them over her hips, and regrets even that small movement. She remembers being spry and flexible and quick to recover from such small offenses of the flesh as sleeping upright in a wardrobe.

When she's done and dressed she heads for the door, cradling her ex-husband's shoe in her arms like the baby they were never able to have. She's not sure what she intends to do with it. Throwing it into the lake feels disrespectful, to the lake. Surely the house comes with garbage service, one more question she should probably have asked before coming here, one more mystery to unravel. Most of life's mysteries are boring ones, she's found, barely worthy of the name. Maybe there was another word for those little, boring enigmas once, but it's been lost. The English language undergoes constant simplification, words escaping and running home to their root languages with dire tales of their time held captive by the American tongue.

She opens the door and steps out into sunlight that hits like maple syrup drizzled on a plate, heavy and somehow sticky, clinging to everything it touches. The light is different here. She's not sure how; give her time and she'll decode it. She's sure of *that*, if nothing else. Just give her time.

The teen from yesterday is waiting outside, accompanied by two older people dressed in similar clothes that she takes for their parents. One of them has a bristly mustache, and that's the one who steps forward and says, "I'm sorry the place wasn't perfectly ready for you when you arrived. We must have read your letter wrong. We were expecting you tomorrow. Did you sleep well?"

"Yes, absolutely." The lie is as natural as breathing, born from the same deep, awful place as the many other lies over the years, the ones about walking into doors or being so clumsy, really, she shouldn't be trusted out on her own. She stops, and grimaces, and says, "Not really. Something spooked me in the middle of the night, and I slept in the wardrobe in the bedroom where I'd gone to bed. My back really hurts."

Telling the truth feels like lancing a wound. The teen exchanges a look with their parents, complicated and silent, and Millie doesn't resent that silent communication as much as she should. The sunlight is still falling on her arms, still burning the curdled sickness of her marriage out of her, all those years of silence and lies slipping away like mist in the morning. She cradles the shoe to her chest, faintly embarrassed by its presence, wishing she had left it inside until she knew the day would hold no further guests or surprises.

"Julie here is ready to finish cleaning the place," says the one with the mustache, presumably the Papa the teen had gone looking for the day before. "If you'd like to come walking with me and Eunice, we can help you find a place to dispose of that nasty old shoe."

"I know the best places for throwing things away," says the teen—says Eunice, and smiles. For a rural teen in the middle of nowhere, she has remarkable dentistry, as clean and white as the moon that hung over the lake the night before.

"This old thing?" Millie lifts the shoe, looks at it like she's never seen it before, like it's something foul and unspeakable. "Yes, that would be best."

"And when we get back, I'll make sure the generators are up and running," says Papa. "You'll need it if you're planning to stay past the end of the summer."

Millie, who has never felt quite this safe or quite this at peace in her life, tilts her face back and breathes in the thick, honeyed sunlight.

"I think I may be staying forever," she says, and the three locals smile, and all of this has happened before, and all of this will happen again, and all of this is precisely as it's meant to be. They are standing in the open, so near to the deep woods, and the sunlight falling there has been waiting patiently, and after years and miles spent so far away that the deep woods were only a dream, she is finally home.

The light is different here.

A Hundred Miles and a Mile

Carmen Maria Machado

W HEN Lucy thinks back to her childhood, she knows
she's getting close to the memory—not even just the
memory, the *words*—when her pulse picks up, a fat bluebottle
fly bumping around a lampshade, urgent and lost. If she doesn't
stop, it gets worse; a string being pulled away from the guitar's
neck. Her blood feels alive, alien, spooked as horses. She knows
if she looks in a mirror she'll see her throat humming its own
crazed tune. So she doesn't look. Would you?

It's strange, the knowing-not-knowing. It twitches like
something that won't die. When china shatters. When someone
offers her milk. She feels like she's drifting away, like she'd simply
disappear if not for the inconvenience of her limbs and organs.

She thought, for sure, that these spells would leave her when childhood did—that she would outgrow them, as she did night terrors and an allergy to cats. And it's true that they changed—became less about broken ceramics and dairy products and, inexplicably, quaint roadside restaurants—and became odder, more diffuse. More of a mood than a fear; a sense of oncoming doom, like the seconds before death by drowning.

It got truly bad just before the wedding—well, the almost-wedding—when she and Pete's mother visited the rental hall. The owner offered her tea, which she accepted; as they walked, discussing the space, she sipped. When it was over—when she drained the final swallow—she saw a design of Cassiopeia on the bottom of the cup. Then, a wave of nausea and panic, a darkening around the edge of her vision. Then, a whisper dropped into her ear.

Don't do it. Once they have trapped you—

When the vignette faded, she asked the property manager if he had a telephone. That was how Pete's mother knew she was leaving Pete before Pete did.

She thought Pete's mother would be angry—furious, even—but when they got into the car Pete's mother grabbed her hand and said, "I wish I could have done the same," and then turned on the radio. They sang the whole way back, windows down. (Months later, tangled up in Meredith, she considered that that was it—she knew on some level that to submit to Pete's bed, sweet and gentle a man as he was, was unthinkable. But why that moment at the wedding hall? Why not when Pete kissed her the first or fifth or fiftieth time?)

Shortly after, Lucy began seeing a psychotherapist, a shriveled little German woman named Dr. Krämer who conducted her appointments from the top of her desk, cross-legged on a zabuton. She was very interested in the story; kept making Lucy return to it, examine it from new angles. Was it simply the reality of the wedding intruding on the fantasy? The knowledge of marriage as yoke, and a larger sense of what was being lost? Or was it the realization no amount of ceremony could make Pete to Lucy's liking, not in the necessary way? Or was it—she said this carefully, pointedly—the cup, with its scrolled handle and thin lip and delicately rendered constellation?

You will never see it again. Don't do it.

But that would be insane, Lucy thought, releasing her skirt from her white-knuckled grip, smoothing it over her knee. It would be insane if it was just the cup.

A few weeks before her nineteenth birthday, Lucy took off with Meredith for a long weekend. They laughed as the city receded behind them and were in Niagara by sundown. This was three years after Liberace held the button to little Debbie Stone's nose to detonate the dynamite, three years before little Roger Woodward survived a barrel-less plunge over the falls. (Polio had frozen Debbie, and fate had saved Roger; even back then, nothing was fair.) They rode the *Maid of the Mist*, ate too many hotdogs, made love in a motel lousy with honeymooners.

On the way home, they stopped for lunch at a little inn somewhere near Syracuse. As soon as they crossed the threshold, Lucy realized something was wrong, terrible. She collapsed into the chair and held the napkin against her cheeks; she traced the velvety contours of the fork at her place setting. Meredith was feeling tired and irritable and had no time for one of Lucy's moods. When the waitress came over to see if everything was all right, Lucy stared at her with such naked—well, naked *something*, not desire, but an expression so open and vulnerable that Meredith stood up in exasperation. "I'll wait in the car," she said. Lucy ate in a daze (refusing milk, of course) and after that they drove home in total silence. They broke up just before they reached the city, and the next time Lucy saw Meredith, she was hanging off a blonde at the Bag and looking like a million dollars.

After that, Dr. Krämer asked Lucy if there was something special about the inn, the table setting, the waitress.

"Nothing," Lucy said. "I mean, nothing that I put my finger on."

"A memory, maybe? Perhaps you went there as a child?"

"It's possible. We took trips all over, my mother and father and brother and I."

Dr. Krämer didn't say anything but watched Lucy over her bifocals.

It wasn't that Lucy had a bad childhood. She knew people who did, who wore their past miseries like a winter coat, subtly altering their shape. But no—her parents were good people. She had never been beaten or neglected. She never went hungry, she always had shoes that fit. Her mother's death—well, she was technically an adult when that happened, wasn't she? And sometimes such things could not be helped. Her father was a content if lonely widower, her brother in love with his new wife.

Dr. Krämer asked her to think back—relax her mind, come to the moment cautiously, like you'd approach a dog that bites.

Brave girl. Wise, brave girl.

"I wouldn't approach a dog that bites," Lucy said.

Dr. Krämer held up her pen like a switchblade. "Then how do you know it's a dog at all?"

A few days into her thirties, Lucy woke up in the middle of the night already sobbing, as if she were rounding off a two-day post-heartbreak bender. She put on her mother's old mink and took a walk. It kept her warm, and every time the wind ruffled the fur she thought about how it was unfair that inheritances so often hinged on death. Why did people choose to wait?

The sky was the color of milky tea and scattered with a handful of stars. She walked past street vendors, drunks, people pouring out of jazz clubs and bars; over puddles and vomit and grates ejaculating steam. She walked until dawn began to thin out the darkness; until waitresses were pouring coffee through the restaurant windows; until shopkeepers unfolded sidewalk signs with a clatter and a sigh.

Sometime after the sun was fully up, she found herself in front of a Gimbels. She hadn't been in a department store in years, and it was breathtaking—as if she'd entered some dusty, crowded market in Baghdad. She fiddled with some gloves, examined some scarves. She wandered into the perfume department and touched her fingers to the bottles and stoppers. She uncapped a lipstick and twirled it free, then bent to a mirror and circled her mouth with the wax.

It was there that she spotted the child—across the room, rosy cheeked, wrapped in a smart white coat.

The child's mother was trying to decide on a watch for her husband. She was examining them closely, asking questions, holding them up to the light. She was distracted because she did not want the clerk to know how little she knew about watches. It was very easy to lure the girl away.

The police were called. They thought they were looking for a small child who had wandered from her mother, which is why they didn't notice Lucy at first, kneeling in the corner of the shoe section on the third floor, whispering something frantically to the girl. The girl was not squirming away—she was, in fact, listening with a solemnity and intent her own mother would not have recognized—and so she did not stand out. It was only when the manager recognized the girl in the white coat that they were separated. The girl waved goodbye to Lucy, and Lucy waved back.

When they were reunited, the rescuing officer assured the mother that the eccentric woman did not appear to have been harming the little girl in any way. She appeared to be merely speaking to her, telling her something. He almost ended with another word —telling her something *urgent*—but he stopped himself. He didn't know why. The mother crushed her daughter to her breast; didn't noticed the way his sentence trailed off.

The police took Lucy to their station. She told them she simply needed the little girl to understand. To understand what, they asked her, but she had fallen asleep in her chair. She stayed asleep for three days.

When the little girl in the white coat became a woman, she would, on occasion, think back to her own past and come across the memory of the department store for reasons she did not fully understand. Her mother. The watch. Her own reflection in a glass case. Only when she looked at it sideways would she remember that it held something else entirely: a hulking, sorrowful creature—red-mouthed and sleek as an otter—extending her hand and whispering the thing she needed to hear.

Quiet Dead Things

Cassandra Khaw

I T began with a murder in the late summer, which is to say it started with a natural repudiation of the act. When news came forward of what had transpired—the woman, tidily flayed and bolted to a tree in the adjacent village—the village of Asbestos woke with rage. How dare their neighbors. Rural living was already besieged by sneering gossip about how cousins would marry their way into monstrosity, allegations of nonconsensual coital relations with the livestock, claims that its parishioners lacked both education and adequate hygiene routines, had bad politics and worse music and nothing like common civility.

It did not need this.

To add homicide to their dossier of purported sins; it was unthinkable.

Like Asbestos, the township of Cedarville was incensed. Mr. Carpenter, who, despite his family name, had no facility with timber but made up for such inadequacy—at least in his own head—by having more than a passing gift for people, sent out little personalized letters to each of his constituents. As the mayor, it was his responsibility to provide order, dispense reassurance, and sustain morale. What happened in the village wasn't just shocking, it was disgusting too, a reminder of how flimsy civilization was, a veneer under which still rutted and writhed all kinds of paleolithic barbarisms. To be human, Mr. Carpenter believed, was to work relentlessly from dawn to deep dusk, perpetually vigilant against the shadow-self.

If any of you hear of such repugnance, wrote Mr. Carpenter, *please make use of official council channels to inform us of what you've discovered. Your anonymity, of course, will be preserved.*

The channels in question were, in actuality, a small bird box installed outside the local arboretum, much too small to fit every one of the township's missives, but luckily only a handful of the population were properly civic-minded. Over the years it had been a square of farmland, a community garden, a green house, a short-lived manor torched to its bones by the young daughter of the last family to inhabit its walls, several pubs, a graveyard for the pets of the township's rich, and, prior to the inauguration of the arboretum, a corner store operated by an immigrant pair. Cedarville had especially fond memories of the last. Mr. Wong and his late sister were, though no one would admit such feelings in sober company, novelties. Up until their arrival, Cedarville was comprised entirely of Irish, French, Russian, Swedish, and German immigrants, all of whom produced children who then enjoyed romances with one another, creating a population who were, to a man, a heavily dilute salmon in color.

To see that much melanin and the refugee gods the Wongs brought with them, wages of a superstitious life unburdened by Christ, was invigorating. It was a reminder there was a world outside the fishbowl of Cedarville, lives outside the schedules of almanacs and shipping routes, places to go and things to do that did not require going home and were far, far from even the scrutiny of the things that lived on Mr. Richardson's farm. Exotic, the township of Cedarville understood, was an egregious description when applied to another human being.

But they all thought it.

Mr. Wong and his sibling were *very* exotic.

No one else in the township kept a shrine in memory of a deceased relative. At most, the local Catholics lit votives while murmuring sheepish orisons, aware the baptized dead had absconded to a better place. Mr. Wong, his round face ablated into a massif of grief, jowls and haggard cheeks hanging low as his spirits, brought his late sister—six years younger than him once, and only sixty-two when she died—food, too: soft white buns, spiced cakes, austere bowls of sour vegetables, white rice, ladders of fatty pork belly.

And incense.

Always those joss sticks to be lit with her morbid repast.

The people of Cedarville knew to anticipate Mr. Wong by the smoky attar of camphor, which clung to him like a malaise of the spirit. Not that anyone saw him with any regularity anymore. Loss had converted Mr. Wong into a hermit, and regressed his life to native pleasures: ethnic cooking, calligraphy, foreign movies, Allegra the postwoman said, which cost a fortune to import. He avoided his neighbors, lived frugally on the profits from the sale of his store, reserved his chatter for the altar over which a monochrome portrait of a teenaged Ms. Wong—nineteen, with a stratospheric bouffant, and makeup too old for her gravely cherubic face—presided.

I think they were lovers, came an anonymous note, printed on periwinkle cardboard and neatly sleeved in a long cream envelope. Were it not for the daub of rose perfume, a wet storm-tossed summer scent, Mrs. Gagnon might have kept her identity secret. But like so many others in Cedarville, she was an animal of habit. *It's why they never married anyone else. Fifty years of living here and neither of them could find a spouse? They must have been fornicating.*

The use of the word "fornicating" was a very Mrs. Gagnon thing, Mr. Carpenter noted, as were her lavender fascinators with their taxidermized nightingales, as was her insistence the Old Testament provided better instruction than its successor, and the way she took sacrament like a harlot traversing her wedding night: with gusto, without hesitation, with the pleasure of years of practice. Mr. Carpenter and Mrs. Gagnon were not friends but Mr. Carpenter trusted in her instincts and carefully inventoried her indictment of Mr. Wong. If nothing else, it was proof that Cedarville had at last acclimatized to Mrs. Gagnon.

For years, it was Mrs. Gagnon who was hounded by the gossips. Over fifty years ago, she had come to Cedarville like a portent: thrice divorced, a pageant alumni, richer than was courteous, a woman to be envied and thus, one to resent. Now? Now, she was part of the body of Cedarville, holied by their church, distrustful as any native of foreign intrusion.

Mr. Carpenter made a note to relay his congratulations. It was nice to see Mrs. Gagnon finally accepted among her peers; he liked it when good things happened to deserving people, "deserving" being the operative word here. Mr. Carpenter, though he understood such ideology was unpopular, even untenable in the current epoch, believed virtue was a currency. Kindness should not be extended to those who did not provide commensurate payment. Love, divine or otherwise, was a privilege to be earned. And that was the problem with the world these days. People expected too much for too little and that avarice, Mr. Carpenter believed, was the reason they'd all be found one day nailed to a tree, throat and temples and trunk woven with a stigmata of thorns.

The days yielded to weeks. Summer fallowed to autumn and Mistress Smith's dogs grew restive in their kennels, eager to be done with the soporific heat and set loose on their annual hunt. Traders came and went. The township fattened with imports. Cedarville was beginning to forget what had occurred in that little village to the west when a man from Asbestos arrived. He was not a tall man, not a handsome one save when he smiled, stocky in that way farm boys often got, with a genial face and clever green eyes, a flurry of soft black curls for hair, the kind in which hearts and fingers so often become entangled.

Mr. Carpenter met the man—Mr. Jacobson—at Cedarville's only gas station.

"Harvest ain't for weeks," he said. "I didn't expect anyone from Asbestos to be here so early."

"The harvest?" said the man, clearing his throat. "No, no. I'm not here for that. I came by to offer some news from Asbestos."

Mr. Carpenter cocked his head. "News?"

"News," said Mr. Jacobson.

The two shared a quiet like a last cigarette, night ashing the dusk sky, that glorious wine-gold leaching into a dead man's grey. The gas station squatted beside the bridge which led into Cedarville, scabrous with rust, a spindly thing still waiting for permission to die.

"What kind of news?" said Mr. Carpenter, when it became clear the man would not speak unless prompted.

"Well, Asbestos had a meeting several weeks ago and we discussed what'd happened, you know?"

Mr. Carpenter nodded. "Yes. We all know."

"We figured," said the man. "It had to be an outsider. One of those truck drivers who pass through sometimes. The guy who comes by twice a year to buy ceramics from Mary Sue. The rich couple with that big cabin in the woods. Someone like them."

"But not," said Mr. Carpenter with the care of a man fording barbed wire, "someone like Mr. Wong."

"Probably not."

A non-answer but not unexpected.

"Could be the teenagers who come for their yearly retreats. They're feral at that age."

Mr. Jacobson nodded and scratched under his chin, his nails raking florid rows down the white road of his throat. They were filthy with what could have been grease or gore, a deep jammy dark that seeped softly along the cuticles. Exactly like blood, Mr. Carpenter thought. But Asbestos, though starved of good farmers, had slaughtermen and butchers and ranchmen. The blood, if it was blood, likely had justifiable cause to be there. And if it did not, there were ways to deal with a murderer so striking.

"Maybe."

"So how does Asbestos plan to deal with this revelation, then?"

"Well," said Mr. Jacobson, and Mr. Carpenter wondered if the man sang when he was not in the abattoir, entrails gnarled along his forearms, a slop of red scudding along the floor beneath his feet, greasing the drains so the chum from his work escaped with ease. No reason for him to *not* sing in the knacker's yard; entertainment wasn't sacred, not like the grain or good earth. "We decided it wouldn't be a bad idea to close off Asbestos for a few months. Make certain whoever it was who did it knows we won't stand for such behavior. That they're not welcome here."

Mr. Carpenter waited. He could tell a request was coming.

"Anyway," said the man. "We were wondering if you'd do the same. Show of solidarity and all that. We'll give you discounts on meat and wool."

"Could even try setting up some kind of barter system," said Mr. Carpenter. "Meat and wool for cider, pies, preserves, whatever else you want from our orchards."

"And your fields."

Mr. Carpenter bobbed his head. "Depends on if you can talk Mrs. Taylor into coming around to check our generator every now and then. The turbines are starting to fall apart."

"What happened to Mr. Smith?"

"The repairman?"

"Mm."

Mr. Carpenter said nothing further until the man took the hint.

"I'm sure we can figure out something. Between you, us, the other communities in the county, we should be able to keep ourselves going for a while," said the man.

Mr. Carpenter thought on this, aware that when he spoke, he spoke for two thousand and fifty-six other individuals, and that he held this responsibility because none of them desired any culpability in municipal affairs; that he was, in some respect, an effigial figure, something to burn should the winter linger past its welcome. It was a knowledge that had left him anchored to cowardice for too many decades.

But today felt different.

Today felt like an occasion for change.

Months from that pivotal instant, Mr. Carpenter would replay the encounter in his head, wondering how he'd come upon the epiphany, if his subconscious had received instruction from the dying summer, some sign necessitating rebellion. If he had read those augurs in his morning oatmeal, in the calamities listed in the morning news, in the flight of the crows of Cedarville, who had always been uncommonly large and eerily astute. Regardless, whatever possessed him did so with a vigor that'd become alien to him, and Mr. Carpenter, there in the ruin-sodden dark, said to the man, vehement for the first time since his youth:

"I think so too."

It was easier than anyone thought it would be.

A few calls made in an apologetic tone, citing half-true excuses and old sins, altercations between Cedarville and this truck driver or that. A number of emails dictated to the Elliots' oldest daughter, a brittle melancholic girl precociously married to the manners of mid-age, then sent through the only computer in the township's solitary school. A single somewhat obsequious letter, mailed to those in charge of the county; more formality than anything else. Both Cedarville and Mr. Carpenter could not recall the last time the administration even took note of their existence.

The matriarchs of the church ran bake sales like wars, organizing them with autocratic pomp, all manners of kitchens conscripted into the effort and not one allowed the freedom to refuse. This was about community. There was no opting out. So for weeks, Cedarville smelled warmly of butter and baking pies, gingerbread and blackberries cooked down to syrup, mulled wine steeping in vast stock pots, their surfaces pitted from long use.

Men and women and giggling children came from adjoining communities, bringing with them money and other oblations, the latter far, far more precious to Cedarville than currency. After all, there would be amnesty from the outside world. No point to money if it can't be spent to acquire things you couldn't trade for, luxuries like Parisian coffee grounds or fresh books.

Slowly, a frenetic joy developed through Cedarville, spreading as gossip might, and all at once, before anyone knew how, there were wreaths on every door, windows garlanded with red, fairy lights threaded along the roofs, and a nightly choir who sang hymns in lieu of carols, most of them in languages Cedarville still spoke. It felt like Christmas although Christmas was still a few months away, and also something older, something old enough that it could not be named, only observed as an absence. Some of the younger people joked about agrestic paganism and how memory could be held in the marrow, how bucolic practices were often scaffolded on grisly traditions, and wasn't it true that everything Christian has its beginnings in blood? Perhaps it was that.

But no one looked too deeply into their postulations, not even them. No point in doing so when there were dances to attend, visitors to entrance, meals to share, drinks to sip and guzzle and splash onto one another, whether in ecstasy or rage or some amalgamation of the two. By the time winter arrived, cauling the branches with frost, everyone was convinced they could do this forever.

Except Mr. Wong.

Where the rest of Cedarville was nourished by the recent changes, Mr. Wong withered. The fat slicked from his small frame. He no longer brought food to his sister's altar, migrating the paraphernalia into the cottage he'd shared with her. He avoided his neighbors; he shrunk. As much a wraith now as the memory of his sibling, Mr. Wong, for a while, seemed like he would grow smaller and smaller, until at last he was nothing but a faint unhappy noise.

Then, Mr. Carpenter made the error of calling a town hall, six weeks after he brokered a deal with Mr. Jacobson, the man from Asbestos. It was not the first of such meetings, but it was the largest, the most officious of the lot. Everyone came, dressed in their festive best, and they stayed even if they could not find room to fit into the church, haunting the windows. The children, Mr. Carpenter thought, were especially darling. Though Cedarville was enjoying a surfeit of largesse, it remained a pragmatic township, taught at the crib to ration and take care of how it made use of its bounties; the winters here could be cruel. As such, most of the finery was reserved for the youngest, and how radiant they were under a patina of such doting! The girls wore embroidered bonnets, the boys damasked waistcoats, and there was satin for accents and goose-down in the lining of their velvet coats, and mother-of-pearl shining from their buttons. Mr. Carpenter, who'd never wanted his own offspring, ached nonetheless at the cherubic vision, full of pride, filled with saudade for the life that ended with his wife's own. Had the Devil provided him the option of being preserved here, in the thick resin of this moment, Mr. Carpenter would have begged for him to take his soul.

It was perfect up until Mr. Wong spoke.

"This is wrong."

His voice, rarely discerned save as a mumble, was atonal and clamorous. It skidded along the higher registers, becoming shrill, but was otherwise arthritic in the way typical of the aged. But for all its thinness, Mr. Wong's voice was not lacking in volume. His declaration boomed through the chatter, and Cedarville collapsed into a watchful quiet.

"Sorry," said Mr. Carpenter from his vantage at the podium. "But how so?"

Mr. Wong strode down the corridor, a finger jabbed at Mr. Carpenter, or perhaps the wizened Christ looming behind the latter. The town halls were, by and large, held in the settlement's only church. Whoever had commissioned the building had worshipped authenticity, and so the Messiah, starved to his pith, possessed not a beatific expression but one of pained ecstasy, the Holy Spear still jutting from beneath his ribs, viscera unspooling from the wound while stained-glass angels gaped longingly.

"This is wrong," said Mr. Wong again. "Closing the borders like this. It's wrong."

"It sends a message," said Mr. Carpenter calmly.

A hoarse bark of laughter. "What message? That we are stupid? If there is a wolf here trying to eat us sheep, what do you think it is going to do? It is going to laugh. It is going to be so happy to know that the sheep won't make contact with their shepherds."

Mr. Carpenter decided then that what grated at him was neither Mr. Wong's diatribe nor the content of his soliloquy, but the architecture of his grammar, his sentence construction, the lack of flow in his speech. His delivery was stilted for all its passion, his enunciation lamentable. It troubled Mr. Carpenter as Mr. Carpenter believed elocution was a vital practice, and if one wanted to speak in public, one owed it to their audience to speak well and with great charm.

"The authorities believe the murderer has moved on," said Mr. Carpenter. "Unless you have reason to believe differently."

The furnaces kicked in. A low hum suffused the church and to Mr. Carpenter, made briefly superstitious by his vexation, it seemed like the building despaired of Mr. Wong's presence too. Why, Mr. Carpenter could not be sure, although the more he interrogated the notion, the more ill-ease he experienced. To a great degree, he understood this to be subconscious projection, a trick of the mind, much like the movement of the seraphs in the corner of his eye. Nonetheless, it is impossible to witness a holy place passing such sour judgment on an individual and not feel a frisson of caution.

Mr. Carpenter said none of this, of course.

"I think the killer could be a local," spat Mr. Wong. "You people don't need to look at me like I'm crazy. You know it's true."

"Our county is small," said Mr. Carpenter, so very carefully. "And we are blessed for that reason. We know each other and we know one another to be good."

The crowd murmured agreement.

Mr. Wong swore loudly, in a tongue none but him and his dead sister spoke. Then, in English again: "Fuck off. Fuck off with your stupid ideas. You think you're all saints? I know who you all have been fucking. I know what you do. I know which of you beat your children and which of you cheat the tourists. Don't think I haven't been paying attention."

Had that bitter statement been spoken under different circumstances, Cedarville might have done nothing but scrunch down, abashed to have its fabrications and its pretenses at genteel behavior so bluntly shucked. But there, in the church, amid those festive days, with so many of them garbed like country kings, a very different emotion took root. It was not horror that burgeoned in the breasts of Cedarville's finest, not self-loathing, not guilt, not introspection or mawkish repentance; no, nothing constructive at all.

It was rage instead, subtle yet consuming, even righteous in its timbre. Rage at the insult of being laid bare without consent. Rage at being coerced into examining old sins when the wise knew better than to exhume the past; at being named for what they were. Spouses glanced warily at their partners while adulterers looked meekly to old lovers. Parents glowered at their brood, daring them to author complaint, to suggest that the punitive measures they'd doled out were disproportionate to the error. Liars smoothed the creases of their fine suits. Cedarville's wealthy, what few there were, consoled themselves with a familiar paean: that there were occasions when they had been kind, that they were, at least, more pious than their neighbors. And all of them, they kept a sliver of their fury for Mr. Wong, for without him they would not be made so uncomfortable.

This was his fault. This unwanted accounting of misdeeds, their sudden uncertainty, the crumbling of their faith in not just each other but themselves. This was Mr. Wong's doing and some manner of reparations would need to be made.

"These are serious allegations you're levelling against the community. *Your* community," said Mr. Carpenter, mouth pinching. "Unless you think yourself better than us somehow."

Mr. Wong drank in the unhappy crowd. He had lived in Cedarville for so long, the memories of his birthplace felt like an abstract, a story told to him and misremembered as his own. He understood this thought as false but fact had little to do with reality. Truth was merely raw material. It was the story, the consensus belief, that mattered.

"I think," said Mr. Wong, aware things would be very different by the end of the sentence. "That I am more honest than the rest of you."

The first month of isolation bore a celebratory air despite the blizzard which came as escort. Cedarville kept its houses bedecked with decorations, though by the second week there was no one to admire their colors, not with how the ice grew in sheets, laminae of glass pressed thickly to the walls and the pavement. The municipal committee tried at first to salt the walkways, only to have their work undone in minutes, and after that consigned themselves to reserving their supplies for emergencies. There were many more days of this algor weather to survive. Likely, there would be tragedies too: people to unearth, the ailing to migrate from home to hospital. They would need the salt then to ward against slippage.

The blizzard howled on.

Snow rose to the knees of the rare few who persisted in trudging their way through the biting cold. Then it went higher, barricading families within their homes. The mood remained jovial, nonetheless. Children sang from second-story windows. Their fathers gossiped for hours on the phone as their mothers clumped in the kitchen, straining for news, for anything, the barest gasp of change, from static-plagued radios, half-filled mugs of lukewarm tea spread over every surface. This was a strange time, a new epoch, one without apparent compass, and Cedarville moved rudderless through each pale week. If not for what happened with Mr. Wong, they might have felt an incursion of despair. But Cedarville persisted, propelled by something not dissimilar to hope.

However, even optimism requires feeding. The congeniality ebbed as the blizzard seared away to blue sky. In the beginning, Cedarville regarded this as a reprieve. Though the temperatures were too arctic for anything to melt, snowfall at least was no longer accumulating. But it was cold in a fashion it had not been for decades and the air lacerated skin. To breathe was to abrade lungs, leave mouths bloodied from the kiss of the chill. Cheeks did not pink but inflamed. And it hurt to be outside so people withdrew indoors, burrowing close to their radiators and their fireplaces, wrapping themselves in promises this would be over soon.

For this reason, it took a week for Mrs. Gagnon's body to be found.

The corpse was discovered crammed into a woodshed, propped upright against the back wall so that, from afar, it appeared as though Mrs. Gagnon was surveilling the stacked timber, and perhaps disapproving of what she saw. The old woman bore no wounds; her death was prescribed to exposure. What no one could answer was the why of the circumstances leading to Mrs. Gagnon's passing. She had no cause to be in the woodshed and while foul play was not improbable, it seemed a negligible hypothesis. When Mrs. Gagnon's cadaver was extracted, it had worn a small thoughtful frown: the expression of a woman grappling with an inconvenience rather than her murder.

But if not murder, then *what* drove Mrs. Gagnon to squeeze herself into that dark space and wait there until her blood blued under her skin? And wasn't that the same look that dressed the face of the corpse they had found in the homestead? That poor woman with her similarly frost-smudged stare, mouth bloodied into a new shape; she had been beaten first—tenderized—before being affixed to the tree by the hems of her flayed skin. It had been ritualistic and cruel and inhospitably strange, even here where farmers talked sometimes of black dogs in the woods, hounds with a corona of headlight eyes floating where they shouldn't. Despite what had been visited on her body, she had looked more thoughtful than tortured, even melancholy. "Pitying," someone had told Mr. Carpenter, who wished immediately he had not been told such; it unsettled him to think of a corpse despairing over the fortunes of the living.

As much as he found such thoughts alarming, what troubled Mr. Carpenter more were the maudlin rumors seeping through Cedarville. He foresaw misfortune coming for the township if he did not mitigate their transmission. So, as best able, Mr. Carpenter steered the bavardage, first to the notion that Mrs. Gagnon, weary of an illness she'd kept private, might have killed herself; and then, when that failed to take hold, to the idea her demise could be attributable to whoever was responsible for the travesty in the neighboring homestead. The thought brought no comfort but that was not its purpose. Mr. Carpenter's intention had been to circumvent any belief that the culprit, if there was indeed one, might have been one of Cedarville's own, and at this he succeeded.

A new energy shortly possessed the township, replacing the malaise. When Mr. Jacobson returned, bringing with him meat in exchange for produce, he was run out of the township before he could cross the bridge to Cedarville, chased back down the road by a coalition of laughing youth with beautiful antique rifles and the chatter of the latter's spent casings upon the shining ice. No one chastised the boys—and they *were* boys, could not be anything but boys, their sisters having lost too much sleep counting the dwindling cans in the pantries to come out— when they returned. Instead, the girls queued at their windows to wave, as though it were war heroes they were welcoming home.

Mr. Carpenter wrote letters to his constituents the following day, reminding them there were deer in the forests, elk and fat grey rabbits, turkey even—for those lucky enough to spot what rare few remained following the harvest culling. If such game wasn't sufficient, there were fish under the ice of the lake: fat trout, walleyes, needle-teethed pike, all dreaming sweetly of summer. Cedarville's larders would stay filled if not fat from Asbestos's tithing. It was unfortunate, yes, but Cedarville, he noted, had survived worse recently: the tragedy of Mrs. Gagnon's passing, for one, and the more regrettable elements of what happened with Mr. Wong. Things would be well.

Then the phone lines went.

The constable quickly established the damage as natural, the wires a casualty of the blizzard. Ice had toppled several utility poles, taking with them a snarl of cables. Satellite service continued to function, albeit at reduced capacity, and Mr. Carpenter wrote again to the residents of Cedarville, suggesting that the community take this period of inconvenience as an opportunity for reflection, a chance to interrogate one's interiority as the year shambled to the solstice. It was so easy to deprioritize family, to forget oneself and one's values in the capitalistic existence espoused by the urban elite. This new silence, even if flawed, should be treated as what it was: a homecoming of a kind, a reversion to a more naturalistic state.

In support of this, the church began hosting Mass daily. When the pastor, Mr. Lambert—soot-haired, despite his advancing age, but spry still in that way some men became when sapped of youth's insecurities—grew too hoarse from the new schedule, the municipal council enlisted volunteers to create a rotation, and the nature of the services—although never deviating from Christian phylum—diversified infinitesimally. The residents of Cedarville, between boarding up their properties, brought tea cakes and book clubs, ad hoc celebrations to the church, and for a few weeks things were as Mr. Carpenter prophesied: they were well.

Up until the Sunday when they discovered Mr. Lambert pinioned to the Christ in the church, belly split from the floor of his throat to the roof of his groin, his entrails the same festive crimson as the decorations limply garlanding the gutters trimming the roof outside. There were no messages, no meaning in the butchery, no calling cards, no clues as to who might have killed him or why;

only a knife on the ground beneath where his viscera drooped. Flies clotted his flayed body and sang as piously as any choir. The Elliots' oldest daughter, who had been the one to find Mr. Lambert's corpse, said she saw a woman's silhouette flickering in the window of the dead man's office. She claimed too that there had been a smell: incense, thick as what clung to Mr. Wong's skin.

But the old man was gone, as was the altar he had built for his sister, and the house in which he lived alone with her ghost was gored of its contents; its doors were locked, strung with police tape. As such, it was a surprise to Cedarville when a pack of teenagers, looking for privacy, discovered the body of the Elliots' oldest daughter dangling from a rope lashed to a ceiling beam, her expression pensive and unexpectedly relieved.

Mr. Carpenter called an immediate assembly. The township gathered to comfort the Elliots, who endured the knowledge of their daughter's suicide with a pragmatic silence, husband and wife clinging to one another, neither shedding tears. Their sons stood in a line behind them. Like their parents, they did not cry, although their eyes gleamed wetly in the wan grey light of the afternoon. Upon delivering his condolences, Mr. Carpenter proceeded to warmly remind his constituents that they were not alone, that the church still operated, that there were neighbors, that there was no cause to succumb to grief as that poor girl had, and that he himself was there and available at any hour, ready to provide company to anyone in need.

At the close of his speech, Mrs. Elliot rose from her seat.

"What happened with Mr. Wong wasn't right," she said. Mrs. Elliot had lived in Cedarville for twenty-five years, but her accent was still that of her bayou past. "The woods know it.

It's punishin' us for that."

Mr. Carpenter, who believed in nothing save the tangible, nodded. "Sometimes, tragedies happen."

"It wasn't right," said Mrs. Elliot with more insistence. "My daughter's dyin' wasn't right either."

Mr. Carpenter nodded again. "You have our condolences."

The woman went silent. She tucked grey curls behind a small round ear, looking to her husband for support, before speaking up again, this time with oracular diction, her expression grave.

"We're going to die for what happened."

"Mrs. Elliot."

She shook her head. "It's just how it is. We did wrong. It's going to make it right."

"Mrs. Elliot," said Mr. Carpenter. "I understand that it is easy to catastrophize during moments of such grief, but, believe me, there is no magic adjudicator waiting invisibly to pass judgment on us."

The woman laughed then, a bitter noise. "Naw. Of course not. S'because it already has."

"Mrs. Elliot," said Mr. Carpenter for the second time.

"We're going to die," she said, as though the statement alone was sufficient explanation, and sat down again. "And it said you're next."

No one said anything after that.

The postwoman, Allegra, found Mr. Carpenter the next morning, with the door to his cottage slightly ajar. He sat slumped, very delicately, in his favorite armchair, a bloom of grey brain coating the wall behind him. The interior admitted no evidence of robbery. It stood as neatly as the bowl of cold oatmeal, the glass of milk, the gun, and the stack of unopened letters atop the late Mr. Carpenter's desk. Like Mrs. Gagnon, like the Elliots' oldest daughter, like Mr. Lambert, like Ms. Wong when they dragged her from the water all those years ago, he was found adorned with a small, thoughtful frown.

The constable died the subsequent day.

Then the Elliots, immolated in their farmhouse.

Then Mistress Smith, whose corpse supplied one last meal to her hounds.

As Mrs. Elliot had predicted, the deaths continued, inexorable as time.

Something Like
Living Creatures

John Langan

JENNA sat cross-legged at the top of the ladder, where it was nailed to the loft. Either of the beds at her back would have raised her another two feet into the air, but she didn't think the extra height would make much, if any, difference. Besides, she liked the spot here, where the ladder connected the house's two levels, at the gap in the railing which ran the length of the loft. It allowed her to survey the house's living room, dining area, and kitchen. The only parts of it not visible to her were under the loft: the bathroom, on the far side of the front door, and her parents' room, directly beneath her, behind a heavy yellow curtain. Her position allowed her a view out the large window set high in the wall opposite the loft. Through its expanse of panes, she could see the crowns of the trees staggered down the hill below the house, and beyond them the broad Penobscot River, its surface flat gray under the overcast sky. A line of fog hid the far shore. Faintly, Jenna could hear the foghorn droning. She wasn't certain of its location. Mother and Father liked the sound: like so much in this part of Maine, it reminded them of the old country.

From where she was sitting near the foot of the ladder, leafing through her Catholic Bible, Samantha said, "Do you see anything?"

"Not yet," Jenna said.

"She isn't trying," Kayla said. She was seated at the kitchen table, her back to the scene out the kitchen window, her attention focused on the deck of playing cards that she continued to turn over in front of her. She had wrapped one of the bath towels around her hair because she said it made her look like a psychic. Jenna thought it made her look as if she had just come out of the shower. She said, "I *am* trying," though she wasn't, not the way she did when she truly wanted to look *far.*

"This Bible talks about creatures with four faces," Samantha said. "Actually, it says they were something like living creatures. How is something *like* a living creature?"

"I don't know," Jenna said.

"Beats me," Kayla said. "That's why I prefer to stick to Virgil. Plus, you know, tradition."

"You and Virgil," Jenna said.

"It says the creatures had the face of a human being in the front, the face of a lion on the right side, the face of an ox on the left side, and then it says they had the face of an eagle, but it doesn't say where. It would have to be on the back, right?"

"Makes sense," Jenna said.

"If you say so," Kayla said.

From the nearer edge of the curtain across Mother and Father's room, a finger of buttery light stretched across the living room floor, fading as it approached the opposite wall. Samantha was turning the onionskin pages of her Bible on the oval rug to the left of the light. Jenna wished she wasn't so close to the reaching light.

"Not that anyone's asking," Kayla said, "but the cards are talking."

"What are they telling you?" Samantha said.

"The hearts are gathering," Kayla said. "The four kings are in alignment."

"Hearts mean family, right?" Samantha said.

"And kings mean power," Jenna said.

"Yes," Kayla said. "But."

Samantha snickered. "You said butt."

"Shut up," Jenna said. "It isn't that kind of but."

"I know," Samantha said.

"The ace of spades keeps showing up mixed in with the hearts," Kayla said.

"He means violence, doesn't he?" Samantha said.

"It's a card," Kayla said, "not a 'he.' But yes, it does mean violence."

"Bad violence," Jenna said.

"Is there any other kind of violence?" Kayla said.

"I mean," Jenna said, "violence so bad, it tears everything apart, throws everything down. Like an earthquake. Or a hurricane."

"Or one of the living creatures," Samantha said. "At least, I think so. They have four wings, too. Did I mention that?"

"No," Jenna said.

"Do you see anything?" Kayla said.

"Not yet," Jenna said.

"She isn't trying," Samantha said.

"Shut up," Jenna said, "I *am* trying."

The finger of light on the floor dimmed, as if something was occluding it.

"This Bible," Samantha said, "says that if you cook a fish's heart, it will drive away devils."

"How did they find that out?" Kayla said. "Did they experiment? 'Let's try a bird's heart. Anything? No? Okay, what's next? I know! A fish!'"

"It says the fish was a monster," Samantha said. "Well, monstrous."

"Which just means it was big," Kayla said.

"Not necessarily," Jenna said, although she thought Kayla was probably right.

"So will any fish's heart work," Samantha said, "or does it have to be a monster fish?"

"Monstrous," Kayla said.

"You can also use its gall bladder to cure blindness," Samantha said.

"That's some fish," Kayla said. "I wonder what its small intestine does? How about its spleen? Its left eyeball?"

"This Bible mentions Asmodeus," Samantha said.

"Hush," Jenna said.

"Which one is he?" Kayla said.

"You know," Jenna said.

"He's the limping one," Samantha said. "He has a chicken foot." Jenna couldn't help herself. "Rooster."

"Right," Kayla said. "His domain is *lust*."

"Okay," Jenna said.

"Lust," Samantha said, and giggled.

"I'm going to try to see now," Jenna said.

"I thought you *were* trying," Kayla said.

"You said you were," Samantha said.

"I'm going to try harder," Jenna said.

"Whatever you say," Kayla said.

The finger of light on the bare wood floor brightened, as if whatever was in its way had moved.

"There's the ace of spades again," Kayla said.

Jenna gazed out the large window across from her. She looked over the quiet treetops, over the calm river, to the fog bank. She looked past green leaves, past gray water, to white fog. She looked over emerald, over pewter, to silver. She felt her connection to her body loosening. In the fog, in the white, in the silver, there was a speck, a spot, a figure, tiny then bigger then life-sized, as if Jenna was sitting beside it, beside her, beside a woman, a tall woman, a grown-up woman, her mother. Her mother was wearing a dark green sleeveless dress. Her mother's arms were circled by serpents with flashing green scales. Her mother's hair was piled high on her head and threaded with smaller green snakes. A dark green blindfold obscured her mother's eyes. In her right hand, Mother was holding a short knife with its curved blade pointing down. In her left hand, Mother was holding a knot of writhing serpents. Mother's mouth dropped open, and ebony pearls poured over her lips. The vision retreated, speeding away; as it did, Jenna had the impression of a shape looming behind her mother, something with a shaggy pelt and dull eyes, canted to one side. She returned to her body feeling as if she had plunged down a steep slide into a pool of cold water. Her head swam. She gripped the railing to steady herself.

"You saw something!" Samantha said.

"Did you?" Kayla said.

"Yes," Jenna said.

"What did you see?" Samantha said.

"Well?" Kayla said.

"Wait a minute," Jenna said.

The yellow curtain in front of Mother and Father's room rustled and flapped. The finger of light on the floor widened to two, three, four fingers, then dimmed as Mother stepped into the living room. She hauled the curtain closed behind her. Mother was dressed in her white housecoat, over which she had tied the green apron on which white letters demanded, DON'T MAKE ME POISON YOUR FOOD. Apron and housecoat were heavy with blood, as were Mother's slippers. Blood dribbled from the heavy kitchen scissors in her right hand. Because of where she was sitting, Jenna couldn't see what her mother was holding in her left hand.

"Girls," Mother said past the cigarette between her lips. "Come here."

Samantha closed her Catholic Bible and slid it to one side. Kayla left her cards in their placement on the kitchen table. Jenna uncrossed her numb legs and descended the ladder haltingly. Together, she and her sisters formed a half-circle around Mother. Mother's cat's-eye glasses, Jenna saw, were speckled with blood. Mother cast what was in her left hand onto the floor. It landed with a meaty splat. For a moment, Jenna saw the twisted, bloody mess and thought it was the snakes from her vision.

"We're going to learn haruspexy," Mother said. Ash dripped

from the end of her cigarette as she talked.

"What's that?" Samantha said.

"Organ divination," Kayla said.

"Divination with organs," Jenna said.

"Same difference," Kayla said.

"Pay attention, now," Mother said.

For Fiona

Money of the Dead

Karen Heuler

LAURA and her three elderly neighbors had been living in a West Village tenement for over forty years. They weren't close friends, but as the tenants in the rest of the five-story walkup came and went, they clung to their shared connection to the building's history and their own place in it. Each floor had a slightly different odor, created—Stella on the fourth floor once told Laura—by the skin cells they each shed every day over the decades. She said that the cells stuck to the walls and produced an odd stippling effect after a fresh paint. There would be the smell of paint for a week, and then the old smells would creep back like spiders repairing their webs.

"The fifth floor has wallpaper showing through," Alberto pointed out. Stella remembered that wallpaper, with its pattern of foggy trees and mountains. She recalled the janitor who had put it up, who later fell off a ladder, who had been taken away and never came back. The four old people had, over the years, known neighbors who had died behind their closed doors. The smell had given it away. Stella, for instance, had moved into an apartment where someone had died. She still had a tendency to sniff suspiciously on damp days.

It was best not to think about that.

Alberto lived down the hall from Laura, and when she found a package wrapped in red paper outside her door, she naturally asked him about it. He had found one as well. As did Stella. As did Gerald on the first floor. They all contained flimsy but beautiful dollar-sized papers, of various denominations, with *Money of the Dead* written in script on them. Laura invited her neighbors over for coffee or brandy, whatever they chose, so they could discuss the situation.

"At first I was afraid it was some notice from the landlord," Stella said. She was in her eighties but stood straight and slim, with hair cut short like a boy's. "Is someone pointing out that we're all old? Is that what it is?"

"It might be a joke," Alberto agreed. "There's an old story where I was born, that ghosts get tired of the places where they died, and search for a nicer place to live. Ghosts are restless."

"And do they pay rent? Is that what the money is for?"

He shrugged. "Someone knows the story and is making a joke? Could be."

"Maybe not. Maybe they're giving it to us to use it for something," Gerald said. He had a bad habit of winking, which he did then.

They had all brought their packages and they sat around the table, counting and studying the money. "There are no signatures on any of the bills, and no serial numbers. Just the amount, and

Money of the Dead, and a dark image." Alberto was the most meticulous of the bunch, neat and analytical and, sometimes, slow.

"It looks like a road at sunset," Laura said. She considered herself sensitive to the arts.

"That would be fitting."

"And dark shapes at the end. Indistinct. Trees? People?"

"No one ever knows what's at the end," Alberto suggested.

They had different amounts, ranging from one hundred to five hundred, and no one knew whether it was better to have more or less of it. Who wants to have dead wealth? Were they supposed to *buy* something with it and *pay* someone for it?

"We should wait a day or two," Gerald said, "in case we get a catalog." He winked again.

"Not everything is funny," Laura said.

"I believe this is money *for* the dead," Stella said. "But what do they want us to do with it?"

"Exchange it for someone who's dead?" Laura asked.

A sudden chill ran through each of them.

Yes.

Laura went through her photo albums, turning pages to look at her little boy. She had very few of Brian as an adult, and those she did have showed a steady growth of depravity. She chose one photo when Brian was eight and studied it. He had turned into a cold, impatient man and he had dabbled in crimes she could only imagine. He gloated about cheating people. One of his victims had killed him.

She decided that having her son back—the good son, the boy

she remembered—was worth every bit of money she had.

She told the others what she was thinking.

"Don't do it," Stella said. "I wouldn't. No good can come of it."

"But what else is the money for? They left it for us because we know so many of the dead. *They gave it to us for a reason!*" She looked around at them, waiting for them to agree.

Alberto shook his head. "I don't know. There's something bad about this."

Laura blushed in irritation. They had lived down the hall from each other for almost forty years, and they had little in common. She felt, very often, that he disapproved of her. For what? For the failure that was her son?

"What else would the money be for?" Laura repeated. "Why else would they choose us?"

They looked around uneasily; Gerald even raised his eyebrows instead of winking. Stella believed they were the only ones in the building to get the money. Everyone else was young, and the dead don't matter to the young. But these four were old, and they knew some of the dead.

On one side, life; on the other, death. It was almost, sometimes, as if they could see across the divide, or hear a furtive, melancholy whistle. Their friends were there, as were their enemies. Did the dead think about them? How often?

"Maybe we're supposed to do something special," Alberto said, lifting his head. They had each been lost in thought. "But I wouldn't be hasty. We can remember our beloved dead the usual way. Candles. Prayers. No exchange. You're suggesting an exchange."

"I don't know what to call it," Laura said. "Reaching out—that's how I think of it. Like sending money so my boy can visit me."

"I think we should be very cautious about this," Stella said softly. "I imagine there's a right decision and a wrong decision here, and, since we each have the money, we're in it together. Let's think about it some more before we act."

The debate continued. Laura sat there, watching it fly around from one insistent neighbor to another. They weren't going to agree that night, and she had already decided what to do. They could get angry, it didn't matter. She could recall the years when she was happiest, when Brian still loved her, and here was a chance to have it again. She thought he would come, stay for a while, and then leave. Maybe fade away, like a memory.

That night she took all the money, folded it in the red paper along with a note that said, *Brian, age eight*, and the photograph. He was all smiles, looking happy. She placed it outside her door.

Anxiety kept her awake. She was torn between feeling stupid, regretting such a risky, unpredictable move, and hope. He used to look at her with love, with unrestrained confidence; he used to check in constantly, assuming she knew everything and would always know everything. Perhaps he had never recovered from the realization that she didn't. It was so hard to believe that a cruel man had been waiting inside that gentle little boy. He had been a radiant child.

What had changed that child into a thug, a monster, a bully, and a cheat? She had seen nothing—no, there was nothing to see when he was a child, none of what he would come to be. There was no point in blaming herself, was there? They had loved each other then. She had done her best with him and he had repaid that by growing into a man who had stolen from her, threatened her, ruined people she knew, and died in a fight on a dark corner.

In the middle of the night she regretted offering all the money. Why hadn't she held some back, just in case? Money might be needed for something else, something she couldn't imagine yet. She tiptoed out to the door, opened it, and saw the package was still there. A longing suddenly overtook her, a longing for the sweetest part of her life. It didn't matter how much it cost.

It might be wrong to change her mind, anyway; it might be insulting to remove some money. She left it.

Brian was filling her head. How she missed that boy, how she missed the love they'd had for each other. No other love had rivaled that—certainly not the love she'd had for Brian's father, who had died when Brian was two and had been easily forgotten. The boy had been all that mattered, and had made her life whole.

Such good thoughts! She slept for a while and woke with anticipation. She got up, her heart beating wildly, and opened the door. The hallway was empty.

Nothing. Laura was hit by disappointment. She would not see the boy she cherished so much. She had a quick image of the adult Brian, pushed it away, and then flushed in shame. But she hated to think of him as an adult. It was better to forget what he'd become. Over time, he had changed and she had changed too, holding herself back as the ten-year-old, the twelve-year-old, the fourteen-year-old stared her down with contempt. She had lost control totally at fifteen, with his piercings and shaved head or dyed hair, his ripped clothes, and the snarl in his voice. At sixteen, he took her money and a credit card and left. Just left. She hadn't the heart to cancel her card (it was the one way she knew he was still alive) until the bill came. It took her two years to pay it off. And after that, it got harder. Phone calls, threatening letters, all from people he had cheated. And police visits.

She turned to make herself some coffee, and stood staring blankly at the wall when Brian came in, rubbing his eyes, asking for cereal. "Mommy," he said. His voice was soft and familiar and cozy, as if this had been going on every morning of his life—as, of course, it had, at that age. She had missed the sound of it so much, had missed the ease of it.

She held her breath at the first sound of his voice; she finally let it out. "Eggs?" she asked. "We're out of cereal."

His childish eyes looked at her with attention. "Did you forget me, Mommy?"

"I didn't forget you," she murmured, getting out the eggs. "I forgot the cereal."

From the moment of his return, Brian shadowed her. That was soothing at first, and confirmed how good they were together. But he never gave an inch. After a week, she was aware of how he crept up behind her and startled her with his breath on her neck. He would push in beside her when she sat on the sofa, and drape his arms around her shoulders and across her chest. How much he loves me, she thought at first, but day after day his hands got tighter and his breath got hotter. "Let me breathe," she would murmur as she untangled him.

"Don't you love me?" he asked sadly and then, once, "Don't you love me as I am?"

What did that mean? Why did her heart drop? Had he ever asked her anything like that when he was a child?

Of course not. She would have remembered. Or would she? Was this love and she had forgotten?

"Who was that?" he asked when Alberto knocked and asked to meet the following night. "He doesn't like you. He thinks you're a pushover."

"Brian!" she had said, shocked.

"Well, I think you are, too," he said without rancor.

Just that morning he had told her she shouldn't go out so often, that it was careless. "Why do you always go away? Why won't you stay here with me? I'm always alone. Is that what you want—to leave me? You can't stand to be with me?"

"Never!" she had said, anxiously sitting down beside him so she could hug him. He held his body stiffly, however. Had he felt unloved as a child, is that what he thought? He had been everything to her; what had she been to him?

And then one day, without preparation, without thought, after he had accused her of staying away too long—he didn't want her leaving, he said; ever—she blurted out, "And where have *you* been?"

All sounds stopped; nothing came through from outside, no sound from the street, no sound from the hallway. Nothing in the sky, even though she couldn't see the sky. She knew it. The silence layered into deeper and deeper thicknesses, and her heart beat with each ratchet down into the silence. He looked at her as if he'd been waiting for a long time for this question, as if it would all turn on what happened after this moment. What would turn? She wondered that in the side of her mind, a mere notation.

"You know," he said, "I was so lonely. You sent me there, didn't you? You wanted me there. There's no one there, Mommy. I was all alone. Don't send me back, Mommy!" He sobbed in a dry voice that still managed to pierce her.

"I would never," she told him. "I would never." They held each other even as she recalled what a relief it had been when he died. She held him tighter. But how relieved she had been!

"Don't send me away, Mommy! Please, Mommy!" His teeth showed like a madhouse clown's and he repeated that "Mommy" a few more times.

Then he started using that word relentlessly, lisping it, snarling it, saying it dreamily or even lustily. Oh how she learned to hate it. "Where have you been, Mommy? Did you talk to anyone, Mommy? Mommy, there's no more milk. Mommy, why were you gone so long? Don't you love me, Mommy?"

There were times when he looked heartbroken, his eyes gleaming, and cried out, "I don't think you want me here, Mommy. Do you?"

Did she? Had she made a terrible mistake? This wasn't the Brian she remembered, the charming boy who giggled at their private jokes. This Brian was challenging, complaining, and possessive. She had always wondered how Brian had become such a brutal adult, whether she had somehow contributed to it, formed him, influenced him. Had she? How?

She ran into Alberto a few weeks after Brian arrived, as she was leaving her apartment—or, she thought later, maybe Alberto had been waiting outside her door for a while. His apartment was in the front of the building; hers was in the rear by the staircase.

He cleared his throat and asked, "Any problems? I mean, with the, with the—the package?"

She had never much cared for Alberto's stiffness, but she felt lifted up to see a person who wasn't Brian. "It's not what I expected," she admitted. "I asked for my son as a child again, the best age, and it's not what I remembered. You?"

"I had a friend who killed himself, a long time ago, when we were in college. He was the most interesting person at school. I've never been able to stop thinking about him, about how I might have said something, one word, one sentence, that would have made a difference. I remember him as remarkable and vibrant."

"How is he now?" she asked, touching him lightly near the elbow. She had never touched him before, but it felt good; human.

She was afraid for a moment that Brian might see it, somehow. She let her hand drop.

Alberto stood there, frowning, his eyes looking into the air. "It's not what I thought," he said finally. "I've always wondered if I might have made a difference. He says I would. He says he gave up because of me."

They both were silent until she said, "Alberto, I'm so sorry. Do you believe it's true?"

His eyes, which had been staring almost absently away, turned back to her. "What else can I believe?"

Even if Brian couldn't see them, maybe he was listening on the other side of the door. She motioned to move down the hallway; surely they couldn't be overheard there. Still, she dropped her voice. "Are we sure that they are who we think they are?"

He nodded. "Or the reverse. I sometimes wonder if I am who I think I am."

"Oh," she said, nonplussed. They were who they'd always been. Of course they were. "I haven't seen Stella or Gerald lately, have you?"

"I saw Gerald a few days ago. He was coming out or going in—at any rate, in his doorway. He said he had found someone to buy his share of the money. He had listed it on eBay. I don't think that was wise, do you? But he's always been that way. Out for himself, I mean."

Who isn't out for themselves? Laura wondered, but that was Alberto—disapproving. Although she didn't care for Gerald either.

Stella lived on the fourth floor, and Laura followed Alberto upstairs to check on their neighbor. They stood outside her door while he tapped once, twice. There was no answer. What a weak knock he has, Laura thought, and pounded loudly. "Stella!" she called. "Stella! It's Laura and Alberto! Talk to us."

And then they heard the lock turn, and Laura repeated, "It's us, Stella. Your neighbors."

The door opened and Stella blinked at them. "Thank God it's you," she whispered. "Has it been you each time? Are you banging on my door every night?"

"No," Alberto said. "We haven't seen you in a while, so we came by to check. What's going on?"

She shuddered. "Every night. All night. Someone pounds on the door, then it stops. Another pound. Then it stops. At first I looked, but there was no one there. But I won't look any more. I thought about why this was happening, and then I thought maybe it's about the money of the dead. I know you two put out money and got what you wanted, but I didn't put anything out. It seemed sacrilegious. So, I put out half of it because of all the banging, and the next night it was two knocks each time. I put out the rest, and it was three knocks. All night long. Does that make sense? The money is gone, so why are they so mad? What do they want from me? How do I make it stop?"

"I don't know," Alberto said. "I'm sorry. Laura and I asked for specific people, and that's what we got. They obviously knew you had the money. I don't know why they won't stop."

"And who *are* they?" Laura asked. "Do you have any idea?"

Stella's eyes blinked. "I think it's the woman who died here. I think it's her and anyone else who died here. I think they want to come back in."

She looked away for a second, then gathered herself together. "I'm leaving," she said. "I'll stay at a hotel until I decide where to go. The rent's paid. I'll get someone to come for my things."

"But you've been here so long!" Laura said. "And all they do is knock?" She bit her lip as Stella glared at her.

Three days after Stella left, the screams began in Gerald's apartment. They were sickening. Laura stood in the first-floor hallway, on her way out to the store, her heart thudding. She couldn't bring herself to knock on his door—what could she do? She glanced through the front door and saw Alberto outside, his shoulders hunched. He lifted his head and saw her, and came in.

"I hear it," he said stiffly. He took her elbow and they walked back down the hall, to the stairway. "But it's his own fault. It was all a lie, this whole business. He told me yesterday. He put the money outside our doors, as a joke. He said he found a package outside a funeral home in Chinatown." He frowned. "He took someone's offering to the dead."

"But the screams—"

"I told you. He said he had a buyer. Maybe whoever that money was originally meant for, I don't know. There's nothing we can do now. We've invited them in, each of us, in one way or another."

Laura looked back along the hallway to the glass front door. She would have to go past the screams to reach the street now. If she actually made it outside. There was a new heaviness weighing her down when she left Brian, a weariness and worry. What was he doing; was he calling her? She wanted to be free of him, beyond the door, outside, but didn't that prove her failure as a mother? How could she feel the way she did? What kind of person hated their son, dreaded him, hated the sound of his voice?

He called for her a lot now, sometimes just repeating, "Mommy Mommy Mommy," from across the room or right next to her, and nothing she did would shut him up. She was beginning to hate that looming face and the sound of his voice. "Mommy Mommy Mommy Mommy."

Another scream tore through the hallway, and Alberto drew his breath in. "We're stuck with what we've done," he said finally.

But *she* hadn't stolen the money. And she had returned it, after all. Was that true? Had she returned it? Or used it?

Upstairs, a voice called from inside her apartment. "Mommy!"

They stood still, heads cocked, listening. There was another scream from Gerald's apartment. Laura felt a layer of regret folding the two of them together. "Can we send them back?" she asked. Was there any way to undo this, to change what she'd done, to go back to a time when she could have made a different choice? But which choice had been the one to bring her to this point? "Can we?" She could see that small face, those eyes of his—her child, her tormentor. The question was aimed at herself more than at her neighbor.

Behind her, upstairs, she heard him again. "Mommy!"

They lifted their eyes upwards, the lines of bannisters and railings like the inside of a telescope, narrowing and narrowing their vision. Alberto's eyes met hers and he stepped under the stairway to hide, in a move that seemed perfectly justified, and she called up to Brian and rose slowly back to him.

"Why were you talking to him about me?" he asked, once she was inside.

"I wasn't," she said immediately, but he looked annoyed. "I mean, we know each other and we ask about each other's lives. That's what neighbors do."

"Really?" he asked, his eyes shining with calculation. "You were talking about how to get rid of me. Us."

Her heart lurched.

"What does your friend say to you?" Laura asked Alberto. She didn't know if "friend" was the right word.

Alberto winced. "That he would have lived if I'd been kind to him. I don't remember what I told you. We argued. I swore I would never see or speak to him again."

"And yet you called him back now."

"He left me a suicide note," Alberto continued. "I've never been able to forget that note."

When they met, they often found themselves standing silently together, lost in thought.

"I told Brian once that I hated him," she said finally. "More than once. He was a cruel man. Evil. I said I wished he was dead."

He nodded, and after a while he said, "It isn't love that haunts us, but regret."

She found it increasingly hard to leave the apartment, and she often stopped at the building's front door, too uncertain about where to go and what to do.

The tenants on the first floor and on the second floor above Gerald's apartment moved out because of the screaming. The owner came through one day, knocking on doors and asking those who were left about the screams, which didn't happen while he was there. "Yes," she said, "there are screams." Brian came up next to her. "I didn't hear any," he said. "Mommy."

"He doesn't go out very much," she said weakly.

The owner looked thoughtfully at Brian. "Cute kid," he said. "That's a good age. Wait till he's a teenager." He grinned, cast a last look around, and left.

She remembered those years, of course, the constant fights and threats and stealing and everything else. Was it her fault he'd turned out that way? Had she given up on him and left him to crumble? She looked at Brian. "Are you happy?" she asked. "Were you ever happy?"

He frowned and said, "I'll always love you, Mommy. Mommy, Mommy, Mommy, Mommy!" His voice kept getting louder.

"Stop that," she whispered.

The next day she woke up choking, and found Brian in bed with her, clutching her, his hands wrapped around her throat. She reached up and grabbed his fingers, prying them off as she gasped. "What are you doing?" she finally cried.

"I missed you. I wanted to be close to you."

He had crawled into bed twice before, and she had told him not to do it again. He had said the same thing: "I missed you." She sat up, her back to him, trying to make it seem normal somehow. But it wasn't normal.

"You're too old for this," she said, and he pressed against her, his arms reaching around her shoulders. "Mommy Mommy Mommy," he said.

From that night on, she locked her bedroom door. She pulled pillows over her head, but she would wake in the middle of the night and hear him whispering through the door, "Mommy."

She found Alberto standing at the front door again, looking out. "How far can you go?" he asked, and she realized then that her orbit had been closing in. Now, she only went to the small grocery store across the street.

"I'm getting extra food every time I go out," he said. "Stocking up. You should do the same."

She had thought that once and then forgotten it. When she was away Brian filled her head completely; she could only think of him until she returned. There was no reason for her to put up with any of it. He might be her son (she certainly recognized him) but she had wanted the kind son and he certainly wasn't that. He was the adult Brian in the boy's body. That wore her out.

The next time she met Alberto it was at the bottom of the stairs, where he told her more about his friend.

"He said I never cared for him, still don't, that I have no ability to feel for another. Do you think that? He says there are other people I've affected, he knows it, other people I've driven insane. He says I pushed him to it, after all." He cast his eyes down and frowned, then looked at her intently. "I can love people, don't you think? He says I can't, but I've been a good friend, a good neighbor, haven't I?"

She wanted to say yes—she wanted to shout it and touch his hand, but her throat hardened and all she could say was, "I always found you kind of reserved, but we're just neighbors. Some people are like that." On another day she might have made it sound better; but this was, she thought, still a fair statement. They were neighbors, not friends.

It was getting harder to leave, and Alberto stood next to the front door the next day, just standing there. He nodded, and she stood beside him, looking through the glass-paned door. She supposed they would stay there until someone came in or out.

She had not seen anyone else in weeks. "Have all the other tenants left?"

"I think so," Alberto said. "Or they don't come out when we're around."

She drew in her breath. What a strange thing to say.

"Haven't you noticed how quiet it is? Even Gerald's screams are getting quieter."

Alberto tapped on the front door; it made a very faint sound. She reached out and touched it too, as if to make sure it was real. They stood there in the quiet until they gave up and turned back.

She could no longer hear her own footsteps in the hall.

That was the last she saw of Alberto, or anyone except her son. The front door to the building had become too heavy to move. When she gave up and went back to her apartment, the door opened easily going in, but after a few days it wouldn't open out at all. Brian stood there grinning and saying, "You were never enough, Mommy. You were never enough!" and he'd scream with joy, then, his face contorted, and she felt her body grow heavy too, with the weight of his hatred. Never enough? She had wanted that part of her life back, the part she'd thought was successful. She had wanted his love back, and she had assumed he'd wanted hers. But all this time he'd judged her. She had thought he was the one who'd failed! Imagine that!

She could barely walk and began to crawl, and he watched with glee. "Try harder, Mommy, try hard as you can!" and she thought, finally, that there was no end to the hatred the dead held for the living; that no matter how much she had tried (had she tried?), she had no real love for Brian, and he would never forgive her. She would be stuck with him for as long as she lived, and then, she was certain, for even longer after that.

Hag

Benjamin Percy

THE rental home was a cedar-shingled Cape Cod, one of many on the forested island. In the driveway sat a Mercedes, polished to an opal glow. Several suitcases waited on the porch. In an hour, the ferry would take them back to the mainland.

A girl walked down the steps—eight years old, wearing a yellow dress with a matching ribbon in her hair. She carried a stuffed tiger, a pillow, and a small backpack. She opened the rear door of the car and hefted everything inside. Then a voice sounded behind her, and she startled.

"You can't go already," it said.

The fog was thick this morning, and it took her a moment to see through the gray filter of it and find the stranger standing among the trees that edged the property. The two of them were about the same age, both with brown hair, but the other girl wore sneakers and jeans and an overlarge sweatshirt. "Not until we've played," she said.

"*My dad says we have to get ready to go.*"

"*There's plenty of time,*" the girl said and reached into her pocket, withdrawing a bandana that would serve as her blindfold. "*Come on.*"

The gulls were screaming. They swirled overhead, winging the air, their gray and white bodies dodging past each other, and the sand rippled with their shadows. Their hunger had been interrupted.

The deputies would only allow Ellie to get so close. Crime tape rippled in the wind, staking off an area roughly thirty square feet. But she could see, from her vantage at the top of the dune, the remains.

A jogger had spotted them near the damp line of sand that marked high tide. An arm, laced with seaweed, the skin grayed and blackened with rot. Crabs and gulls nibbled at it.

This wasn't the first time this had happened. That's why *The Globe* agreed to send her here—to the coast of Maine.

A deputy named Wallace with a thick black brush of a mustache said, "Sometimes it's just a foot. Sometimes a hand. One time a head. For as long as I been working here, the ocean likes to cough up its dead. Usually happens this time of year, too. Really gets you in the holiday spirit."

This was December, and Ellie wore a fleece and jeans, her hair in a ponytail knocked around by the chill wind. She gripped a notebook. The pages fluttered as she scratched down fast ciphers. She once lost an entire interview to a digital error, so she preferred the permanent memory of paper and ink.

"Do you mind if I take a closer look?" she said. "I came all the way from Boston."

"What do you think you're going to see there you're not going to see here?"

She shrugged her answer. "Devil's in the details, we like to say."

Wallace hesitated a moment, before lifting the tape and waving her through, saying they had already searched and bagged and photographed the area, so what the hell.

She wore flats and the sand seeped into them when she descended the dune, making every step feel like a chill uncertainty. "To be honest," Wallace said, "kind of surprised to see you up here."

"I specialize in this kind of thing," she said, and he said, "Crime beat?"

"I'm an investigative reporter. Part of the spotlight team at *The Globe*." She had a reputation for reviving cold cases, some of which led to prosecutions. Everything from the Long Island serial killer to the highway murders of the Tri-state to the missing boys of the Catskills. She helped the dead finish the stories they couldn't tell themselves.

Wallace missed a step and nearly tumbled down the rest of the dune before righting his balance. "Well, then I guess you're in the right place."

A woman in a windbreaker that read *Forensics* across the back was in the process of readying a bag to place the arm inside. "Hold up," Wallace told her. "Press. Take a smoke break or something." And then he said to Ellie, "But no pictures, okay?"

"Okay," she said.

Waves boomed. Sand fleas bit at her ankles. The air was cold but her nose was hot with the smell of rot. A gull swooped near, screeching a warning, but she barely noticed.

A bone stuck whitely out of the purple, fish-bitten flesh. The fingers curled into a claw. Some of the nails were broken, others gone.

"What is that?" she said, and Wallace said, "What is what?"

"In the hand," she said, aiming at it with her pen. "In the palm."

Wallace waved over forensics. The woman wore shoe-shield booties that whispered in the sand. "Says she sees something."

The woman—her hair styled short and spiked—crouched beside Ellie and snapped on a fresh set of latex gloves. She nudged the dead hand, cranked two of the fingers stiffly back. The skin tore, the grip unlocked. "She's right."

From the hand she withdrew a carved totem. A wooden gull with oversized eyes and a beak that took the shape of a snarl.

Ellie lived in a Cambridge townhome that was never clean. There were always toys or clothes or books underfoot, post-it note reminders stuck to the walls, crayons rolling off counters, dirty dishes waiting in the sink. Now, to add to the mess, there was a half-decorated Christmas tree and a tangled ball of lights.

There was never a time she and her husband didn't have something hurriedly to do. She was a journalist, he was a financial consultant. They were parents to a busy seven-year-old.

In the kitchen, her husband chopped vegetables and tossed them into the wok with a sizzle. NPR played from his phone and the noise of the market roundup knotted up with Christmas carols projected from the iPad her daughter was watching in the living room.

Ellie sat at the kitchen table now with her laptop open. She was studying tide charts, mapping currents. She cross-checked this tab with another open to Google Maps. She dragged it northeast and homed in on a cluster of islands off the Maine coast, then zoomed in until a single island dominated the screen.

At *The Globe*, she sat in a hive of cubicles and constant noise, so despite the news blaring and the carols fa-la-la-la-la-ing and the silverware rattling in a drawer, she remained lost in her own zone of concentration.

"Ellie?" Ron said, and she realized only then that her husband was hovering beside her.

"I'm sorry, what?" she said.

"I was just asking you what's so interesting about Gull Island."

"Oh, nothing really—it's just a story I'm working on."

He held a stack of plates in his hands. "Mind shutting it down? So I can set the table?"

Five minutes later, they scooted in their chairs and hovered their faces over their plates. The chardonnay was cold and crisp and the chicken stir-fry was hot enough to steam on their forks. Their daughter chatted happily between bites. Her name was Lyra and she had a mess of black hair and a gap-toothed smile that couldn't contain her constant stream of questions. She was always asking things like, "What's the difference between nice and good?" and, "What's the difference between mad and angry?" and, "What's the difference between fun and satisfying?"

On the one hand, it was endearing and made Ellie proud that she was raising her own little reporter. But at the end of the day, her brain felt gray and frost-bitten and sometimes she had to start a timer and say, "For fifteen minutes, there will be no questions."

Ellie had stowed away her laptop, but her notepad was never far from her hand. She had it open beside her now and jotted down a note: "Feed the hag."

She startled—and the tail of the *g* scritched off jaggedly—when her husband again called her name.

"What?"

"Have you heard anything I said?"

She crossed out what she had written. "I'm sorry. I just—I'm going to take a few days to chase a story. Is that okay?"

"It's getting close to Christmas," he said.

"I'll obviously be back before then. Obviously."

He didn't say anything. He only wiped his mouth and stood to clear his dishes.

Lyra jogged her eyes between them, and when Ron marched away to the kitchen to scrape the leftovers into a Tupperware container, she said, "Don't go. Please. I hate it when you go."

"I have to. For work."

"But all you do is work."

"Yes," Ron said from the kitchen. "All she does is work."

"Finish up, okay?" Ellie said, neglecting her own unfinished plate, standing and retreating to the bedroom.

She closed the door behind her and walked immediately to her bureau, the top of which was a clutter of perfume bottles and scarves and jewelry and medicine bottles. She found her prescription for Lorazepam. She strangled off the cap and dry-swallowed a pill.

She stared at herself in the mirror for a long minute before opening up a polished wooden jewelry box. She pulled open its bottom drawer and pushed past the bracelets and necklaces and watches until she found what she was looking for, dusty and unseen after so many years.

A carved totem. In the shape of a nightmarish gull.

The girl in the yellow dress wore a blindfold when she stumbled through the woods. She took high steps to avoid tripping. Her hands were out before her, feeling the air, as if her fingers were worms struggling through the dark. Her shoe caught on a stone. Her shin bashed against a log. But she wasn't afraid. Giggles punctuated her words when she called out, "Ten… nine … eight… seven… six…"

Though she couldn't see the pines and hemlocks and tamarack around her, they were cloaked in a fog that swirled in her wake. The ground was moist with it, the rocks slick. And the moisture in the air carried sound strangely. A gull cried and a tree creaked and a stick snapped and her voice called out its countdown and everything sounded both faraway and dangerously near.

The other girl was up ahead. She did not wear a blindfold, so moved much more swiftly, kicking through bracken that dampened her jeans with dew. She leaped over a moss-furred log. She made it almost to the ruins up ahead—the stony ruins of the first settlers on the island—when the voice behind her finally called out, "One!"

Now the girl stopped, rooted in place. And began to count aloud herself, despite her panting breath. Because these were the rules of the game. An old game of tag called Hunter/Hunted, similar to Marco Polo. "Ten… nine… eight… seven… six…" she began and watched, in the near distance, as the blindfolded girl in the yellow dress tripped and shuffled toward the sound of her. "I'm going to get you," she said, laughing. "I'm getting closer!"

Back and forth they went with their countdowns, with their halting pursuit and escape, until the leader among them, the hunted, rushed out of the woods and onto a basalt ridge. The hush of the forest gave way to the shush and boom of the ocean.

Before her was a peculiar landmark, known by the locals as the Witch's Cauldron. A ringed and recessed section of shoreline that looked exactly like its name. At high tide, the sea came crashing through an eroded arch and into this basin, frothing and surging, rising up into a boiling mass of water. The cauldron was thirty feet wide and just as deep.

The girl in the jeans only hesitated a moment, because a voice could be heard behind her, yelling, "Five... four... three..."

She scrambled out onto the rim of the Witch's Cauldron, sometimes upright, sometimes on all fours, crabbing her way to its far side. The blindfolded girl on the shoreside of the ringed gap cried out, "Hello? Are you there? You're supposed to be counting."

For a moment there was only the crash and salt spray of waves, and then the girl began her countdown once more, beckoning the blindfolded girl forward.

"Ten... nine... eight... seven... six..."

And the blindfolded girl marched toward her, seeking her voice, with the mouth of the Witch's Cauldron gaping only a few steps before her.

The ferry was rust-pocked and mildew-stained. The small garage in its belly was empty except for one other car. Ellie walked to the deck to take in the blustery view. She pulled on a wool cap and zipped her jacket to her neck and tucked her hands into mittens.

The sky was the same concrete gray as the ocean. Rain-misted. The air tasted like aspirin. The ferry chugged through waves that rose and dipped. She walked slow laps around the deck. After thirty minutes, the tree-studded, fog-cloaked island was visible in the distance, like a castle with a boundless moat.

Two months ago, the sun would be burning down and the ferry would have run several times a day, jammed with tourists in white tennis shoes. But this was December, and now the ferry only ran in the late morning, so she didn't have to jostle anyone for the bow of the ship.

She leaned over the railing to take in the chop. Something caught her eye. A flash in the murk. The smear of a pale face staring horribly up at her.

She pulled back and counted to ten, then looked again and saw only the cold nowhere of the sea. The ferry blew its horn, the air throbbing with its bass. She could see lobster boats chugging through the water. The wharf that awaited them and the dark-windowed buildings squatting beyond it.

She returned to her car and tucked herself into her seat and dug around in her purse until she found the bottle of Lorazepam. She shook out another pill, swallowing it down with a gulp of cold coffee.

She blew out a sigh—and reached for the rearview mirror to check her makeup. But when she readjusted it, a face curtained with hair appeared behind her.

She screamed and the face in the mirror screamed too. The high-pitched yelp of a girl. Her daughter, Lyra.

Ellie drove off the ferry and parked in the first spot she could find beside the wharf. Boats bobbed in the water when she said, "Will you please stop crying?" and dug out her phone.

She always kept her cell on mute. She couldn't stand the constant distraction of calls and texts and notifications. When she checked it, the screen brightened with voicemails and messages from Ron. All about how he couldn't find their daughter.

"That's because she's sobbing in the back seat," she said through her teeth. And then, louder, "Lyra! Stop! That's enough!"

Her daughter was curled up in a ball, her face red and damp with tears, her breath hitching when she said, "But you're mad at me."

"Just because I'm angry doesn't mean I don't love you." The cabin of the car amplified all sound and made her head feel too full of noise. "Now stop crying! Please!" This she said at a shout, and it only made Lyra wail louder.

A white splat of bird shit hit the windshield as a gull swooped past. Ellie closed her eyes and took a deep shuddering breath. She quieted her voice when she said, "Hey. Hey, Lyra. Come up here. It's okay. Climb up in the front seat by Mommy."

The girl's cries lowered to a whimper. With her sleeve she wiped away a slug of snot. Then she clambered over the console and into Ellie's lap. "It's all right. It's okay."

"I just," Lyra said. "I just wanted to spend time with you."

"I know, I know." She combed her fingers through her daughter's tangled hair and kissed the crown of her head. Another gull swooped past the car and distracted her gaze. Her eyes focused on a figure in the middle distance. Big and box-shaped. A long silvering beard that looked like something washed in with the tide. His face was so deeply creased it appeared scarred. He wore black bibs and a gray wool sweater. He was in the process of docking his boat. He swung a leg over the gunwale, a coil of rope in hand. He knotted it swiftly around a cleat. It was difficult to tell from here, but his hands appeared gloved in blood.

"I'm going to call Daddy, okay? Because I'm sure he's worried about you."

She kept one arm curled around the girl, while the other brought the cell to her ear. The signal was weak, and it took some time before they were connected. His panicked voice said, "Please tell me she's with you?"

"Stowed away in the back seat."

He blew out a heavy sigh. "I was this close to calling the police."

"If I put her back on the ferry, will you be there to pick her up?"

"What?" he said, his relief giving way to anger. "That's a two-hour drive. I can't believe you're even asking me that."

"I'm on assignment. How am I supposed to work?"

The man with the silver beard dragged a shark out of his boat. It left a blood trail on the rough brown planks of the docks. He approached a hitching post with oversized hooks hanging from it. He hoisted the fish and hung it from its gills. Some gulls dropped down—called by the blood—and roosted nearby, hoping the guts might get tossed aside.

"Ron?" she said. "What am I supposed to do?"

"Try being a mother," he said.

For a moment she believed the call cancelled, but then his voice, softer than before, said, "I'm sorry. But I have to work too. Can it wait until tomorrow?"

"If it has to."

"It has to."

"The morning ferry," she said. "Be there."

From his belt the man with the silver beard withdrew a filet knife that flashed silver. He jammed the blade into the shark, prodding the anus and then ripping upward, unzipping its belly. He reached his hands into the gap. He withdrew a sodden mess of what looked like hair jeweled with teeth. He sniffed at it before heaving it aside with a splat.

The gulls descended to feast.

The fog poured off the ocean like a second tide out of rhythm with the noise of the crashing waves. On the coastal side of the Witch's Cauldron stood a girl, counting down, "Five… four… three…"

Inside the formation, the sea foamed and whirled. Toward it walked the girl in the yellow dress. Blindfolded, her arms out before her, hurrying along a little faster as the countdown neared its end.

"Two…"

But the other girl never yelled out, "One!" Maybe she was afraid to. Or maybe she was hoping to draw her pursuer a few more paces.

Then the girl in the yellow dress tripped, fell hard to her knees, only a foot from the drop.

She cried out in pain and nudged off her blindfold, but any injury she felt was soon forgotten when she saw the cauldron yawning before her—and the girl on the other side of it, staring miserably back at her.

There were two parts of Gull Island. The wild place studded with evergreens and knuckled with rocky ridges and creamed over with fog. And the domesticated face of it. Which was mostly clustered along the western shore.

Here, along a single street, stood a cedar-shingled inn, a small brick library, a chowder house, an ice cream shop, a mercantile and knick-knack shop, a tavern called The Lonely Gull, and a seafood shack called The Lobster Pot.

They were all shuttered or posted signs for reduced hours. Because the tourist season was long over. These were the thin times. A tiny windmill turned slowly and creakily at the mildew-spotted miniature golf course. A rusted collection of rental scooters and bikes had been left out like abandoned toys.

In The Lonely Gull, an old man in a flannel jacket hunched over the bar, nursing his beer, while the jukebox played the same song over and over, and on the beach there was a single set of footprints bothering the gray-black sand.

Ellie and Lyra took all of this in as they walked the town and poked their heads in and out of buildings. They desperately wanted a cup of cocoa but the best they could find was a dry-mix packet for sale at the mercantile. They bought it, along with some black-spotted bananas, a bag of bread, and a faded box of granola bars.

The man behind the register had only a few hairs on his head and wore a denim shirt and glasses with thick, yellowed lenses. A fly swatter hung on a nail behind him. He did not greet them when he rang up the order. He paused his hand on the granola bars when she said, "Funny question, but do you know of any missing persons cases? Here on Gull Island?"

"I'm sorry?" he said in a reedy voice.

"Has anyone gone missing here?"

"That *is* a funny question."

"I just—you know how unreliable memory can be—I *seem* to remember a news report from back when I was a kid? About a missing girl? Or a drowned girl? Or maybe I'm misremembering."

"A missing girl, you say?"

"Yeah. Maybe twenty-five years ago?"

"Twenty-five…" His lower lip quivered. "I don't remember anything about that."

"Just curious. Who has police jurisdiction here?"

"There's no police here."

"But if there was a problem, who would you go to?"

"There's Thatcher," the clerk said and finished totaling up the cost.

"Who's Thatcher?" she said and counted out some bills and change.

"Works a lobster boat. But he's our constable."

"Is he a big old guy? With a gray beard?"

"That's the very one."

She thanked him as he bagged up their food. From here they traveled to the inn, walking down the middle of the street, because there was no traffic. The blacktop was spotted white from the gulls. Feathers swirled and revealed the shape of the wind. A face peered out of a foggy window and she remembered the face staring out of the water.

"You know I came here once," Ellie said, "when I was your age. On vacation."

"Was it fun?" the girl asked and Ellie took a long time to give a hollow-voiced answer. "No."

"Then why did you come back?"

"Because I think there might be a story here."

"A funny story? I like those the best."

"No."

"A scary story?"

Ellie did not answer and her daughter said, "I don't like scary stories."

Though it was December, there were no wreaths or sleigh bells or menorahs anywhere. Instead, strange decorations hung from porches and dangled in windows and spiked the hillside and beaches. They were gulls. Carved wooden gulls. Some were as small as a brooch, others were as big as a man. All were of a similar design, with their eyes wide, their beaks open, their wings outstretched.

Such an ornament hung in the inn—near the reception desk, on the wall, like a crucifix. "I don't have a reservation," Ellie said. "I hope you have a room for us?"

The old woman behind the desk coughed out a laugh. Her breath smelled like the ghosts of a thousand cigarettes. "That's funny." She motioned a hand at the cabinet behind her. In every cubby hung a brass key. "Nothing but room here."

Her eyes were milky. She wore a cardigan sweater over a dress with anchors printed on it. She moved slowly, as if her joints were full of rust, when she hefted the ledger onto the counter with a thump and asked Ellie to fill it out.

"How many people live here?"

"Well, there's the people who own houses here, and then there's the people who *live* here. You see a big house? That belongs to someone who vacations here or rents out to tourists. You see a fish shack or an apartment over a shop? That's the rest of us."

"Year-round residents," Ellie said. "That's what I meant."

"Few dozen. Housekeepers. Bartenders. Cooks. Fishermen." The old woman smiled and showed off a gap in her yellowing smile. "Servants."

"It's so quiet here now."

"Thin," the old woman said. "Things get thin here in the winter."

Footsteps thumped down the stairs, and a woman appeared carrying a bucket of cleaning supplies. She had no eyebrows. She wore a paisley scarf on her head and her skin had gone the thin yellow of old paper. Maybe she was in her thirties, maybe her fifties; it was hard to tell. She stared at them without a hello and then disappeared through a door that flashed a glimpse of the kitchen.

"Thin," the old woman said again.

Ellie offered a credit card and the old woman ran it through an old flat-bed imprinter and had her sign the carbon paper. "Haven't seen one of these in a while," Ellie said, and the old woman said, "Sometimes the old ways are best."

Lyra stood beneath the gull hanging on the wall. It was nearly as big as her, anchored by big screws that fissured the wood. She ran her fingers along the detailed ridges etched into its claws. "Don't touch that, sweetie," Ellie said and the girl pulled back her hand as if burned.

"It's all right," the old woman said. "It's pretty, isn't it?"

"It's kinda pretty but kinda also freaky," Lyra said.

"Can you tell me about that carving?" Ellie said. "I noticed quite a few of them decorating the storefronts."

"Oh, it's an old pagan tradition here. Connected to the winter solstice."

"The solstice. On the twenty-first."

"Two more days." The old woman winked. "Not everyone who came across the Atlantic was a Puritan, you know."

"Mommy's a writer," Lyra said, followed by an "Ow!" and it was only then that Ellie realized she was digging her fingers into her daughter's shoulder.

"A writer?" the old woman said.

Ellie's words came out in a quick tumble. "I never really get a vacation. Always on deadline, you know. So I thought I'd get away. Do a touch of work. But mostly get away." She tried to neaten her daughter's hair and then gave up. "We'll get some quality time in—right, Lyra?"

"Until you get rid of me."

Normally, Ellie used silence as an invitation; when people were uncomfortable, they said too much too quickly. Now she was falling victim to her own techniques. This whole island felt like one big watchful silence, and she had to be careful not to give herself over to it. "This little one—she'll be going back on the ferry tomorrow, but I'll stay on."

The old woman made a sound that could have been the clearing of phlegm or the uttering of disapproval.

"Maybe we'll get a few good walks in."

"Don't turn your back on the water," the old woman said. "You'll want to take care at this time of year. The ocean is... unforgiving."

~

After they collected their key and dropped off a bag in the room, they headed out again. Ellie had asked about the library—noting it was closed—and the innkeeper said if they were curious, they'd find the back door unlocked.

"It's an honor system, of course," the innkeeper said, and Ellie said, "Of course."

The building was small, square, and rowed neatly into sections. The lights buzzed on, one of them flickering. The air had the musty tang of a cellar. They found the children's section in a corner. Somehow it seemed hard to believe they had one at all. She set up Lyra in a beanbag chair with some *Frog and Toad* books before searching the stacks.

She found what she was looking for near the rear of the building. A few dust-coated shelves of local history. Some of the books—published by presses she had never heard of—featured photos and illustrations of shipwrecks, fishing boats, trees, gems, birds, and lobsters. They concerned the Maine coastline or the surrounding islands more generally. But some of the older volumes—bound in cracked cloth, a few leather-backed, even a finer vellum—gave her the particulars of Gull Island.

She sat cross-legged on the floor and pulled books down and scribbled what she found in her notebook. Here was a book of recipes on everything from blueberry lattice to fish stew to lamb bake. Here was a ledger that simply listed years of population counts, taxes, goods traded going all the way back to the 1700s, the same family names listed over so many years that today they might as well be one blood. She traced her way back a few decades, looking for births that might match up with her own. Here was one. A Haddie Ragnar. She jotted down the name. And then tried to plug it into Google, but her phone wasn't picking up a signal inside the brick building.

Here was a book of photographs without any captions or dates. She thumbed through it once, and then again. Boats in the harbor. A pile of lobsters as tall as the frowning man who stood beside it. The construction of the inn. A dead tree on a rise with children standing in a ring around it, holding hands and wearing gull masks. Stone ruins in the woods. A dead seagull with flies crawling all over it. The Witch's Cauldron. There it was, as if ripped right out of her memory. The ring of stone splashed full of surf resembling nothing so much as a boiling pot. She would find it. Tomorrow.

Her daughter appeared at the end of the aisle, silent and watchful. She was normally so full of questions, but since they arrived on the island, she had gone mostly silent. Her face was slack and her eyes distant. "Are you okay?"

Lyra pulled a curl of hair into her mouth and chewed on it. "I'm okay."

"Don't you want to read?"

"I'm bored of reading."

"Here." Ellie ripped some pieces of paper out of her notebook and popped the cap off a pen. "Then draw."

A cold draft bothered her ankles and spiked its way like hoarfrost up her legs and through her body. She gave a shiver and returned to her reading. There was a book—a black book—but she couldn't read whatever writing was within it. The rough ink characters might be Old English, but she didn't know for sure. At its center was an illustration that spilled across two pages. At first she thought it was an ocean current—or perhaps the wind—

for the way the black tendrils swirled across the paper.

But then she spotted eyes and teeth within it and determined that it might be hair.

Her daughter was scraping the pen back and forth with such speed, soaking the page with so much ink that the paper tore. "What are you doing?" Ellie said. She snatched up the messy scribbles and made out the words *Feed the Hag*.

"Lyra? Why did you write that?"

The girl's shoulders rose and fell.

"Did you see Mommy writing that?" Ellie waited only a half-second before raising her voice to a yell. "Answer me!"

At their room at the inn, wind hissed through the cracks around the window and trembled the curtains. Above the bed hung a painting—framed in driftwood—of a fisherman dragging up his fish-fattened net in a storm. "It's cold in here," Lyra said when they closed the door behind them.

Ellie dropped her backpack—heavy with a few books she had borrowed from the library—and cranked up the thermostat, and the baseboard heaters began to tick and glow orange.

"No TV?" Lyra said and opened the drawers of the bureau one by one. "Then what are we supposed to do?"

"Here," Ellie said and offered her cell phone. "Watch some YouTube videos. You might need to stand by the window for them to load."

The girl snatched the phone and climbed up onto the bed and pulled the quilt over her. "What are you gonna do?"

"Mommy needs to think," she said as she entered the bathroom and cranked the hot water to a steaming roar.

There were two mugs on the bureau next to a coffee maker, and she dipped them each under the faucet and stirred in the packets of cocoa. "One for you," she said, passing it along to Lyra. "And one for me. Don't spill, okay?"

"Okay," her daughter said, the glow of the screen on her face.

In the bathroom, Ellie stripped off her clothes and lowered herself slowly into the tub. Wisps of steam danced on the surface of the water. Her skin prickled with the heat. She leaned back and closed her eyes—and remembered.

The gulls seemed to eddy and surge in the same patterns as the ocean below. Their voices came together into one voice that sounded like crying.

The girl in the yellow dress—Ellie—threw down her blindfold and the wind caught it and swept it out into the Witch's Cauldron, where it vanished into the frothing crowns of water.

She marched out onto the ring of rock—the width of the walkway only six feet or so, with a perilous drop to either side— toward the girl who had drawn her there. But who was the Hunter and who was the Hunted seemed suddenly confused.

Both of them were crying, their hair knocked about by the wind. "What are you doing?" Ellie yelled. "You could have killed me. What's wrong with you?"

The nameless girl hunched in on herself, as if expecting a blow. The fog clung to the air like wet cotton. The waves boomed below. The wind whistled all around. Ellie almost didn't hear her say, "She made me do it."

"Who?"

The girl spoke in a low voice, as if afraid someone might be listening. "She's hungry. The island is hungry."

"Who?" Ellie said. "What are you talking about?"

"The hag," the girl said. "We have to feed the hag. Or she feeds on us."

"You just hate the fact that I'm rich and you're poor," Ellie said. "You hate the fact that I can leave this place and you're trapped here."

Right then the girl slapped Ellie—and Ellie wheeled around and slapped her right back.

And the girl lost her balance and fell.

The bathwater was growing cold. Ellie lifted her foot and used her toes to grip the knob. The faucet churned out more hot water. But then there came a moan and a sputter as the stream lessened to a dribble and choked off entirely.

Ellie sat up, the water streaming off her chest, and used her hands to fiddle with the knobs. Squeaking them back and forth and back and forth. The faucet visibly shuddered—and then began to expel a yellow and then brown and then black trickle of water.

"Old pipes," she said, but then something else appeared, oozing out, draining slowly into the tub. A thick clotted mess of hair. Barnacled with what looked to be fingernails.

She didn't realize she was screaming until Lyra hurried into the bathroom, the phone clutched in her hand and blaring cartoons. When she saw the hair spreading its black tendrils through the water, and her mother scrambling back in the slick tub to avoid it, the girl dropped the phone and the screen shattered on the tile floor.

There was no landline in the room, and the innkeeper didn't respond when Ellie called down the stairs. She looked over the railing, still wrapped in her towel, and found the reception desk empty, as revealed by the golden glow of a lamp.

Night came early, and the thick darkness beyond the windows could have passed for midnight.

She dressed and threw the gelatinous mess of hair—what felt like seaweed—out the window of the bedroom. She then scrubbed her hands with soap three times over. Her whole body felt unclean.

"You're mad," Lyra said. "You're mad about me sneaking into the car and now you're mad about the phone too."

"I'm frustrated. That's all."

Lyra buried her head beneath a pillow and Ellie rubbed her back and said, "Hey. How about we get some dinner. I bet that would make us both feel better."

"Okay."

Ellie dressed and they went downstairs and walked outside, leaving the front door yawning open, because they could see from here that all the storefronts were dark. So they returned inside and ate a dinner of mushy bananas and stale granola bars while sitting cross-legged on the bed. The phone wouldn't turn on—and Lyra didn't pack anything of her own—so Ellie read her a copy of the *Atlantic Monthly* she had brought along, until eventually they fell asleep in their clothes.

She wasn't sure what time it was when she awoke, nor was she sure why her pulse was thudding in her ears. She sat upright, her face tipped toward the window. Her dreams still clung to her like cobwebs, but she felt certain a door had closed somewhere, the sound shivering through the inn.

She climbed carefully from the bed, trying not to disturb her daughter's sleep, and crept to the window, the floorboards cold and creaking beneath her feet. The waves could be heard even through the glass, a shush and boom, shush and boom, as if the island were breathing.

There was nothing at first, just the side yard of the inn, a patch of meager grass. Then a figure appeared below, moving across it. The innkeeper, Ellie was almost certain. But the darkness was so severe—a clinging black that washed away all color and acuity.

Whoever it was, she was heading toward the road. The road that led away from the town and along the shore studded with vacation homes. But before she stepped onto the blacktop, she turned, as if she could sense someone watching. Ellie pulled back from the window with a sharp intake of breath. When she looked again, there was nothing, but it appeared the woman was wearing a mask. With big hollow eyes. And a hooked beak.

Ellie tried to go back to sleep but couldn't. This was what she had come here for, wasn't it?

She slipped on her shoes and zipped into her jacket and hesitated over her daughter, wondering if she should wake her and tell her she was going out for a bit. Back at home, she and Ron could be streaming a movie in the next room and no matter how many gunshots or explosions shouted from the screen, Lyra never woke. Ellie was counting on her being such a sound sleeper now.

She locked the door behind her and stepped gingerly down the staircase, cringing at every squeak and moan. Outside, she wished for her phone's flashlight, but the moon soon cracked through the clouds and offered a silver glow. The waves lulled.

The farther she walked, the farther out the houses were spread. Cottages and cabins mostly, but a few gothic revivals set up on basalt ridges or tucked back in the woods. She had gone nearly a quarter-mile when she saw lights up ahead. The yellow rectangles of windows burning through the dark.

She remembered what the innkeeper had said—about the bigger houses belonging to those who didn't live here—and this was one of them. A Victorian revival with gables and a turret and many chimneys knifing toward the sky. Inside there were bodies moving. Dozens of them. A holiday party, perhaps.

But when she crept off the road and up the broken-shell driveway, she noticed that several inside wore masks. Gull masks. They were dancing to a music Ellie couldn't hear, their bodies throbbing and writhing.

One person—she thought it was a man at first, but no, no, it was a woman—wore no shirt. Her chest was scarred over from a double mastectomy. Her skin was yellow where it wasn't a raised, angry pink. The housekeeper—it must be her—though her face was hidden, masked like the others.

Before Ellie could get any closer, headlights flared down the road and a truck pulled up the driveway. She scrambled off into the brush before she could be spotted.

~

Back at the hotel, Ellie keyed open the door, but forgot to try the knob first, so maybe it was already unlocked? Because the bed was empty. The room was empty. The bathroom was empty. The closet was empty.

Lyra was gone. Her daughter was gone.

She called out her name as she wandered the halls and pounded up and down the stairs twice in the bewildering dark. Her shoe caught on the edge of a rug. She banged a hip into a table. She felt like she was breathing too much and not enough.

"Lyra?" she said one last time, and heard a noise then. In the bathroom. Slowly she entered and stepped toward the tub. Nestled in its bottom was her daughter, whispering into the drain.

Ellie scooped her up and said, "Thank God, thank God," and hugged her hard. The girl complained—"Stop it"—in a sleep-slurred voice.

"What were you doing? Didn't you hear me when I was calling for you?"

But the girl was not really here, still lost to some dream, and Ellie tucked back into bed. Then she chewed down two pills and climbed under the sheets herself. She wrapped herself around the girl as much for warmth as to hold her in place.

That night Ellie dreamed of gulls pecking her skin down to the bone and a long-haired hag who squatted on her chest and crushed the breath from her lungs as she leaned in for a hungry kiss.

In the morning, while waiting for the ferry, they walked up and down the wharf, breaking up pieces of bread to throw to the gulls that followed them in a shrieking cloud.

"They like me," Lyra said, hurling a handful of crumbs into the water, laughing when they gulls dove and fought.

"That's only because you're feeding them." This was said by a hunchbacked man in a buffalo-plaid flannel jacket. "You've got to feed them or they'll turn on you." He walked to the end of the dock and untied a rope. Hand over hand, he dragged up a netted pot he had left out overnight. He had hair like gray straw. He clamped a pipe between his teeth and puffed smoke that smelled like fried oysters.

The pot oozed and dribbled when pulled from the dark water—hand over hand, six feet, three feet, onto the dock with a *clunk*. Lyra crouched down to study what was trapped inside and said, "Gross."

Ellie at first believed them to be crabs or lobsters. But they were something else. Black- and white-shelled. Insectile. One like a crab crossed with a spider, another like a lobster crossed with a centipede. Barbed and terrible. With long mandibles and pulsing stingers.

Lyra said, "Can you eat them?"

"No," the man said and hoisted one out to show her. With no more effort than it would take to tear apart a sodden piece of paper, he ripped the crustacean open and black and green guts squiggled in his hands. "No, you can't eat them." He tossed the mess into the water. "There's not much to eat during the thin time. But the seasons turn. And the island gives back."

"Do you know where I could find Haddie Ragnar?" Ellie asked.

"Haddie, you say? Well, you might have already met her. At the inn."

"How'd you know we were staying at the inn."

"Fair guess."

"Haddie is the housekeeper, then?"

"Ah yuh." The man cleaned out the pot. Then he pulled a plastic bag from his pocket. In it was a chopped-up fish. He used the chunks to bait the pot and kicked it off the dock again.

A boat motored by and Ellie made eye contact with its captain. The man from yesterday. The one the grocery clerk called Thatcher. He stared at her in his passing, and her eyes were the first to drop.

The wind was picking up. It ripped the spume off the waves and whipped Ellie's hair across her face when she spoke to the ferry captain directly. She paid him an extra twenty dollars, if he wouldn't mind watching after the girl, keeping her in the cabin. She would be no trouble. It was only a half-hour passage and Lyra's father would be waiting to pick her up on the mainland.

She kissed Lyra on the forehead and told her they would finish decorating the tree when she got home, probably tomorrow. Did that sound like fun? The girl nodded, but then dropped her eyes to the floor and asked if she could stay. Please. Please, could she?

"I wish you could," Ellie said, but the words came clumsily. "I wish that too. But remember? Mommy has to work. So we can have nice presents under the tree."

"But I'm supposed to stay," the girl said under her breath.

"You mean you *want* to stay?"

The girl did not respond, and so, with another kiss to the forehead, Ellie wished her goodbye and headed off.

~

The front desk of the inn was empty, but Ellie followed the smell of cigarettes to the door behind it and gave a gentle knock.

"Yeah?" a voice said.

Ellie pushed open the door. She stepped halfway into the room and paused at the sight of the woman with the headscarf. The housekeeper from yesterday. She was sitting at a round table in the kitchen. She smoked a cigarette and ashed its red tip into a coffee mug.

"You're Haddie Ragnar."

"I am."

"I'm Ellie Templeton."

"You don't need a formal introduction to ask for fresh towels or a roll of toilet paper."

Ellie stepped fully into the room. "I think we might know each other?"

The other woman inclined her head, waiting for an explanation.

"When I was a girl, I came here."

"Okay."

Ellie blurted the story out in the rush of a few minutes. Then she was quiet for a beat before saying, "It was you, wasn't it? You were the girl? At the Witch's Cauldron?"

"It was." She took a deep drag and blew out a cloud of smoke that ghosted around her. "I was."

"I'm sorry… I can't tell you how happy I am… You don't know how sick I've felt…" She suddenly seemed unable to pin words together.

"Sick? Hmm." Haddie danced her cigarette around in the

air as if to trace out an explanation with the smoke. "Way I remember it, it happened a little differently, though."

Ellie took another step forward. "Can I buy you a coffee?"

"Grill's closed through the winter." Haddie reached into her cardigan and pulled out a flask and set it on the table and indicated Ellie should take a seat. "So this'll have to do."

Ellie ran away. She ran back through the fog, back through the woods, past the ruins, and eventually into the yard of their vacation rental, where her parents loaded their suitcases into the trunk of the car.

She had left the girl behind. An island girl. Haddie. That was her name.

Ellie had slapped her and the girl lost her footing and slipped and skidded and fell. And now here Ellie was, clinging to her father's leg as he said, "Was it a fun vacation?"

"Yes. But I'm ready to go home."

"Me too," he said, and then reached into the pocket of his jacket and offered her something. "I got you this. A souvenir." It was one of the gull totems, the wooden carvings she had admired in the shop near the wharf. "So you'll always remember."

Ellie took it and her mother said, "Who was that girl you were playing with?"

"Nobody," Ellie said.

She was already trying to shove the memory deep into a closet of her mind. To forget about the girl. To forget about what happened. It hadn't seemed real, so she made it unreal.

What she didn't know then—or all this time later—was that the girl, Haddie, had not fallen into the water. She caught herself. She clung by her fingers to a stone ledge. The waves boomed below her and wetted her shoes. But she was very much alive.

In the kitchen at the inn, Haddie brought down another coffee mug from the cupboard—and poured the flask into it. "You can't trust memory. Life's taught me that much." In her version of that morning, they had paused their game in the ruins—and Ellie had taken off her blindfold as the two of them explored—and from there they walked out onto the Witch's Cauldron. Haddie slipped and fell, but it was the wind that did it. "Not you, Ellie. Not that I recall."

"I should have tried to help you."

"It's hard to blame a child," Haddie said and toasted the flask. "Besides. I'm still here."

Ellie cupped both hands around the mug and brought it to her mouth. The liquor was spicy and lit a candle-flame in her stomach. "I can't tell you how glad I am to hear that."

There was a flicker of a smile. "If you can call it living. But there's always a spring that follows winter. A fat time after the thin time. That's what keeps me going. That's what keeps us all going." She wore earrings, Ellie noticed, carved in the shapes of gull heads. They swung and dangled as she spoke as if riding invisible currents of air.

"Health to follow sickness?" Ellie said, and Haddie nodded and said, "Let's hope."

Ellie almost told her that she had been carrying this wound around with her ever since then, that she became a crime reporter because of Haddie, became a person obsessed with investigating secrets and dark impulses. And for her entire career, it's been a necessary comfort to take the microscope away from herself and analyze other horrors.

But she didn't say any of this. Because she had always been more of a writer than a talker. "There was a body," she said instead.

"What's that about a body?"

"Multiple bodies, actually. They wash up. On the coast of Maine. Sometimes it's just a leg. Sometimes an arm."

"Okay."

"A few days ago, there was a hand. Looked like a shark had chewed it up and spit it out. It had something in its palm." She reached into her jacket pocket and removed the gull totem she had received so many years ago from her father. When she set it on the table, there was a *clunk* that made its weight seem heavier than it was. "It was a gull totem. Just like this one. The one my father gave me as a souvenir when we visited."

"So that's why you're really here, then?"

"I studied the tide charts."

"What's your theory? An old sad lady with cancer is chucking people in the drink?" She let out a wheezy laugh.

"No. I don't know."

"You don't know much, do you? Maybe you should have been a fiction writer instead? Then you can bend the truth however you want it."

"There was a party last night," she said.

Haddie barely had any eyebrows left. They were more like faint feathers. But she raised them now. "What's that?"

"You went to a party last night? What was it for?"

"How do you know about a party?"

"Your mother told me," Ellie lied.

Haddie studied her a long few seconds before dropping the spent butt of her cigarette into the mug. "That old bat is losing her mind. She'll be telling people her social security number and bank account next."

"What was it for? The party?"

"Solstice of course. The most important holiday of the year."

Ellie parked in the weed-choked driveway. She had driven past the overgrown lot twice, but now she was certain this was it, the vacation home where she had stayed as a child. The windows were gone and gulls swooped in and out. The cedar shingles had fallen off in places like old teeth. A tree grew through the roof.

She felt strangely light and warm—and not just from the whiskey—when she stepped out of the car. A smile teased the edges of her lips. Her feet barely seemed to tap the ground before springing her forward. She had been unburdened. She peered through the front door and glass-fanged windows. She sat on the porch but felt as though maybe there was no real reason for her to be here anymore. The plain gray light of day washed away her sense of urgency. What mystery was she even trying to solve anymore? Was it her own guilt, now allayed, or the severed hand on the beach that had brought her here? Any deadline she had in her mind seemed to be dissolving by the second.

Then she pulled a book from her backpack to review, and that old feeling soaked into her again. The nerve-shredding anxiety she had experienced on the beach when she saw the totem clutched in the sea-rotten hand. *Early Tales of Gull Island*, the cover read. She thumbed through its pages, learning about how settlers crashed a boat against these shores one brutal winter. And here they were stranded for several dark, cold months as squall after squall rolled in off the ocean, battering them. Their provisions ran out and the fish wouldn't bite and so they ate one of their own. A woman they had brought over as a servant. Their camp overlooked the Witch's Cauldron, and that is where they threw her bones when they finished with her.

It was said that she still haunts the island, that the cauldron became an extension of her, like a terrible gaping throat. And it's in the winter—when the wind sharpened with ice, when the shadows lengthened and the island was at its most desperate—that her spirit grew especially tempestuous. The ocean won't give the islanders fish or lobster or scallops if they don't give back to it.

The hag can only be sated when fed. She gave to the island and now the island must give to her. The solstice was a platter upon which sacrifice must be served.

Ellie closed the book with a thump. Her legs were numbing in the cold and she thought to stretch them in a hike through the woods. Beneath the trees all sound hushed. She could see the crowns of the pine and hemlock trees shaking with the wind, but she felt protected here. The light was dim and her footsteps hushed by the needles carpeting the ground.

After two hundred yards of clambering over logs and kicking through dried tangles of ferns, she came upon the ruins. They were roofless. The stone walls had crumbled unevenly, but still patterned out a clear collection of dwellings with sunken foundations. There was a staircase that rose to nowhere and another that descended into the dark. She moved among the buildings and discovered a round stone recession, what she assumed to be a well, but when she looked into its shadow-thick bottom she gasped at the sight of two black eyes gleaming back at her.

Her vision took a moment to adjust—and then the doe solidified below. It had fallen down and broken its rear leg. When the deer tried to stand, the joint bent wrongly. A cry sounded, a rasping whine like metal drawn across a file. There was corn and hay strewn about—both below and above—and around the same time Ellie recognized this was a baited trap, she heard a crackling in the woods behind her.

Someone was coming.

She ducked and slunk over to the stairs she had spotted earlier, hurrying down into the shadows herself, where her nose twitched from the mildew. There were ciphers etched into the stone here. Scars of the past. Glyphs that told a story she didn't quite understand, but seemed to indicate a story of solstice and sacrifice.

A minute later the light shuttered as someone passed by overhead. She only caught a flash, but that was enough to recognize the big body of Thatcher.

She could hear his heavy footsteps approach the deer, and she crept up a few paces and peered over the lip of the foundation and watched him unspool a rope and knot it swiftly into a kind of noose. He lowered it down and then yanked up. The deer's hooves clacked and skittered against the stone when he fished it out—and then stilled it with a jab of his filet knife. There was a soft mewl, and then silence.

After a minute, he hefted the deer onto his shoulder and started through the brush, toward the treeline, where the forest gave way to the basalt cliffs and the ocean beyond.

She snuck after him, staying low. Blood oozed down his back when he stood at the edge of the Witch's Cauldron. He didn't fling the deer carcass so much as let it slip off his shoulder and into the roiling surf.

The clouds were thickening and dropped thick flakes that the windshield wipers sloshed arcs through. Her car came around the bend, and the road sloped down toward the harbor, where she saw—as big as a building—the docked ferry.

A ferry that shouldn't be here. She said as much when she parked out front and hurried up the steps of the inn and found the old woman seated at the front desk. "There's a Nor'easter coming," she said. "Captain decided it wasn't worth the trip."

"I put my daughter on board that ferry. It was supposed to take her to the mainland. My husband was waiting for her."

"I don't see what that's got to do with me."

"My daughter would have come here. She would have asked about me. She would have gone to our room."

"What daughter?"

"The daughter I had with me. Right here. When I checked in with you."

"You never checked in with no daughter."

"I did," Ellie said at a shout. "I—what are you even talking about? You're not making sense."

"You're not making sense. I remember it like it was yesterday, because it was."

"She was right here."

"You were right here. But not with any daughter. No, miss."

Ellie knew she needed to stay calm, to think rationally, to remember what Haddie said earlier about her mother's mind fraying at the edges. The old woman had probably just forgotten. Ellie herself had lost—seemingly—the memory of what happened to her as a child, so couldn't this woman conceivably lose what happened to her yesterday?

"Where's your daughter? Where's Haddie?"

"Oh, now it's my daughter you want, is it?"

"Where is she?"

"How am I supposed to know?"

The old woman's voice grew severe. Her lips peeled back to reveal a gray, uneven line of teeth. "You tourists. You come here and you think you can tell us what's what. I've seen it my whole life. You come here and you use us. You use the island. You wring all the pleasure from it like a wine-sopped dishrag. Then you leave." Her eyes went someplace faraway and her voice grew sad and thoughtful. "But we need you to come back."

She focused her eyes on Ellie again and flicked her hand dismissively, as if to say *away with you*. "Because we *use* you just as you use us. We'll keep using you. Without you, the island starves."

Her phone wouldn't work. She punched her thumb at the cracked screen and a few shards stuck to her. She tried voice commands. She tried powering on and off. It wasn't just the signal—spotty yesterday, gone today, maybe interrupted by the rising storm—it was the phone itself, broken after being dropped. Dropped by her daughter. Her daughter had been here. Her daughter was here.

She checked every room in the inn, with the old woman pacing her and berating her. She ran down to the ferry and—as it sloshed in its moorings—walked its empty deck and checked its cabin. There was no one to be seen in the harbor and no lights on in any of the windows when she walked along the quay and pounded on doors.

She tried the back door to the library and the wind ripped the knob out of her hand. She rushed inside. Hundreds of pages stirred at once as the wind bullied its way through the shelves. Origami gulls—hung from fishing line—wobbled from the ceiling.

She left and jogged the rest of the way to the inn. Along the shore, waves crashed like thunder. The wind carried sharp drops of sleet in it and knocked the trees into a frenzy. At the inn, she found the old woman gone and the phone behind the front desk dead. From her purse she dug out her prescription bottle and shook it with a rattle. Only three pills left. She took them all.

Night fell. The storm worsened. Silver stripes of snow collected in the cracks of rocks, the bark of trees. Ellie stood at the lip of the Witch's Cauldron, because this time she would be the one who waited, not the one lured. There was more than once that she doubted herself—with the night pressing in all around her and the pills fizzing in her veins—wondering whether her mind was broken, if her memories were as confused as the swirling dark. Who knew what was real anymore? Maybe she didn't have a daughter. Maybe she didn't have a husband or a career either. Maybe she had been the one who had fallen into the Witch's Cauldron all those years ago.

But then a figure came out of the woods. A shadow bleeding

out of the shadows. Wearing a bone-white gull mask.

Ellie's whole body shook, soaked and chilled, her teeth chattering so hard she felt they might crack. "Ten, nine, eight, seven…" she said, and the figure paused at her voice and tipped her head and yanked at a rope.

And out of the trees followed her daughter, Lyra. Her wrists bound and her mouth gagged. Her hair was a damp, seaweedy mop. Any tears she shed were lost to the sleet melting down her face.

Ellie stepped forward and said, "Please." In that one word trying to say, *She didn't do anything*, and, *I'm the reason we're here*, and, *Stop acting like a crazy person* all at once.

Haddie pulled off her mask. Her eyes were black hollows. Her skin looked so insubstantial it might have been painted over bone. She told Ellie the rest of their story then. About how, so many years ago, after she fell, she managed to curl up on a ledge, but found herself trapped, unable to climb out of the cauldron. It was a day later that someone found her. Half-dead from hypothermia. "Maybe you think I deserved it. Because I brought you here. Because I tried to make you fall. But I didn't have a choice. *She* made me." With the utterance of that word—*she*— Haddie gestured toward the cauldron. The hag haunted her, just as she haunted them all, demanding to be fed.

"I know you think that's true," Ellie said. "But it's not."

The waves crashed so hard the stone below them vibrated.

"You think I'm terrible. But after I fell, you left me. You left me to die. You're no better."

Ellie risked getting closer, and closer still, small steps as she reached out her arms pleadingly. "It's like you said. We were just girls."

"I didn't want to hurt you before. But maybe I want to hurt you now."

"This isn't real. You don't have to—"

"Did you not see us? Did you not take a look at the people who live here? We're sick. The island is starving. If we don't—"

Before she could finish, Ellie lunged and grabbed hold of her daughter. She yanked at one of the girl's arms, while Haddie snatched at the other, with Lyra screaming between them.

Near the edge of the cliff, Haddie lost her grip, but recovered by staggering forward, dropping Ellie with a tackle. "She's hungry!"

Ellie fought for control—and swung around—and their entangled momentum carried them toward the chasm. They threw jabs, ripped at each other's hair, rolled over, and then over again, and over once more. And here—at the edge of the cauldron—Haddie slid over.

For a second she seemed gone. Lost to the seething bowl of whitewater. But when Ellie leaned forward, she saw the woman dangling, her arm curled around a knob of rock.

She didn't help before, but she would now. She would save Haddie, and somehow they would put the past and this night behind them. "Come on." She reached for Haddie, seizing her wrist. "Take hold of me. I've got you."

But her grip was slippery. And Haddie was too heavy. And when Ellie tried to yank her up, the woman fell, plunging into the water below. She struggled there for a minute or more, thrashing in the waves, trying to stay afloat. And then—but it couldn't be—something rose from the water. Something with long black kelpy hair. Something that wrapped an arm around her throat and pulled her down into the froth with a gargling scream.

The hag.

Ellie staggered to her feet and called out for her daughter and saw that, along the cliffside, impervious to the driving sleet, stood the other islanders. Dozens of them. All wearing gull masks. They made no effort to stop her when she ushered her daughter away.

Ellie drove at perilous speed to the harbor, nearly skidding off the road more than once. Her right hand gripped Lyra all this time as if something might crash through the window and rip her away.

She thought about rolling directly onto the ferry, but didn't know how long it would take to unmoor from the docks, let alone how to negotiate its navigation system. She had grown up in a family that loved waterskiing and fishing, so she abandoned the car at the wharf and raced Lyra onto a lobster boat that surged and thudded in the storm. She untied its ropes—peeling back a fingernail in her hurry—and cranked the engine to life. There was a scrape when the bow nudged against the stern of another boat. She cranked the wheel and eased the throttle, spinning them around to chug into open water.

Then the boat lurched and the motor whined. The anchor. She had neglected the anchor. The island didn't want to let go of her yet.

She chased her way to the back of the boat, searching for the anchor crank, and then scudded to a stop. Because he stood at the end of the dock. Thatcher. Watching her in the sleet-blurred darkness. The boat was only ten yards offshore and he leapt into the sea and surged his way toward her, his big arms scissoring the water.

She said, "No, no, no," and unlocked the anchor reel and began winding it in as fast as she could manage. She dared a glance overboard just as a big hand rose out of the water and snatched hold of an algae-slimed fender. Up from the chop rose the bearded face. Thatcher spit water from his mouth and tried to haul himself up to the gunwale.

And then, in a rush, her daughter appeared beside her. Holding a filet knife. She slashed once, twice, three times at the anchor line—and it snapped free. The boat chugged suddenly forward. At that Ellie charged and kicked Thatcher full in the mouth, knocking him back into the waves that rose into points like teeth.

The ship motored blindly out to sea and Ellie blinked through the sleet at her daughter, already worried about the scars she would carry inside her and how the memory of this place would stain her, as the girl gripped the knife and stared blankly out into the windswept night and said, "We can go now. We fed her. And now, for a little while anyway, she's done being hungry."

Take Me, I Am Free

Joyce Carol Oates

T HE mistake must have been, the child woke too soon from her afternoon nap.

Really she knew better, for she'd been scolded previously for waking too early, and interfering with her mother's schedule. And now, coming downstairs unexpectedly, in her fuzzy pink slipper socks, she hears her mother on the phone: "No, it *is not* postpartum bullshit. It isn't physical at all. It isn't mental. It isn't genetic, and it isn't *me*. It's her."

The voice on the other end of the line must have expressed surprise, doubt, or incredulity, provoking the mother to speak vehemently: "It's *her*. She's defective. She's perverse. She hides it—whatever she *is*." Another pause. "You can't see it. Her father can't see it. But *I see it*."

And, as the child stands frozen on the stairs, in her fuzzy slipper socks, groping her thumb against her mouth to suck (though *disgusting thumb-sucking* is certainly forbidden in this household): "Of course my mother-in-law, the doting grandmother, refuses to 'see' it. The woman has a vested interest in denial."

Now, the mother notices the child on the stairs. A flush comes into her face, her green cat eyes glare with fury that the child has (once again) wakened too soon from her nap and come downstairs too soon, intruding upon the mother's private time. "I've told him, it's her or me. Preferably *her*."

Carrying the phone in one hand, the furious mother seizes the child by the wrist and tugs her down the remainder of the stairs—"You! Are you eavesdropping, too?"—giving her a small shake of rebuke while continuing to speak into the phone in an incensed voice: "I didn't sign up for this. I didn't understand what was involved—'motherhood.' Before I knew what was happening *she* got inside me and kept growing and growing and now she's everywhere—all the time. Always I'm obliged to think of *her*—sucking all the oxygen out of my lungs."

Guiltily, the child tries to apologize. She is a small inconsequential girl, just four years old; tears leave her face smudged, like a blurred watercolor. She should know better by now—indeed, she does know better. *Waking at the wrong time. Coming downstairs at the wrong time. Bad!*

In a flurry of activity, focused as a tornado, the mother gathers the child together with the week's trash to set out on the sidewalk in front of the buffed-brick rowhouse on Stuyvesant Street. In the neighborhood there has been a longstanding custom of setting out superannuated household items—old clothes, chairs with torn cushions, battered strollers, children's toys, occasionally even a toilet seat, or an entire toilet—beside a hand-printed sign reading *TAKE ME, I AM FREE.* Mocking this phony-charitable custom, the mother sets the weeping child down amid a gathering of unwanted useless things, of which some have been on the sidewalk for weeks.

"Just sit here. *Don't* squirm. I'll be watching from the front window."

Trying not to sob, feeling her lower face twist in a spasm of grief, the child sits on the chilled pavement through the remainder of the day as strangers pass by, pausing to stare at her, even to (rudely) examine her, or to ignore her altogether, as if she were invisible. Some laugh nervously—"Well—hell! You're a *real girl.*" A rusted tricycle, a soiled lampshade, a red plastic ashtray with a plastic hula girl on its rim, a box of old clothes, shoes, books are met with more enthusiasm than the shivering child who remains obediently where her mother positioned her even after a cold rain begins to fall.

If only she hadn't wakened too early from her nap!—the child recalls with shame. *That* was the mistake, from which her punishment has followed.

Each time a pedestrian approaches her the guilty child peers up with an expression of yearning and dread—yearning, that someone will take pity on her, and bring her home with them; dread, that someone will take pity on her, and bring her home with them. Though she should know better, she can't help but think that, in another few minutes, her mother will relent and lean out the front door of their house to call her in a lightly chiding voice—"*You!* Don't be silly! Come in out of the rain right this minute."

Eventually it is sunset, and it is dusk. There are fewer pedestrians now. The child has virtually given up hope when she sees a tall figure approaching—"Good God! What are you doing here?"

It is the child's father, returning from work as he does each weekday at this hour. He is astonished to discover his beautiful little daughter curled up asleep on the filthy damp pavement beside the crude hand-printed sign TAKE ME, I AM FREE.

"Darling, I've got you now. Don't cry—you're safe."

But the child begins to cry, clutching at the father's arms as he lifts her and carries her into the house which is warmly lit and smells of such delicious food, the child's mouth waters.

"Well! Nobody wanted her *again*, eh?"

In the dining room the mother has begun setting the table for dinner. She does no more than glance at the indignant father and the fretting child in his arms—their appearance hasn't surprised her at all.

The father says to the mother: "You aren't funny. You know very well that we wanted this child—we want her."

"What do you mean—'we.' *You*—not me."

"Well then, yes—*I* want her."

"But did you want *her*? You couldn't have known who she would be, could you?"

"Yes."

"Oh, come on—don't be ridiculous. Do we 'want' what we are given, or are we merely resigned to it? In the matter of children it's a lottery—losers, winners—'blind fate.' You can't say that we deserve her simply because we had her, as you can't say we had her because we deserve her. *She* has no say in the matter, either—but she doesn't realize, yet. As one day she will."

"You have no reason to come to such conclusions. In a

civilized country like ours—each child is *precious*."

"'Civilized!'"

The mother laughs derisively. Her laughter is sharp and cruel as a cascade of falling glass.

The father says, stung: "I said—you aren't funny. Just stop."

"*You* stop. You're the Platonist in this household."

Though the mother speaks in a bright brittle accusatory voice, she is really not unhappy. She is not in what the child knows to be a *bad mood*. The glassy-green cat eyes gleam with less malice than before.

For it seems that while the child has been outdoors in the rain, the mother inside the warm-lit cozy house has prepared a special meal. Moist pink flesh upon a platter sprinkled with fresh parsley, which the child identifies as grilled salmon; wild rice with shiitake mushrooms, Brussels sprouts sautéed in olive oil—a feast. The mother has brushed her lustrous dark hair, brightened her sullen mouth with red lipstick, changed from the shapeless slacks she wears around the house into a soft heather-colored wool skirt that falls to her ankles; around her slender neck is a necklace of carved wooden beads carved to resemble tiny hairless heads.

How many places are set at the dining room table?—the child blinks back tears, desperate to see.

A Trip to Paris

Richard Kadrey

Houston, Texas 1963

Roxanne Hill cut her finger on a broken teacup while finishing the dishes. She went into the bathroom and doused the injury with iodine, grimacing as it burned, but not making a sound. The pain was her penance for being clumsy enough to shatter one of her late mother's cups. When she was done, she returned to the kitchen, but left the rest of the dishes to soak rather than ruining the bandage she'd carefully wrapped around the wound. She would finish the cutlery and plates tomorrow; at the same time she would scour the wall clean where a small patch of mold was beginning to grow on the wall behind the faucet.

The house was quiet. It was always quiet now. However, some days seemed heavier with silence than others, and this was one of them. Glancing at the calendar on the cupboard door reminded her why. It had been exactly a year since her family had died. How could she possibly have forgotten a date like that, she wondered. But she forgave herself because there had been so much to think about since her husband and children left her. The police, for instance. She worried about them every day, though the fear had diminished greatly over the last few months. If the authorities didn't know that she'd poisoned them by now, they weren't likely to ever know. It was thrilling to think. She was free. Roxanne said the word once.

"Free."

And in filling the silence it felt as if she'd broken a dark spell that had surrounded her for the previous three hundred and sixty-five days. She took a long breath and turned on the burner under the kettle. There was time for a cup of tea before she had to be at church.

After Wednesday evening services, she went down into the church basement with four other women and began sorting boxes of donations for the parish's clothing drive. While the four other women babbled, Roxanne noticed that their voices were more hushed than usual. It was clear that while she'd forgotten the significance of the day earlier, the other women had not. Jeanette Morgan tried to draw her into the conversation by asking Roxanne's opinion about an elegant evening dress she'd found in one of the boxes. There was no reason for the question, of course. Roxanne knew very little about fashion, much less about evening wear. It was an obvious attempt by Jeanette to draw her out. So, to break the tension mounting in the room, she said, "It's beautiful. I wish I'd had something like that for my wedding."

As she'd guessed, mentioning her marriage quieted the other women and they worked most of the rest of the evening in relative silence. Around eight p.m., Delilah Montgomery drew Roxanne aside and confided in her that she and the other women were worried.

She said, "You've been strong, honey, for a whole year. But we know it's been hard on you too."

"What do you mean?" said Roxanne, not liking the comment one bit.

"It's your skin, darling. It's so pale. And your eyes. We can tell you don't sleep."

In fact, Roxanne slept soundly every night. Still, she played along with the other women's worry, hoping they'd leave her alone. They'd become intolerable to her over the past year. Such tiny people with such tiny lives, wanting nothing more than a clean house and mowed lawn to complete them. But she held her tongue and gave Delilah a smile that could be taken for grateful.

"I suppose it has been hard," Roxanne said, hoping that would end the discussion. But it didn't.

As if on cue, Jeanette approached her with a large aluminum pot she took from the refrigerator where they kept juice and snacks for Sunday school.

"We didn't want you to have to cook tonight," she said. "So we got together and made you a beef stew. Enough to last for a few days. And you don't even have to return the pot. It's yours. Our gift to you."

Roxanne never dropped her grateful smile. She accepted the pot, saying, "Thank you so much. You're such good friends."

That was all it took. The other women swooped down on her,
hugging her and kissing her cheeks. Roxanne tolerated it, knowing
that soon enough, she'd never have to see any of them again.

After that, the other women shooed her from the basement,
insisting she go home and rest. She didn't need to be told twice.
With the cook pot on the passenger seat, she drove home
and went straight to the kitchen. When she sniffed the stew,
it actually smelled rather good, if a bit spicy. That would be
Delilah's doing, she thought. The woman believed that a few
jalapeno flakes in a dish made her a daring chef. Roxanne shook
her head at the foolishness of it.

She put the stew on to warm and poured herself a glass of
wine. What truly disgusted her about the other women in the
church group was the thought that if she hadn't acted to save
herself, she might have ended up just like them.

Idiots. Letting themselves be trapped by laziness and fate.

Roxanne remembered when the doctor had told her she was
pregnant the first time. She thought she was going to faint. Dr.
Powell had to help her into a chair so she wouldn't fall on her face.
She was sure that Sean, her husband, had tricked her somehow.
She wasn't ready for babies. Wasn't sure she even wanted them,
yet there she was. It wasn't fair.

*I was drowning, and when you're drowning, you'll do anything
to keep from going under. You can't blame a drowning victim for
simply wanting to live.*

When the stew was ready, she heaped a good-size portion
into a bowl and ate on the sofa while looking through travel
brochures. She'd been collecting them for months, and now that a
year had passed it was time to move on. But to where?

An hour later, still as undecided as before, she put the rest of the stew away and the bowl in water to soak. As she did, she remembered the thumb-sized patch of mold on the wall behind the sink. Roxanne got out the bleach from the pantry and scrubbed thoroughly until the wall was immaculate. Afterward, she went upstairs to bed, where she fell into a deep and pleasant sleep.

Thursday was always grocery day. Roxanne took the car to the Piggly Wiggly with a short shopping list in her pocket.

Living on her own these days, she never spent much time in the grocery store and seldom filled her cart more than a third full. Today was no different, especially since she was anxious to get home to her brochures. She'd been leaning toward moving to New York, but now she was thinking about Europe. She had plenty of time to decide. The house had to be sold before she could leave and that might take months. The idea of another summer in Houston depressed Roxanne, but she was determined to be patient. She'd been patient about dealing with the family. She just had to do it one more time.

There were few enough items in her cart today that Roxanne headed for the express lane. However, on her way over, Jeanette from church cut her off.

She smiled at Roxanne with surprised delight, and she smiled back sunnily, thinking, *Pack mule*, at the sight of the other woman's nearly full cart.

"Are you coming to Delilah's ladies-only lunch this Sunday?" said Jeanette excitedly. "Her roses are coming into bloom and it should be beautiful."

Roxanne nodded. "She does love those roses."

"Then you'll be there?"

I would rather die than be there, Roxanne thought. "I'll try to be."

"Did she ask you about the library book drive?"

Anxious to get out of the store and the inane chatter, Roxanne said, "Of course. I'll put a box or two together this week. Sean and the kids' books, mostly."

"Oh," said Delilah, going quiet. "Will you be all right doing that?"

She took a breath and said, "It's healthy, don't you think? Time to let go and move on."

Jeanette shook her head. "You're so strong. I don't know if I could ever do it."

I am. I am stronger than you, thought Roxanne.

Bored and wanting to get out of the conversation, she glanced at her cart as if she'd forgotten something. "You know, I have some frozen things I should be getting home."

"Of course, dear. I'll see you Sunday."

"Goodbye."

When she arrived home, Roxanne put away the groceries, heated up some of the beef stew, and froze the rest. Later, when she went to wash her bowl, the patch of mold was back on the wall. A larger patch this time, as big as the palm of her hand.

Annoyed, she wiped it away, this time with ammonia.

To get away from the smell, she went into the living room and pulled books from the shelves, piling them on the sofa. She'd been in a foul mood since running into Jeanette. It was getting harder and harder to maintain a placid public face for these people. That's why the book drive was such a godsend.

The books were one less thing to worry about when she finally escaped to wherever the brochures would take her.

The next morning the mold patch was back on the wall, larger and thicker than ever. It spread out in all directions, like the branches of a tree. The mold was thickest where the branches separated, with bulges and little hillocks. Looking at the foul mess was like gazing at a toxic cloud in the sky. Roxanne could almost make out shapes in the filth. The sight of it made her feel queasy.

She pulled a bucket and scrub brush from under the sink and got the bleach from the pantry. She mixed it with scalding hot water and tried to wipe the mold off the wall. Where before it had come off easily, this time she had to scrub as hard as she could to dig down through the rancid tree trunk to the wall beneath. Eventually, the mold disappeared under her insistent brushing, but Roxanne saw that she'd damaged the wallpaper. Where two sections met, they now pulled apart, trailing glue like a scab coming off a wound. Worse yet, she found that some of the mold had worked its way into the drywall. Furious, she scraped at it with a butcher knife. When it didn't come off immediately, she threw open the cupboard looking for something stronger than the bleach and ammonia she'd tried earlier.

And then she saw it.

It was a small glass spice bottle labelled "Garlic Salt." But what it contained was much stronger stuff. She stared at it and thought of Sean and the kids. She was certain she'd disposed of the poison, yet here was the concoction she'd used that night, in a bottle of the one spice she wouldn't ever use in a million years.

Roxanne took the bottle off the shelf and held it in her hand.

I forgot the date the other day and now this. Things have gone so well up to now. What is it that people say? That some murderers want to be caught? No. I don't want that, she thought, wondering in a mild panic what else she might have forgotten.

She looked back at the wall, at the shapes in the mess, like silhouettes of animals and people. There were definitely faces forming in the moldy tree branches. Roxanne stared at one in particular.

Sean, she thought.

Now angry as well as scared, she twisted the top off the garlic salt.

Why won't you stay dead?

She shook the bottle, throwing some of the poison directly onto the moldy face. It bubbled briefly and began to shrink and dissolve. When it was almost gone, Roxanne scrubbed the spot with bleach again. When she was done, she carefully threw the bottle into the kitchen trash and shoved it all the way to the bottom of the bag. Exhausted and sick to her stomach, she went into the living room and pushed the books off the sofa so she could lie down.

She knew she had to be more careful from now on. She'd waited months for people's obsession with her tragic story to die down. She couldn't afford any mistakes. Not when she was so close to finally escaping this stupid town and these ridiculous people.

To relax, she looked through the brochures and decided on Paris as her first destination. Between the family's life insurance and what she would get when she sold the house, Roxanne was sure she'd be able to have a grand life there.

Feeling more relaxed, she went into the kitchen and made

herself a cup of chamomile tea.

In bed, she dreamed of the Eiffel Tower and the Champs-Élysées. As happy as Paris made her, dark skies dampened her mood. It always looked as if the city was on the verge of rain. Worse, she saw things in the scudding clouds overhead. Silhouettes of animals. A neighbor's dog. A horse she'd ridden as a child. Human faces, too—some familiar—their features constantly changing in the roiling mist. Their mouths moved as if they were trying to speak, but all Roxanne heard was the rushing of the wind.

The next morning, mold covered almost the whole wall behind the sink, reaching to the ceiling. Twisted bodies and faces were clearly outlined in thick patches. Her children's faces. A gnarled mass at the lower corner thrust out like a hand reaching for her.

Her heart was beating so hard that she had to sit down at the kitchen table and catch her breath. She wanted to run from the wretched house. Better yet, burn it to the ground. In her head, she calculated how much insurance she had left in the bank. It wasn't enough. If she simply left and abandoned the house, the money wouldn't last for more than a year or two. Besides, simply running would raise suspicions. She'd worked so hard to tamp down gossip, she didn't want it to start now. No, mold or not, she had to sell the house. Be patient and play the shattered widow and mother for a while longer. But to do so, she'd need a useable kitchen. Between the mold and the damage she'd done to the wall, that was impossible without help.

Roxanne spent half an hour leafing through the phone book before settling on a repairman named Jameson. She called and arranged for him to come by the next morning.

Before retreating to the living room, she reached up and tapped at the mold with a polished fingernail. A few wet bits of it fell away. She reached up and touched her son's face, then drew her nails across it until his features were unrecognizable. Sean and her daughter's faces were too high to reach, so she gave up on them. On her way to the sofa, she found bits of the mold stuck to her fingertips. She wiped them clean with a rag, threw it in the trash, and put the bag in the garbage can sitting at the end of the driveway.

Mr. Jameson arrived at nine the next morning. After a brief, polite greeting, Roxanne led him straight into the kitchen. When he saw the wall, he set down his toolbox and whistled. The mold now crept across the ceiling over the sink.

"I wish you'd called me earlier, ma'am. I might have been able to help before it got this bad."

"Can you fix it?" Roxanne said.

Jameson frowned for a moment, put on a pair of rubber gloves, and approached the wall. He pinched some of the mold between his fingers, tearing off a narrow section of her son's corrupt leg, and letting the mess fall into the sink. He pressed his fingertips to the wall and pushed gently. It gave a little. Jameson shook his head.

"I'm not sure I'm going to be able to save the wall right above the sink. It'll have to get replaced."

Roxanne swallowed a stab of panic. She didn't like the idea of a stranger creeping around her house, especially now that she could plainly see her family staring down on her. She wondered what Jameson saw in the mold.

"Are you sure?" she said. "Isn't there anything else you can do?"

"I can knock some of this down with a chemical wash I have in the truck. But that doesn't fix things. You see, ma'am, if the mold is this bad by the sink, it's likely it's spread. You might have to replace the whole wall."

No, no, no, no, no, she thought, but said, "How long would that take?"

"If I do it myself, a few days. If I call in a crew, one or two."

The panic returned, a cold wave that washed through her body. She looked at her dead family and said, "A crew? No. I can't have people trampling through the house. I need to think."

"Take your time," said Jameson. "I'll get some things from the truck. See if I can clear up some of the mess. You don't need to be breathing that stuff."

When he returned, Roxanne sat at the kitchen table and watched him work. Whatever cleaning supplies he had were much stronger than hers. The mold quickly disappeared under the mop he used on the wall and ceiling. Seeing her family vanish from the kitchen, she began to feel like herself again.

She said, "Oh my. That's much better. Maybe you won't have to do the whole wall."

Jameson looked around. "We'll see. Let's let this dry for now and I'll come back tomorrow. This stuff is strong. If anything is going to handle that mess, it's this."

Roxanne leaned her elbows on the table, suddenly tired. Still, the clear wall made her smile.

"What do I owe you for today?" she said.

Waving a hand at her, Jameson said, "Nothing. Let's see where things stand tomorrow."

"Do you do that with all your customers?"

He shrugged. "It's a nice town. Why not?"

"Aren't you afraid someone will cheat you? I mean, you cleaned my wall already. What if it stays clean and I didn't let you in tomorrow?"

Jameson smiled for the first time since he'd entered the house. "You wouldn't do something like that. You're a good person, Mrs. Hill."

She looked at the man, concerned. "How do you know that? What do you mean?"

As he gathered up some tools, Jameson said, "You don't remember me, but we were in high school together. You, Sean, and me. It's how I know you're a good person. You were nice to me when you didn't have to be."

Roxanne wracked her memory and then it came to her. "You're not Billy Jameson, are you?"

He took off his hat and did a small bow. "Billidiot the Idiot," he said. "Dumbest kid in our year. I thought it might be why you might have called me. You recognized the name."

"I didn't. I'm sorry," said Roxanne, relaxing. If he was the Billy she remembered, he was as thick as tar. "But now I'm glad it was you. If I'm going to have someone in my home, it should be an old friend."

Jameson nodded as the picked up his equipment. "See? A nice person."

Roxanne walked him outside and they agreed for him to come by the next morning.

"With luck, that will be the end of it," Jameson said.

She waved to him as started the truck. "Thank you, Billy."

Back inside, she examined the kitchen. There were black smears here and there where the mop had wiped away the mold but, aside from that, the wall didn't look too bad at all.

She sat down at the table again and flipped through the phone book to the Realtors section until she found the company that had originally sold them the house. She circled the name and decided to call them tomorrow afternoon about putting the place up for sale.

With the excitement over, Roxanne wanted a cup of tea. She put the kettle on, but when she opened the cupboard to get the teabags, she knocked over something leaning against the box— the jar labeled "Garlic Salt". Her breath caught in her throat. She was positive she'd thrown the stuff away yesterday. But, no, that had been yet another mistake. No longer in the mood for tea, she turned off the burner and took the bottle to the garbage can and, again, pushed it to the bottom of the trash bag. She put the top of the can on firmly before going back inside.

That afternoon, Roxanne went to see a movie. She couldn't bear being stuck in the house right then.

When she got home, the wall was still clean. She made tea and called a travel agent to set an appointment over the weekend to talk about Paris. Tea in hand, she took her brochures upstairs to bed with her and stayed there for the rest of the day.

The mold was back in the morning, along with the taunting faces of her family. When Jameson arrived and saw the state of the wall, he set down his toolbox and made a grunting noise.

"I'm sorry, Mrs. Hill. I've never seen a mold patch like this before. I'm going to have to replace the drywall."

She stood behind him, hands clasped nervously. "The whole wall?"

"I won't know till I take down the worst of it over the sink."

"All right," she said. "But I'd like you to do the job yourself. I couldn't bear to have the house full of strangers and noise right now."

"Okay then. I'll pick up some drywall sheets and can start tomorrow morning."

"And it will take a couple of days, you said?"

He looked at the wall. "That depends on the damage."

"Of course."

Throughout their conversation, Roxanne's attention was pulled back to the edges of the mold. She could swear that it pulsed and changed shape, as did the large mounds of filth that were her family's bodies, so that it looked as if they were writhing in pain.

Am I crazy or has it always been moving and it's something else I missed?

Then a dark thought hit her. If she could see the movement, could Jameson? Was he able to make out Sean and the kid's contorting bodies and was keeping it a secret? She looked at him. He didn't seem any different, but she had to be sure.

She pointed to a patch on the side and said, "It's strange how the mold is like clouds. Full of shapes. Do you see the arm over there?"

Jameson looked where she pointed for a moment, then scratched his chin. "You're right. It's an arm. Isn't that funny?"

"And a leg over there."

"I see it."

Roxanne pointed to where the mold touched the ceiling. "And up there. It's almost like a face. A man's face, don't you think?"

"It's funny you mention that one," he said. "I actually noticed it earlier but didn't mention it on account of it being sort of strange."

"Strange how?"

Jameson tilted his head up and looked again. "Well, it looks a little—and I feel funny saying it—but it looks kind of like Sean. I swear those are his eyes."

Roxanne felt a cold weight in her stomach. She wasn't hallucinating. They were there. Her whole family looking down on her. Spying on her. And now Jameson had seen them too. Her mind raced, trying to figure out what it meant and what she might have to do about it. But she couldn't think of a thing.

Jameson frowned. "I'm sorry. I shouldn't have said anything. It's just, I was surprised. It wasn't right, though, me bringing up bad memories like that."

"Don't worry," said Roxanne. "I was the one who brought it up."

"I guess," he said, still frowning. He picked up his toolbox and headed back out of the house in a rush. Roxanne followed him to the truck.

"I'll see you tomorrow?" she said.

"I'll be here. And, like I said, I'm sorry."

"Don't think anything of it."

As he drove away, Roxanne thought, *He knows what happened. If he doesn't go to the police now he will soon. I'm going to have to kill him.*

She went into the kitchen and looked around, hunting for just the right implement. Rummaging through the drawers she found the butcher knife, a large pair of shears, and a hammer. But none of those would do. She would be caught instantly. She needed something subtler.

Maybe the skillet? *I could say that he attacked me.* No. She recalled that Brainless Billy had always been a good boy. If he'd done anything inappropriate with anyone else in town, she would have heard about it.

Roxanne put down the skillet and went into the living room and stood by the front window looking over the row of houses she hated. Same lawns. Same mailboxes. Children's bikes on the lawns. It made her sick.

Later, she wondered if she might be overreacting to Jameson's words. Even if he suspected something, all he had for evidence was some strange mold. And he wouldn't have said anything about that if she hadn't prodded him. After going over it in her head a few more times, she thought, *No. He's no threat.*

Later, she called the travel agent's office and bought a one-way ticket to Paris on a flight leaving at the end of the month. Her mood lifted instantly. When the wall was repaired, she could let the realtor handle everything else. She didn't need to be here. Taking a deep breath, she let it out slowly. It would be her first time on a plane.

I'm doing it. I'm really, finally doing it.

Though her mood was light when she went to bed, her dreams were troubled. One by one, each member of her dead family stepped from the wall and fed her the same poison she'd used on them. Jameson held her and let it happen.

Roxanne woke early and went into the bathroom. While washing up, she found small patches of mold under her nails and on her fingertips. She scrubbed her hands clean with alcohol and hot water.

Knowing she wouldn't be in the mood to cook later, Roxanne took the stew from the freezer and left it out to defrost. Jameson arrived at nine, his truck weighed down with gray slabs of drywall. In the kitchen, he carefully measured the area over the sink, making notes on a pad he kept in the breast pocket of his overalls.

"Would you like some tea?" said Roxanne, watching his every move, waiting to see if he reacted to the figures protruding from the mold. Her family moved all the time now. Hands grasped at the air. Mouths gaped as if screaming. Yet Jameson didn't appear to notice any of it.

"No thanks," he told her. "I'm more of a coffee person."

"I have that too. It's instant, but I could put on some water."

As he spread out a tape measure across the wall, he said, "Thank you. That'd be real nice."

She went to the cupboard for the Folgers. When she opened the door, it was there again. The little bottle of garlic salt. It felt like there was a frozen lump in her stomach. She put a hand on the counter to steady herself and took out the coffee. Roxanne smiled, but inside she was screaming.

Someone is doing this to me. I threw this away. Twice. I know it. Someone keeps putting it back.

She glanced at Jameson. He had his back to her.

Besides me, who else has been in here? Who else has seen the faces? No one but idiot Billy. What kind of game is he playing?

As she heated water on the stove for coffee, she glanced at the skillet. He still had his back to her.

I could do it. Right now. Scratch my face. Tear my dress. Tell everyone it was self-defense. I could do it.

Jameson turned then and, seeing his face, Roxanne's courage flagged. No. There had to be another way. Some way to be absolutely sure.

On the wall, her family writhed and shrieked.

Standing on the edge of the sink, Jameson picked at the mold that touched the ceiling. The lump in Roxanne's stomach tightened. He was practically face-to-face with Sean. Yet he didn't appear to notice anything. She relaxed at the thought that Jameson was simply too dumb to see the grotesque miracle right in front of his face.

When the water was ready, she poured some over the coffee crystals and offered Jameson the cup. She considered pouring herself one too when Jameson said, "Your family got sick. Isn't that right?"

Roxane held herself very still. She turned to him and leaned on the counter, trying to effect a relaxed air.

He knows. The bastard knows. He's playing with me.

"Yes," she said. "Why do you ask?"

He frowned with concern. "I'm sorry. I shouldn't have brought it up."

"It's fine. But I'm curious about what made you think about it."

He turned the tape measure nervously over and over in his hands. "My sister and the kids went apple picking and ate a bunch of them. Got real sick. Maybe the apples were bad or maybe it was pesticide. Anyway, they ended up in the hospital."

Roxanne raised her eyebrows in feigned concern. "I hope they're all right."

"They're fine. Though little Andy had to stay an extra day on account of he kept throwing up."

"But he's better now?"

"Yes, Mrs. Hill. He's just fine."

"How wonderful."

Her mind raced. Was this part of his game, bringing up pesticide? She looked back at the garlic salt on the shelf, thinking, *I have to know. I have to be sure. What if he really is just an idiot?*

Jameson said, "I hope you don't mind something."

"What's that?"

"Well, this job is so odd that I mentioned it to a couple of folks, including Jeff Delano. Do you know him? He was in school with us too. These days, he's a cop."

"No. I don't know him," said Roxanne quietly.

"He helps me out with jobs sometimes. You know, on the weekend for extra money. Jeff might come by in the afternoon. That is, if it's okay with you."

Roxanne sat down at the kitchen table wondering what it would take to get her family's bodies exhumed. Not the word of an idiot, certainly, but perhaps the testimony of a busybody cop.

"It's perfectly all right," she said.

"Did you hurt your hand?" said Jameson.

She looked down at her fingers. There was mold under her nails and smeared on her fingertips again. Using dish soap, she washed them in the sink and said, "How funny. I must have touched the wall when I came in."

"You'll want to be careful. Mold like that is bad for you."

Yes. He is playing. Being coy until the police arrive. I should have seen it coming.

She wished she'd followed her instincts and simply abandoned the house, letting the realtor deal with repairs and the sale. She could have flown to Paris days ago instead of being trapped at home between a dimwitted monster and her screaming family. Still, she wasn't caught yet.

While Jameson made drywall calculations in his book, Roxanne put the stew on the stove over a low flame.

She said, "Do you like stew, Mr. Jameson?"

He glanced at the pot. "Call me Billy."

"Thank you, Billy. Call me Roxanne. So, do you like beef stew?"

"I do. A lot."

"Then you'll have to stay for lunch."

"Thank you, Roxanne. That'd be nice."

"What time did you say your policeman friend was coming by?"

"This afternoon sometime."

She glanced at the kitchen clock and said, "Maybe we should eat an early lunch so we'll be ready for him."

Jameson said, "I wouldn't mind that. I didn't get any breakfast."

"Then we'll feast as soon as possible."

He bustled around her in the kitchen while she stirred the stew on the stove, careful not to let it burn on the bottom. When it was warm and the comforting smell filled the kitchen, Roxanne took a bottle from the cupboard and poured the whole thing into the stew.

"What's that?" Jameson said.

She stirred the pot, relaxed and resigned. Jameson had won their little game. The police were on the way.

"Just something to add a little spice to our lunch," she said.

Roxanne ladled out two bowls and they sat together at the table. Jameson dug his spoon in eagerly and ate big mouthfuls of the stew. Roxanne left her spoon beside her bowl and stared up at the wall where her family screamed at her.

Jameson cleared his throat. "The other day, when I first got here, I saw a bunch of travel brochures in the living room. Are you going somewhere?"

"Yes, I am. Paris."

Jameson stopped eating and leaned back in his chair.

"Wow. I've never been farther than Galveston. Will you tell me about Paris?"

"I haven't been there yet."

"Yeah, but you know a lot more about it than I do."

"I suppose I do."

Roxanne sat quietly, a finger on her spoon, her mind racing for a way out, but her mind was blank. The police were on the way. If she ran, Jameson would no doubt stop her. *Yes. That's exactly what he'll do*, she thought.

Jameson said, "Jeff would love this stew. Can we save him some?"

She didn't think about it for long. "What do you say we finish it ourselves and I'll give him the recipe."

"Sure. But you're not eating."

Roxanne looked at the mold on her fingers and up at her family. She picked up her spoon. "I wasn't sure I was going to, but I think I will after all."

With a half-full mouth, Jameson said, "What's the first thing you're going to do when you get to Paris?"

She thought for a moment. "I'll check into my hotel and go out onto the balcony where I'll have a view of the Eiffel Tower. I'll breathe in the air and think, *I'm free*."

She took a bite of the stew. It was just as good as she remembered.

They ate and talked like old friends until the pot was empty.

The Party

Paul Tremblay

"I'M leaving my purse under the seat. Don't let me forget. Ugh, we're so late," Jacqui says. She proclaimed they were going to be late every five minutes during the drive down from their apartment near Central Square in Cambridge; *you're not driving fast enough* the unspoken accusation.

With the prophecy fulfilled, they exit the car. Frances says, "It's fine. No one is late to a party."

"Look at all the cars parked on the street and driveway. Everyone is here already."

Jacqui is a generally charming, but socially anxious, extrovert. When the anxiety builds toward a boil, Frances has found asking a simple, borderline annoying question helps Jacqui to release some of the steam. "Who is everyone?" Frances asks.

Jacqui smirks and narrows her eyes. "I know what you're doing. Thank you and you can stop." She clutches the bottle of merlot Frances picked out. Neither of them is sure if it will be to her boss's liking.

"I'll answer for you: work people. People you see and talk to every day. People who like you and admire you and on occasion steal your lunch from the office fridge." Frances takes Jacqui's free hand (her fingers are shockingly cold) and leads her up the long, woods-flanked driveway clogged with SUVs and luxury sedans.

Jacqui wriggles her hand free, nervously adjusts the scarf hanging loosely around her neck, and says, "I didn't want us to be the last people here. Everyone staring at us as we go in. Maybe we should stay outside—you can have a smoke—until someone else shows up and we'll sneak in behind them."

Frances runs a hand through her shoulder-length, graying hair. "Oh, we're definitely the last ones here." She tries to say it with a smile, or to pluck one from Jacqui.

"We should go home," Jacqui says. "We have this bottle of wine."

"I don't like wine."

"I meant for me."

They have been living together for almost a year, dating for nearly two. They met when Jacqui tornadoed into Frances's *House of Brews*, a small café by day and specialty beer bar by night. Jacqui ordered a large black coffee to go and accidentally left her phone and purse on the counter. When she returned twenty minutes later, Frances was sitting at a small table with the phone and purse along with pastries on two small plates. She had taken off her apron and put on a black blazer in an attempt to look more like the owner and less like she'd been behind the counter for the prior sixty hours the place had been open. Jacqui missed her conference call and they sat and talked as she finished her coffee. Jacqui returned later that night for a free beer at Frances's insistence. Frances is fifty-one years old, which is fifteen years older than Jacqui. There are times when that gap feels like an epoch. She knows Jacqui's anxieties are the root of how she is reacting to their lateness and it's not that she's embarrassed to be seen with an older woman at a work party. However, Frances is tired of the it-doesn't-matter-if-they-stare-at-us conversations and tired of her own teen-like insecurities that pick and nag and doubt and never seem to go away.

"Can't go home now. The Work People—" Frances pauses here, accentuating the playful, purposeful nickname, "—have seen us already."

Jacqui surprises Frances by laughing. As though reading her mind and purposefully tweaking it, she says, "You're my old lady," and hauls up Frances's hand for a mock chivalrous kiss.

The seventies-style ranch sprawls atop the private hilly lot like an inkblot. Twin floodlights illuminate the cobblestone walkway at the end of the drive and the home's dark brown exterior, which shows if not its age, then its yearly battles with the extremes of New England weather. Rigorously landscaped shrubs flank the front entrance.

Frances says, "Cute, but smaller than I imagined."

"Wait until you see inside. She's shown me pictures."

"I bet she has."

"You're not funny." The front door is ajar, leaking conversation and laughter from the party. "I guess we just go in."

"This is your party. You can cry if you want to." Before following Jacqui inside, Frances looks behind them. Beyond the floodlights and walkway there is only the dark. She cannot see the street or the length of the drive. It's a silly thought, one reflecting her own unspoken anxieties of having to be *on*, of having to—in her mind—justify who she is to a group of strangers, but it's as though nothing exists beyond the house and this point in time.

Frances says, "That's what I call an open floor plan." From what she can see from the foyer, the only walls in the house are the exterior walls. An expansive kitchen, dining room, and living room flow into each other and overlap, the boundaries ambiguous and arbitrary. The interior is brightly light, almost garishly so. Yellows and golds mix with copper and other earthy tones. Elegant, modern light fixtures drop from the ceiling. The massive kitchen island is quartz-topped and has a deep farmer's sink. The wall to their left is all windows and glass, floor to ceiling, offering a view of the lantern-lit backyard. Bookshelves ivy the rear wall in the living room area. Well-dressed revelers fill this space, everyone drinking and showing their teeth.

One of the guests rushes over, gives Jacqui a hug, waves hi at Frances, and within the same breath of the greeting, offers to take their coats and wine. The rules of the party house always to be fumbled through and figured out as one stumbles along, Frances is about to ask if they should take off their shoes, but the younger woman disappears with her arms full of their coats. Jacqui is stunning, as always, in her little black dress. Frances wears her threadbare blazer over an untucked, white button down, and her best skinny jeans.

An older man in a gray suit appears next to them with a tray of red-tinged drinks in tumblers. He explains that it's a cocktail made especially for the party: Four Roses bourbon, Campari, sweet vermouth, and orange zest. Frances asks if the drink has a name. "It's called simply 'The End.'"

"As in, if you drink one it'll be the end of your night?" Jacqui accepts a glass with a little bow of thanks.

"Festive," Frances says. She declines as she's driving. She asks if there's any beer, the hoppier the better. The man points her to a lonely table set up against the wall of windows.

Upon returning to Jacqui's side after the beer run, Jeanne Bishop, the owner of the house and the CFO of Jacqui's company, stands in the middle of the great room and taps her glass with a fork until the party quiets. She says, "Thank you all for coming. I'm generally not one for speeches." The party laughs at the irony or self-deprecation as they are supposed to. Frances is self-aware enough to know her predisposition to not like Jeanne Bishop isn't entirely fair, but thinks, not without some satisfaction, that she is made of sharpened, uncompromising angles, and that she sounds as dry-cleaned as she looks. "I'll keep it brief and to the point. Eat, drink—" Jeanne pauses to sip deeply from her half-empty glass, "—and fuck, for tomorrow we die."

The party in the great groom roars and claps its approval.

"Is the head of HR here? I'd like to lodge a complaint," Frances whispers into Jacqui's ear.

"I don't think that line was in Corinthians," Jacqui says. She's clearly more relaxed having walked through the pre-party fire of anxiety, and she links arms with Frances.

At the physical contact, Frances smiles, she can't help herself.

"She's using the new living translation."

"Why are we here again?"

"She's your boss."

"Right. You should've told me to say no. Really, you're supposed to protect me from things like this."

"I failed. That toast was kind of weird, right?"

"Rich white people are weird. She's not like that in the office."

"Do you mean she's not rich and white, or she's not drunk in the office?"

"Shh. We should go say hi. Those are the rules, right?"

They wait politely in an informal greeting line that has gathered around Jeanne, who wears a red sequined gown. Another man in a gray suit carrying what looks to be a straw-woven picnic basket comes by asking for cell phones. Most of the people around them hold up empty hands, signifying they'd already complied with the demands of the basket.

Jacqui looks at Frances expectantly, or is it questioningly? Frances cannot tell. Earlier, Jacqui made a show of leaving her purse and apparently her phone under the passenger seat. Did she know this phone request would be made? Frances says, "There's no way in hell I'm giving up my phone."

Jeanne steps between them and says, "Putting phones out of reach is one of my office rules when we have meetings. I'd rather people fully engage with one another without distraction. Hello, my dear." Jeanne hugs Jacqui quickly. "I'm so glad you made it." She holds Jacqui at arm's length and drinks her in. Jacqui apologizes for being late, muttering something about the drive being longer than they anticipated. Jeanne turns her attention to Frances and says, "I've heard so much about you, Frances, it's wonderful to finally meet."

They hug and Jacqui widens her eyes, clearly enjoying Frances's discomfort.

"It's very nice to meet you too, Jeanne," Frances says. "I'm sorry about the phone thing. But if something goes wrong at my café, like if it catches fire or something—" she laughs at her own joke that she knows isn't all that funny, "—I need to know."

"Of course, of course. But, even if it did go up in flames tonight, god forbid, we know it wouldn't matter since the world is ending tomorrow." Jeanne laughs.

"I guess that's one way of looking at it." Frances drinks from her beer bottle. She's either not in on the joke or is the butt of one.

"Oh Jesus, Frances, I'm sorry." Jacqui nervously darts her eyes between the two women. "I don't know how I forgot, but I did. I didn't—" she pauses, gestures at Frances, and speaks directly to Jeanne, "—I didn't tell her there's a theme to the party."

Jeanne's rigid posture momentarily curls. "You didn't tell her?"

"Yeah, you didn't tell me?" Frances's voice goes higher pitched than she intended. She did not want to sound so obviously hurt.

"Surprise? I'm sorry. I feel awful. Jeanne, I don't think I've told you, and it's not a big deal, really, but I tend to stress out and my brain can shut down before—before gatherings like this—"

"Oh, Jacqui, I'm sorry, I had no idea."

"No, it's okay, please don't apologize. I'm fine. It just takes a little extra work to get me to the party. Once I'm there, I'm always fine, and I have a great time, and I'm usually the last one to leave, right, Frances?" Jacqui grabs Frances's hand and squeezes.

"Well, I'm glad you're here, Jacqui, and please let me know if you need anything. And, yes, Frances, the theme of the party is the end of the world. We're not celebrating apocalypse per se, and I don't mean it to be morbid, but think of this as more a celebration of living in the here and now. Now that I'm talking about it this way, it's a terrible theme, isn't it?"

Frances says, "No. Not at all. Maybe we'll try it out at my café sometime. Offer to serve everyone their last cup of coffee or pint of beer."

Jacqui says, "Ugh, I'm the worst. I'm sorry to you both."

Jeanne fusses and insists Jacqui stop apologizing. Frances does not.

After a silence of some length that wilts polite smiles and glows with the embers of confusion and resentment, Jeanne says, "I am disappointed no one dressed up like Mad Max or Imperator Furiosa."

Frances says, "If I'd only known. I'm big into cosplaying."

Jacqui rolls her eyes, and says, "Your home is absolutely gorgeous, Jeanne. I can't stop looking at that wall, all those beautiful windows."

"Thank you, Jacqui. You're too kind. It was a lot of work. Worth it in the end, I think. But—" she pauses to sip, and, while swallowing, points a thin finger, "—with all that glass, we'll be totally exposed tomorrow when the world ends. Maybe we'll be kept as pets, like fish in an aquarium, and they'll watch us as we either slowly starve or go mad. I'm just kidding, sorry. We're not planning on staying in this room. Too exposed. Okay, I'll stop joking. I do get into the spirit of my themes. Perhaps too much. Jacqui, I'm guessing you did not mention to Frances my offer to stay the night? I have plenty of room and it's such a long drive back to the city. And for what?"

"Why didn't you tell me the theme?" Frances holds up quote fingers around "the theme." "Am I making too much of this? I don't think I am. You had weeks to tell me."

"I don't know. I'm sorry."

"What do you mean, you don't know? There has to be a reason. Did you think I'd make fun of it or say I wouldn't want to go?"

"I really don't know."

"I don't get how you don't know."

"I'm not lying to you."

"You could've told me when we got here. You could've told me when that guy brought you 'The End' drink? Jesus, why not tell me then?"

"Look, I'm sorry. You know how I get before social gatherings and my answer isn't going to change even if you keep asking."

"What about the collecting phones thing? You left your phone in the car. I saw you do it. Why not warn me about that? I mean, it's like you brought me to a—to a secret cult party."

"Seriously? You're being ridiculous."

"Am I?"

"Yes. 'Secret cult party' was last year's theme."

"I knew it. Total cult. Work People Cult. You have your glass of Jim Jones juice. Plus that Caligula toast/speech she made. And the shit about being in the aquarium is more than kind of fucked up."

"Now you're being a jerk. I can't even deal with you right now." Jacqui's arms are crossed over her chest and she smirks, likely trying to appear more bemused than she actually is.

"Fine. I'll stop. But there's no way we're culting here overnight."

"Yes, I know. Give me a little fucking credit."

Frances has pushed far enough, if not too far. Their brief but intense argument ran its course from stung feelings to resigned attempts at humor but is in danger of heading back out toward hurt again. She shakes her empty beer bottle regretfully. "If I go outside to smoke will I be the first one sacrificed?"

"Only if we're lucky."

Past the kitchen and down a narrow hallway, Frances finds the bedroom currently serving as the coatroom.

The ceiling lamp has been left on, but the fog of decorative frosted glass dims the light. The walls above the wainscotting are creamy yellow. The darkly stained headboard, the prow of the king-sized bed, claims much of the rear wall. Guest coats and jackets have been carefully if not obsessively arranged atop the white duvet-covered mattress. The number of coats is overwhelming. Are there that many people here? And there's something about the way the coats are laid out, like trophied pelts. She makes a mental note to make a joke to Jacqui later that she would've been back to the party sooner but finding her coat was like finding a needle at an archaeologist's dig site. She finds her overcoat right away though and retrieves her cigarettes and lighter.

Across from the bed, tucked into a corner of the room and beneath a large window, is a sitting area; plush chair, small bookcase, and a circular, one-post, wooden table. Atop the table is, well—she's not sure what it is. The red, lumpen, smooth-surfaced thing is shaped like a strawberry yet is the size of a birthday cake. Bigger, actually. Frances decides it is a cake as she walks around the bed to the sitting area.

With the cake designation clear in her mind, she assumes the red exterior is fondant icing, but upon closer inspection the surface isn't smooth. The longer she looks, the more organic the thing appears, although there is no sign of stem or stalk. There are random patches with small, raised bumps and with black dot-like pits, or pores in its skin. She does think of the outer layer as a skin. Sitting briefly in the plush chair, she wonders if the skin would be as soft as the cushion beneath her, or crusted and hard. There's a sickly-sweet compost smell, almost smokey, that initially stings her eyes with its unpleasantness. She quickly becomes used to it. Beneath the object is a porcelain platter or serving dish, and pooled at the object's base is a dark red, almost purple, glistening liquid. Frances leaves the chair but maintains a crouch, and maneuvers to the other side of the table, the side facing the window. The skin here is acned with pustules and weeping sores.

Frances stands and shimmies a few fleeing steps away from the sitting area, wringing her hands together absently. She doesn't turn on a heel and leave the bedroom. She instead returns to the chair, bends, and reaches a finger toward a section that appears the smoothest, the most unblemished. The surface breaks at her touch as though it was made of rice paper. Liquid saps out from a fingertip-sized hole. It felt like touching a rotted tomato, only worse, because it is not a tomato.

Outside the bedroom and standing in the middle of the hallway is Jeanne. "Did you find everything you need?" she asks.

Frances says, "Yeah," and holds up her pack of cigarettes with one hand. She wipes her other hand on her jeans. Witty rejoinders die on the pad of her greased fingertip.

"You're welcome to go out back. I left a standing ashtray at the edge, where the brick meets the grass. It looks like a tall, skinny birdbath. Can't miss it. The glass doors to the patio are unlocked."

"Thank you. I will." Frances walks past Jeanne, almost pressing against the wall to avoid any glancing contact with her.

"I know it's a lot," Jeanne says, "but my offer stands for you and Jacqui to stay overnight. You can have my bedroom if you like. I don't mind."

It's a clear, cold night. Unlike being in the city, bubbled within its desert of light, there are stars visible in the sky. Some of the pinpricks of light are larger than others. Some flicker and waver, others are hard, steadfast, unblinking.

A breeze enables the grass and trees to speak. Standing at the edge of the bricked patio but not on the grass—she will not step onto the grass—her back to the house, Frances stares into the wooded lot. The ankle-high grass leads to a thick grove of trees. She does not look at their heights and tops and wonder how long the trees have lived, how long they have left to live. She instead strains to identify the mishappen mounds crowding around the bases of their trunks until she can't bear to stare at them any longer.

Can anyone from the party see her out here? Would she,

undetected, be able to watch them revel while in—how did Jeanne put it?—their aquarium?

Frances mutters, "Shouldn't it be a *terrarium*, Jeanne?" She throws the cigarette butt onto the grass and not the ashtray. A small act of defiance, one that twitches a smile.

Frances turns around and looks inside the teeming, glowing house. Jeanne and Jacqui are standing together by the patio doors and looking out into the yard, presumably at Frances. They are far enough away that their faces are featureless blurs. Judging by the hand gestures and her bobbing head, Jeanne is doing all the talking.

The man with the drink tray comes by and offers Jacqui another red glass of The End. She takes it. She raises the tumbler in the air, tipping it out toward Frances, toasting her.

Refinery Road

Stephen Graham Jones

Y EARS later, at a trivia game in the bar of the hotel Jensen's company had him at for three days, *An Officer and a Gentleman* would roll up on every screen. The title and the poster both. The movie was the answer to whatever the obscure question had been—Jensen hadn't really been interested, was just riding out the cheers and groans, trying to finish his drink without getting jostled too much. The room and meals and cab fares were all expensed, but this drink, all nine dollars of it, was his and his alone.

He left it sitting there, along with two singles for the bartender.

It wasn't because he could have won that round if he'd been quicker on the draw. Even if he'd been tuned in, he wouldn't have called *that* movie out. He'd never even finished it. According to the screens still assaulting him from all sides, it was from 1982, Richard Gere and Debra Winger, but when Jensen, seventeen then, had pushed it into his family's VCR in 1988, he didn't know

Gere or Winger by name, by face, any of that. He just knew he'd liked *Top Gun* enough his sophomore year, and according to the back of the box this was another fighter pilot thing, and had been on ninety-nine-cent rental at the grocery store, so why not.

Jensen had just been getting into the movie when Cara called him. The whole time she was telling him where she was, he was staring at *An Officer and a Gentleman* paused on-screen, the video barely holding on, the tracking lines and static juddering this drill sergeant scene.

It was bad for the tape, but Jensen left it paused like that all the same.

Why Cara needed Jensen to pick her up now now *now* was that when she'd come home with a tattoo of her dead little brother's name on the inside of her left wrist, so she could touch it with the fingertips of her right hand, her dad had lost it, called her every name he had coiled up inside, and when Cara finally ran out the front door he'd fired his welding truck up, chased her through all the empty lots on their block, trying to run her down. He only stopped when she stumbled across the railroad tracks and his truck was too long, high-centered on the rails, both the front and back tires spinning in the air.

When Jensen picked her up at the gas station, Cara huddled in, just told him drive, drive, she didn't want to be here anymore. Her lip was busted. Jensen offered her a tissue from the little pack his mom kept in the center console. He wasn't supposed to take the Buick out without explicit permission, but this was an emergency. He was already making the argument in his head. But if he got ragged on for taking it, so what. This was Cara, his best friend. She'd been there for him on the playground in fourth grade when he wet his pants, and she'd held his hand once at the mall, to try to make a girl Jensen liked jealous, and when her little brother had overdosed in his bedroom last year, Jensen had held her head to his shoulder for all of one afternoon, and let her hit the side of her fists into his chest and shoulders every few minutes, when it all rose for her again.

They picked Mote up once Cara was calm enough. His parents had decorated the front of their house for Halloween, and the reason Jensen turned the headlights off while Mote was locking his front door was that dads being *Halloween decoration*-cool like that wasn't what Cara needed to see right then.

Mote slipped into the back seat like ducking out of a bank he'd just robbed, and that wasn't all wrong: he had a six of his dad's beer.

"Where to?" Jensen asked all around.

"Just go," Cara told him.

They made the usual circuit: up the drag, back down the drag, turning around at the auto parts store, but the night was dead. It was Tuesday.

"Let me see," Mote said, taking Cara by the chin.

He ran the back of his knuckle under her bloodied lip.

"It's gonna fat up," he told her, leaning back.

"Thanks, Einstein," Cara said back, and was just taking his proffered beer when the cop car that they didn't know had pulled up alongside flashed its light.

"Shit," Jensen said, both hands finding the wheel.

"Shh, shh," Mote said.

Cara snaked her bottle down, let it hide alongside her thigh, but the cop hadn't lit up for them. He was already accelerating away, blasting through the light.

"Go see," Mote said to Jensen.

"What, are we moths?" Jensen said back. It was what his mom always told him, about being drawn to what she called "episodes of trouble."

"More like fireflies," Cara said softly, and Jensen sneaked a look over at her, like her face was going to be as wistful as her voice.

He waited the red light out, followed that cop car, Mote calling out its right turn.

It took them back by the gas station Jensen had picked Cara up at.

"No," she said, leaning closer to the windshield.

"What?" Jensen asked.

"Where'd he go?" Mote said, leaning over the front seat, his beer dangling from his fingers for all the world to see.

"Left," Cara said, so certain Jensen could only follow.

They could see the blue and red lights a block and a half before they got there.

It was the train tracks.

Cara's dad's welding truck was crumpled, smashed. Jensen knew the trains slowed, coming through town, but even slow was enough to plow through a truck caught up on the tracks.

Jensen turned his headlights off, crept as close as they could get away with.

The firemen were extracting a body from that truck.

"He stayed?" Jensen said, not really believing this.

"He was drinking," Cara said back flatly, shrugging her left shoulder.

"Shit, your *dad*, you mean?" Mote said, finally clueing in.

"Serves him right," Cara said, and before Jensen or Mote

could stop her, she was stepping out her side of the car and running forward a few feet to hurl her half-full beer.

She screamed behind it, not words, just anger, and the bottle popped way on the other side of the tracks, drawing all the firemen and cops' eyes.

They followed the arc that bottle had taken back to Jensen's mom's Buick.

"No, no," Mote said, slumping down as far as he could in the rearview mirror.

"C'mon, c'mon," Jensen said to Cara, though she was too far to hear him.

She came back all the same, her hands balled at her sides, her gait not nearly urgent enough. The moment she was in, Jensen reversed hard, spun them around in what he hoped wasn't a guilty manner, and eased away, pulling his headlights back on.

"What were you doing?" he said to Cara.

"I hate him so much," she said back, reaching to the back seat for another beer.

"Listen, I can just get out—" Mote said, but Jensen turned hard, shutting him up for the moment.

"They'll all be looking for us now," he said, and instead of taking them back to the drag, which would be an invitation to get pulled over, he took smaller and less likely streets, all the dead ends and cul-de-sacs finally spitting them up at the city limits.

"Yeah, the sticks," Mote said. "Great. Wonderful. Nothing bad ever happens out here. Not to people my color."

"Mine either," Jensen said.

"But girls are *completely* safe out here," Cara said, playing along—almost grinning, even.

Jensen considered her grin: was she even registering what was happening? Her dad was dead. He'd been run over by a train.

Or maybe she was registering it. Maybe that was why she had that grin.

"You good?" he said across to her.

"Excellent," she said back, looking straight ahead, which kind of put the lie to her words.

Still, "My mom's going to see the gas gauge," Jensen said out loud, to break the awkwardness, and for some reason—he'd never figure it out—it was him saying that that made Cara start in crying. Not hard crying, not even letting herself cry, really. But there were tears she couldn't help slipping down her face, now. She wiped them away, kept her lips pulled in tight, her eyes still so straight ahead.

Jensen knew he should put his hand on her knee, or do *some*thing, but the excuse he gave for just driving was that, like his mom said, he was responsible for the lives of everyone in the car, so he couldn't be distracted, since it only takes a moment of inattention to kill everyone.

"It's not your fault," Mote said to Cara, like just stating a fact. "Anyway, he was… I mean, I don't want to—"

"It's better this way," Jensen filled in. "You don't have to worry about him any more."

"Yeah," Mote chimed in, evidently even less sure than Jensen what to say.

"My mom," Cara said, closing her eyes like for calmness. "First it was my brother, who I was supposed to have been babysitting. And now it's my dad, who was—"

"He was trying to run you *over*," Jensen reminded her.

"Train's like an act of God," Mote said. "The world calling in his ticket, yeah? Nothing you did, Care Bear."

She looked down, sort of grinned again, like trying to fake it until it was real, or real enough. When her head came up, she was drinking long from her bottle, like punishing herself.

"He, he—my little brother, I mean," she said, having to stop to burp. "My grandma showed me the pictures once. He looked just like my dad at that age."

It was funny to her. Or, she laughed after saying it, anyway.

"That's where he grew up," she said, chucking her chin down a dirt road Jensen had never seen.

"Your brother?" Jensen asked.

"My dad," she said, something disconnected about the way she said it, like she was really just talking to herself.

"Serious?" Mote asked, looking down that dark road.

Jensen slowed so Cara could take a snapshot with her eyes, and then, because there was only blackness opening up before them, he came to a stop, backed up into that road to turn around.

"No, stop!" Mote said. "Headlights!"

Without asking why, Jensen turned them off.

It was just in time for the red and blue lights already coloring the trees to become a cop car, speeding up the road.

"How'd they find us already?" Jensen said, his heart jackhammering awake.

"It's me they want," Cara said, her finger to the door handle on her side, like she was going to step out into the road, await judgment.

The instant the dome light glowed on with her door starting to open, Jensen reached across, pulled it shut again, his body seatbelting her in.

"No, no, I have to—!" she said, but now Mote had his hand over her mouth, and Jensen knew that if this cop managed to smear his dummy light through their windshield, it would be obvious what was happening: two guys were abducting this girl, one of them holding her down, the other keeping her quiet.

The cop car slammed past, tore a hole in the night and drove right through it, the sirens lasting only a moment longer.

When Cara was calm enough, Jensen drew back to his seat, checking Mote in the rearview.

"Clear?" he said, and when Mote nodded, Jensen turned the headlights back on.

At which point a cop car that had been speeding around the curve turned *its* headlights on, along with its blue and reds.

Even though he was in Park, Jensen still stood on the brakes, washing the darkness behind them red.

This cop car slowed as if expecting them to pull out in front of it, and then, maybe two hundred yards past them, *its* brake lights flared.

"It's me they want," Cara said. "I killed him. I killed both of them."

"Shut up!" Jensen told her.

"Go go go!" Mote was saying, making everything worse.

Jensen shook his head no, but it was his job to keep everyone in the car safe, wasn't it? He sucked his headlights back in, dropped his mom's big Buick into Reverse, and stomped the gas, the rear tire that got the torque having to spin for two or three seconds before finding purchase.

Fifty yards back, he whipped them around again, the nose

of the car sliding in the dirt, the car fishtailing when he had it back in Drive.

"We're gonna dead-end back here, we're gonna get stuck," Mote said, practically in the front seat with them now.

"It comes back into town by the refinery," Cara said blankly. "That's where my granddad worked when he was alive."

Jensen registered that "when he was alive" and it caught. Was it really necessary to have added that? So… what, then, did her granddad do when he *wasn't* alive? Did dying not mean the same thing to people out here in the sticks?

Jensen didn't ask.

Driving this narrow dirt road without headlights was enough to deal with.

Mote was sitting up in his open window now to look behind them from a higher vantage point, see if they were being chased down.

"Anything?" Jensen called back.

"Drive, man," Mote told him.

Jensen accelerated.

Cara was calmer now. Like something inside her had turned off. Was this what shock was? Jensen had never seen it this up-close. What he did know was that she didn't seem to care if they got caught or not. She kind of even wanted it, maybe.

Not tonight, he said inside, which was when… Cara didn't so much throw up as vomit just started leaking out her mouth. Frothy beer, with veins of blood shot through it, probably from her lip.

"No, no, the window!" Jensen said, and slid them to a sideways stop.

Cara held as much of the vomit in her cupped hands as she could and Mote slithered the rest of the way out, opened her door for her so she could stumble out, fall to her hands and knees by the three-strand fence, empty the rest of her stomach.

Moving on automatic—Cara needed to *see*—Jensen turned the headlights on, then realized the beacon they were, switched them off just as fast.

"Watch," he told Mote, and Mote nodded, his head on a swivel: up the road, back down the road.

Jensen slid across the seat, careful not to spill his beer, and stepped out, knelt by Cara, tried his best to hold her hair up and away. When she finally collapsed against him, shuddering, he reached back for his beer so she could wash her mouth out.

Looking over her head, over the fence, there was a house-shaped empty space where there were no stars.

Slowly, Cara became aware of it too.

She chuckled, then laughed, then stood into whatever this was.

"Of course we're here," she said.

"Your dad's old house?" Mote said—the obvious thing.

It was empty, long-abandoned, it looked like.

"I hated him," Cara said, looking around to Jensen, her eyes fierce, her hair lifting around her on the breeze.

"It's not your fault," Jensen told her. It was all he could think to say.

She took a drink of his beer, swished it, spit it out, and then she ran forward, slung this bottle ahead of her as well.

It disappeared almost instantly, shattering seconds later against the house.

They all watched, Jensen shaking his head no about the

chance of a light coming on in there, which would mean her dad had already come home to where he'd grown up.

It was just an empty old house in the country, though. All the windows stayed dark.

"The refinery?" Jensen prompted to both of them.

Cara stared the house down a few more seconds then nodded, turned her back on it, and the three of them piled back in.

"I'm sorry for getting you two involved in my stupid family drama," she said.

"Best Halloween *ever*," Mote said, closing his door.

"Wouldn't be anywhere else," Jensen said, and dropped the car into gear.

Mote held the last two beers over the seat for them.

"Your dad's gonna—" Jensen started, about the stolen beers, but stopped himself before "kick your ass."

So it just hung there between them, dead.

"It's okay," Cara said, and cracked her beer open with the seatbelt tongue—a trick of *her* dad's, Jensen knew. But still, it was pretty cool.

Her window was down, the ends of her hair stinging the side of his face, and he could have gone faster, on a straightaway like this, but he didn't.

This is good, he was telling himself.

It was just the three of them, same as it had always been. Same as it would always be.

He switched hands on the wheel, which gave him a different angle in the rearview.

The first thing he saw was that Mote wasn't where he'd been. He was pressed all the way to the passenger side of the car.

"What's—?" Jensen said, adjusting the mirror to see the back seat directly behind him.

Cara's dead little brother was sitting there.

Jensen let his foot off the gas and swayed his back in, away from this, the car's momentum carrying them.

"C-C-Ca—" he said, and she looked over at him like she had a hundred times in geometry, like she had a hundred more times on the drag on a Friday night, like she'd been doing for all of the twelve years they'd known each other.

And then she saw the way he was crowding the steering wheel, and—slowly, as if realizing in increments—she looked from Jensen to the back seat, for whatever he was trying to get away from.

Her expression didn't change.

"Ben," she said, so calmly. "What are you doing out here?"

Jensen turned around enough to see Cara's brother shrug his left shoulder like that was the wrong question, and then level his eyes on Mote.

It was the dome light coming on that told Jensen that Mote had opened his door to get away from this.

Ben had already reached across, though, had Mote by the wrist.

Mote coughed from that contact, and thin blood sheeted down over his chin.

Now Ben let him go.

Jensen, not looking ahead anymore, not keeping his passengers safe even a little, all his attention facing the wrong way, locked all four tires.

His mom's Buick stopped across the road, the caliche dust it had been dragging swallowing the distant silhouette of the refinery Jensen had just registered—all spires and darkness against the dim glow of the city.

If they could just make it there and turn right, he knew, then they'd be home free.

Except Cara was still talking to her dead brother, sitting in the back seat.

"I should have been watching you better," she was saying, her eyes full now, the window beside her powdery white for the moment.

Jensen leaned forward more, knew Ben was going to touch him next. When that contact came, though, it was Cara.

She was leaning across—she was kissing him softly on the cheek.

"Thank you," she said, and then had already stepped out, was holding Mote's door open for her little brother.

Jensen saw Ben cross from one side of the rearview mirror to the other, and then both doors closed at the same time.

"Tell your mom I'm sorry," Cara leaned down to say through the window.

She was holding Ben's hand in hers, now. And not coughing blood. Yet.

"*No, no, Cara, don't!*" Jensen said.

In reply, Cara looked back down the road, through the settling dust. "Mote," she said, like just making him out.

Jensen looked too, and when he couldn't see Mote, he came back to Cara.

She was already gone, fast as that.

He shot up through his window and sat on his door, looked across the top of the car, his hands leaving drag marks in the white dust coating the roof, but all around them it was only the night.

He was breathing hard, couldn't steady his hands, his heart, and after looking for Mote and not finding him, which didn't make sense, after sweeping the darkness with his mom's headlights for Cara and Ben, he finally eased back into town, took that right at the refinery, its fences tall and spiky.

But that too dropped out of the rearview after another mile or two.

His mom was already asleep when he crept in. She'd turned the television off, turned all the lights of the house off.

Jensen sat on the couch where he'd started that night, and he didn't press play on *An Officer and a Gentleman*, and he didn't understand anything, he was pretty sure.

The next day wouldn't help.

The fireman hadn't just pulled Cara's dad from that welding truck the train had smashed into. Cara and Mote had been there as well, it turned out.

Jensen's mom hugged him when he couldn't stop trying to tell her that that's not how it *was*, that Mote fell out the back door of the car, that he was never in Cara's dad's stupid truck.

"You took the car out?" Jensen's mom asked.

"And Ben was there, only it wasn't Ben, it was Cara's dad when he was a kid, they looked just the same!" Jensen insisted.

"*Ben?*" Jensen's mom said, holding him out at arm's length. "Dear—Ben's been dead for months, he couldn't have—"

Jensen didn't go to school for the rest of the week, and didn't go to the funerals either, and nothing made sense anymore, but after a few years he was able to tamp it down enough that it didn't rise behind him every day, anyway.

He got a job, then he got another job, then he hired on somewhere with benefits and business trips, and then he washed up in a hotel bar, a trivia game all around him, and then there he was sitting in front of *An Officer and a Gentleman* again.

And then he wasn't.

He was two blocks away from the hotel already, and then a mile, and then, just past where the industrial district of this town petered out, there was a shape out in the darkness where there were no stars.

Jensen stood there and watched it to be sure it was what he was already sure it was: the refinery. Not looming, just distant. What it being there again meant, he knew, was that he was, somehow, still pulled over on the side of Refinery Road that night. He hadn't so much walked out past the city limits of this town his work had delivered him to, he'd... he'd walked into a memory. No—more than that. The past. He'd found a fissure, a seam, a door left open, and slipped through. Maybe because, in his heart, he'd never really left.

"Hey," Jensen said aloud to this moment, this night, this part of the road, and tilted the bottle of beer up ahead of him, in greeting—the bottle of beer he hadn't walked away from the hotel with, but that was the least of the wrong things happening.

A quarter mile behind him, along the ribbon of blacktop he'd drifted away from, a police cruiser flew past, its blue and red lights strobing the yellow grass and trees and fence line.

"Hello," Jensen said to this officer, lifting his beer that way as well.

When he looked back to the grass swaying in the slight breeze, he could taste the scorched brakes of his mother's Buick on the air—acrid and oily, but kind of good, too, the kind of pain you sort of like a little, at least at first.

The kind of pain you *need*, when you know something was your fault.

He was supposed to have kept his passengers safe, wasn't he?

He nodded to his mom that yes, yes, that had been his main and only job.

And he hadn't done it.

So he'd had to go out into the world alone, without his two best friends in the world.

But now he could go back, couldn't he?

That's what this was: a do-over.

He took a long drink of his beer—it was warm, flat—and then, his bottle dangling by his leg, he slouched down through the ditch and up into the pasture. It was the only place that felt right anymore. Without the silhouette of the refinery stabbing up through the horizon, never any closer no matter how fast he drove, how desperately he ran, he felt he might just fall up into the sky, never stop.

Standing knee-high in the swaying grass about twenty yards out were two shadows he knew.

First the girl lifted her beer to him in greeting, and then the guy, like he was embarrassed to be out here, doing this, and Jensen was smiling now, smiling and swishing faster through the grass, his own bottle falling behind him, his own blood coating his chin now, but that's just because you can't go back alive, but you *can* remember what it was like to punch through the darkness in a great heavy car, your headlights off, everyone you care about there with you, and so what if by the end of that road you're sitting in the cab of a welding truck, the world bright white from a train's lone headlight, its air horn screaming loud enough to split the night in two?

The man who just woke behind the steering wheel of that welding truck is struggling to get his door open, is panicked because he thought he was alone, and because the train is almost here, but the three of you packed in beside him are just serene, are just watching up those rails, holding each other's hands, because this is how forever happens.

It's going to be wonderful.

It always has been.

The Door in the Fence

Jeffrey Ford

THERE was an old couple who lived behind us when I was a kid—Rolly and Rita. They had the place on the other side of our back fence. Whereas most of the suburban yards were a quarter acre, treeless grass rectangle, their lot was bigger than usual and covered with trees. Rolly was a short, stout guy with a block head and three days' white beard. He wore glasses and his face was usually red with a distinct line of sweat on the brow. In retrospect, he looked like Hemingway from the tenth dimension. His wife, Rita, was a quiet woman in a drab housedress with an apron over it. Her dark hair hadn't yet started to go white and a faint mustache adorned either end of her upper lip. She never said much to us when we were young. Rolly was the one with the personality, of sorts.

He built a doorway in our back fence so we kids could go over to his yard when we wanted to ride on the giant, homemade lawn glider. It was like a chariot, swinging through the breeze, and although this was about sixty years ago, I still remember the sense of freedom. The other item Rolly had that drew us through the fence was a small cannon. When I say the cannon was small, I mean the size of a toy truck. It did pack a boom and a wallop, though. Sometimes, depending on what time of day, whether Rolly was drunk or not (he kept a bottle of Chivas Regal in the well shed), we could talk him into shooting it off.

On Saturday afternoons when my father was out in the back, cutting the grass or raking leaves, he would go through the fence into Rolly's yard. He'd meet up with the old man in the well shed and they'd bullshit and drink Chivas. One time I accompanied him on his visit, and I got a seat between them, right in front of the stonework encircling the open well. Rolly told me to look into it. He said no one knew how deep it went. He instructed my father to hold me while I peered in. "It'll draw you to its heart," he said. I leaned over the stones, put my head beneath the bucket attached to the windlass. Instead of it being uniformly pitch, the view was more psychedelic, as in it glowed in patches along the walls of the well like the black light posters my brother and I had. "There's lights," I said.

"It's some kind of lichen or mold," Rolly said. "That well has been here a long time. The house is a hundred and fifty years old. I imagine the well, in one form or another, would have to be a lot older."

"Do you drink from it?" my father asked.

"Are you kidding? This is my water, right here." He dashed off what was left in his glass. My father followed suit, and then they poured a couple more.

I met Rolly when I was about five, and he went the way of all Rollys when I was around ten. I recall him showing us his photos from WW2 and photos of his dog, Mumps. I don't think I went to the funeral. My parents probably did. As far as I remember, it was like Rolly was there and then he wasn't. The cannon was probably still there unless they buried it with him. The glider was also still there, but we no longer went through the fence. Someone had nailed the door shut from the other side. We were sure it was Rita, who didn't want us playing in her yard. With that, a whole episode of my life fell away and drifted off. Once in a rare while, usually in winter, I'd look down through the empty tree branches into their yard from our upstairs bathroom window. No matter how many times I did, I never saw a single footprint in the snow. I'd watch the glider swing back and forth, empty, and it would bring to mind the sound of the cannon going off in some distant other country of my memory.

At the end of the following summer, I was in the car with my mother, and we were driving back from the grocery store, when a bike pulled out of one of the side streets right in front of our car. My mother hit the brakes hard, and she dropped her cigarette into her lap. Retrieving it, she said, "Could you possibly…" which was one of her stock lines for any kind of bullshit life threw at her. I was in the back seat and, pre-seatbelts for kids, I'd smashed my face into the headrest of the seat in front of me. As I was rubbing my forehead, I looked out the front windshield and noticed the bike rider was more familiar close up. I tapped my mother on the shoulder and pointed. "It's Rita," she said, and we watched in silence and followed as she pedaled up the street, her white mumu flowing. She'd lost the apron, but gained a pair of green moccasins and a pair of knee-length white athletic socks. Just before we pulled into the driveway, Rita lifted her legs in front of her and rested them on the top of the handlebars. My mother tooted the horn in appreciation of the stunt.

Later, at the dinner table, my mother told my father what we'd witnessed. He widened his eyes but said nothing. "She's like sixty-six now," said my mother. "I guess since Rolly's gone this is her idea of stepping out. While he was still alive, I never saw her do anything but sit out on the glider with her hands folded in her lap and her hairnet squeezing her head too tight."

For the rest of the summer and then autumn and through the winter, we spotted Rita at every and any time of the day or night riding that old bike—high, wide handlebars, pedal brakes, reflector on the back, basket in the front, one of those bells you worked with your thumb instead of a horn. She pedaled fiercely, undeterred by rain or snow, as if the work of her legs was responsible for the motion of the sun and moon and stars. In the winter, she put on a woolen Rangers hockey hat and wore a padded, insulated jacket, black rubber boots over the moccasins. More than once during this time, I heard my mother say, "Well, I gotta hand it to her, she's getting in great shape." When I looked down at her yard through the leafless branches, I'd see her shovel the snow from the concrete drive to her garage, and once it was clear, she'd go back and forth the length of it, sideways, doing the Karaoke step, like they made us do in football practice. At other times, I'd see her on the cold cement, her knuckles pressed into it, doing push-ups.

This was all rather odd for the late 1960s, especially for a woman closing in on seventy. To tell the truth, though, as entertaining as watching Rita was, she was low on my list of real interests. The way I experienced her was more like brief bouts of surprise. She'd pop into my field of view and as quickly pop out and my teen head would backfill and obscure her. There was one incident, though, that happened in early spring and made an impression. I was in the car again, this time with my father. We were heading home down our block and we had to creep along because there was a guy, running right in the middle of the road in front of us. My father, in situations like this, just chilled. He didn't beep the horn, he didn't get pissed off, he just drove slowly. He'd told me once it was a way of being he'd learned in the army, since you always had to wait on lines for everything.

Eventually, the runner, dressed in a sweatshirt with the arms cut off, sweatpants, grocery store sneakers, realized there was a car a few feet behind, and moved out of the way. We passed him, and lo and behold it wasn't a guy after all, it was Rita, but she had her dark hair cut into a crew and the mustache that had always been poised to happen wasn't waiting any longer. Her biceps were impressive for such thin arms. She wore a red headband and a whistle on a string around her neck. "Who's that?" said my father. "It's Rita," I said. He drove a few yards, checked the rearview mirror, and said, "Yikes."

It seemed she stayed with running for a year. My mother, working on her fifth glass of cream sherry, cigarette in hand, opined from her spot in the dining room, "I saw Rita yesterday. I think she's getting younger."

"Crazy is obviously good for your health," said my father. "She doesn't stop long enough for Death to snatch her." The two of them would be dead in fifteen years, at sixty and sixty-one. Rita was moving toward seventy, looking like Charles Bronson.

You could see she was old, but she was ripped, and she moved with agility and speed. Not grace, though, as she had a slight limp in her gait from the time Rolly set the cannon off just as she walked in front of it and it gave her a great and lasting punch in the thigh. Her movement side to side, the motion of her arms when she ran, was like a crab playing a violin.

As summer came on again, the first Saturday after the start of vacation, I took my bike early in the morning over to the grade school around the corner. There was a lot of concrete there that was good to ride on. When I crossed the basketball court and looked toward the school, I saw into the alcove created by the giant brick box of the gym jutting out from the main building and the lower wall of the cafeteria. There was Rita, playing against herself in handball. I stopped my bike to bear witness. She had on a pair of black gloves with no fingers, a black leather biker vest over a white, man's T-shirt, her red headband (her hair had grown out frizzy), a pair of gym shorts with the local high school's iconic lion on the left leg, and those crappy sneakers. She moved around the asphalt, suddenly jumping side to side, talking to herself. I think she was celebrating her best shots. "Here we go," she'd say and slam the ball against the wall with her left hand. At least in her mind, the game was on. I took off before she spotted me.

In all the time I had been intermittently, half unconsciously, charting Rita's changes, there'd never been an instance when anyone in our family had spoken with her. Sometimes my mom would wave and beep the horn when driving by, while Rita was either running or on the bike. Never once did she acknowledge the gesture—which was odd because before Rolly died, although she'd been quiet, she often stood on her side of the back fence and chatted with my mom on the occasions both would be hanging laundry.

In late June, my mother came home from the grocery store one day and told us Rita had been on the warpath there. Apparently, she'd had the manager of the deli department up against a wall and was threatening him because the cold cuts scale didn't show the shopper what the weight of their purchase was. It had long been broken and an issue at the store, but the deli guy, who was tall and broad, was such a bully no one did anything about it. My mother said, "Rita had him by the tie and was pulling his head down to her level. She was shouting at him, spit flying from her lips. She had on her Hell's Angels outfit." I'm pretty sure my mother meant her leather vest and black handball gloves. The police were called, and when my mother saw them pull up outside, she walked over to Rita and took her by the arm. Softly, she whispered, "It's okay. I think he's got the message." She led her down the aisle and took her out the back door as the police entered through the front. She told us, "Rita never once said a word to me, but the minute she hit fresh air, she took off running at a dead sprint. I'm telling you her arm was hard as a rock."

Whenever I rode through the schoolyard on my bike on a late summer afternoon, I'd stop for a while and watch the handball games in the alcove by the gym wall. The guys and girls who played there were pretty much in gangs and were the black-leather-wearing, Colt-45-drinking, cigarette- and pot-smoking, knife-fighting, bottle-busting crowd. If someone like me stopped to watch, usually they got beaten up and rolled for whatever money they had. I was an exception because the head tough guy there, Bobby Lennon, protected me. It seems my father had picked him up hitchhiking one day and taken him all the way to Bayshore. Because of that kindness, nobody at the handball court messed with me.

Lennon was a long-haired tough guy, strong but a lot of fat at the same time. His handball attire was a dirty white wife-beater T-shirt, black jeans, and black boots with steel toes for when kicking the beaten. He was a sloppy drunk, and when he'd be two 40s deep and losing at handball, it wasn't unusual for him to stumble over and punch his opponent viciously in the face. Imagine this scene and then Rita showing up, which she did one evening, ready to play. I had an advantage over the others present since I'd been tracking her changes. The assembled kids didn't know what to make of her at first. "Is that like a kid or an old lady?" I heard someone whisper behind me. There was snickering and quiet laughter.

She arrived in between games and, instead of figuring things out, she stepped onto the court and said she was there to take on whoever had just won. It was the first I'd heard her speak in years. Her voice was high pitched and had a quaver to it, completely different than the retiring hush of her past. What she'd proposed wasn't the way things usually went down. Games were planned out in advance for almost the entire afternoon and evening. I watched Lennon push off the wall he'd been leaning on, put down his bottle of beer, and walk slowly toward her. "'Scuse me, Granny," he said, blowing his cigarette smoke on her. "But you're not playing." He got close and leaned down. "What the fuck are you supposed to be, anyway?"

She grabbed a shock of his hair with each fist and jerked his head down to meet her kneecap, which was thrusting upward.

Lennon went over like a sack of rocks and was out before he hit the ground. Rita's mouth hung open, her eyes wide with a distant stare, a wooden mask of both age and fear polished to a thin veneer of vibrant health. She looked down at Lennon, who lay face-up, and blew her whistle. Kids crowded around him as blood gushed from his nose. A moment passed, and when I looked for Rita, she was running in the distance across the baseball diamond.

I lost track of her for a while, busy in my last year of high school. We didn't see her jogging past the house anymore or on her bike down by the library. The once or twice I looked from the upstairs bathroom window down through the branches at the snow, there was no sign of her. Nothing until the winds of April brought news of an attempted robbery at the pizza place in town. Two guys walked in with stockings over their faces and guns drawn. Rita happened to be sitting at the counter. It also happened that she was carrying a Browning 9mm in her coat pocket. She turned to catch the action, and Phil, the pizza guy behind the counter, who was interviewed afterward, said he could tell the gunmen were stunned by a glimpse at her face. He described it as "haggard, yet smooth, the wrinkles shining and waxed like a car." One of them even cried out, "Jesus." She pulled out her gun and blasted both of them in the head. One fell. One kept walking, though dead, and got off a shot at the ceiling before tumbling onto a table. Phil told the cops he'd probably be dead if it wasn't for Rita. They wanted to question her, but she was gone.

Years passed and there was no more about Rita save for her popping up in a nightmare once or twice. It's not that I never thought about her, but life was coming at me fast—school, marriage, kids. One night, my wife asleep on the couch next to me—we must have been in our late thirties because I know, within the boundaries of the memory, the kids were asleep upstairs in their rooms—I watched *I was a Fugitive from a Chain Gang*. In it, Paul Muni is on the lam from a prison breakout and being hunted constantly. There's a scene at the very end at night where, outside her apartment, his girlfriend asks him how he lives. He hisses, "I steal," and then falls backward, swallowed by shadows. For some reason I thought of Rita and felt a sense of closure about her weird saga. Then time came down like a blizzard, burying the whole crazy thing from my notice.

Until, in the early 2000s, I was teaching a creative writing class at a community college in mid-Jersey. I would end up teaching English there for about twenty-five years. It was generally a good gig, but there were a shitload of papers to read and mark. In this particular semester, they'd booked my fiction writing class Tuesday, late at night (it didn't get out till 10.30 p.m. and I had a two-hour drive home) in a weirdly shaped room on the top floor of a three-story building out by the last parking lot. It was known as the Sank Building, named for some freeholder, Bradley Sank. The students called it the "stank" building because you could get high there and the campus police never patrolled it.

It was a spring semester, so the class started in winter, and that year there'd been a pile of snow. All the walkways were covered with ice, and the wind shrieked across the big open parking lots at night. The evening classes on campus usually had quite a few older students along with the usual eighteen- to twenty-five-year-olds. I'd gone around the room and read off the names, and they all seemed pretty eager to get started. I asked them, in honor of the first night, to write me their life story in three handwritten pages as a way for us to get to know each other. The class was three hours, and I told them they could take the first two writing and then we'd read a few of them out loud. They set to it, and I opened my notebook and made believe I was writing.

When two hours had passed, I asked, "So, who wants to read?" People smiled and shook their heads, but one arm went up, in the back, at the juncture of the room where it was impossible for me to see the entire student. The arm was clothed in a purple jacket sleeve. He scooted his desk to the left and into my field of view. It was an old guy, and he looked, no shit, just like Salvador Dali. His face was sagging and sad, his fashion style was low-key pirate—ruffles at the cuffs and down the front of a white shirt. His mustache was waxed and twirled at either tip. I asked him his name and he said, "Samzibar."

"Is that a first name or last?" I asked.

"Only," he said.

"Okay, have at it."

He started reading from his pages, and two lines in he dropped the fact he'd been born with the name Rita, in a small, upstate New York town. The mere mention of her name, and my memories of her came up in the field of my imagination like soldiers from dragon's teeth. The story went on through the thirties and came to where she met Rolly and they fell in love. She told about the children she tried to have, Mumps the dog got a mention, and then she told about a well on their property inside a little shed, and how she drank from it regularly. Rolly wouldn't and warned her not to because of the strange glowing lichen on the inner walls of it, but all she could think about was the beautiful glow, the warmth of it. The water was ice cold and electric in its freshness. There was a buzz to it in more ways than one. She had just begun to tell about the changes it wrought in her when Samzibar stopped reading. "I ran out of room," he said. "I think I lived too much." The students clapped for his imagination. He nodded and leaned back in his chair.

A few more people read and we discussed their life stories. I called class after that. The students filed out, and as I put my papers and books in my bag, I looked up and saw Samzibar heading toward me. A chill went up my spine and through my right eye.

"You know who I am, don't you?" I asked. We were alone on the upper floor and the wind howled outside.

He nodded. "You came through the fence to ride the glider."

I looked to the door to see if I could make a break for it. I had no idea how Rita, aka Dali, had ended up in my classroom. I was pretty certain it wasn't a dream. "Why are you here?" I said.

"I have a favor to ask."

"You're going to have to answer some questions first," I said, surprised at myself for getting uppity with the one who took down Bobbie Lennon, not to mention plugging two pizza thieves.

He nodded and sighed. Taking the nearest seat, he settled in and I began. "The water, did it make you a man?"

She laughed. "The water filled me with energy. It built up over the years in me, and just about the time Rolly died, the power blossomed and I became something other than human. As for dressing like a man and growing a mustache, I'd long had the desire for it, well before I even met Rolly or tasted the water from the well. I never wanted to be a man, if I had I would have become one. What I wanted was simply to be my own kind of woman. The water had nothing to do with that. Some people, when they get old, all they can think about is dying. Some, on the other hand, find freedom."

"The water seemed to have made you very physical, aggressive…"

She nodded. "I optimized my physicality. I was dangerous."

"Why did you have a gun?"

"It had been Rolly's. The ultimate personal means of aggression. And I'd begun traveling amidst unsavory elements."

I looked at her in silence for a few seconds and thought I could almost see Rita's face from a time before her change. "Why Dali?" I asked.

"What do you mean?

"You're telling me you're not trying to look like Salvador Dali, the painter?"

"Stop abusing me," she said and appeared to be substantially upset.

"Okay, okay," I told her. "You have my apologies. I misread you."

"I've had a lifetime of that. Only since I stopped taking the water have I slowed down and begun aging again. I've shaken its overwhelming effects and settled back into humanity."

"You should probably be like a hundred and twenty by now," I said.

"Probably. I'm here to ask you to edit my memoirs. When I finish writing them, I'm going to shoot myself. I've had more than enough. Who knows, I could go on living for another hundred years before death finally catches up with me."

I couldn't believe it. At the end of this great mystery, what the whole thing added up to was me reading and marking more pages of someone else's writing. "Why me?" I asked.

"Because you know my story is true. And you're a writer. Your work is published." She reached into the bag she wore over her shoulder and took out a thin sheaf of papers. Holding them out to me, she said, "Here's just a piece of it to give you an idea of what's coming."

I took the pages from her and she left. I don't know if it was the result of one of her secret powers, but I was dazed for a minute, couldn't move, overcome with memories of the door through the back fence, the glowing well, the boom of the cannon. When I finally got it together to stand, I staggered to the window and looked down across the parking lot. I saw her shadowy form trudging along, limping slightly, the white ruffled shirt catching the security light, glowing from beneath a long pirate coat. The figure never stopped at a car. By then, my car was the only one left in the lot. She just kept walking to the asphalt's edge and stepped across the boundary into the woods.

Here, then, is what she handed to me and I read on the spot—

It was 1983. I was just about at the height of my powers and was working for gangsters, killing people they wanted killed. Mind, I never killed anybody but other gangsters, no women and children, but men? Shit, they hardly had to pay me. I had all sorts of methods, from strangulation to making blood spurt out their ears with a single punch to the forehead. And just think, I was in my late eighties.

Have you heard this saying? Absolute power corrupts absolutely. Zero morals. I'm not proud of it, but my person was taken over by a biological entity, if you know what I mean? Everybody in the crew thought I was a guy. I tried to tell them at first, I was my own kind of woman, but they'd just grin and nod, mostly out of fear I might turn my savage talents upon them. I had my head shaved back then and wore a black, form-fitting sweatsuit. Also, I added yellow-lensed ski goggles to my outfit. I never looked as sharp as that again.

So my boss, a tub of shit with a ketchup stain on his shirt and a vast overestimation of his own capabilities, told me one day he had a job for me coming up and we all stood to make a fortune from it. It was about this time I started to regret my life of crime. From the moment I'd plugged those two goons in the pizza parlor, I'd been on a tear through the underworld, killing, wreaking havoc—some days for one gang and on other days against that same gang. I was enamored of the action, the opportunities to mix it up with so-called tough guys. God, I wrecked a hundred and a half of them.

The gist was one of the other crime bosses had his own special fighter who they wanted me to fight. The purse was two million. There was a lot of talk about my opponent. He was called Thriller, I think because Michael Jackson's song came out at the end of the previous year. It was hugely popular. The others in the crew tried to explain my opponent to me, but I wouldn't let them.

The day finally came and we drove down to a spot at the end of Jersey, an abandoned warehouse near a town called Shell Pile. The place was a dump. Inside the old building, they had a large circular chain-link cage. My boss told me to go inside it. As I did, he yelled after me, "To the death. Do you understand?" I didn't even turn around. I was standing there for a few minutes, and then music started blaring from unseen speakers—the Jackson hit. Other people filed into the warehouse. I didn't bother to look for my opponent. Finally, I sensed someone standing behind me, and it was him, Thriller. I hadn't noticed, but there was another

*opening on the opposite side of the cage through which he'd
entered. My defenses came up instantly, the adrenalin, the other
chemicals from the well water, and I was growling, as back then
I had a tendency to do in such situations. I went from poised to
leap to complete stillness in an eyeblink. My opponent, the killer,
Thriller, was a kid, at best twelve years old.*

*He was naked, and his body was covered with long blond hair.
He had dog ears instead of human and they came to points. He
had the saddest dog face I'd ever seen. Then he charged me, and
I knocked him back onto his tail. He came at me again, snapping
and frothing. I gave him a love tap on the chin and he went
sprawling. By then it was clear to me that I wasn't going to kill a
child, no matter how screwed up it was, and so I climbed to the top
of the cage, thirty feet in the air, and exited through a small hole
at the very center. From there, I jumped and somersaulted down
the side of the thing. This all happened fast as lightning, but it only
took an instant for my boss and the crew to see I was abandoning
the bout. They had their guns drawn and weren't about to let me
escape. I skipped and leaped around and over them and a couple
wound up shooting each other.*

*I got out of the warehouse and ran off across a field into the
thick woods of the pine barrens. Once in under the trees, I slowed
down and caught my breath. I'd only rested for a heartbeat before
I heard a twig crack behind me and knew Thriller was on my trail.
I took off through the barrens like a shot, leaping fallen trees,
vaulting creeks, and for a while swinging from branch to branch so
as not to leave tracks. Still the kid stayed with me. Around dawn, I
realized there was nothing behind me and slowed down. Running
away would have been easy, but I had a strange thought, one that*

wasn't about myself. I had what I believed to be a feeling of worry
for the poor kid lost in the woods by himself.

I retraced my steps and found him curled up, beneath a tall
black-jack oak. I lay down next to him, and when we woke he
followed me, and I took him in as both my pet and my son. It was
the moment I started caring again. He ate ravenously and the cat
litter cost a fortune as I could never get him to go on the toilet. I
had to get us an apartment and I needed a job. He only lived for a
brief time, a few years, before succumbing to splintering bones and
organ failure. He'd been poorly bio-engineered by mob doctors in
search of the perfect assassin. Some clandestine botched scientific
experiment. At the end, the result of it all broke my heart. I'd given
him the name Hector and I think we loved each other.

I have to tell you, the walk through the decrepit Sank Building
and across the dark and inhospitable parking lot at 11.30 p.m.
had me looking over my shoulder and sent me images of a deep
dark stone well, able to draw you into its heart and not let go.
On the two-hour drive home, I wondered if the story could be
real. It seemed, even for having to do with Rita, a tad far-fetched.
Let's face it, I was a fiction writer and teaching a class in fiction
writing. Even though she said it was her memoir, she might
have developed a sense of ironic humor. Perhaps all her physical
power was subverted into a glowing intellect. Or fiction was the
only way she could capture the staggering epic of her life. Either
way or any way, I thought about it and reread the piece more
than a few times through the week. I almost told my wife, but the
whole thing was far too complicated to explain. The following
Tuesday night at the stank, I waited for Rita to show up, even

held up the start of class in anticipation of seeing her again. Of course, she never returned.

Now I'm in Ohio, living out among cornfields and tumbledown red barns, nobody to see for miles. I'm retired from teaching more or less, although I still do a class every now and then at a fairly close-by university. I can't see very well, but I talk to the dogs a lot, especially when I sit out back on the nice days beneath the apple trees and face out into the two-mile green field. Yes, I have a notebook with me and a pen, and I'm supposed to be writing but, to be honest, I do more thinking. Though you'd expect me to be fed up with all the Rita nonsense by this age, I admit she comes to my mind more than she should. I daydream she lives in a trailer in the wind break in the middle of the vast field before me. In that island of white oak and hickory she passes her considerable golden years, enjoying the experience of aging, of falling apart. She works on her memoir, and I wait patiently for the day she will bring me a jar of freezing water. I keep an ear out for the shriek of her whistle.

Pear of Anguish

Gemma Files

KNOW *what a pear of anguish is?* Imogen asked me, that last day we spent together, and I shook my head. *I'll show you. Take a look.*

She opened up her book and thumbed through it quickly, spreading its dog-eared pages to display two illustrations set next to each other, one a sketch, the other a photograph. Both were indeed roughly pear-shaped, as advertised; the one on the right spread out in petals, weirdly organic, while the one on the left was black iron, spiked all over, sharper outside than in.

You use the screw, here, she said, pointing. *Tamp it down, tight, and thrust it up inside, anyplace that's big enough to take it. Could be the mouth, like a gag, that's why people in Holland called it the choke-pear… but other people, they say they used it during the Burning Times, on women. Down there.*

Jesus, that's gross, I said. *Seriously, what—why? Why would anybody—*

—stick that inside someone and pull the screw, let it open up, see what happened? Her eyes were still on the page, half-slit and dreamy, like she was hypnotized. *It's no different than cutting yourself, Una... all on the inside, though, instead of the outside. No scars. None that show.*

And somebody else doing it to you, instead of you doing it to yourself, I pointed out. Cutting, I could have said—would have said, later on, when I finally knew how to say things like that out loud—was all about control in a world without it. Hurt yourself to dim or stem the pain you already knew was coming. What kind of control would shit like *this* give you?

It's dumb, I told her, finally. *That'd kill you. Totally different.*

Imogen smiled then, her smile that looked more like a snarl, skewed left and upwards, in a way that made her look as if she was having a stroke. *Like you've never thought about it,* she replied. *Steal your Mom's booze and a bunch of pills so it wouldn't hurt as much, slit your wrist the right way and let them find you like that. I used to plan on setting myself on fire with the gas can my dad kept in our shed, back in Gananoque, but it's harder here.*

Why not throw yourself off the bridge, you want it that bad?

Maybe, one day. Maybe.

Around us, the Ravine wasn't quiet so much as full of a very different sort of noise. As part of a system of watersheds downtown Toronto sat overtop, the section we knew best ran underneath the St Clair Ave East bridge, bisecting our shared neighbourhood for a mile in either direction—trace it far enough south and it blended into Rosedale, eventually becoming part of the Don Valley Parkway, which an enterprising hiker might trace almost right on down to Lake Ontario. The trees grew so close they strangled the sky, and the creek rushed by at full flood over rocks and trash, striking liquid against the runoff tunnel's concrete walls. Green dusk here at the bottom of the slope, true dusk starting to show up above. The insects sang and the leaves rustled, and for half a heartbeat I thought I heard a cicada whine so loud it cut through my skull like a skewer.

Seriously, I said, at last, *don't be so fucking stupid; don't pretend like it even matters* how. *You'd still be just as dead.*

Sure. But think about how they'd all feel, if we did.

From "me" to "we," in one small slide. That was Imogen, all over.

They'd laugh at us, Im, is all, I told her, after a long minute. *Look sad in public and make fun of us in private, for being weak-ass losers who couldn't stay alive long enough to get into high school. Like usual.*

But Imogen simply sat there studying those horrible pictures, as if she thought somebody was going to test her on them later, ignoring me entirely.

The very first day I met Imogen, I followed her down under the St Clair West bridge without even thinking twice, straight into the Ravine's heart. She let herself out of the recreation yard through a crack in the fence and moved downwards into the green shadows through weeds that grew big as bushes, clumps of nettle and deadly nightshade, scrums of birch with big torn strips of bark hanging down from their trunks like loose bandages. There was a path, but she avoided it, preferring to make her own.

I'd been coming back from lunch when I spotted her, still reading that book she'd been nursing under her desk all day in the corner of the recreation yard, ignoring a clot of "popular" girls discussing her from near enough to make it obvious, yet far enough away to make objecting to being discussed more work than it was worth. I didn't know any of their names yet, but I recognized their faces from earlier; I didn't know *anybody* here yet, given I hadn't known I was changing schools until Mom had told me the week before, when she'd picked me up at the airport after coming back from Melbourne only to take me "home" to a completely different house from the one I'd left a month before.

"You'll like it, Una," my mom told me, "it's a whole fresh start."

"Sure," I agreed. No point in arguing.

Arguing never helped.

One p.m. on Day One at the new school near the new house, and the only one in class whose name I'd managed to learn thus far besides the teacher—Miss Huergath, roughly my height but twice my width, sporting red plastic frames and a big cross at her neck—was Imogen, who nobody seemed to like and everyone seemed to be afraid of. She didn't seem all that scary to me, but then again, why would she? Usually, *I* was that kid.

That alone made me want to follow her, to see what all the fuss was.

"And what did you do over the summer, Imogen?" Miss Huergath had asked, that morning, after the national anthem was over and we'd all sat down again. I followed her gaze to see who she was curving her mouth at and found it was a girl sitting almost beside me, head cocked and long, pale hair half-shading her face, eyes glued to whatever she had in her hands. She barely looked up, flicked her eyes back and forth, before replying.

"I spent most of my time reading mythology," she said. "Norse, Greek, Egyptian, Aztec, African. Christian."

"Christianity isn't mythology," Miss Huergath said.

Imogen twitched one shoulder, not quite a shrug, but not quite *not* one. "All right," she said.

One of the other girls snorted. "But *why*?" she asked, as if the answer implied: *Because you're the most giant geek who ever geeked, obviously.* And for a minute she seemed like she might go on, but Miss Huergath raised her hand instead and snapped her fingers at the same time, silencing her.

"Jennifer Diamond," Miss Huergath said, "do we talk out of turn in this class? No, we do not." And then she was turning my way, scanning the attendance sheet. "So," she began. "Mmm… Una, is it? And how did you spend *your* vacation?"

Everybody looked at me, then, the way I'd been praying they wouldn't, freezing the breath in my lungs and thoughts in my brain together at once, for one painfully long moment, as I struggled to form my next sentence. "In Australia," I told her, at last, when I was able. "My dad lives there." Which drew a snicker, of course, courtesy of what sounded like the same girl as before: *Australia? But why?*

I felt my face heat, all my pimples flaring up at once, and tried to distract myself from the strong, immediate urge to throw something at her by looking back at Imogen, whose eyes were back on her book. That was good; I remember thinking how I wanted to know what the title was, whether it was one I'd already read, and tried to crane my neck to see. But the light on the spine was too strong for me to make anything out, even if she hadn't had it opened so wide.

Around us, the class went on with Miss Huergath's Q&A, a steady drone, busy-dumb as bees in a hive. And I was able to sink back into myself, invisible, or at least as much so I ever could be—me, with my adult height and full pubertal shift at age ten and a half, almost eleven. Me, so gawky and inconveniently well-developed, my face painfully sunburnt from that last trip to the beach before boarding the flight back to Toronto; I still wore the horrible navy-blue acrylic turtleneck I'd spent a day and a night travelling home in, if only so nobody had to gape at those long strings of red-brown skin working their way off the back of my neck and into my cleavage, let alone the scars on the insides of my wrists.

Which was uncomfortable, but no more than anything else, really. The glasses with lenses so thick they sometimes fell off when I leaned too far; the braces, rubber bands linking my top to my bottom canines, tending to snap when I yawned. The stretch-marked C-cup breasts I'd somehow grown over those last two weeks of August, so fast I had to wear one of my mom's bras until we could take a trip downtown to the Eaton Centre, with her underwire cutting into me every time I slumped.

And all that fucking blood, that was the worst of it. The way it always seemed to catch me by surprise after that first time, with an acne flare-up, a pre-migraine squint and a general feeling of having been punched in the crotch as heralds that I'd yet to get used to tracking. Not to mention the rage that came with it, stronger than it had ever been before, which is saying something.

I hated it all, hated my body, hated myself. Didn't help I'd always felt like a monster, long before looking like one—never in on the joke, not until I figured out the joke was always me. Like a bomb with a timer anybody could wind up, a storm made from screams, thrown fists and broken furniture. Like anyone could make me explode by looking at me the wrong way. Like everyone *would*, eventually, because it was oh-so-fun to watch when I did.

My last school had been like that, from Grade One on. *You make it so easy for them,* Mom used to tell me, and I guess I did. I guess I always had.

So yeah: if there was someone else who already filled this new class's mockable outsider slot, I'd love to make sure she was the person I had to make fun of in order to keep the roving eye of social malevolence securely away from *me*, for once.

Down into the Ravine, therefore, trailing after Imogen. I didn't even know her last name then, and it didn't matter—I wanted to see what she'd do. My plan was to spy on her, take notes, carry stories back to the clot of "populars." Be practical and start out on the right side of things, for whatever good that turned out to do me.

Didn't work out that way, though.

You've been hanging around with Imogen, Jenny Diamond said, as I put my glasses back on after drying my hair, still huge and naked from my post-swimming-lesson shower—I surfaced blinking, taken aback to find her there and horrified to see she had the whole fucking pack with her, all the "populars" at once: Fazia Moorcroft, Nini Jones, Peri Boyle. *I mean… we wanted to make sure you knew about her, before you made a mistake. It's not too late.*

I already knew I was blushing again, probably all over, clutching my wet towel like a shield and wanting to hit her so hard she'd cough blood, so hard I had to breathe a moment, deep, before I spoke. *Too late for what?* I asked her, finally.

Nini and Faz grinned at each other. *You know she's a witch, right?* Faz asked.

Witches aren't real, I said.

That's what a witch would say, Nini told me. *You a witch too, Una?*

No, I snapped back, already knowing it was the wrong answer.

Later, after they'd gone—after I'd screamed at them until they left me alone, at last, hard enough to hurt myself, hard enough that swallowing felt like something scraping the inside of my throat—I retreated to the toilet and crouched there crying slow, hot tears, re-reading the back of the cubicle door top to bottom like a litany: *le freak c'est chic, heather sucks dick, frig yourself, imogen = witchie-poo.* Pretty soon my name would be up there too, probably misspelled. So I bit into my thumb until I could taste salt, until the tooth-marks were deep enough to sink an entire nail into, until I knew I'd still have bruises two weeks on, purple-grey in yellow. Like swearing blood brothers, I guess, but without the other person.

When Imogen saw what I'd done, saw the marks I'd made on myself, her otherwise unreadable eyes got all wide and soft, as if I'd handed her a ring or something. And: *I knew it,* was all she said, quietly. *I knew you were like me.*

Nothing to say to that but, *Yes, obviously,* so I nodded instead. Knowing that from now on, we'd be the same in everybody's eyes. Kicking myself for thinking I could ever avoid it.

I know why I am the way I am now, and part of me managing to figure it out eventually involved teaching myself to forget—to place that time, those events, my entire childhood, at one remove, behind a scratched and dirty porthole through which I could either view things without actually having to feel them, or feel things without remembering what caused those feelings. To recall my experiences without getting caught inside them, forced to re-live them on a loop for what seems like hours, pinned in an endless useless churn of post-dated embarrassment and rage and hate.

From where I am now, my adult perspective, I can see that what I once thought was spite on others' parts was actually fear that if they let me get away with being abnormal, then what use was the standard of normality they kept their own status by clinging to? We were all women, at least prospectively... but since puberty made me the only one with overt female characteristics, I was the one who stood out. So why not be a cop instead of a criminal, the "populars" must have thought, policing the tall poppy for crimes we'd all share a year or so later? Slut-shame the girl who thinks of herself as a brain on top of a spine, who barely notices boys except as noisy distractions; raid her locker for maxipads because she never remembers to bring her lock, then stick them to the inside of her desk so she'll find them when she flips up the top, a mocking message written underneath with shoplifted drugstore lipstick: *These belong to you, hee hee hee.* Since they all purported not to know what these things were, because none of them had to, yet.

Similarly, I can see that what I used to think was my own innate evil—the evil Imogen obviously shared, which called her to me, and me to her—was simply a long-inculcated belief I'd been somehow born *wrong*, a bullied bully, book-smart but street-stupid, violent from puberty on, but always uncontrollable, an egotistical liar who could never be relied upon to do the right thing, mainly because she was incapable of understanding what the right thing was. After years of therapy and some chemical help, I now understand I wasn't *bad*, different, blind to what most people apparently came into this shitty world knowing about how to fit in, how to get along.

But even only glimpsed through the porthole, the feeling sometimes comes back without me even knowing what it's about, in waves. A tidal wave submerging me, but it's all faceless, formless, attached to nothing. It's like I'm being haunted by the ghost of a feeling; I don't know who I'm angry at, or why; I don't know what I hate them for, but I do, and that seems illogical, selfish, weird. So it turns into me hating myself, being angry at myself, for being weak enough to want to trust, to make friends, to find *love* somewhere outside the divorce-broken ring of my own family, in the first place. For laying myself open, so stupidly, again and again and again.

My parents thought they were each other's best friend, too. That's why they thought they never needed anybody else, till suddenly they did, but didn't have anybody to turn to. And while I told myself even back then that I'd never live like that, if I could help it… really, how could I have ever expected things to turn out differently? They never taught me how to manage to live with other people without hurting them, not even by bad example.

You scared them, Una. (Good.)

You made them scared of you. (*Good.*)

(They fucking should be.)

Things I did in the moment, that passed through me like a storm, so fast and hard I could barely remember I'd done them, later on. Like: oh yeah, *that* happened. I cut holes in other people's clothes. I pissed in other people's shoes. I stuck someone else's Barbie's head up inside me, then put it back on the doll for her to find. I smeared my own blood on the wall, wrote things in it. The same year I met Imogen, I picked up a cat by its tail while listening to a record on headphones, then couldn't figure out how my mom could have known what I was doing; even after I left Imogen behind, I strangled a girl and knocked her head on the floor because she said my whales looked more like tadpoles. Later, in yet another "new" school, I got sent to the principal for interrupting class by describing how to do a lobotomy in detail—which I'd picked up by reading a biography of Frances Farmer—then threatening to do it on one of my classmates with a compass.

IknowwhyIamthewayIamnow,butonlybecauseI'vemanagedto livelongenoughtofigureitout.That'sthesimpletruth. AndIwish—I *do* wish, even after everything she did, I did, *we* did, together—that Imogen had been able to do that, too.

Eventually.

"Come out," Imogen told me that first day, as I crouched in the bushes, watching her. "You're Una, right? Think I can't see you? I can see everything."

That seemed unlikely, but I instantly felt dumb for being there, so I stood up instead; crossed my arms and scowled at her, *fuck you* face screwed on hard, expecting her to be frightened. Which she very much obviously wasn't—beckoned me over, peremptorily, and showed me what she was doing: how she'd set creek-washed rocks in a circle with a baby-doll's detached plastic face in the middle, looking up, blue eyes blind in the green-dark diffuse sunlight slipping down around the bridge.

"The fuck is *that* for?" I asked, and she giggled.

"You swear like a boy," she said. "Is that because you're so tall?"

"I don't know, I fucking like it. So what *is* that, anyway?"

"I'm making a scrying mirror. Watch."

She turned it over, then, showing me a small, round mirror she'd carefully fitted inside the face, probably from somebody's make-up kit. "First you have to cure it, see—take a flame and melt the edges so it won't fall out: the sign of fire. Then leave it all night where the wind can get at it, especially if it's blowing past a graveyard; the sign of night, the sign of air. Then wash it in the creek and leave it down here under a bunch of leaves, looking down into the dirt: the sign of earth, and water. One thing left to do, now: anoint it, and see if it works."

"Anoint it with what?"

Another giggle. "What do you think?" she asked, pointing to where my sleeves had rucked up, glued with sweat, to show off the scars inside both my wrists—those scratches I always told people came from the cat, if they asked, which they mostly didn't. Not to mention the deeper cuts, treated with Bactine and band-aids, which I never told anybody about at all.

I had a hook I'd stolen from my nana's embroidery kit once, meant for ripping seams; Imogen had a penknife, the kind that folds out, its handle wrapped in tape she'd coloured black. She stuck its point into the pad at the base of her pointer finger, between heart- and head-lines, and twisted till she had to pull it out sideways, freeing a drop of blood the size of a dime. "Now you," she commanded, and I didn't even think to disobey. I was far too interested, at that point—I wanted to see if it would work. Nothing I'd ever tried by myself had, up to that point, and I'd always wondered why.

(*All little girls try practicing magic, eventually,* my first girlfriend would tell me, in our second year of university. *That's because magic offers power, and they don't have any... magic tells you things can change, if you want it bad enough. They haven't figured out yet how that's a fucking fairy tale, and fairy tales aren't real.*

(And I remember nodding, but that was mainly because I was drunk and she was beautiful, enough so I wanted to agree with her. Thinking, as I did, how I could sure tell her some stuff to the contrary, if I wanted. If I felt like I had the right to.

(*I used to have a friend who'd disagree,* was all I ended up telling her, though, so low I don't think she actually heard me.)

Imogen squeezed her wound until she'd painted a triangle on the mirror's surface, point up. "Now you," she said, "but widdershins, opposite, other way 'round. Point down."

"I know what widdershins is," I told her, grumpily, sticking the hook between my index and middle fingers. To which she laughed again, full-on this time, loud enough to startle a nearby pigeon.

"Of course you do," she said.

And what did you see in the scrying mirror, Una? a voice asks, from deep inside my mind—that first psychiatrist Mom sent me to, maybe, with her sad, smart eyes. To which I answer, internally: *Nothing. I saw nothing. I never saw anything at all. Not even when I said I did.*

And what did Imogen *see, do you think?*

I can't know that. I only know what she *said* she saw, over and over: a way out, an escape. A door to somewhere better than this shitty world we both knew we were trapped in, the place where one step forwards always led two steps back. Where everyone else got away with everything and we got away with nothing, not even with being two similarly inclined weirdos lucky enough to find each other, to share an affinity, to make up stories together and lie our way into believing them... acting like we believed them, anyhow. On my part.

And yes, we hurt ourselves; we hurt each other. Why not? Pain was already a constant. Imogen's fairy tales at least promised that pain could be harnessed, used as currency. They promised it could be bartered for entry into the numinous. No different from any other religion that way—any other mythology. All the ones we'd studied and discarded on our own, before finding each other.

I mean, pain really *should* count for something, don't you think? Considering how much it hurts.

Think about it, Imogen told me. *Why do other people hurt us? To get what they want, which is for us to hurt. Cause and effect. So when we hurt ourselves, Una, what do we want out of it? What can we* possibly *want?*

...to... not hurt, anymore? She didn't answer, simply waited, which is how I knew she must be disappointed in my reasoning. *Okay, no—no, obviously; that's too easy. To hurt, so long as it hurts them, too. Like they hurt us.*

And? she prompted.

And get away with it.

That's part of it, sure... witchcraft, all that. Baby steps. But I want to go farther, as far away as possible. To a place where my pain makes me queen, empress. To a place where my pain makes me—

—what, fucking god? *Good luck with that, man.* She wouldn't look away, which meant I had to, eventually. Asking her, after a beat: *And besides... what about me?*

Well, you too, Una—come on, did you really think I didn't mean it like that? We're sisters now. Of course, you too.

(*So long as you're willing to pay the same price, that is,* she didn't say, and didn't have to.)

This thing we were after didn't have a name, but we knew we'd know it when we saw it. It felt like... some prospective culmination for all that leprous, unchannelled pubertal fury I felt, that crazy rage to procreate held completely separate from true sexuality, never thought about in conjunction with other people, because they all hated me and I hated them. All those "hunky" boys whose attention Nini and Faz competed for, never understanding they knew even less about the whole shebang than *they* did; I'm not saying I didn't think about sex at all, but not with *those* idiots. I mean, I already knew how to masturbate—"gouging," I called it, for some reason, probably because everything that appealed to me at that age was about secrecy and humiliation, revenge and freedom from consequences, a toxic antique glamour wrapped in blood and gold and jewels. And power, power, power, like my girlfriend-to-be would say.

I remember how I used to stand in the bath looking upwards into the shower's spray and touch myself till the blood rushed so far out of my skull I blacked out: *that's* how it felt, the thing Imogen wanted us to find, together. I'd wake up in the tub, cold and wet with the back of my head ringing against the porcelain, and believe me, it's not like it never occurred to me I was probably killing brain cells, or risking I might crack my head…

But because it felt so good, I kept on doing it—chasing that high, the mounting buzz and pixelation, the letting go, the refreshing dark. Even more like dying, I suppose, than the little death itself.

"Blood's what opens a door," Imogen used to say. "Did you really think you wouldn't have to pay for something like that? Something *wonderful*?"

"No."

"No, that's right. I knew you understood. That's why we're friends."

So every day we'd go down into the Ravine, look in her scrying mirror and try to find a place where the world wore thin, a crack through which to reach somewhere else. We looked for it everywhere. Under the bridge, through the trees, inside the downwards slope of the walls, the deepest part of the creek. We mapped things out in either direction, a mile or more south and north, down towards Rosedale, up towards the Mount Pleasant Cemetery. We broke through thickets of willow-whips and blackberry thorns to emerge into what had looked promising from below, only to have it turn out to be yet another slice of some too-quiet side-street lined with twin-garage houses and speed bumps, its offshoots all cul-de-sacs, for absolute minimum public access.

Imogen would always be the one to see it first, of course; she'd cry out, point with her free hand and set off running, pulling me along. Hand in hand with our wounds pressed tight, grating, throbbing: the lope and the stagger, faster and faster, lungs burning, until it finally blinked out almost as we reached it. And I'd bend at the waist to spit on the ground, coughing as Imogen cursed, damning everything she could think of.

"It shut again," she'd say, finally, once she'd calmed enough to form new words. "We weren't fast enough. We have to be faster."

And I'd nod, still gulping. "I know," I'd reply. "Next time, maybe. Maybe next time."

A third voice, now: Imogen's, of course. Who else?

You never saw anything, Una? That's not what you told me.

Well, no.

Because sometimes... sometimes, I did. Almost.

Probably a shared illusion born of mutual self-hypnosis, or whatever—but I got scared after a while, because increasingly I fooled myself that if I squinted at the exact right angle, I eventually might be able to catch something forming in the air, superimposed over whatever supernatural beacon Imogen was leading us towards. Because, on one particular day, at the very moment dusk turned to twilight, I genuinely thought I could see the threshold... a thin, bright line starting to trace itself around what could only be a frame, hanging high in the air with light from another world spilling out as the door it came attached to began to crack, just a fraction. Before it slammed tight once more.

A fingernail of new moon shining down on us where we stood, and stars, so many stars, caught in the trees' darkness like glitter in a woman's hair. And Imogen grinding her thumb into my wrist, wringing my already-stinging hand so hard it spasmed: *Fucking faster, Una, goddamnit. It's like you don't even* want *it.*

I do, though, Im, I swear. You know I do.

She gave a long sigh, then, almost a snarl. Ragged and ugly. It scraped me inside, like sandpaper.

You'd better, is all she said.

Here's what I *do* know: when someone disappears, no matter the reason, they leave a hole. Wait long enough, and that hole is all you have—it's all you're left with. The assumption that they're gone, and they're not ever coming back. It creates its own gravity, like every other anomaly; everything left over revolves around it, forever.

It's like a scratch on a record, it leaves a groove. It'll never play right again. So every time you hear this wounded song you associate with that gone person, you'll remember she *is* gone—remember she might be dead—and it'll hit you all at once, everywhere, over and over again. Shake you like a bag full of rocks. You'll be one big bruise.

The dead hate the living. We have what they want: time. We have choices, chances. The dead are hungry, always. They resent us everything, even our pain.

By remembering what you've forgotten, by trying to see what it is that happened objectively, what is it that you invite back into your life? Do you open a door, summon a ghost? Do you announce yourself as open to being haunted?

The past is a trap and memory is a drug.

Memory is a door.

Blood holds the door open longer, Imogen realized, after we'd not-quite-done it enough times to have some statistics to work with. *We need* more *of it, that's the key.* Which is how we ended up poring over *A History of Torture and Execution*, which—in turn—is where Imogen found her pear of anguish. And it wasn't as if I really believed she'd be able get ahold of one, but who knew what she was capable of, or what she assumed *I'd* be capable of? I really didn't feel like stabbing myself (or her, or both of us) in the vagina as part of some *Let's Go! Narnia* craziness any more than I felt like throwing myself from the bridge with her on the off-chance a door might open in thin air, halfway down...

I wouldn't tell on her, though. That was never an option.

That evening, however, my body decided things for us. I stole an empty jar from the kitchen and squatted over it for an hour after lights-out, reading *Salem's Lot* by the streetlight leaking through my bedroom window. The result was clotted red-black, thick and dreadful; I'd filled it halfway by the time I stuck the lid back on and screwed it tight, wrapping it three deep in plastic bags before stowing it away at the bottom of my backpack.

Suffice it to say, nobody ever told me that, much like any other sort of dead flesh, shed uterine lining really does need to be refrigerated.

Nini Jones. If someone had given me a gun, even at age twelve, I truly think I'd've shot that bitch right in the face. The strange part is that when I think of her now, I see her as she was—plain, not pretty: rake-skinny and dishwater blond, weird eyes, weird angles. But back then, she was really, really good at convincing me and everybody else that she was perfect, the righteous social arbiter of everything "in" or "out." Jenny Diamond had money, supposedly from the fleet of cabs bearing her last name; Faz was born glamorous, a lovely brown girl centre-set in a bright white trio of semi-pro assholes. And Peri Boyle, I eventually figured out, simply trailed along behind all three of them, avoiding censure through protective coloration. A low-grade trick, I guess, but I sure couldn't manage it... Imogen, either. So, good for her.

"The hell's this?" Nini drawled, the next day, down in the Ravine—and grabbed the jar from Imogen, who'd barely started to twist its cap. The force of the move alone was enough to make it spring the rest of the way open, releasing the worst stink I'd ever smelled, a whole hot summer day's worth of fermentation. Nini sprang back, dropping it; the jar shattered against the ground, sprayed rocks, dirt and glass shards coated with decaying menstrual blood everywhere, including across her white canvas shoes. "Jesus, *fuck*!" she screamed, kicking out at Imogen with one stained foot, who kicked back, hitting her in the knee. Nini started to fall and caught onto Faz, who flailed, almost upsetting them both, while I saw Jenny Diamond retch in the background as the wave reached her, coughing: "Oh holy shit, fuck *me*, is that—? Una, *god*, you *freak*."

I laughed long and loud, hyena-harsh. "Medical waste, bitches," I growled, "same as your mom throws out every month. You stupid fucking retard *children*." To which Faz replied, too loud, at almost the same time, with her one arm wedged under Nini's now and the other hand tugging at Jenny's skirt-waist, trying to pull them both away: "Seriously, guys, c'mon—what do you want, like... some *disease*, courtesy of the St Clair coven? A serious case of Tampax cooties?"

"Cooties don't exist, you dumb-ass," I threw back. "Or witches."

"Yeah? Tell that to *her*."

I glanced over my shoulder, in time to catch Imogen in mid-crouch, coming up with two fresh handfuls of creek-bed rocks, wet-slick and twice as heavy. She flung them at the "populars" underhand and barely aimed, as if she was pitching the world's worst softball game. One glanced off Nini's shoulder to whack Jenny in the chest, both of them squeal-braying in protest as Faz broke into a run, dragging them with her, straight past Peri Boyle, who'd been hanging back all this time behind a nearby tree; she whirled to yell after them, but I didn't hear what she said.

That was because the other rock collided with the side of my head, opening a gash in my scalp that ripped open the top of my ear and sent my glasses flying, leaving me face-down in the dirt with blood in my eyes, functionally blind and howling. Already in half-Hulk mode to begin with, I felt myself *go off*, top of my head exploding into metaphorical flames; I rounded on Imogen with both hands clawed, ready to rip, to tear, to knock her head on the ground until it broke. "I'M GONNA FUCKING *KILL* YOU!" I vaguely remember roaring, even as Imogen saw my face and cried out like some weird bird, half in guilt, half in ecstasy. Like…

Fresh blood, Una. That's exactly what we needed. Not that old stuff, that garbage you brought—fresh. Because it doesn't count if it's too easy, right?

(Right.)

It has to *hurt*.

It was Peri who found my glasses, in the end, and gave them back to me in the nurse's office, once I'd blundered up out of the Ravine with Imogen still screaming after me—Peri, who was never really my enemy, and became my friend after both of us ended up in the same Alternative High School, a few years on. Her mom was a French teacher who thought she was extraordinarily cultured, I later found out, always rabbiting on about Yeats and Robert Bresson, and married to this asshole writer, penniless but culturally approved; he was award-winning, her reward for putting up with Peri's dad all these years, a "mere" journalist. The two of them would go after Peri tag-team style, work her like a nine-to-five, trying to convince her that because she was physically rather than mentally inclined, she must be genuinely stupid. And while I do think Peri might indeed have had a learning disability, she had more heart in her finger than her bitch of a mom had in her whole body.

For a while, every time we met as adults, Peri would always end up reminding me how brave I was, how much she'd admired the way I wouldn't lie down and take it back in school, even if she'd never done anything about it. And every time she'd tell me this, I'd wonder what exactly she was on—until the night I finally made myself peer back through the past's dirty porthole at it, and remembered a dinner with Peri's mom and stepfather during which I'd spent three courses smouldering at the way they baited her before finally erupting, yelling at them both at the very top of my voice: "She is *not* dumb, but *you* are a pair of assholes who deserve to die alone!"

They don't know, though, do they? Imogen sometimes asks, from inside my scarred ear. *That you're not brave, never have been, but get you mad enough and you'll leave anyone behind.*

People can count on it. You make it so easy for them, Una, after all. You always have.

Fuck you, Im.

Like that, yeah. See what I mean?

Which is when I see her, or think I can, through whatever door her own blood eventually opened, smiling at me sweetly from whatever black-jewelled throne she sits on, pointing a finger at me with its long, gilded, cormorant-claw nail. Then shrugging, and returning to whatever duties she has on the other side of the crack: organizing a library made from cured rolls of human skin, maybe. Writing new spells in gold-dust and quicksilver. Mummifying her enemies alive, or flaying them, or flaying some to mummify others. A twelve-year-old sociopath with a crown serving gods who run on rage and hate and pain, never quite grown old enough to bleed herself, except with a ceremonial knife: powerful, finally, enough so she can probably order rain to fall and mountains to rise, if she wants to; a suitable reward, no doubt, for all her effort. But alone, now and forever, in every way that matters.

The same way we both are.

So the school nurse called my mom, and the look on her face when she saw me... I don't have to try to remember *that*. She made me tell her who all the other kids were, marched to the principal's office to tell him she was keeping me out of school for a week, and booked us an assessment at the Clarke Institute for Psychiatric Health. After it was done, the doctors told Mom they thought that if I actually believed I was a witch, I might have anything from narcissistic personality disorder to early-onset schizophrenia. They recommended she commit me for observation, to be sure. "We're not doing that," Mom said, which is why she's my hero. Instead, they gave her the name of a child psychiatrist I ended up going to for the next five years, as well as suggesting I should stop seeing Imogen. Mom agreed.

Then it was Monday again, and I was coming back to school for one last day, essentially to pick up whatever stuff I might have left behind. I walked across the bridge and through a side-route I often took in order to avoid the "populars," a wind-tunnel triangle between the Ravine's west slope and two residential apartment buildings in an L-shaped arrangement, following along the Ravine's side until it blended into the yard's back fence. But today, this path wasn't empty like usual. Instead, it was crowded with kids, teachers, even janitorial staff, all pressed up close to the fence and staring down through the trees, the green shadows, the close-knit weeds and bushes. An ambulance was parked at one edge of the crowd, flanked by two police cars, their lights on and blinking; someone had strung crime-scene tape through the fence from one end to the other, suturing the hole Imogen and I used to go down through.

I couldn't see what they were looking at, not from where I stood. So I edged my way around the outer rim of the crowd instead, a loose arrangement of younger-grade kids in clumps of two, three and four apiece. There I eventually found one boy I didn't think I'd ever seen before, and approached him. "What's happening?" I asked, quietly. "What are they all doing here? Are those the cops?"

"Yeah," he said. "Somebody called them this morning, after they went down through the Ravine coming to school. I hear they found a girl's clothes down there, all covered in blood, like she'd had her throat cut or something. No girl, just the clothes."

"No body, huh?"

"Nope." He paused for a moment, not even looking at me, before adding: "The cops think it might have something to do with this girl whose mom reported her missing last week: Imogen, the one everybody thinks is a witch. They think maybe her friend Una did it."

I don't have a lot of memories I'm never quite sure I didn't make up after the fact, but this is one, if only because I've thought about it so long as a series of descriptive sentences—no emotions attached, not even images, simply a string of events: this, then this, then this, then this. I know I must have found out the facts of what happened to Imogen, at least so far as anyone else knows them, but I might as well have read them in the papers, or seen them on TV. I do know I switched schools almost immediately afterwards, though we didn't move house until three years later, and the new school came with a new bus route that went literally in the opposite direction from my old one—it meant I never really had to interact with any of these people or places again, not unless I wanted to. And I had no reason to want to.

I do think it happened, though. Maybe the very flatness of it proves that it happened.

I certainly don't have any reason to doubt that in real life, things aren't as dramatic as either Imogen or I would have liked them to be.

I'm still here, and she's not. That's all I know. And I know myself, the way she never got to. And whatever happened, I wasn't there.

It had nothing to do with me. It still doesn't.

Nothing, or everything.

So, if I slip my fingernail down the inside of my wrist sometimes, along the closed seam of a long-healed scar, what does it matter, as long as I leave it shut? So long as I only *think* of unpicking it, of shedding blood and seeing what might happen? What light might leak in, and from where, over the lintel of the invisible? What door might begin to form, haloed in shared wounds, opening at last to let me through, even after I left her alone to make her own key?

Pay the price, make it hurt; reap your reward, fast or slow. That's how magic works, or so I've always heard.

Isn't it.

Special Meal

Josh Malerman

I T was that time of year again when I had to pretend I didn't know math.

We were at the dinner table, me on my side, my elbows barely reaching the wood, Brad across from me with his silly spiky hair. Dad was to my left and Mom to my right, but I don't like talking about rights and lefts because directions scare me: they're a little too much like math.

How many of us were there?

I don't want to say.

We were eating Chicken Kiev, my favorite, because the butter squirted out of the bird and it made me laugh and I loved the taste and because Mom said, "Amy, I've never met someone who loved something like you love Chicken Kiev." That's nice, isn't it? The smallest compliment.

But let's not talk amounts.

Let's talk family. And dinner. And the television on in the living room, where *Buckle Up* was playing silently, Dad having put the record on the machine, the one with all the strings and swells and slow moods. The light of the TV was all over Mom, painting her blue, as there was no wall between the kitchen and the living room, that being my favorite place in the house, the exact spot where a wall might've been, but wasn't.

Brad didn't like Chicken Kiev, but Brad was "late to everything," Dad once said and Mom said, "Is it okay to know what *late* means?"

I remember that discussion. They didn't think I heard them, but in a house as small as ours, you hear. Mom was worried Dad had used math. *Late*, she said, *implies time passing.* I remember that. Dad said it was okay to know time. Mom said it wasn't, though.

It was harder for them to pretend they didn't know math because they grew up with it.

"And green beans," Dad said, putting some on my plate. I loved green beans almost as much as I loved Chicken Kiev. It was like a birthday dinner but of course I couldn't be sure when my birthday was.

We ate, quiet, for a while. Brad didn't speak much anyway. I think it's because his friend Melanie got in trouble. I would be quiet too if I kept remembering the time my friend told me she knew math. What was Brad supposed to do with that secret? He did what he was supposed to do.

He turned Melanie in.

"We need more milk," Mom said. That was often how our conversations began. Little things. What we needed. What we didn't have. What we'd used.

"Okay," Dad said.

"And other things."

"Okay."

Yes, half of Mom's face was painted blue by the television. I remember worrying about that word: *half.*

I was so busy stuffing my face, I hadn't noticed the mood was off. Brad wouldn't look me in the eye. Which was okay. Which was normal. But Mom and Dad, there was something there, too. The way they kept looking across the table, asking if I was okay, asking if I wanted more, then going quiet again. They didn't even get up to flip the album when it came to a stop. One of them usually said, *Wanna play the other side?*

Because who would be caught saying they knew which side was which?

"The car sounds funny," Mom said. She knew all these things. What we needed. What sounded funny. And there was always hesitation, before every time she spoke, when she considered what she was going to say. I overheard Dad tell her once she was thinking too much about it. When they said we couldn't know math, they didn't mean we couldn't know when it was midday. Mom shushed him when he said that. But Dad continued, saying there was math in everything, literally everything, and people couldn't be expected to not know that a couple made two.

Mom freaked out when he said that. Hurried Brad and me into the basement. Locked the basement door. Waited. While we were down there, she talked about colors. She sat on a stool under the light bulb and talked about moods and feelings and colors, all stuff that Dad would call *safely vague.* Dad was upstairs then. Mom was waiting to hear sirens, I think. Waiting for someone to come ask Dad what he knew about a couple being equal to two.

He was angry up there. Pacing. Dad didn't yell, wasn't a yeller, but you knew when he was upset. He couldn't sit still. He talked to himself, but really he was talking to Mom, knowing we could hear him down below. Brad hadn't done what he was supposed to do with Melanie at that point in our lives, so he was talkative still, talked with Mom about colors.

But I listened to Dad. I heard him say, *It's in everything. Age, time, space, outer space, nature, work, rest. Everything!*

Except feelings, Mom said, her head cocked to the ceiling, and we knew she was talking to Dad whether or not Dad could hear her.

That night was bad. But nobody came to ask Dad what he meant by two.

"More beans," I said. I couldn't get enough of them. The chicken, the beans, and the bread rolls. Oh my. Mom worried I ate too much but Dad said no, it was fine, it was good, it was nice to see.

"Oh, wait," Dad said, getting up from the table. He went to the refrigerator and came back with a pitcher of grape juice.

"Oh," Mom said, "I almost forgot."

"Amy," Dad said. "Your favorite."

"Is it my birthday?" I asked.

Brad looked up then, only for a moment. Mom and Dad exchanged a look and then Mom smiled my way and it looked like her face might crack in half.

That word again: *half*.

That's math.

It's in everything.

"Do you really not know what today is?" Dad asked. "It's okay if you don't."

"No," I said. "Stop being silly."

"Amy, honey," Mom said. "Tonight's your test."

I set my fork down.

Oh.

Had it been a year? What was a year anyway?

"We received a letter a few…" She considered how to put it. "We received a letter recently. Remember I told you about it?"

Dad looked like he was going to cry.

"Oh yeah," I said. I picked up my fork and started eating. It was so good I thought I could eat that dinner forever. "When are they coming?"

"Well," Dad said, pouring the grape juice. "We don't know that kind of thing. Not exactly."

"Right."

Brad's fork scraped the plate and it sounded bad.

"Tonight," Mom said. That smile again.

Dad sat down.

"So," he said. "Amy. You know we gotta ask you a question before they come by. Right?"

"Yes."

"And you know what that question is, right?" Mom asked.

"Yes." Then, "You need to ask me if I know math."

Silence. Not because I'd said something shocking. I was right, this *was* the question. But because now that I'd said it, it had kinda been asked, and they were waiting for the answer. Even Brad.

How could they not know if I knew math, right? Well, I think it has to do with kids being young. And getting into things. And who knows what they do all the time and what they think and what they pick up, too.

Maybe even what they teach themselves.

That's what I'd done. I'd learned math on my own. It wasn't from a book. It was from listening, closely, to Mom and Dad. They used numbers all the time, even when they didn't mean to. Dad was right, of course, there was math in everything. And if you kept quiet and listened, you could hear it. Math. Want an example? One night in Mom and Dad's bedroom, a storm outside, Brad and I were in bed with them. And Brad asked if we could stay that way forever, if we could stay in their room and make jokes and watch television. Dad said, no, Brad. One day you won't need us. One day you'll be on your own two feet.

You catch that? Of course you did. *One* day. *Two* feet. Brad had two feet. I supposed that meant I did, too.

Mom didn't catch that one. She didn't catch a lot. Like when I asked if we could get a dog and Mom said, *Can you imagine a four-legger in this tiny house?*

Four.

The numbers came to me like this, over time. And I was open to them. I learned two, four, seven, three, nine, one, eight, five, six in that order, I think. I don't know for sure if there is an order. I think there is. Because I know we have eight shoes. Two each. See? That's math. Mom used to smile and ruffle my hair and tell me I was cute the way I liked to play with all our shoes. But I was adding. I was subtracting. I was learning there on the carpet. I wondered how Melanie learned math. I wondered what she looked like when she told Brad she did.

"No," I told them. A lie, of course, but I didn't want them to have to do what they were supposed to do. And not just because I didn't want to be taken away... I didn't want Mom and Dad to become quiet like Brad became quiet because of doing what he was supposed to with Melanie. So:

"No. No math."

"That's good," Dad said.

But they exchanged another glance, and I knew they knew.

"Is there dessert?" I asked.

"Of course," Dad said. "Are you done with the chicken?"

"No. Not at all. I just wanted to know."

"Amy, honey," Mom said. "Can I ask you another question?"

"Yes."

"How many forks are you holding?"

Yes, they knew.

"I don't know," I said. "My fork."

Brad was staring at me now. Mom and Dad couldn't stop with the worried glances across the best dinner of my life.

"Amy," Dad said. "How many fingers am I holding up?"

He held up three.

"Don't do that," Mom said.

"Come on," Dad said.

"*Please*," Mom said. "Use a different example."

Terrible silence then. The kind when you knew Dad felt really bad inside.

"How many windows are in your room, Amy?" Dad said.

"Just stop it," Mom said.

She got up and went to the refrigerator and opened the door. Dad eyed me, sadness all over his face. Worry. He looked like he still wanted an answer.

The answer was one.

"It's just the window," I said. "I don't know."

Dad nodded but he kept his eyes on me as Mom came back

from the fridge and said, "We need cheese."

I think Mom did this, took stock without numbers, to constantly prove to herself (and the world) that she didn't know math. Because if she and Dad didn't, how could Brad and I?

"This is the best meal of my life," I said. I gobbled up more chicken and beans, stuffed half a roll in my mouth, and washed it all down with grape juice.

Mom sat down again. Half of her in blue.

"How many shoes are we wearing?" Brad said.

So sudden. So mean.

I turned red. I've never been able to stop myself from turning red. Mom and Dad saw it and I felt the entire room get hot and I cried. Through the tears I saw anger on Brad's face. Guilt, too. Then he was crying and Mom was at my side, kneeling on the carpet while Dad had a hand on Brad's shoulder.

"We talked about this, Brad," Dad said. He sounded scared. "You promised not to do it again…"

"Amy," Mom said. "We saw the drawings. We saw the numbers."

Can people freeze? Even without cold weather?

I froze.

One of them found the papers. Brad?

Had to be. I knew I shouldn't have kept them in the drawer in the playroom. I knew I shouldn't have written it down. But math isn't easy when it's only in your head. Mom looked to Dad and Dad pulled the papers from his pocket and I turned even more red because they knew I'd lied.

They knew I knew math.

Dad went to the record machine and flipped the album and came over to my side of the table and knelt there, too. Mom on one side, Dad on the other, but I don't like to say right or left.

"Listen," Dad said. "Tonight, you're going to learn an important lesson. Okay?"

I nodded but I didn't feel good. I kicked at Brad under the table, but my legs didn't reach him and all I did was kick the table and knock over my juice.

Dad was sweating.

"Stop it," Mom said. "You listen to your dad *right now.* This is the most important conversation of your life, Amy. Okay?"

But it wasn't okay. They'd caught me lying. I couldn't stop turning red.

"I'm gonna tell you why it's good that you lied," Dad said.

This surprised me.

"Good?" I said.

"Yes. Very good. There's no changing what's been done, okay?" He was talking quiet, his mouth near my ear. "You learned it, that's what happened. No changing it."

He got quieter with each word.

Is that math?

"You lied," he said. "And you did a good job of lying. If we didn't know better, your mom and I might have believed you."

Dad looked to Mom. She didn't look like she might've believed me.

"And when they come tonight?" Dad said. Now his lips did touch my ear. "*You're going to lie again.*"

I looked to Brad, saw he was still crying, pretending to eat now, though. The chicken on his plate looked good. The whole meal. So good.

"Really?" I said.

It's what I'd planned on doing, of course. It's what I was going to do. But Dad, Mom, Brad; it's not what they were supposed to do. They were supposed to tell them I knew math.

"*Yes*," Mom said. Just like that. Urgent. Her lips touched my other ear. "*You're going to pretend you don't know math.*"

I didn't tell them I did that last time, too. Did they know? Could they tell how old the paper was, the paper in Dad's pocket?

"Burn it," Mom whispered.

The album played.

Dad nodded.

He got up. Went to the stove, already on for the chicken, put the pages inside. Despite everything that was happening, it made me sad, the idea of all that being burnt up. That was an amazing time for me. Me and the shoes in the playroom.

Then Dad was back beside me and both his and Mom's lips were touching my ears.

"Their questions will be harder."

"They'll try to trick you."

"Answer like you answered me before."

"You don't have to answer fast."

"Take your time."

"Not too much time."

I smelled the pages burning.

"Hey," I said.

But there was a knock at the door.

Mom shot up. Brad wiped the tears away. Dad kissed my ear before rising.

"I'll get it," Dad said.

I looked to my plate. To the chicken, beans, bread. The

best meal of my life.

Mom sniffed the air. Looked to the oven.

Dad opened the door.

"Hello," he said. "We were just having Amy's favorite meal. Come on inside."

There were six of them. Sorry, but there were.

They dressed like they dressed last year. Shirts and ties. Coats and hats. No beards. No rings.

I worried they might be able to tell I knew what zero meant.

"Evening, ma'am," one of them said to Mom. Mom nodded.

Dad and Mom hated these people. They wanted to kill these people. They would if they could.

Brad kept his eyes on his plate.

"Do you mind?" the man said. He wore glasses. Removed his hat. He was older than Dad.

Is that math?

"Not at all," Mom said.

But she did. You could hear it.

The man picked up Mom's chair and brought it over to me. Another man sat in Dad's chair. Another stood by the door. Another stood by the front window. Another stood where there was no wall between the kitchen and the living room. And the other went deeper into the house.

See? Six.

"Amy," the man with glasses said. "How many fingers am I holding up?"

He held up one.

I looked at it. Saw the wrinkles where his finger bent. Counted those, too.

"I don't know," I said. I laughed a little. "It's your finger, I guess."

"How many people are in your family?"

I looked to Mom and Dad. Brad. They all looked back. There was sweat at Mom's hairline.

"I don't know," I said. I giggled nervously. "They're my family is all."

"How old are you?"

This one I didn't know.

"I don't know. I'm a kid."

"How many hours do you sleep?"

This one I sort of knew. Because Mom and Dad talked about time more than they realized they did. They said things like *afternoon* and *midnight* and you could start to work your way out from there.

"I don't know. I sleep."

"Are you afraid of the two men in your living room, Amy?"

He almost tricked me. He was so close. I looked to the man on the couch but stopped myself before looking to the one by the window. That would mean I knew two, right?

"Two?" I said.

I shouldn't have said it. I was being obvious. I should've just said I don't know.

"How many times does Mommy tell you she loves you at night?"

Almost got me again. One. She said it once. Every night.

"I don't know. I love you, Mommy."

She looked away. I saw more sweat on her cheeks.

The man who stood where there was no wall sniffed the air. He looked to the oven.

"What's in there?" he asked Dad.

Dad looked to the oven.

"Where? The oven?"

The man on the couch spun to look. They all did. Even Brad.

"Yeah. The oven."

"We made chicken," Dad said. "Amy's favorite."

"That's not chicken," the man said.

Then the man who was in Dad's chair was up and he went to the oven and he opened it and he looked inside.

Is there a number for when numbers don't end? For time going on and on and on? It felt like he looked into the oven for that long.

He closed it.

"Nothing," he said.

Zero.

"One more question," the man with the glasses said.

"Good," I said.

The room went quiet.

They all looked at me. Everyone.

"Why is that good?" he asked.

And I knew he'd tricked me.

I'd showed him I knew what *one more* meant. I turned red. I couldn't stop it. I've never been able to stop from turning red.

"Amy?" Dad said.

The man by the oven shook his head no at Dad.

"Amy?" Mom said.

The man who stood where the living room met the kitchen held up a hand to keep Mom quiet.

The man in the glasses, though, he just waited for my answer.

"Amy?" he said.

"I don't know why good," I said. "I just said it is all."

The man on the couch made the music on the record machine stop.

"Amy," the man with the glasses said. "Do you know math?"

I did know math. I knew it and I liked it, too. It was fun, counting the objects in the house, taking one away, counting them again. It was fun, thinking of things in halves and wholes, as nine, eight, five. It was fun, measuring things in the house by shoes. Stacking the shoes, marking the wall, stacking them again, until I'd reached as tall as me. I was nine shoes tall, four times over. Isn't that fun? Dad told Mom once that we couldn't know math because math was *science's older brother.* Brad was my older brother. Sometimes I worried I didn't know Brad.

"Does anybody in this room want to do what they're supposed to do?" the man in the glasses asked.

"I don't know math," I said.

But he only waited. Waited for my family to answer him.

"What do you mean?" Mom asked. "Amy doesn't know math."

But the man just looked to Dad.

"This is madness," Dad said. "Amy doesn't know math. She's a child."

He looked to Brad.

"And you? Do you want to do what you're supposed to do?"

Brad looked to me, looked to his fork, looked to the man with the glasses. I could tell he was thinking of Melanie and the time he did what he was supposed to do.

"Amy doesn't know math," Brad said.

The man with the glasses stood up. He put his coat on. The other men did the same.

"Thank you," the man with the glasses said. "For having us."

Then they were out the door. And Dad closed the door behind them.

There were six. Now zero.

We sat in silence. I looked at my plate. The best dinner of my life. Chicken Kiev and beans and dinner rolls. Grape juice, too, but spilled across the table.

Dad went to the record machine.

"How about dessert?" Mom said. Her voice shook when she spoke.

"Yes," I said. "Dessert."

Brad stood up.

"Brad?" Mom said.

"Brad?" Dad said.

I looked at my plate.

"I'm doing what I'm supposed to do," Brad said.

"*Brad!*" Mom shouted.

But Brad was already out of the kitchen. Dad must've ran there because they fought near the front door. Then Mom was there, too.

I looked at my plate.

Dad shouted and someone hit someone and Mom screamed that Brad said he would never do what he was supposed to do again.

I looked at my plate.

The front door opened. Dad and Mom shouted.

I looked at my plate.

I thought how amazing it was, the chicken, the beans, the bread. There was even a little grape juice left in the glass. Enough for a sip, anyway.

Outside, Brad shouted to the men who had left our home. Sirens. Mom and Dad shouted, too. I heard my name. I heard "math."

Brad did what he was supposed to do.

While I stared at my plate.

Even when the men came back inside. Even when they crossed the living room, heading toward me alone at the table, I stared at my plate.

Chicken Kiev. Green beans. Bread rolls.

It was the best meal of my life.

"She knows math," one of them said.

One.

"They knew," a second one said.

Second. Two.

Even as they carried me out, past where there was no wall between the living room and the kitchen, I stared at my plate.

"I love math," I said.

And it felt good to say. Good like the meal.

The best meal of my life.

Sooner or Later, Your Wife Will Drive Home

Genevieve Valentine

Bess stood outside the gas station for ten minutes before she got up the nerve to knock, heels sinking into the mud while the sun dropped out of sight. By the time she made up her mind, she had to lift her shoes carefully out of the squelching mess, drag through it as if against the tide.

The rain was over, too late; her car had already slid off the road. It sat in a trough of its own making, waiting for the earth to dry, and she had already determined never to tell her father about it. He had feelings about women driving, much less driving alone. She'd nearly thrown a vase at him. You weren't supposed to talk about it now that the men were all home, but she'd driven the carpool to the factory just fine for three years. Even in the pounding rain she'd steered for the shallowest incline, hadn't she? She'd gotten out of the car in one piece, hadn't she? She'd gone for help, hadn't she? She'd made it a mile alone through the bog before she'd seen this place, the neon trembling but alive.

She adjusted the lapels of her jacket to be more presentable. Bess was careful to be presentable. She was plain, and she understood the duty to pay all the attentions to herself that nature hadn't. No man respected a slovenly woman. The seams of her stockings were perfectly straight; she'd put on fresh powder as soon as the rain had stopped. Her gloves were goners, but she brushed the last of the mud off her hem before she tapped the service station door.

The man who answered didn't seem at all surprised to see her. But he was young, with acne scars at his temple and pale hair glued back and a face that looked slightly elsewhere, so perhaps he was just the sort of young man who hated to look caught out. He glanced at her hands.

Bess smiled. A lady always started out polite with a man if she needed things done, her mother said.

The young man's shirt had a name patch on it, but she didn't want to presume. "Good evening, sir. I'm afraid I need help with my car."

After a second, the young man stepped aside. Bess crossed the threshold, feeling as if there was something important she'd left behind.

The door closed gently in the cool dark room. The neon sign went out. She and the young man were alone.

Lizzie opened the car door just enough to determine the Beetle was axle-deep in mud.

She didn't dare go hiking back down the road. She knew better than to wander from the safety of her car at night. Her dad had taught her how to change tires, and how to break a man's nose if he came up behind her, and warned her never to hitchhike no matter how many of her friends had tried it; she'd been raised cautious by a man who should know. She would wait until morning, and go searching in daylight.

In the car she shook off the rain, opened her sleeping bag, and poked through the wreckage of her snacks: potato chips, three Red Vines. She made herself chew a hundred times. She wished she'd done wilderness training last semester. (Her father hated the idea of her out in the woods with boys, and she'd given up the idea; every time she stood outside registration and thought about it, his voice somehow got louder than her voice.)

Lizzie could never tell him she'd gotten stuck in her Beetle with nothing but Red Vines. That was more frightening than the dark. She'd been raised practical—she knew how fast everything went downhill once you were starved out. And her father had never liked the Beetle; said it was impossible to take seriously, that you couldn't do any hauling in a car like that. Lizzie didn't care. The magazine ads for the thing made it sound like women couldn't be trusted to use the fucking brakes, but she'd wanted a car she could push herself, if it came to it, and it certainly had.

Four hours later, when the truck pulled over and the guy with an umbrella in hand slid out and jogged across the road, Lizzie made herself look welcoming. She was hungry, and alone, and her father helped women on the side of the road when he could. This guy had a face like a father. She couldn't be rude to a man who wanted to help. And what were her options, out here alone, if things got bad? She could brain him with the wrench,

296 · GENEVIEVE VALENTINE

probably. She clamped it under one armpit, so she could reach it if she had to.

"Looks like you could use a ride to civilization," he said, grinning. He seemed like a man who had daughters.

She left the sleeping bag. She'd warm up soon.

Betty frowned up at the motel. In the rain, the sign bled into the air like someone had draped a blue scarf across a lamp. She'd been to a party last year where the girls who lived in the house did that. Very bohemian, to stand around in red and blue light, watching everyone laughing and talking loudly over some sitar record, standing close enough to touch each other. Those bohemian girls touched any boy they liked. Fearless. Tacky. Fearless.

Her car had begun to make wet rattling noises as the storm got worse, and rather than risk getting stranded on the road—you couldn't trust any man at all who you met on the road, not even a policeman, her brother had said—she had pulled over here, where from the road the sign had looked bright and safe.

She shifted in her loafers; her skirt brushed her calves. This motel didn't look like the sign had looked from the road. It looked haunted, she thought, before she could get hold of her imagination. She'd promised her brother she wouldn't lose her head about going all alone. It was only five hours to her sister's; without the rain she'd already be there, and when she heard trouble she pulled over right away, just as her brother had told her. Never be stuck on the road alone, that was the rule.

Two of the rooms had lights on, yellow teeth in an empty mouth.

The night clerk had opened the door when she pulled in. Now he stood frowning into the drizzle, glancing down the row of rooms like he could figure out her hesitation.

Behind the drapes in one of the occupied rooms, a man's silhouette paused like a shadow play. She could feel his eyes on her, even from here. Betty wasn't like those slender bohemian girls, who made up their eyes and smiled unkindly at her for showing up with white gloves and her hair in a French twist, but she knew what an unkind glance from a man felt like. You had to, if you were alone.

"I'll take a room, please," she said, already knowing whose room she'd end up beside. The clerk looked like the sort who enjoyed making a woman uncomfortable.

So Betty didn't stay there. She was a university girl, and she knew better than to stay in a place with men who couldn't be trusted. She'd left that bohemian party after an hour, to make sure she could catch a bus home before any of the boys thought she was the sort to touch a man she barely knew. She knew when to get out of a bad situation.

There was a restaurant beside the motel—almost empty, but warm and well-lit. There were only two other tables, and the waiter appeared silently at her elbow any time Betty even thought about wanting something, like magic, like the place was a Michelin star; she never even felt him watching her.

Liz figured it was just as well her husband wasn't coming with her—he got so sour whenever she was distracted on a home visit.

He'd be sour with her gone, too, but the farther away she was, the less that bothered her. If there was something he didn't like doing, it was always better to leave him where he was. She was in for an argument when she got back, but at least she'd have a little quiet on the drive.

"You shouldn't be starting out on a long drive so late," he said. He hadn't come home with the car until seven, and now the last of the light was going. "You shouldn't even be going to this thing, he's barely your brother."

That was an old fight, and it was already too dark for them to have it again. Her father had made it clear he expected her there for the pictures. It wasn't going to rain until tomorrow, and the headlamps were in good condition. She didn't like it—driving at night was frightening for a woman alone—but she had to get back home. Graduation wouldn't wait, not even for the rain.

"I'll be all right," she said.

She said it like a promise; she'd learned a long time ago that she could only say that when it sounded like she was promising something to him.

(He'd come home one night last winter and seen her crying about Rachel, their setter. A car hit it. That was fine with Liz, honestly; the dog had been her husband's idea, and it ran after cars so often it was obvious what would happen. But she'd named it after Rachel from high school, who'd had the same hair, so red Liz could always see her in the crowd as she walked away from school back wherever girls like that went, making a horizon when Rachel leaned close to spy on her notes.

"Shouldn't have named it after a person, what'd I tell you," he'd said, slamming the two videos he'd rented onto the kitchen table.

He'd decided it was date night, and now she'd ruined it by crying and he couldn't enjoy his surprise and she really wished the dog had waited a day to die. She was so terrified by how it sounded—like he knew her—that she said, "I'll be all right," so brightly she'd started laughing at herself even though he just scowled harder and took one of the tapes upstairs to watch by himself.)

He didn't move from the couch when she brought her suitcase out. He threw the keys so hard they stung her palm.

Liz was so nervous she had to stop halfway down the driveway to stretch her shaking hands. She wasn't even afraid—there were interstates, there were lights, there were pullovers and policemen. It was just that going meant giving in to something, and staying meant giving in to something else, and what she really wanted was to take the car and drive wherever she felt like and not have anyone ask things of her ever again, which was the kind of thing she'd had tantrums about before she got taught better than to have them, and it was all stuck so high up in her throat she thought she would vomit.

She watched a few exits pass, clutched the wheel with white knuckles, but she didn't stop. She had to get home. They expected her.

Ellie smoked a cigarette after her boyfriend left, for her nerves, before she started cleaning up the books.

At first he'd thrown glasses—well, at first he hadn't thrown anything, but that was before Ellie realized that once you get settled with a man it gets harder to keep him happy—and it had been awful, until she worried they'd have to drink water out of coffee mugs. But he had better control of himself now. Now he reached for her books when he was angry; they didn't break, so it was more economical, and it was much easier to pick them up than to sweep glass off the floor twice a month.

She twisted back her dark hair so it wouldn't fall into her eyes. It was too long, and it felt longer every time she saw a girl in the street with her hair bobbed, but he liked it long; "Virginal," he said, and laughed when she didn't laugh. That was back at high school—before she dropped out, after she'd given up the goods.

She didn't rush, because once he was out at a speakeasy that was it for the night, and thinking of all the time she had to fill made her think—sudden and so wild she nearly dropped her armful of books—of getting in the car while he was out, turning onto the first long road she came to and driving west until this entire city vanished and he could never reach her. She'd start over from nothing. (She wouldn't even take the car—he might not chase her, but he'd definitely chase the Ford—but she knew how unsafe it was to get on a bus with strange men.)

The impression rose as she tidied, until the broom felt like the gear shift and she had goosebumps from the breeze. She could make it to Chicago without stopping. There were boarding houses there. Chicago was lousy with boarding houses—the paper talked about how awful it was that so many young women lived in them alone.

Ellie's hair was bobbed, in this imaginary city; bobbed hair with bangs, and a long necklace she wore at night to go watch Theda Bara, and a job as a social secretary. Dancing at night if she wanted. Maybe she would really go, she thought as she set the plant back. Maybe it was time.

She was packing when he came home.

The first thing Bet did when she realized her car was screwed and her cell phone was dead was to find a scenic pullover still visible from the road, with working streetlights. Then she jammed her jacket in the back window like she'd already gone for help, and crouched out of sight on the passenger's side so she could still reach the horn, just in case.

She wasn't an idiot. Dudes on the road would say they could help you or offer you rides and then you ended up like that girl from Robinson High who went missing from the school parking lot after a field trip, and they found her three weeks later in the river. Maggie something. Meredith? She had long blond hair and the picture on the front page of the city paper—not the little paper you got at the post office, the big one that everybody got delivered—was of her in a princess dress from *Into the Woods*, like the cops wanted to make it clear she was special. Not special enough for the guy who kidnapped her to dump her body somewhere besides the fucking river, but still.

For a while it was a whole Thing just to go outside. Everybody had decided that killing one young woman wasn't going to be the end of it, like killing young women was something everybody was secretly itching to do and after somebody broke the seal on that all the adults assumed it was open season. When Bet went to the library to research her history project, she had to call her mom when she got there and again when she got home, like she couldn't drive a mile without being snatched.

(She'd decided to make her history project about old ads that made women sound totally hopeless. She'd seen an ad for a blender and thought it was hilarious, and it was faster to read ads than articles. The librarians loved the idea. There was so much terrible food; she'd thought it would be fun.

It sucked, actually. After seeing the Volkswagen one that bragged about all the cheap replaceable parts with a picture of a smashed-up car—"Sooner or later, your wife will drive home one of the best reasons for owning a Volkswagen," it said; "You can conveniently replace anything she uses to stop the car. Including the brakes"—she thought about selling hers. She hadn't. It was a new Beetle, so it wasn't the same. People these days knew better. History was just history.)

They never caught the guy who killed what's-her-name. After six months, everybody acted like it was a serial killer who left town and it was a near miss for everybody else. But there were still a lot of curfews that never let up, and prom was moved from a hotel to the gym. When Bet left for college, all the dads on her block frowned at their daughters for leaving. Bet's dad had bailed on them when she was four, and she'd been happy to skip all that shit—dads got weird about things. A girl in her biology class had gone to a purity ball with her dad in seventh grade and she looked like she hadn't gotten a good night's sleep since.

A dad can kill his daughter and probably never kill again, but Bet was smart enough not to say. Nobody wanted to hear that.

That fall, Bet waved to her mother and got in her car with pepper spray in the ashtray and that was it. In three years she'd used it twice—some dudes just did not want to hear "No," and so you had to explain it again—and her car had never broken down before, but it was fine. This was part of having a car. This was just life. She wasn't somebody's shitty wife in a Volkswagen ad from forty years ago. The fear was just some bullshit that somebody else's dad had shaken into her when she wasn't looking.

When the cop pulled up and knocked on the window, she was so startled that she grabbed the pepper spray, pointed it right at him. "Shit!"

But he just laughed, bending closer and narrowing his eyes like this was a game they'd agreed on, and shook his finger at the pepper spray. For a second Bet went cold all over, but she pushed it aside. She'd have sprayed anyone else, but—he was a cop. What was she supposed to do, say no? Spray him in the mouth and bolt onto the interstate?

She left it in her car when she got out to meet him. No point in giving him something to arrest her for.

The woman's hair was wet through. There were leaves tangled in it, from where she had been dragged across the ground. When the coroner turned her over, it made the most horrible sound Eliza ever heard.

The woman was naked, except one shoe dangling off her right foot. Her back was torn up so badly the coroner hissed sympathetically. Eliza clasped her hands behind her back.

"Bet you a dollar that's deliberate," one of the detectives said to the other, pointing at the shoe. "No way it stayed on the whole time."

"So what, we're looking at the Cinderella Killer? Jesus Christ." The other one rubbed at his eye. "Bob, any ideas where she was murdered?"

The coroner winced and glanced over at Eliza. She didn't know why. Her hands were shaking, but that was more from the cold by now than the surprise. There were so many empty places, so many shallow ponds and stretches of woods, so many trucks, so many roads. You could kill a woman practically anywhere.

One of the detectives was peering through the trees. This was the narrowest part of the woods behind her house; she'd worn a path in it, a few years back, thinking about going down to the road one night and hitchhiking out. Her brother had caught her one night. She hadn't tried again.

"There's that junction a few miles down the road," he said.

The other one sighed. "Fuck. Women are always trying to travel alone." He turned to Eliza, one sharp look up and down. "Did you hear anything?"

She hadn't heard a thing. She'd slept deeply the whole week. Her brother hadn't been back home for five days; it had been so quiet, all that time.

Elizabeth's husband loved movies with ghosts in them. He saw as many as he could. Good, old-fashioned ones, not the new ones. He took her to the kind where everyone still dressed for dinner, except most of the women were dead.

It had been such an awful trip—her mother was sick, and of course she couldn't go alone (everyone knew what happened to women who traveled alone), so he'd driven her. But there was nothing for him to do while she nursed her mother and tried not to be obvious about crying, in the kitchen making coffee for everyone.

"Buck up," her husband told her sternly, the one time that

weekend he caught her at it, and she'd nodded and swallowed and wiped her eyes. They hadn't come down here to snivel. It was just that her mother was dying, and she was so afraid.

"I've been wanting to see this one," he said on their way back, and pulled into the cinema two towns north of home. It was starting to rain; he hated driving in the rain, because he wasn't good on slippery roads, and never let her drive when he was angry. She thought it was a little mean—so late, after such a long day, in a town she barely knew, and a movie about something so dreadful—but she'd been thinking of ghosts all weekend anyway. One more wasn't going to matter.

So Elizabeth sat next to him and watched translucent women in white wandering the haunted manor at night doing whatever they wanted, and thought how funny it was to be an actor, having to pretend to be afraid.

She was never scared at movies. Sometimes he got mad ("Jesus, what is it with you, you made of lead? What's the point of a scary movie if you won't even be afraid?") so occasionally she held his hand, because it made him happy to think she was a little frightened.

This time she skipped it, even when he held his hand out, even when she could see in the line of his jaw that he was angry. But it had been a long day. She was allowed to have long days.

The women onscreen were talking about men. Women were always talking about men, or thinking about men, everywhere you went. One of the men was a killer. One of the women was going to die. Everybody seemed to know already, despite all the music and the wandering around.

Her husband subscribed to a movie magazine he told the

mailman was for her; he told her a lot about making movies, as if she hadn't read it herself. Sometimes an issue had photos of the actors sitting in their cafeteria in costume, the monsters and the women side by side, eating dry hamburgers and pretending not to see the camera while someone talked about how everyone got along so well.

Elizabeth thought it was awfully odd to have to scream and faint and do that kind of thing with people after you'd been eating lunch with them—she couldn't even hide it whenever she was mad at her husband, he always knew a mile away and the whole house filled with a dark cloud until she apologized—but that's why she wasn't an actress. She'd pick whatever role was easiest and line up for hamburgers. Probably the ghosts. The women who played ghosts only had to raise their arms to show off their hands and make sure the trains of their nightgowns kept out of the way. The actresses who stayed alive had to run and breathlessly explain themselves to men who didn't believe them and scream and scream and scream. The dead had no fear. You could point as many fingers as you wanted.

The murderer was finally cornered. Once he was dead, the ghost women vanished. (Definitely ghosts, she thought. They got to go home early.)

His fist pressed against his leg the whole rest of the movie, as if Elizabeth would want to hold it eventually and he wanted her to know she'd missed her chance.

"I hope you enjoyed it," he snapped when the lights came back on, and she didn't bother to argue whose idea it had been. She was still thinking about how easy it was for a woman to disappear, once the right man was dead.

It was dark when they got out, and still raining. It would be a long ride home.

Tiptoe

Laird Barron

I WAS a child of the 1960s. Three network stations or fresh air; take your pick. No pocket computers for entertainment in dark-age suburbia. We read our comic books ragged and played catch with Dad in the backyard. He created shadow puppets on the wall to amuse us before bed. Elephants, giraffes, and foxes. The classics. He also made some animals I didn't recognize. His hands twisted to form these mysterious entities, which he called Mimis. Dad frequently traveled abroad. Said he'd learned of the Mimis at a conference in Australia. His double-jointed performances wowed me and my older brother, Greg. Mom hadn't seemed as impressed.

Then I discovered photography.

Mom and Dad gave me a camera. Partly because they were supportive of their children's aspirations; partly because I bugged them relentlessly. At six years old, I already understood my life's purpose.

Landscapes bore me, although I enjoy celestial photography—high-resolution photos of planets, hanging in partial silhouette; blazing white fingertips emerging from a black pool. People aren't interesting either, unless I catch them in candid moments to reveal a glimmer of their hidden selves. Wild animals became my favorite subjects. Of all the variety of animals, I love predators. Dad approved. He said, *Men revile predators because they shed blood. What an unfair prejudice. Suppose garden vegetables possessed feelings. Suppose a carrot squealed when bitten in two… Well, a groundhog would go right on chomping, wouldn't he?*

If anybody knew the answer to such a question, it'd be my old man. His oddball personality might be why Mom took a shine to him. Or she appreciated his potential as a captain of industry. What I do know is, he was the kind of guy nobody ever saw coming.

My name is Randall Xerxes Vance. Friends tease me about my signature—RX and a swooping, offset V. Dad used to say, *Ha-ha, son. You're a prescription for trouble!* As a pro wilderness photographer, I'm accustomed to lying or sitting motionless for hours at a stretch. Despite this, I'm a tad jumpy. You could say my fight or flight reflex is highly tuned. While on assignment for a popular magazine, a technician—infamous for his pranks—snuck up, tapped my shoulder, and yelled, *Boo!* I swung instinctively. Wild, flailing. Good enough to knock him on his ass into a ditch.

Colleagues were nonplussed at my overreaction. Me too. That incident proved the beginning of a rough, emotional ride: insomnia; nightmares when I *could* sleep; and panic attacks. It felt like a crack had opened in my psyche. Generalized anxiety gradually worked its claws under my armor and skinned me to raw nerves. I committed to a leave of absence, pledging to conduct an inventory of possible antecedents.

Soul searching pairs seductively with large quantities of liquor.

A soon-to-be-ex-girlfriend offered to help. She opined that I suffered from deep-rooted childhood trauma. I insisted that my childhood was actually fine. My parents had provided for me and my brother, supported our endeavors, and paid for our education; the whole deal.

There's always something if you dig, she said. Subsequent to a bunch more poking and prodding, one possible link between my youth and current troubles came to mind. I told her about a game called Tiptoe Dad taught me. A variation of ambush tag wherein you crept behind your victim and tapped him or her on the shoulder or goosed them, or whatever. Pretty much the same as my work colleague had done. Belying its simple premise, there were rules, which Dad adhered to with solemnity. The victim must be awake and unimpaired. The sneaker was required to assume a certain posture—poised on the balls of his or her feet, arms raised and fingers pressed into a blade or spread in an exaggerated manner. The other details and prescriptions are hazy.

As far as odd family traditions go, this seemed fairly innocuous. Dad's attitude was what made it weird.

Tiptoe went back as far as I could recall, but my formal introduction occurred at age six. Greg and I were watching a nature documentary. Dad wandered in late, still dressed from a shift at the office and wearing that coldly affable expression he put on along with his hat and coat. The documentary shifted to the hunting habits of predatory insects. Dad sat between us on the couch. He stared intently at the images of mantises, voracious Venezuelan centipedes, and wasps. During the segment on trapdoor spiders, he smiled and pinched my shoulder. Dad was fast for an awkward, middle-aged dude. I didn't even see his arm move. *People say sneaky as a snake, sly as a fox, but spiders are the best hunters. Patient and swift.* I didn't give it a second thought.

One day, soon after, he stepped out of a doorway, grabbed me, and started tickling. Then he snatched me into the air and turned my small body in his very large hands. He pretended to bite my neck, arms, and belly. *Which part shall I devour first? Eeny, meeny, miny moe!* I screamed hysterical laughter. He explained that tickling and the reaction to tickling were rooted in primitive fight or flight responses to mortal danger.

Tiptoe became our frequent contest, and one he'd already inflicted on Greg and Mom. The results seldom amounted to more than the requisite tap, except for the time when Dad popped up from a leaf pile and pinched me so hard it left a welt. You bet I tried to return the favor—on countless occasions, in fact—and failed. I even wore camo paint and dressed in black down to my socks, creeping closer, ever closer, only for him to whip his head around at the last second and look me in the eye with a tinge of disappointment. *Heard you coming from the other end of the house, son. Are you thinking like a man or a spider? Like a fox or a mantis? Keep trying.*

Another time, I walked into a room and caught him playing the game with Mom as victim. Dad gave me a sidelong wink as he reached out, tiptoeing closer and closer. Their silhouettes flickered on the wall. The shadows of his arms kept elongating; his shadow fingers ended in shadow claws. The optical illusion made me dizzy and sick to my stomach. He kissed her neck. She startled and mildly cussed him. Then they laughed, and once more he was a ham-fisted doofus, innocently pushing his glasses up the bridge of his nose.

As with many aspects of childhood, Tiptoe fell to the wayside for reasons that escaped me until the job incident brought it crashing home again. Unburdening to my lady friend didn't help either of us as much as we hoped. She acknowledged that the whole backstory was definitely fucked up and soon found other places to be. Probably had a lot to do with my drinking, increasingly moody behavior, and the fact that I nearly flew out of my skin whenever she walked into the room.

The worst part? This apparent mental breakdown coincided with my mother's health tribulations. A double whammy. After her stroke, Mom's physical health gradually went downhill. She'd sold the house and moved into a comfy suite at the retirement village where Grandma resided years before.

The role of a calm, dutiful son made for an awkward fit, yet there wasn't much choice, considering I was the last close family who remained in touch. Steeling my resolve, I shaved, slapped on cologne to disguise any lingering reek of booze, and drove down from Albany twice a week to hit a diner in Port Ewing. Same one we'd visited since the 1960s. For her, a cheeseburger and a cup of tea. I'd order a sandwich and black coffee and watch her pick at the burger. Our conversations were sparse affairs—long silences peppered with acerbic repartee.

She let me read to her at bedtime. Usually, a few snippets from

314 · LAIRD BARRON

Poe or his literary cousins. *I've gotten morbid,* she'd say. *Give me some of that Amontillado, hey?* Or, *A bit of M.R. James, if you please.* Her defining characteristics were intellectual curiosity and a prickly demeanor. She didn't suffer fools—not in her prime, nor in her twilight. Ever shrewd and guarded, ever close-mouthed regarding her interior universe. Her disposition discouraged "remember-whens" and utterly repelled more probing inquiries into secrets.

Nonetheless, one evening I stopped in the middle of James's "The Ash Tree" and shut the book. "Did Aunt Vikki really have the gift?"

Next to Mom and Dad, Aunt Vikki represented a major authority figure of my childhood. She might not have gone to college like my parents, but she wasn't without her particular abilities. She performed what skeptics (my mother) dismissed as parlor tricks. Stage magician staples like naming cards in someone's hand, or locating lost keys or wallets. Under rare circumstances, she performed hypnotic regression and "communed" with friendly spirits. Her specialty? Astral projection allowed her to occasionally divine the general circumstances of missing persons. Whether they were alive or dead and their immediate surroundings, albeit not their precise location. Notwithstanding Dad's benign agnosticism and Mom's blatant contempt, I assumed there was something to it—the police had allegedly enlisted Vikki's services on two or three occasions. Nobody ever explained where she acquired her abilities. Mom and Dad brushed aside such questions and I dared not ask Aunt Vikki directly given her impatience with children.

"I haven't thought of that in ages." Mom lay in the narrow

bed, covers pulled to her neck. A reading lamp reflected against the pillow and illuminated the shadow of her skull. "Bolt from the blue, isn't it?"

"I got to thinking of her the other day. Her magic act. The last time we visited Lake Terror..."

"You're asking whether she was a fraud."

"Nothing so harsh," I said. "The opposite, in fact. Her affinity for predictions seemed uncanny."

"Of course it seemed uncanny. You were a kid."

"Greg thought so."

"Let's not bring your brother into this."

"Okay."

She eyed me with a glimmer of suspicion, faintly aware that my true interest lay elsewhere; that I was feinting. "To be fair, Vikki sincerely believed in her connection to another world. None of us took it seriously. God, we humored the hell out of that woman."

"She disliked Dad."

"Hated John utterly." Her flat, unhesitating answer surprised me.

"Was it jealousy? Loneliness can have an effect..."

"Jealousy? C'mon. She lost interest in men after Theo kicked." Theo had been Aunt Vikki's husband; he'd died on the job for Con Edison.

I decided not to mention the fact that she'd twice remarried since. Mom would just wave them aside as marriages of convenience. "And Dad's feelings toward her?"

"Doubtful he gave her a second thought whenever she wasn't right in front of his nose. An odd duck, your father. Warm and fuzzy outside, cold tapioca on the inside."

"Damn, Mom."

"Some girls like tapioca. What's with the twenty questions? You have something to say, spill it."

Should I confess my recent nightmares? Terrible visions of long-buried childhood experiences? Or that Dad, an odd duck indeed, starred in these recollections and his innocuous, albeit unnerving, Tiptoe game assumed a sinister prominence that led to my current emotional turmoil? I wished to share with Mom; we'd finally gotten closer as the rest of our family fell by the wayside. Still, I faltered, true motives unspoken. She'd likely scoff at my foolishness in that acerbic manner of hers and ruin our fragile bond.

She craned her neck. "You haven't seen *him* around?"

"Who?" Caught off guard again, I stupidly concluded, despite evidence to the contrary, that her thoughts were fogged with rapid onset dementia. Even more stupidly, I blurted, "Mom, uh, you know Dad's dead. Right?"

"Yeah, dummy," she said. "I meant Greg."

"The guy you don't want to talk about?" Neither of us had seen my brother in a while. Absence doesn't always make the heart grow fonder.

"Smart-ass." But she smiled faintly.

In the wee hours, alone in my studio apartment, I woke from a lucid nightmare. Blurry, forgotten childhood images coalesced with horrible clarity. Aunt Vikki suffering what we politely termed an episode; the still image of a missing woman on the six o'clock news; my father, polishing his glasses and smiling cryptically. Behind him, a sun-dappled lake, a stand of thick trees, and a lost trail that wound into the Catskills… or Purgatory. There were other, more disturbing recollections that clamored for attention, whirling in a black mass on the periphery. Gray, gangling hands; a gray, cadaverous face…

I poured a glass of whiskey and dug into a shoebox of loose photos; mainly snapshots documenting our happiest moments as a family. I searched those smiling faces for signs of trauma, a hint of anguish to corroborate my tainted memories. Trouble is, old, weathered pictures are ambiguous. You can't always tell what's hiding behind the patina. Nothing, or the worst thing imaginable.

Whatever the truth might be, this is what I recall about our last summer vacation to the deep Catskills:

During the late 1960s, Dad worked at an IBM plant in Kingston, New York. Mom wrote colorful, acerbic essays documenting life in the Mid-Hudson Valley; sold them to regional papers, mainly, and sometimes slick publications such as *The New Yorker* and the *Saturday Evening Post*. We had it made. House in the suburbs, two cars, and an enormous color TV. I cruised the neighborhood on a Schwinn ten-speed with the camera slung around my neck. My older brother, Greg, ran cross-country for our school. Dad let him borrow the second car, a Buick, to squire his girlfriend into town on date night.

The Vance clan's holy trinity: Christmas; IBM Family Day; and the annual summer getaway at a cabin on Lake Terron. For us kids, the IBM Family Day carnival was an afternoon of games, Ferris wheel rides, running and screaming at the top of our lungs, and loads of deep-fried goodies. The next morning,

Dad would load us into his Plymouth Suburban and undertake the long drive through the mountains. Our lakeside getaway tradition kicked off when I was a tyke—in that golden era, city folks retreated to the Catskills to escape the heat. Many camped at resorts along the so-called Borscht Belt. Dad and his office buddies, Fred Mercer and Leo Schrader, decided to skip the whole resort scene. Instead, they went in together on the aforementioned piece of lakefront property and built a trio of vacation cabins. The investment cost the men a pretty penny. However, nearby Harpy Peak was a popular winter destination. Ski bums were eager to rent the cabins during the holidays and that helped Dad and his friends recoup their expenses.

But let's stick to summer. Dreadful hot, humid summer that sent us to Lake Terron and its relative coolness. Me, Greg, Mom, Dad, Aunt Vikki, and Odin, our dog; supplies in back, a canoe strapped up top. Exhausted from Family Day, Greg and I usually slept for most of the trip. Probably a feature of Dad's vacation-management strategy. Then he merely had to contend with Mom's chain-smoking and Aunt Vikki bitching about it. Unlike Mom and Dad, she didn't do much of anything. After her husband was electrocuted while repairing a downed power line, she collected a tidy insurance settlement and moved from the city into our Esopus home. Supposedly a temporary arrangement on account of her nervous condition. Her nerves never did improve—nor did anyone else's, for that matter.

We made our final pilgrimage the year before Armstrong left bootprints on the Moon. Greg and I were seventeen and twelve, respectively. Our good boy Odin sat between us. He'd outgrown his puppy ways and somehow gotten long in the tooth. Dad turned onto the lonely dirt track that wound a mile through heavy forest and arrived at the lake near sunset. The Mercers and Schraders were already in residence: a whole mob of obstreperous children and gamely suffering adults collected on a sward that fronted the cabins. Adults had gotten a head start on boilermakers and martinis. Grill-smoke wafted toward the beach. Smooth and cool as a mirror, the lake reflected the reddening sky like a portal to a parallel universe.

Lake Terron—or Lake Terror, as we affectionately called it— gleamed at the edge of bona fide wilderness. Why Lake Terror? Some joker had altered the N on the road sign into an R with spray-paint and it just stuck. Nights were pitch black five paces beyond the porch. The dark was full of insect noises and the coughs of deer lurching around in the brush.

Our cabin had pretty rough accommodations—plank siding and long, shotgun shack floorplan with a washroom, master bedroom, and a loft. Electricity and basic plumbing, but no phone or television. We lugged in books, cards, and board games to fashion a semblance of civilized entertainment. On a forest ranger's advice, Dad always propped a twelve-gauge shotgun by the door. Black bears roamed the woods and were attracted to the scents of barbeque and trash. *And children!* Mom would say.

The barbeque set the underlying tone; friendly hijinks and raucous laughter always prevailed those first few hours. Revived from our torpor, kids gorged on hotdogs and cola while parents lounged, grateful for the cool air and peaceful surroundings— except for the mosquitos. *Everybody* complained about them. Men understood shop talk was taboo. Those who slipped up received a warning glare from his better half. Nor did anyone remark upon news trickling in via the radio, especially concerning the Vietnam War; a subject that caused mothers everywhere to clutch teenaged sons to their bosoms. "Camp Terror" brooked none of that doomy guff. For two weeks, the outside world would remain at arm's length.

Mr. Schrader struck a bonfire as the moon beamed over Harpy Peak. Once the dried cedar burned to coals, on came the bags of marshmallows and a sharpened stick for each kid's grubby mitt. I recall snatches of conversation. The men discussed the Apollo program, inevitably philosophizing on the state of civilization and how far we'd advanced since the Wright brothers climbed onto the stage.

"We take it for granted," Mr. Mercer said.

"What's that?" Mr. Schrader waved a marshmallow flaming at the end of his stick.

"Comfort, safety. You flip a switch, there's light. Turn a key, a motor starts."

"Electricity affords us the illusion of self-sufficiency."

"Gunpowder and penicillin imbue us with a sense of invincibility. Perpetual light has banished our natural dread of the dark. We're apes carrying brands of fire."

"Okay, gents. Since we're on the subject of apes. We primates share a common ancestor. Which means we share a staggering amount of history. You start dwelling on eons, you have to consider the implications of certain facts."

Mr. Mercer shook his head as he lit a cigarette. "I can only guess where this is going."

"Simulation of human features and mannerisms will lead the field into eerie precincts," Dad said.

"Uh-oh," Mr. Schrader said. "This sounds suspiciously close to op-shay alk-tay."

"Thank goodness we're perfecting mechanical arms to handle rivet guns, not androids. Doesn't get more mundane."

"Mark it in the book. Heck, the Japanese are already there."

"Whatever you say, John."

"Researchers built a robot prototype—a baby with a lifelike face. Focus groups recoiled in disgust. Researchers came back with artificial features. Focus groups *oohed* and *ahhed*. Corporate bankrolled the project. We'll hear plenty in a year or two."

"Humans are genetically encoded to fear things that look almost like us, but aren't us."

"Ever ask yourself why?"

"No, can't say I've dedicated much thought to the subject," Mr. Mercer said. "So, why are we allegedly fearful of, er, imitations?"

"For the same reason a deer or a fowl will spook if it gets wind of a decoy. Even an animal comprehends that a lure means nothing good." Dad had mentioned this periodically. Tonight, he didn't seem to speak to either of his colleagues. He looked directly at me.

"Shop talk!" Mom said with the tone of a referee declaring a foul. Mrs. Schrader and Mrs. Mercer interrupted their own conversation to boo the men.

"Whoops, sorry!" Mr. Mercer gestured placatingly. "Anyway, how about those Jets?"

Later, somebody suggested we have a game. No takers for charades or trivia. Finally, Mrs. Mercer requested a demonstration of Aunt Vikki's fabled skills. Close magic, prestidigitation, clairvoyance, or whatever she called it. My aunt demurred. However, the boisterous assembly would brook no refusal and badgered her until she relented.

That mystical evening, performing for a rapt audience against a wilderness backdrop, she was on her game. Seated lotus on a blanket near the fire, she affected trancelike concentration. Speaking in a monotone, she specified the exact change in Mr. Schrader's pocket, the contents of Mrs. Mercer's clutch, and the fact that one of the Mercer kids had stolen his sister's diary. This proved to be the warmup routine.

Mr. Mercer said, "John says you've worked with the law to find missing persons."

"Found a couple." Her cheeks were flushed, her tone defiant. "Their bodies, at any rate."

"That plane that went down in the Adirondacks. Can you get a psychic bead on it?"

Aunt Vikki again coyly declined until a chorus of pleas "convinced" her to give it a shot. She swayed in place, hands clasped. "Dirt. Rocks. Running water. Scattered voices. Many miles apart."

"Guess that makes sense," Mr. Mercer said to Mr. Schrader. "Wreck is definitely spread across the hills."

Mrs. Schrader said under her breath to Dad, "Eh, what's the point? She could say anything she pleases. We've no way to prove her claim." He shooshed her with a familiar pat on the hip. Everybody was ostensibly devout in those days. Mrs. Schrader frequently volunteered at her church and I suspect Aunt Vikki's occult shenanigans, innocent as they might've been, troubled her. The boozing and flirtation less so.

The eldest Mercer girl, Katie, asked if she could divine details of an IBM housewife named Denise Vinson who'd disappeared near Saugerties that spring. Nobody present knew her husband; he was among the faceless legions of electricians who kept the plant humming. He and his wife had probably attended a company buffet or some such. The case made the papers.

"Denise Vinson. Denise Vinson…" Aunt Vikki slipped into her "trance." Moments dragged on and an almost electric tension built; the hair-raising sensation of an approaching thunderstorm. The adults ceased bantering. Pine branches creaked; an owl hooted. A breeze freshened off the lake, causing water to lap against the dock. Greg and I felt it. His ubiquitous smirk faded, replaced by an expression of dawning wonderment. Then Aunt Vikki went rigid and shrieked. Her cry echoed off the lake and caused birds to dislodge from their roosts in the surrounding trees. Her arms extended, fingers and thumbs together, wrists bent downward. She rocked violently, cupped hands stabbing the air in exaggerated thrusts. Her eyes filled with blood. My thoughts weren't exactly coherent, but her posture and mannerisms reminded me of a mantis lashing at its prey. Reminded me of something else, too.

Her tongue distended as she babbled like a Charismatic. She covered her face and doubled over. Nobody said anything until she straightened to regard us.

"Geez, Vikki!" Mr. Mercer nodded toward his pop-eyed children. "I mean, geez Louise!"

"What's the fuss?" She glanced around, dazed.

Mom, in a display of rare concern, asked what she'd seen. Aunt Vikki shrugged and said she'd glimpsed the inside of her eyelids. Why was everybody carrying on? Dad lurked to one side of the barbeque pit. His glasses were brimmed with the soft glow of the coals. I couldn't decipher his expression.

Mood dampened, the families said their goodnights and drifted off to bed. Mom, tight on highballs, compared Aunt Vikki's alleged powers of clairvoyance to those of the famous Edgar Cayce. This clash occurred in the wee hours after the others retired to their cabins. Awakened by raised voices, I hid in shadows atop the stairs to the loft, eavesdropping like it was my job.

"Cayce was as full of shit as a Christmas goose." Aunt Vikki's simmering antipathy boiled over. "Con man. Charlatan. Huckster." Her eyes were bloodshot and stained from burst capillaries. Though she doggedly claimed not to recall the episode earlier that evening, its lingering effects were evident.

"Vikki," Dad said in the placating tone he deployed against disgruntled subordinates. "Barbara didn't mean any harm. Right, honey?"

"Sure, I did… not." From my vantage I saw Mom perched near the cold hearth, glass in hand. The drunker she got, the cattier she got. She drank plenty at Lake Terror.

Aunt Vikki loomed in her beehive-do and platform shoes. "Don't ever speak of me and that… that fraud in the same breath. Cayce's dead and good riddance to him. *I'm* the real McCoy."

"Is that a fact? Then, let's skip the rest of this campout and head for Vegas." Mom tried to hide her sardonic smile with the glass.

"Ladies, it's late," Dad said. "I sure hope our conversation isn't keeping the small fry awake."

His not-so-subtle cue to skedaddle back to my cot left me

pondering who was the psychic—Aunt Vikki or Dad? *Maybe he can see in the dark,* was my last conscious thought. It made me giggle, albeit nervously.

Greg jumped me and Billy Mercer as we walked along the trail behind the cabins. Billy and I were closest in age. Alas, we had next to nothing in common and didn't prefer one another's company. Those were the breaks, as the youth used to say. The path forked at a spring before winding ever deeper into the woods. To our left, the path climbed a steep hill through a notch in a stand of shaggy black pine. Mom, the poet among us, referred to it as the Black Gap. Our parents forbade us to drink from the spring, citing mosquito larvae. Predictably, we disregarded their command and slurped double handfuls of cool water at the first opportunity. As I drank, Greg crept upon me like an Apache.

He clamped my neck in a grip born of neighborhood lawnmowing to earn extra bucks for gas and date-night burgers. "Boo!" He'd simultaneously smacked Billy on the back of his head. The boy yelped and tripped over his own feet trying to flee. Thus, round one of Tiptoe went to my insufferably smirking brother. Ever merciless in that oh-so-special cruelty the eldest impose upon their weaker siblings, I nonetheless detected a sharper, savage inflection to his demeanor of late. I zipped a rock past his ear from a safe distance—not that one could ever be sure—and beat a hasty retreat into the woods. Greg flipped us the bird and kept going without a backward glance.

The reason this incident is notable? Billy Mercer complained to the adults. Dad pulled me aside for an account, which I grudgingly provided—nobody respects a tattletale. Dad's smirk was even nastier than Greg's. *Head on a swivel, if you want to keep it, kiddo.* He put his arm around my brother's shoulders and they shared a laugh. Three days in, and those two spent much of it together, hiking the forest and floating around the lake. The stab of jealousy hurt worse than Greg squeezing my neck.

Near bedtime, we set up tents in the backyard, a few feet past the badminton net and horseshoe pit. The plan was for the boys to sleep under the stars (and among the swarming mosquitos). Mrs. Schrader protested weakly that maybe this was risky, what with the bears. Mr. Schrader and Mr. Mercer promised to take watches on the porch. Odin stayed with me; that would be the best alarm in the world. No critter would get within a hundred yards without that dog raising holy hell. And thus it went: Odin, Billy Mercer, a Schrader boy, and me in one tent, and the rest of them in the other. We chatted for a bit. Chitchat waned; I tucked into my sleeping bag, poring over an issue of *Mad Magazine* by flashlight until I got sleepy.

I woke to utter darkness. Odin panted near my face, growling softly. I lay at the entrance. Groggy and unsure of whether the dog had scented a deer or a bear, I instinctively clicked on my trusty flashlight, opened the flap, and shone it into the trees— ready to yell if I spotted danger. Nothing to corroborate Odin's anxious grumbles. Scruffy grass, bushes, and the shapeless mass of the forest. He eventually settled. I slept and dreamed two vivid dreams. The first was of Aunt Vikki spotlighted against a void. Her eyes bulged as she rocked and gesticulated, muttering. Dream logic prevailing, I understood her garbled words: *Eeny! Meany! Miny! Moe!*

In the second, I floated; a disembodied spirit gazing down. Barely revealed by a glimmer of porchlight, Dad crawled from under a bush and lay on his side next to the tent. He reached through the flap. His arm moved, stroking.

These dreams were forgotten by breakfast. The incident only returned to me many years later; a nightmare within a nightmare.

Over blueberry pancakes, Dad casually asked whether I'd care to go fishing. At an age where a kid selfishly treasured an appointment on his father's calendar, I filled a canteen and slung my trusty Nikon F around my neck and hustled after him to the dock. Unlike the starter camera I'd long outgrown, the Nikon was expensive and I treated it with proper reverence. Film rolls were costly as well. Manual labor, supplemented by a generous allowance and a bit of wheedling, paid the freight. Mom, a stalwart supporter of the arts, chipped in extra. She encouraged me to submit my work to newspaper and magazine contests, in vain. Back then, the hobby was strictly personal. I wasn't inclined to share my vision with the world just yet, although I secretly dreamed big dreams—namely, riding the savannah with the crew of *Mutual of Omaha's Wild Kingdom*.

The sun hadn't cleared the trees as we pushed away from the dock. Dad paddled. I faced him, clicking shots of the receding cabins and birds rising and falling from the lake and into the sky. He set aside his paddle and the canoe kept on gliding across the dark water.

"This is where we're gonna fish?" I said.

"No fishing today." After a pause, he said, "I'm more a fisher of men."

"I don't get it."

"Time to begin reflecting on what kind of man *you* are."

"Dad, I'm *twelve*." I inherited my smart-Alec lip from Mom.

"That's why I don't expect you to decide today. Merely think on it." He could see I wasn't quite getting it. "Ever since you showed an interest in photography, I had a hunch…" He cupped his hands and blew into the notch between his thumbs. Took him a couple of tries to perfect an eerie, fluting whistle that rebounded off the lake and nearby hills. He lowered his hands and looked at me. "I planned to wait until next year to have this conversation. Aunt Vikki's… outburst has me thinking sooner is better. Sorry if she frightened you."

"Why did she fly off the handle? Are her eyes okay?" I hoped to sound unflappable.

"Her eyes are fine. It's my fault. The Vinson woman was too close to home. Anyhow, your aunt is staying with us because she can't live alone. She's fragile. Emotionally."

"Vikki's crazy?"

"No. Well, maybe. She's different and she needs her family."

"She and Mom hate each other."

"They fight. That doesn't mean they hate each other. Do you hate your brother? Wait, don't answer that." He dipped his paddle into the water. "What's my job at the plant?"

"You build—"

"Design."

"You design robots."

"I'm a mechanical engineer specializing in robotic devices

and systems. It's not quite as dramatic as it sounds. How do you suppose I landed that position?"

"Well, you went to school—"

"No, son. I majored in sociology. Any expertise I have in engineering I've learned on the fly or by studying at night."

"Oh." Confused by the turn in our conversation, I fiddled with my camera.

"Want to know the truth?"

"Okay." I feared with all the power of my child's imagination that he would reveal that his *real* name was Vladimir, a deep cover mole sent by the Russians. It's difficult to properly emphasize the underlying paranoia wrought by the Cold War on our collective national psyche. My brother and I spied on our neighbors, profiling them as possible Red agents. We'd frequently convinced ourselves that half the neighborhood was sending clandestine reports to a numbers station.

"I bullshitted the hiring committee," Dad said. He seldom cursed around Mom; more so Greg. Now I'd entered his hallowed circle of confidence. "*That's* how I acquired my position. If you understand what makes people tick, you can always get what you want. Oops, here we are." Silt scraped the hull as he nosed the canoe onto the shore. We disembarked and walked through some bushes to a path that circled the entire lake. I knew this since our families made the entire circuit at least once per vacation.

Dad yawned, twisting his torso around with a contortionist's knack. He doubled his left hand against his forearm; then the right. His joints popped. This wasn't the same as my brother cracking his knuckles, which he often did to annoy me. No, it sounded more like a butcher snapping the bones of a chicken carcass. He sighed in evident relief. "Son, I can't tell you what a living bitch it is to maintain acceptable posture every damned minute of the day. Speaking of wanting things. You want great pictures of predators, right?" I agreed, sure, that was the idea. He hunched so our heads were closer. "Prey animals are easy to stalk. They're *prey*. They exist to be hunted and eaten. Predators are tougher. I can teach you. I've been working with your brother for years. Getting him ready for the jungle."

"The jungle?" I said, hearing and reacting to the latter part of his statement while ignoring the former. "You mean *Vietnam*?" There was a curse word. "But he promised Mom—"

"Greg's going to volunteer for the Marines. Don't worry. He's a natural. He's like me." He stopped and laid his hand on my shoulder. Heavy and full of suppressed power. "I can count on your discretion not to tell your mother. Can't I?"

Sons and fathers have differences. Nonetheless, I'd always felt safe around mine. Sure, he was awkward and socially off-putting. Sure, he ran hot and cold. Sure, he made lame jokes and could be painfully distant. People joke that engineers are socially maladjusted; there's some truth to that cliché. Foibles notwithstanding, I didn't doubt his love or intentions. Yet, in that moment, I became hyper aware of the size of his hand—of him, in general—and the chirping birds, and that we were alone here in the trees on the opposite shore of the lake. Awareness of his physical grotesqueness hit me in a wave of revulsion. From my child's unvarnished perspective, his features transcended mere homeliness. Since he'd stretched, his stance and expression had altered. Spade-faced and gangling, toothy and hunched, yet tall and deceptively agile. A carnivore had slipped on Dad's sporting goods department ensemble and lured me into the woods. *Let's go to Grandma's house!*

Such a witless, childish fantasy. The spit dried in my mouth anyhow. Desperate to change the subject, perhaps to show deference the way a wolf pup does to an alpha, I said, "I didn't mean to call Aunt Vikki crazy."

Dad blinked behind those enormous, horn-rimmed glasses. "It would be a mistake to classify aberrant psychology as proof of disorder." He registered my blank expression. "Charles Addams said—"

"Who's that?"

"A cartoonist. He said, 'What is normal for the spider is chaos for the fly.' He was correct. The world is divided between spiders and flies." He studied me intently, searching for something, then shook himself and straightened. His hand dropped away from my shoulder. Such a large hand, such a long arm. "C'mon. Let's stroll a bit. If we're quiet, we might surprise a woodland critter."

We strolled.

Contrary to his stated intention of moving quietly to surprise our quarry, Dad initiated a nonstop monologue. He got onto the subject of physical comedy and acting. "Boris Karloff is a master," he said. "And Lon Chaney Jr. The werewolf guy?"

"Yeah, Dad." I'd recovered a bit after that moment of irrational panic. The world felt right again under my feet.

"Chaney's facility with physiognomic transformation? Truly remarkable. Unparalleled, considering his disadvantages. Faking—it's difficult." One aspect I learned to appreciate about my old man's character was the fact he didn't dumb down his language. Granted, he'd speak slower depending upon the audience. However, he used big words if big words were appropriate. My deskside dictionary and thesaurus were dogeared as all get-out.

While he blathered, I managed a few good shots including a Cooper's hawk perched on a high branch, observing our progress. The hawk leaped, disappearing over the canopy. When I lowered the camera, Dad was gone too. I did what you might expect—called for him and dithered, figuring he'd poke his head around a tree and laugh at my consternation. Instead, the sun climbed. Patches of cool shade thickened; the lake surface dimmed and brightened with opaline hardness. Yelling occasionally, I trudged back toward where we'd beached the canoe.

He caught me as I rounded a bend in the path. A hand and ropy arm extended so very far from the wall of brush. A hooked nail scraped my forehead. *Look, son! See?* Instead of pausing to peer into the undergrowth, I ran. Full tilt, camera strap whipping around my neck and a miracle I didn't lose that beloved camera before I crashed through the bushes onto the beach.

Dad sat on a driftwood log, serenely studying the lake. "Hey, kiddo. There you are." He explained his intention to play a harmless joke. "You perceive your surroundings in a different light if a guardian isn't present. Every boy should feel that small burst of adrenaline under controlled circumstances. Head on a swivel, right, son?"

I realized I'd merely bumped into a low-hanging branch and completely freaked. By the time we paddled home, my wild, unreasoning terror had dissipated. It's all or nothing with kids—dying of plague, or fit as a fiddle; bounce back from a nasty fall, or busted legs; rub some dirt on it and walk it off, or a wheelchair. Similar deal with our emotions as well. Dad wasn't a monster, merely a weirdo. Aunt Vikki's crazed behavior had set my teeth on edge. The perfect storm. My thoughts shied from outré concerns to dwell upon on Dad's casual mention that Greg planned on going to war and how we'd best keep on the QT. Not the kind of secret I wanted to hide from Mom, but I wasn't a squealer.

He remained quiet until we were gliding alongside the dock. He said, "Randy, I was wrong to test you. I'm sorry. Won't happen again. Scout's honor."

It didn't.

Toward the end of our stay, the whole lot of us trooped forth to conduct our annual peregrination around the entire lake. We packed picnic baskets and assembled at the Black Gap. Except for Dad, who'd gone ahead to prepare the site where we'd camp for lunch. Another barbeque, in fact. Mr. Mercer brought along a fancy camera (a Canon!) to record the vacation action. He and I had a bonding moment as "serious" photographers. Mr. Schrader, Dad, and a couple of the kids toted flimsy cheapo tourist models. Such amateurs! Mr. Mercer arranged us with the pines for a backdrop. Everybody posed according to height. He yelled directions, got what he wanted, and joined the group while I snapped a few—first with his camera, then my own. I lagged behind as they scrambled uphill along the path.

We trekked to the campsite. Hot, thirsty, and ready for our roasted chicken. Dad awaited us, although not by much. None of the other adults said anything. However, I recall Mom's vexation with the fact he hadn't even gotten a fire going in the pit. She pulled him aside and asked what happened. Why was he so mussed and unkempt? Why so damned sweaty?

He blinked, pushed his glasses up, and shrugged. "I tried a shortcut. Got lost."

"Lost, huh?" She combed pine needles out of his hair. "Likely story."

That winter, drunken ski bums accidentally burned down the Schrader cabin. Oh, the plan was to rebuild in the spring and carry on. Alas, one thing led to another—kids shipping off to college, the Mercers divorcing, etcetera—and we never returned. The men sold off the property for a tidy profit. That was that for our Lake Terror era.

Greg skipped college and enlisted with the United States Marine Corps in '69. Mom locked herself in her study and cried for a week. That shook me—she wasn't a weeper by any means. My brother sent postcards every month or so over the course of his two tours. Well, except for a long, dark stretch near the end when he ceased all communication. The military wouldn't tell us anything. Judging by her peevishness and the fact she seldom slept, I suspect Mom walked the ragged edge.

One day, Greg called and said he'd be home soon. Could Dad pick him up at the airport? He departed an obstreperous child and returned a quieter, thoughtful man. The war injured the psyches of many soldiers. It definitely affected him. Greg kibitzed about shore leave and the antics of his rogue's gallery of comrades. Conversely, he deflected intimate questions that drilled too close to where his honest emotions lay buried. Dumb kids being dumb kids, I asked if he killed anyone. He smiled and drummed his fingers on the table, one then another. That smile harked to his teenaged cruelness, now carefully submerged. More artful, more refined, more mature. He said, *The neat thing about Tiptoe? It's humane. Curbs the ol' urges. Ordinarily, it's enough to catch and release. Ordinarily. You get me, kid?* We didn't speak often after he moved to the Midwest. He latched on with a trucking company. The next to the last time I saw him was at Dad's funeral in 1985. Dad's ticker had blown while raking leaves. Dead on his way to the ground, same as his own father and older brother. Greg lurked on the fringes at the reception. He slipped away before I could corner him. Nobody else noticed that he'd come and gone.

Aunt Vikki? She joined a weird church. Her erratic behavior deteriorated throughout the 1970s, leading to a stint in an institution. She made a comeback in the '80s, got on the ground floor of the whole psychic hotline craze. Made a killing telling people what they wanted to hear. Remarried to a disgraced avant garde filmmaker. Bought a mansion in Florida where she currently runs a New Age commune of international repute. Every Christmas, she drops a couple grand on my photography to jazz up her compound. I can't imagine how poster photos of wolves disemboweling caribou go over with the rubes seeking enlightenment. Got to admit, watching those recruitment videos shot by her latest husband, my work looks damned slick.

~

And full circle at last. My coworker startled me; nightmares ensued; and creepy-crawly memories surfaced. Cue my formerly happy existence falling apart. Two a.m. routinely found me wide awake, scrutinizing my sweaty reflection in the bathroom mirror. I tugged the bags beneath my eyes, exposing the veiny whites. Drew down until it hurt. Just more of the same. What did I expect? That my face was a mask and I peered through slits? That I was my father's son, through and through? If he were more or less than a man, what did that make me?

On my next visit, I decided to level with Mom as I tucked her into bed.

"We need to talk about Dad." I hesitated. Was it even ethical to tell her the truth, here at the end of her days? *Hey, Ma, I believe Pop was involved in the disappearances of several—god knows the number—people back in the sixties.* I forged ahead. "This will sound crazy. He wasn't… normal."

"Well, duh," she said. We sat that there for a while, on opposite sides of a gulf that widened by the second.

"Wait. Were you aware?"

"Of what?"

Hell of a question. "There was another side to Dad. Dark. Real dark, I'm afraid."

"Ah. What did you know, ma'am, and when did you know it?"

"Yeah, basically."

"Bank robbers don't always tell their wives they rob banks."

"The wives suspect."

"Damned straight. Suspicion isn't proof. That's the beauty of the arrangement. We lasted until he died. There's beauty in that too, these days." Mom's voice had weakened as she spoke. She beckoned me to lean in and I did. "We were on our honeymoon at a lodge. Around dawn, wrapped in a quilt on the deck. A fox light-footed into the yard. I whispered to your father about the awesomeness of mother nature, or wow, a fox! He smiled. Not his quirky smile, the cold one. He said, *An animal's expression won't change, even as it's eating prey alive.* May sound strange, but that's when I knew we fit perfectly."

"Jesus, Mom." I shivered. Dad and his pearls of wisdom, his icy little apothegms. *Respected, admired, revered. But replaceable.* A phrase he said in response to anyone who inquired after his job security at IBM. He'd also uttered a similar quote when admonishing Greg or me in connection to juvenile hijinks. *Loved, but replaceable, boys. Loved, but replaceable.*

"He never would've hurt you." She closed her eyes and snuggled deeper into her blankets. Her next words were muffled. I'm not sure I heard them right. "At least, not by choice."

Mom died. A handful of journalist colleagues and nurses showed up to pay their respects. Greg waited until the rest had gone and I was in the midst of wiping my tears to step from behind a decrepit obelisk, grip my shoulder, and whisper, "Boo!" He didn't appear especially well. Gray and gaunt, raw around the nose and mouth. Strong, though, and seething with febrile energy. He resembled the hell out of Dad when Dad was around that age and not long prior to his coronary. Greg even wore a set of oversized glasses, although I got a funny feeling they were purely camouflage.

We relocated to a tavern. He paid for a pitcher, of which he guzzled the majority. Half a lifetime had passed since our last beer. I wondered what was on his mind. The funeral? Vietnam? That decade-old string of missing persons in Ohio near his last known town of residence?

"Don't fret, little brother." Predators have a talent for sniffing weakness. He'd sussed out that I'd gone through a few things recently, Mom's death being the latest addition to the calculus of woe. "Dad *told* you—you're not the same as us." He wiped his lips and tried on a peaceable smile. "They gave me the good genes. Although, I do surely wish I had your eye. Mom also had the eye." The second pitcher came and he waxed maudlin. "Look, apologies for being such a jerk to you when we were kids."

"Forgotten," I said.

"I've always controlled my worse impulses by inflicting petty discomfort. Like chewing a stick of gum when I want a cigarette so bad my teeth ache. I needle people. Associates, friends, loved ones. Whomever. Their unease feeds me well enough to keep the real craving at bay. Until it doesn't." He removed a photo from his wallet and pushed it across the table. Mom and Dad in our old yard. The sun was in Dad's glasses. Hard to know what to make of a man's smile when you can't see his eyes. I pushed it back. He waved me off. "Hang onto that."

"It's yours."

"Nah, I don't need a memento. You're the archivist. The sentimental one."

"Fine. Thanks." I slipped the photo into my coat pocket.

He stared at a waitress as she cleared a booth across the aisle. From a distance his expression might've passed for friendly. "My motel isn't far," he said. "Give me a ride? Or if you're busy, I could ask her."

How could I refuse my own brother? Well, I would've loved to.

His motel occupied a lonely corner on a dark street near the freeway. He invited me into his cave-like room. I declined, said it had been great, etcetera. I almost escaped clean. He caught my wrist. Up close, he smelled of beer, coppery musk, and a hint of moldering earth.

"I think back to my classmates in grade school, high school, and college," Greg said. "The drug addicts, the cons, and divorcees. A shitload of kids who grew up and moved as far from home as humanly possible. Why? Because their families were the worst thing that ever happened to them. It hit me."

"What hit you?"

"On the whole, Mom and Dad were pretty great parents."

"Surprising to hear you put it that way, Greg. We haven't shared many family dinners since we were kids."

"Take my absence as an expression of love. Consider also, I might have been around more than you noticed." He squeezed.

As I mentioned, despite his cadaverous appearance, he was strong. And by that, I mean bone-crushing strong. My arm may as well have been clamped in the jaws of a grizzly. I wasn't going anywhere unless he permitted it. "They were good people," I said through my teeth.

"Adios, bud."

Surely it was a relief when he slackened his grip and released me. I trudged down the stairs, across the lot, and had my car keys in hand when the flesh on my neck prickled. I spun, and there was Greg, twenty or so feet behind me, soundlessly tiptoeing along, knees to chest, elbows even with the top of his head, hands splayed wide. He closed most of the gap in a single, exaggerated stride. Then he froze and watched my face with the same intensity as he'd observed the waitress.

"Well done," he said. "Maybe you learned something, bumbling around in the woods." He turned and walked toward the lights of the motel. I waited until he'd climbed the stairs to jump into my car and floor it out of there.

A long trip home. You bet I glanced into my rearview the entire drive.

In the wee desolate hours, short on sleep due to a brain that refused to switch off, I killed the last of the bourbon while sorting ancient photographs. A mindless occupation that felt akin to picking at a scab or working on a jigsaw puzzle. No real mental agility involved other than mechanically rotating pieces until something locked into place. Among the many loose pictures I'd stashed for posterity were some shot on that last day at Lake Terror in '68. The sequence began with our three families (minus Dad) assembled at the Black Gap and waving; then a few more of everybody proceeding single-file away and up the trail.

I spread these photos on the coffee table and stared for a long, long while. I only spotted the slightly fuzzy, unfocused extra figure because of my keen vision… and possibly a dreadful instinct honed by escalating paranoia. Once I saw him, there were no take-backsies, as we used to say. Dad hung in the branches; a huge, distorted figure hidden in the background of a puzzle. Bloated and lanky, jaw unslung. Inhumanly proportioned, but unmistakably my father. His gaze fixed upon the camera as his left arm dangled and dangled, gray-black fingers plucking the hair of the kids as they hiked obliviously through the notch between the shaggy pines. His lips squirmed.

Eeny. Meeny. Miny. Moe.

Skinder's Veil

Kelly Link

Oᴺᴄᴇ upon a time there was a graduate student in the
summer of his fourth year who had not finished his
dissertation. What was his field? Not important to this story,
really, but let's say that the title of this putative dissertation was
"An Exploratory Analysis of Item Parameters and Characteristics
That Influence Response Time."

By the middle of June, Andy Sims had, at best, six usable
pages. According to the schedule he had so carefully worked
out last year, when a finished dissertation still seemed not
only possible but the lowest of the fruit upon the branches
of the first of many trees along the beautiful path he had
chosen for himself, by this date he should have had a complete
draft upon which his advisors' feedback had already been
thoughtfully provided. June was to have been given over to
leisurely revision in the shade of those graceful and beckoning

trees.

There were reasons why he had not managed to get this work done, but Andy would have been the first to admit they were not *good* reasons. The most pressing was Lester and Bronwen.

Lester, Andy's roommate, was also ABD. Lester was Education and Human Sciences. He and Andy were not on the best terms, though Lester did not appear to have noticed this. Lester was having too much sex to notice much of anything at all. He'd met a physiotherapist named Bronwen at a Wawa two months ago on a beverage run, and they'd been fucking ever since, the kind of fucking that suggested some kind of apocalypse was around the corner but only Lester and Bronwen knew that so far. The reek of sex so thoroughly permeated the apartment in Center City that Andy began to have a notion he was fermenting in it, like a pickle in brine. There were the sounds, too. Andy wore noise canceling headphones while doing the dishes, while eating dinner, on his way to the bathroom where, twice, he'd found sex toys whose purpose he could not guess. He was currently in the best shape of his life: whenever Bronwen came over, Andy headed for the gym and lifted weights until he could lift no more. He went for long runs along the Schuylkill River Trail and still, when he came home, Lester and Bronwen would be holed up inside Lester's room (if Andy was lucky) either fucking or else resting for a short interval before they resumed fucking again.

Andy did not begrudge any person's happiness, but was it possible that there could be such a thing as too much happiness? Too much sex? He resented, too, knowing the variety of sounds that Lester made in extremis. He resented Bronwen, whose roommates apparently had better boundaries than Andy.

No doubt she was a lovely person. Andy found it hard to look her in the eyes. There were questions he would have liked to ask her. Had it been love at first sight? In the fateful moment that day, standing in the refrigerated section of the Wawa, had Lester's soul spoken wordlessly to hers? Did she always love this deeply, this swiftly, with this much noise and heat and abandon? Because Andy had been Lester's roommate for four years now, and aside from a few unremarkable and drunken hookups, Lester had been single and seemed okay with that. Not to mention, whenever Andy brought up Lester's own dissertation, Lester claimed to be making great progress. Could that be true? In his heart of hearts, Andy feared it was true. He mentioned all of this over the phone to his old friend, Hannah. It all came spilling out of him when she called to ask her favor.

"So that's a yes," Hannah said. "You'll do it."

"Yes," Andy said. Then, "Unless you're pranking me. Please don't be pranking me, though. I have to get out of here."

"Not a prank," Hannah said. "Swear to God. This is you saving my ass."

The last time they'd seen each other was at least two years ago, the morning before she left Boston for an adjunct position in the sociology department at some agricultural college in Indiana. "Adjuncts of the corn," she said and had done three shots in succession. She'd been the first of their cohort to defend, and what had it gotten her? A three-year contract at a school no one had ever heard of. Andy had felt superior about that for a while.

Yesterday, Hannah said, her recently divorced sister in

California had broken her back falling off the roof of her house. She was in the hospital. Hannah was flying out tomorrow to take care of her two young nieces. All of her sisters' friends were unreliable assholes or too overwhelmed with their own catastrophes. Her sister's ex was in Australia. What Hannah needed was for someone to take over her housesitting gig in Vermont for the next three weeks. That was what she said.

"It's in the middle of nowhere. It's outside of town, and the nearest town really isn't a town anyway, you know? There's not even a traffic light," Hannah said. "There's no grocery store, no library. There's a place down the road where you can get beer and lightbulbs and breakfast sandwiches, but I don't recommend those."

"I don't have a car," Andy said.

"I don't have one either!" Hannah said. "You won't need one. There's a standing grocery order, so you won't need a car for that. I get a delivery every Tuesday from the Hannaford in St. Albans. If you want to make changes, you just send them an email. And I'm leaving a bunch of stuff in the fridge. Eggs, milk, sandwich stuff. There's plenty of coffee. I have an Uber coming tomorrow at five p.m. Can you get here around three? I went ahead and mapped it, it should take you about seven hours to get here. I'll send directions. Show up at three, we can catch up and I can go over stuff you need to know. But don't worry! There isn't a lot of stuff. Really, it's just a couple of things."

"You're not giving me a lot of advance notice," Andy said.

"What's your Venmo?" Hannah said. "I'll send you nine hundred bucks right now. That's half of what I'm getting paid for three months."

Andy gave her his Venmo. The most he'd ever been Venmoed

was, what, around forty bucks? But here it was immediately, nine hundred dollars, just like that.

"So," Hannah said. "You'll be here. Tomorrow, by three p.m. Because promise I will hunt you down and remove the bones from both legs if you don't come through. I'm counting on you, asshole."

He was googling one-way car rentals when Bronwen wandered into the kitchen. She had Lester's old acapella T-shirt on (Quaker Notes) and a pair of Lester's even older boxer shorts. She got a Yuengling out of the fridge and popped it open, then stood behind Andy, looking at his screen.

"Going on a trip?" she said. She sounded wistful. "Cool."

"Yeah," Andy said. "Kind of? I agreed to take over a housesitting gig in Vermont for the rest of the month and it starts tomorrow afternoon. It's out in the middle of nowhere, and even if I took a bus I'd still be over an hour away, so I guess I'm renting a car."

"That's a terrible idea," Bronwen said. "Car rental places will just rip you off, especially in summer. I've got a car and I'm off work the next couple of days. Lester and I'll drive you."

"No," Andy said. He had spent most of the month trying to avoid being in the same room with Bronwen and Lester. Hadn't she noticed? "Why? Why would you even offer to do that?"

"I've been trying to get Lester to get off his ass and go somewhere all summer," Bronwen said. "Just say yes, and I'll tell him it's a done deal. Then he can't weasel out. Okay? We'll drop you off and then camp somewhere on the way home. A lake, maybe. Lots of lakes in Vermont, right?"

"Let me think about it," Andy said.

"Why?" Bronwen said.

There really wasn't anything to think about. "Sure," Andy said. "Okay. If you're okay with it and Lester is okay with it."

"Great!" Bronwen said. She seemed truly delighted by the prospect of doing Andy this favor. "I'm going to go home and get my tent."

He spent the rest of the afternoon avoiding Lester—who despite Bronwen's reassurances was clearly sulking—and going through his piles of reading and research material. In the end he had a backpack and three canvas bags. He stuck his laptop and printer and a ream of paper in his gym bag, wrapped up in underwear and socks, a sweatshirt, his last two clean T-shirts, running shorts, and a spare pair of jeans. A waterproof jacket and a pair of Timberlands and his weights. There was a guy down the street who made regular trips up to various weed dispensaries in Massachusetts to buy merchandise which he then sold on locally at a healthy profit, and after perusing what was on offer, Andy spent a hundred dollars of Hannah's money on supplies. After some thought he also purchased a pouch of Betty's Eddies Tango for a Peachy Mango gummies for Bronwen as a thank you.

Because, really, it was Lester that Andy bore a reasonable grudge against. There was, for example, the time Lester had been complaining about Andy at top volume to Bronwen, not realizing Andy had come home and was right there, next door in his bedroom. "It isn't that he's a terrible person. He's so fucking smug. Has to map every single thing out, but only because he won't let himself think about whether or not he wants any of it. What does he want? Who knows? Definitely not Andy. No interior life at all. You know how people talk about the unconscious and the id? The attic and the basement? The places you don't go? If you drew a picture of Andy's psyche it would be Andy, standing outside of the house where he lives. He won't go inside. He won't even knock on the door."

Which was rich, coming from Lester. That's what Andy thought. And anyway, Lester wasn't a psychologist. That wasn't his area at all.

He texted a couple of friends he hadn't seen in a while and went out, leaving Lester and Bronwen to fight about Vermont or fuck or watch Netflix in peace. It was good to be out in the world, or maybe it just felt good to know that tomorrow he was going to be in Vermont with all the time and space he could possibly need to get some real work done. To all of the questions about the house and its owner, he just kept saying, "No idea! I don't know anything at all!" And how good that felt, too, to be on the threshold of a mysterious adventure. It wouldn't be terrible, either, to see Hannah again.

As if this thought had summoned her, his phone buzzed with an incoming text. *You're still coming right?*

All packed, he wrote back. *So I guess I am.*

You're going to love it here. Promise. See you tomorrow. BE HERE BY 3!!!!

The plan had been to leave no later than six a.m. They got a late start, because Lester needed to find his spare inhaler, then bug spray, then a can opener, and then he wanted to make a second pot of coffee and take out the recycling and trash and check e-mail. By the time they were in the car it was eight a.m., and of course they hit traffic before they were even on the 676 ramp. Lester fell asleep as soon as they were in the car.

Bronwen, checking the rearview mirror, said, "We'll make up the time once we're on 87."

"Yeah," Andy said. "Okay, sure." He texted Hannah, *on my way hooray*, put his airpods in and closed his eyes. When he opened them again, they were stopping in New Jersey. It was 10.30. According to his phone, they were now five hours away.

Andy paid for gas. "I could drive," he said.

"Nah, buddy," Lester said. "I got it." But he took the wrong exit out of the rest stop, south instead of north, and it was five miles back before they were going in the right direction again.

Bronwen, in the passenger seat, turned around to inspect Andy. "One time I missed an exit on 95 going down past D.C. and so I just went all the way around again. It's a big ring, you know? Turns out it was a lot bigger than I thought it was."

There were a lot of trucks on 87, all of them going faster than Lester. No cops.

Bronwen said, "You got any brothers or sisters?"

"No," Andy said.

"Where you from?"

"Nevada," Andy said.

"Never been there," Bronwen said. "You go back much?"

"Once in a while," Andy said. "My parents are retired professors. Classics and Romance Languages. So now they spend a lot of time going on these cruises, the educational kind. They give lectures and seminars in exchange for getting a cabin and some cash. They're cruising down the Rhine right now." No, that had been December. He had no idea where they were now. Greece? Sardinia?

"That sounds awesome," Bronwen said.

"They've had norovirus twice," Andy said.

"Still," Bronwen said, "I'd like to go on a cruise. And once you've had norovirus, you're immune to it for like a year."

"That's what they told me," Andy said. "They were actually kind of psyched after they had norovirus the first time."

"This friend," Bronwen said, "the one in Vermont, what's her name?"

"Hannah," Andy said.

"Did you ever date?"

"No," Andy said.

"Yes," Lester said.

"It wasn't really dating," Andy said. "We just kind of had a thing for a while."

"And then Hannah went off to teach at some cow college," Lester said. "And Andy hasn't gotten laid since."

"I'm just really, really trying to concentrate on my dissertation," Andy said. Sometimes, avoiding Lester, he forgot exactly why he ought to avoid Lester. It wasn't just Bronwen, and sex. It had a lot more to do with just Lester.

"Yeah," Bronwen said. "That makes so much sense. Sometimes you have to keep your head down and focus."

She really was very, very nice. Unlike Lester. "You have any brothers or sisters?"

"Nope," Bronwen said. "Just me. My parents are over in Fishtown."

"Fancy," Andy said. Fishtown was where all the nice coffee

shops and fixed-up rowhouses were.

"Yeah," Bronwen said. "My mom's mom's house. But they're saying they're gonna put it on the market. The real estate tax is insane. But, you know, I think my mom is afraid if they sell the house they'll end up getting divorced, and then she'll have no husband and no house."

"I'm sorry," Andy said.

"No," Bronwen said. "I mean, my dad's kind of a dickhead?"

"I can vouch for that," Lester said.

"Shut up," Bronwen said. "I can say it but it doesn't mean you can."

"Whatever," Lester said. "You love me. It was love at first sight. *Coup de foudre.*"

"I like you a lot," Bronwen said.

"She doesn't believe in love," Lester said to Andy. "She's only with me because I'm ghost repellent."

"Believe it or not, he isn't my usual type," Bronwen said. "I'm actually more into girls."

"Go back a minute," Andy said. "To the thing about ghost repellent."

Lester said, "So we met at the Wawa, remember? There was only one six-pack of Yuengling in the cooler and I got it. And Bronwen came up while I was at the counter to ask the guy if there was more, and there was, but it wasn't cold. So I invited her over and we hooked up and she ended up spending the night but she said that at some point she'd probably have to split because everywhere she goes eventually this presence, this ghost, shows up, and unless she's at work or something and can't leave, she'll just take off again. But the ghost never showed up. It never shows up when she's with me. So, you know, we started hanging out a lot."

"What do you mean a ghost shows up?" Andy said.

"It's just something that happens," Bronwen said. "Ever since I was a kid. Just after my fourteenth birthday. I don't know why it happens, or why it started. It doesn't bother anyone else. No one else sees it. I don't even see it! I don't even really know if it's a ghost or not. It's just, you know, this presence. I'll be somewhere and then it will be there too. It doesn't do anything. It's just there. My mom used to tell me that it was a good thing, like a guardian spirit. But it isn't. It's kind of awful. If I leave a room, or if I go somewhere else, it doesn't come with me right away, but eventually it's with me again. If I stay in one place long enough, like if I'm asleep long enough, then when I wake up it's there. So, yeah. I'm a terrible sleeper. But I went home with Lester and I fell asleep in his bed and then I woke up and it wasn't there."

"Ghost repellent," Lester said smugly. There was a car in front of them that wasn't even doing sixty-five. Lester just stayed there behind it.

"I thought maybe it was gone for good," Bronwen said. "But I went home and took a shower and it showed right up. So, not gone. But any time I'm with Lester it stays away. So, yay."

"Incredible," Andy said.

Bronwen was facing forward again. "You probably don't even believe me," she said. "But, you know. There are more things than are dreamt of."

"I don't *not* believe you," Andy said, equivocating.

But this didn't appear to satisfy Bronwen. She said, "Well, whatever. I bet you've had weird shit happen that you can't explain. Weird shit happens to everyone."

"Except me," Lester said.

"But that's your weird thing," Bronwen said, patting him on the arm. "If nothing weird ever happens to you, then that's pretty weird."

Andy said, "Once a kid knocked on our door, and when I went to answer it, he didn't have a head."

"Right," Lester said. "Last Halloween. We gave him some Tootsie Rolls."

"Both of you are utter and complete assholes," Bronwen said. She put Ariana Grande on the stereo, tilted her head back, and closed her eyes. Apparently she found it easier to ignore assholes than a ghost.

They stopped at a McDonald's just off the highway around three p.m. The map function now said they'd get to the house around 4.15. Andy sat at a table outside and texted Hannah. She called him back immediately. "Cutting it close, asshole," she said.

"Sorry," Andy said. "But it isn't my car, so there isn't much I can do."

"Whatever, I owe you for agreeing to do this at all. It sucks, you know? Having to take off like this. This is such a sweet job. Please don't fuck it up for me, okay?"

"How's your sister?" Andy said.

"She's okay, sort of? Doesn't want to take the good painkillers, because she has a history with that stuff. So that's going to be fun for everyone. Oh, hey. She's calling. See you soon."

Bronwen came outside and sat down on top of the picnic

table. She was dipping French fries into the remains of her chocolate milkshake.

Andy said, "I can't tell you how much I appreciate you guys driving me."

"Not a big deal," Bronwen said, tilting her head up and back toward the sun. She was a tawny golden brown all over, hair and skin. There were little golden hairs all over her forearms and legs. Andy could almost understand why a ghost followed her everywhere. Hannah was long and pale and freckled and sort of mean, even when she liked you. She was funny, though. She changed her hair color when the mood struck her. In her last Instagram post her hair was brown with two red-pink streaks, like a Porterhouse steak.

"Oh," Bronwen said. "Oh, that was quick. Much quicker than usual."

She'd dropped her milkshake. Andy picked it up before much could spill, but when he tried to give it back to her, Bronwen ignored it. She was watching a space on the sidewalk a few feet away.

"What?" he said. "What is it?"

Bronwen said, "I'll go see if Lester's done." She jumped off the table and went back inside the McDonald's.

Did Andy feel anything? Some kind of presence? He went over to stand, as far as he could gauge, in the place Bronwen had been staring at. There was nothing there, which probably meant that Bronwen had some kind of mental health issue, but also she'd just driven him most of the way to Vermont. "I don't actually think you're real," he said, "but if you are, maybe you could go away and stop bothering Bronwen. She's a nice person. She doesn't deserve to be haunted."

Saying this seemed the least he could do. When he went inside to check on the situation, Bronwen was in a booth, slouched down with her face in her arms and Lester rubbing her back. Andy went and got her ice water.

Eventually, she sat up and took a sip. "Sorry," she said.

"No worries," Andy said. "But we'd better hit the road. I need to get there before Hannah's ride shows up. I don't want to cut it too close."

"Dude," Lester said. "Give her a minute." He actually seemed to be irritated with Andy and did that mean he believed Bronwen? That there was a ghost?

"Yeah," Andy said. "Of course." He went and used the bathroom and when he came out again, Lester and Bronwen weren't in the booth. They weren't at the car, and eventually he realized they had to be in the family restroom because there was no one else in the McDonald's and the lock was engaged. It was another good twenty minutes before they emerged, and apparently the ghost had gotten tired of waiting and left, because Bronwen seemed much more cheerful getting back in the car. Lester too, for that matter.

Shortly after that, Andy's phone lost all reception, which was probably for the best, because although Bronwen drove at least ten miles above the speed limit the rest of the way, they didn't reach the address Hannah had given him until well after five.

The place Hannah had been housesitting was off a two-lane highway, the kind they'd been following for the past two hours. There were two stone pedestals on either side of the dirt drive, but nothing on top of them. There were a lot of trees. Andy didn't really know a lot about trees. He wouldn't have minded if there were fewer. It was the first turn-off in maybe half a dozen miles, which was what Hannah's directions had said. If you kept going, you got to the store where you could get sandwiches and gasoline. That would have meant they'd gone too far. But Hannah's directions had been clear, and they hadn't gotten lost once. Nevertheless, they were late and Hannah was long gone.

You couldn't see anything from the turn-off because of all of the trees. It was like going into a tunnel, the way the trees made a curving roof and walls over the narrow lane of white gravel, but then suddenly there was the house in a little clearing, very picturesque, three wide gray flagstone steps leading up to a green door between two white pillars, a pointed gable above. The house itself was a sunny yellow color, two-story with many windows. Behind the house, more trees.

"Nice place," Bronwen said. "Cheerful."

Andy's phone still had no reception. It seemed to him that there were several possible scenarios about to play out. In one, Hannah's Uber had been delayed. The green door opened and Hannah came out. In another, this all turned out to be a substandard prank, and the door would open and a stranger would be standing there. But what happened is that he got out of the car and went up the steps and saw that there was a note on the door. It said:

CAN'T WAIT ANY LONGER. WILL CALL FROM AIRPORT. WROTE UP INSTRUCTIONS FOR YOU AND LEFT THEM ON COUNTER. FOLLOW ALL OF THEM.

Andy tried the door. It was unlocked. Bronwen and Lester got out of the car and began to unload the trunk.

"We must have missed her by, what? A half hour?"

Andy said, "I guess she waited around a little while."

"It always takes longer than you think it will," Bronwen said. This seemed accurate to Andy, but not representative of the whole picture.

Lester said, "Come on. Let's get Andy's stuff in and hit the road. There's a sugar shack near the campground we booked that does a maple IPA, and today's Tuesday so it closes at six-thirty."

"Or you could stay here," Andy said. "Why camp when you can sleep in a bed?"

"Oh, Andy," Bronwen said. "That's so nice of you. But the whole point of this is camping. You can sleep in a bed anytime, you know?"

"Sure," Andy said. "I guess. You want a quick tour before you go? Or to use the bathroom?"

"Here," Lester said. He passed Andy's backpack over and then went back to the car to get the gym bag and the rest. Something about his body language suggested that perhaps Lester was as weary of sharing an apartment with Andy as Andy was of sharing one with him.

Bronwen and Andy remained on the porch. You could see, through the door, an open-plan living room with furniture arranged around a central fireplace and chimney of stacked gray stone. Even though it was summer, there was a stack of firewood piled up beside the fireplace. Everything looked comfortable and a little shabby. There was no reason not to go inside.

"At least come get a glass of water," Andy said.

"No," Bronwen said. She sounded very certain. "I'm good."

"What?" Andy said. "Are you getting a bad vibe or something? Is it haunted?" He was joking. He was kind of not joking.

"No," Bronwen said. "No vibe at all. Promise. It's just I don't think I want to go inside, if that's okay. That's all."

"Oh," Andy said. He mostly believed her, he thought. "Okay, good." On the whole, however, he had liked Bronwen better before he knew she was an authority on the supernatural. He decided he would keep the gummies for himself.

"That's everything!" Lester said. "Have fun, buddy. Get lots of work done. See you in a couple of weeks."

"Will do," Andy said. "Enjoy sleeping on the ground. Bye."

They got back in Bronwen's car, Lester driving again, and turned around, disappearing back into the trees. You could see how the lower branches were practically scraping the top of the car. It was cooler here than it had been in Philly, which wasn't exactly a surprise. The coolness must collect in the trees, little pockets under each leaf. There was no breeze, but the leaves were not still. They flexed and turned, green to silver to black in a shivering cascade as if Lester were catching a glimpse of the scaled flank of some living, crouching thing, too enormous to be seen in its entirety.

Andy picked up the carrier bags and went inside the house. It was a very nice house, very welcoming. He was lucky Hannah had thought of him. He went in search of the instructions she'd left.

Your phone won't get reception here, she'd written, *unless you're online. Then it should be okay downstairs. Upstairs not so great. You'll see the network. Skinder's Veil. No password. Get on and send me a text, please, so I know you've arrived. If you don't, I'm going to have to turn around and come back.*

Sleep in whatever bedroom you want. The one at the back of the upstairs on the left has the most comfortable bed. Also the biggest. The bathroom upstairs is a little finicky. Don't flush if you're about to take a shower.

Don't forget groceries come on Fridays. Driver comes around ten a.m. and leaves everything on the porch. The delivery list and all the info is on the fridge if you need to add anything.

If there's a storm the power will probably go out, but there's a generator. You have to fill it every twelve hours when it's running. It's in the little shed out behind the kitchen. Internet is mostly good if slow.

Help yourself to whatever you find in the cabinets. Laundry is upstairs next to the bathroom.

This house belongs to Skinder. I don't know if that's his first name or his last name. He's eccentric but this is a sweet gig so whatever. He only has two rules for the housesitter, but please take them very seriously. Like, Moses coming down with the stone tablets level serious. All of this was going to be much simpler to explain in person, but you've already fucked that up, so let me hammer this home. TWO RULES. DON'T BREAK THEM.

RULE ONE! IMPORTANT! If any friends of Skinder's show up, let them in no matter what time it is. No matter what or who they are. Don't worry about taking care of them. Just let them in and do whatever and leave when they're ready. Some of them may be weird, but they're harmless. Some of them are actually pretty cool. Hang out if you want to and they want to. Or don't. It's totally up to you! You've got your dissertation to finish, right? Anyway, it's entirely possible nobody will show up. Some summers a bunch of Skinder's friends show up and some summers I don't see anyone at all. No one so far this year.

RULE TWO! THIS ONE IS EVEN MORE IMPORTANT!!! *Skinder may show up. If he does, DO NOT LET HIM IN. This is* HIS OWN RULE. *Why? I have no idea, but for the duration of the time during which he pays me to stay here, Skinder may not enter his own house. No matter what he says, he is not allowed to come in. I know how bizarre this sounds. But, fingers crossed, this will be a non-issue and you won't see Skinder at all. If you do, then all you have to do is not let him in. It's that simple.*

ANDY: This is my favorite place in the world and the easiest job in the world and you had better not fuck it up for me. If you're thinking of fucking it up, then also start thinking about how I'm going to murder you one inch at a time.

Love, Hannah.

P.S. If you look outside at night and there's mist coming up from the ground all over, don't freak out! There are a lot of natural springs around this area, a lot of water underground on the property. The mist is a natural phenomenon. It's called Skinder's Veil which is also the name of the house, which has belonged to the Skinder family for a long, long time. Also, the water here comes from a well. It's spring fed so it tastes funny but apparently it's good for you. It's supposed to, and I quote, "open your inner eye." So, basically, free drugs! There's plenty of bottled water in case you don't like the taste but I always just drink the water from the tap.

P.P.S. Seriously, if Skinder shows up, do not let him in the house no matter what he says.

Andy put the note in his pocket. "Much to think about," he said out loud. This was a thing that one of their TAs had liked to say at the end of every class, back in undergrad. There'd been a certain intonation, and it had cracked Hannah and Andy up all semester. They'd said it to each other all the time. It had been the working title of Hannah's dissertation. Andy couldn't even remember the guy's name.

He found the network on his phone, waited until he had a few bars back. And here were Hannah's texts, increasingly frantic, then terse. Three voicemails. He went back to his bags at the front door and dug through the backpack until he'd found the pouch of gummies. Ate one and then texted Hannah back. *Here! Just missed you, I'm guessing. So so sorry. Call me when you can. I have some questions.*

He investigated his new living situation while he waited for Hannah to call. The kitchen and the living room he'd seen. There was a farmhouse table off to one side of the open-plan space, set in front of a big window overlooking a small area of flagstones, furred with moss. There was an Adirondack chair in case you wanted to sit outside, which Andy was not sure he did. Everything was very green: the mossy flagstones, the chair, the slumped, ferny ground, and trees, trees, trees crowding in close around it all. It had taken Andy some time to get used to the East Coast, the way there were trees growing everywhere, but this was another order of magnitude. Here there was nothing but trees and this house and whatever lived in and among trees.

There was the start of a path, too, heading off into those trees. Maybe it went somewhere interesting. More likely it was just going to be more trees.

There was a flat-screen TV, though, on the wall opposite the fireplace. And there had been a satellite dish on the roof. That seemed promising. They didn't have a TV back in the apartment in Philly. There was a bookshelf with a blue ceramic bowl of small pinecones, a perfectly ordinary and unremarkable piece of granite, and some paperback books, mostly Stephen King and Michael Connelly. No family pictures, nothing sentimental or which might indicate the kind of person who lived here.

Andy set up his printer and his research material on the table. Then he took his small assortment of clothes and toiletries upstairs. There were four bedrooms. The two at the front of the house were smaller, the beds and curtains made up in cheerful floral fabrics, one red and white, the other green and blue. In the green and blue bedroom there was an amateurish painting of some sort of creature standing on two legs beside a river. So, a bear, perhaps? Were there other animals that stood on two legs? But then again, bears didn't have long and luxuriant tails, did they. In the red and white bedroom, instead of a painting there was a framed cross-stitch that said: "WEST EAST HOME IS THE BEAST." He would have to google that.

Above the bed in each room were two dainty bells, mounted just below the crown molding. A wire attached to the canon disappeared into a small hole drilled into the wall. They were called servants' bells, weren't they?

"Much to think about!" Andy said, and went to see the other two bedrooms. These were larger than the front bedrooms and the ceiling sloped down over the headboards of the beds. Here, too, were the bells, but no paintings, no vaguely Satanic cross-stitches. He decided to claim the left-hand bedroom, the one

Hannah had suggested. The bed had been stripped; he found the sheets in the dryer.

Andy made himself a grilled cheese for dinner and had what turned out to be pasta salad out of a Tupperware container. There was a half-bottle of white wine in the refrigerator. He finished that and was sampling the tap water, which was a little musty but perhaps would get him high, when Hannah finally called.

"You're there," she said.

"Eating your pasta salad," he said. "Not sure about the raisins."

"It's my mom's recipe," Hannah said. "You grow up eating something, it's comfort food."

"Mine is grilled cheese," Andy said. "But it has to be Swiss cheese."

They were both silent for a minute. Finally, Andy said, "Sorry I didn't get here in time to see you."

"Never mind," Hannah said. "At least you're there. I started thinking you weren't going to show at all. What do you think?"

"I think I should have brought some sweaters," Andy said. "So what's with the rules? I'm supposed to let everyone in except for Skinder, who is the one who actually owns the house?"

"That's pretty much it exactly," Hannah said.

"So anyone can just show up and I let them in? But then, what if I accidentally let Skinder in? It's not like I've met him."

"Oh, wait, no," Hannah said. "Shit. This would have been so much easier if I'd been able to explain this in person. Look, Skinder's friends show up at the back door. The kitchen door. So, someone shows up and knocks at the kitchen door, let them in. The only person who will knock at the front door is Skinder. It's actually pretty easy. Don't let anyone in if they knock at the front door."

"Doesn't he have a key?" Andy said. "To his own house?"

"I know," Hannah said. "It's freaky. If it makes it easier, think of it like a game. Like Settlers of Catan. Or Red Rover! Or, whatever. There are rules and everyone has to follow them. If you think about it that way, then you just do what the rules say and you're fine."

"Okay, but what happens if I mess up and I let Skinder in?"

"I don't know," Hannah said. "I lose my summer job? Look, I signed a contract and everything. I'd have to give back what he paid me, which means you'd have to give me back the money I passed on to you. Just don't let him in, okay? If he even shows up, which he probably won't do. I've done this for a while and he only showed up three times, once the first summer, and then twice the summer before last. He knocks on the front door and you don't let him in. I didn't let him in. He asked me to let him in and I didn't and so he went away again. It was a little weird, especially when he came back the second time, but it was fine. You'll be fine. Just don't let him in."

"Okay," Andy said. "So what does he look like?"

"Skinder?" Hannah said. "Oh, boy. You'll know it's him. I'm not going to try to explain it because it will sound crazy, but you'll know. You'll just know. For one thing, he always has a dog with him. It's this little black dog. So if you see the dog, that's him."

"What if he doesn't bring the dog? Or what if the dog's dead? You didn't see him last year. The dog could have died."

"It really doesn't matter," Hannah said. "You don't have to know what he looks like to know it's him. He only comes to the front door. Just don't let anyone through the front door and you'll be fine."

"Don't let anyone in the front door," Andy said. He took another swallow of musty water. Perhaps he would acquire a taste for it. "But if anyone knocks on the back door, then I have to let them in, right?"

"Right," Hannah said.

"I don't really understand any of this," Andy said. "I'm kind of feeling like you've gotten me into something here. Like, I thought this was just a housesitting gig. You didn't mention all of this other stuff on the phone the other day."

"Yeah," Hannah said. "I was pretty sure that if I brought all this up then you'd pass on the golden opportunity I was holding out to you. And I really, really needed you to come up so I could get out to my sister."

"And this is in no way a hilarious prank," Andy said.

"I'm paying you nine hundred dollars to stay in a secluded house in the country where you can finally get some real work done on your dissertation," Hannah said. "Does that seem like a prank?"

"Much to think about," Andy said.

"Much to think about, asshole," Hannah said. "I'll call you in a day or two, okay? I have to go catch my flight."

"Safe travels," Andy said. But she had already hung up.

There was a six-pack of some fancy IPA at the back of the fridge, and a jar of Red Vines on the counter beside the sink. He took a couple of those and one of the beers through to the living room and sat at the farm table. He turned on his laptop and put aside thoughts of Hannah and rules and the person who owned this house. He set aside, too, thoughts of Bronwen and the thing she said followed her. Regardless of whatever she felt or thought, it wasn't real. Nothing was following anyone. He had felt nothing. And if there had been something, well then, it wasn't here, was it? It was her ghost, not his, and so it would be wherever Bronwen was, waiting for the moment when Lester wasn't there.

Andy worked for an hour, comparing penalized splines in

various studies, until at last the edible kicked in, or perhaps it was the tap water smoothing down his splines and his thoughts and all the strangeness of the day. He watched TV and at nine he went upstairs to bed. He slept soundly through the night and only woke up because he had forgotten to close the blinds and sunlight was coming through the windows, turning all of the room to auspicious gold.

For the next two days he did not return to his dissertation, though he told himself that he would tackle it after breakfast. After lunch. Before dinner. Instead of doing this, he took naps, got stoned, played Minecraft, and did his sets and reps. After dinner he watched old science fiction movies. He left the television on when he went to bed. It wasn't that he was lonely. It was just that he was out of the habit of *being* alone. On the third night, when he looked out of his bedroom window, threads of mist were rising from the ground below the trees. As he watched, these threads wove themselves into pallid columns, and then a languorous, uniform cloud, blotting out the patio. The Adirondack chair shrank away until only its back and arms remained, floating in whiteness. Andy went to the red and white bedroom at the front of the house and saw that the driveway had already vanished. If Hannah hadn't told him this would happen, he supposed he would have found the phenomenon eerie. But it was perfectly natural. Creepy but natural. Natural and also quite beautiful. He tried without success to get a good picture with his phone. No doubt it would be possible to get better results if he left the house to take a picture at ground level, but he dismissed this idea when it came to him. He preferred not to go stand outside knee deep in something called Skinder's Veil, natural phenomenon or not.

Instead he went to bed and had two hours of sleep before he woke. One of the bells above his head was ringing, ringing, ringing.

No one was at the front door. The TV was on: he turned it off. The bell was still ringing and so he went to the kitchen and turned on the lights. A woman stood at the back door, peering in. She must have had her finger on the bell and Andy, against his better judgment, did as Hannah had said he must and unlocked the door to let her in.

"Oh, good," she said, stepping into the kitchen. "Did I wake you up? I'm so sorry."

"No," Andy said. "It's fine. I'm Andy. I'm housesitting here. I mean, my friend Hannah was housesitting, but she had a family emergency and so now I'm filling in."

"I'm Rose White," his visitor said. "Very nice to meet you, Andy." She opened the refrigerator and took out two beers. She handed one to him and then headed into the living room, sitting down on one of the chintz sofas and dropping her leather carry-all on the floor, plopping her muddy boots upon the coffee table.

She couldn't have been much older than Andy. Her hair, longish and dirty blond, looked as if it hadn't seen a hairbrush in several days. Perhaps she had been backpacking. In any case, she was still extremely attractive.

"Have a drink with me," she said, smiling. One of her front teeth was just a little crooked. "Then I'll let you go back to bed."

Andy opened the beer. Sat down in an armchair that faced the fireplace. Hannah had said he didn't have to hang out, but on the other hand, he didn't want to be rude. He said, "Mist's cleared up."

"The veil? It usually does," Rose White said. "Don't recommend going out in it. You can get lost quite quickly. I was quite surprised to find myself right on Skinder's doorstep. I thought I'd been going in another direction entirely."

"You live nearby?" Andy said. It didn't seem polite to ask why she was out so late at night. "Hannah comes and housesits every summer. Maybe you've met her?"

"Phew," Rose White said. "The big questions! Haven't been through in years, actually. Let's see. The last housesitter I met was an Alma. Or Alba. But I see nothing's much changed. Skinder's not much for change."

"I don't really know much about Skinder," Andy said. "Anything, really."

"A complicated fellow," Rose White said. "You know the rules, I suppose."

"I think so?" Andy said. "If he comes to the house, I'm supposed to not let him in. For some reason. I don't really know what he looks like, but he'll come to the front door. That's how I'll know that it's him. But if anyone comes to the back door, then I let them in."

"Good enough to get by," Rose White said. She began to unlace her boots. "Aren't you going to drink your beer?"

Andy set it down. "I might just go back to bed, unless you need me for something. Going to try to get up early and get some work done. I'm working on my dissertation while I'm here, actually."

"A scholar!" Rose White said. "I'll be quiet as a mouse. Leave your beer. I'll drink it for you."

But she was not, in fact, as quiet as a mouse. Andy lay in his bed, listening as she rattled and banged around the kitchen, boiling water in the kettle and pulling out various pans. The smell of frying bacon seeped under his closed door in a delicious cloud. Andy wished he had his noise-canceling headphones. But they were on the table beside his laptop, and he did not want to go downstairs and get them.

He thought, *Tomorrow I really will get some work done, visitor or no visitor. Otherwise all the time will just melt away and in the end I'll have accomplished nothing.*

Without meaning to, he found himself listening for the sound of Rose White coming up the stairs. It must have been after three when, at last, she did. She went into the bathroom beside his bedroom and took a long shower. He wondered which room she would choose, but in the end it was his door she opened. She didn't turn on the lights, but instead got into the bed with him.

He turned on his side and there was enough moonlight in the room that he could see Rose White looking back at him. She had not bothered to put clothes back on post-shower. "Do you have a girlfriend?" she said.

"Not at the moment," Andy said.

"Do you like to fuck women?"

"Yes," Andy said.

"Then here's my last question," she said. "Would you like to fuck me? No strings. Just for fun."

"Yes," Andy said. "Absolutely, yes. But I don't have a condom."

"Not a concern for me," she said. "You?"

Yes, a little. That was the problem with knowing a fair bit about how statistics worked. "No," Andy said. "Not at all."

But afterward, he wasn't quite sure what the etiquette was. Should he try to get to know her a little better? He didn't even know how long she was going to be staying at the house. It would have been easier if he'd been able to fall asleep, but that seemed to be out of the question. He decided he would pretend to be asleep.

"Not tired?" Rose White said.

"Sorry," Andy said. "A lot to think about. Think I'll go downstairs and watch TV for a while."

"Stay here," Rose White said. "I'll tell you a story."

"A story," Andy said. "You mean like when a kid can't fall asleep. So one of their parents tells them a story? A story like that?" He wasn't a kid. On the other hand, there was a woman in his bed he'd just met, and they'd had sex and now she was offering to tell him a story. Why not say yes? If nothing else, it would be something, later on, that would be an interesting story of his own. "Sure. Tell me a story."

Rose White drew the covers up to her neck. She was lying on her back, and this gave the impression she was telling the story to someone floating on the ceiling. It felt strangely formal, as if Andy were back in a lecture hall, listening to one of his professors. She said, "Once, a very long time ago, there was a woman who wrote books for a living. She made enough from this to keep not only herself in modest comfort but also her sister, who lived with her and was her secretary. She wrote her novels longhand and it was the sister who read the manuscript first, before giving it back to the writer to edit. This sister, who was a romantic with very little outlet for expression, had a peculiar way of marking the parts she liked best. She would prick her finger with a needle and mark the place with her own blood to show how good she thought it was. A little blotch over a well-turned phrase, a little smudge. She would return the manuscript, the writer would do her revisions, sparing the lines and scenes that her sister had loved, and then the sister would type everything up properly and send it along to the writer's agent.

"The writer's books were popular with a certain audience, but never garnered much critical favor. The writer shrugged this off. She told her sister the merit of the books was that they were easy to produce at a rate which kept a roof over their heads, and they served a second purpose, which was to entertain those whose lives were hard enough. But, the writer said, she had in her a book of such beauty and power that anyone who read it would be changed by it forever, and one day she would write it. When her sister asked why she did not write it now, she said that such a book would take more time and thought and effort than she could currently spare.

"As time went on, though, the writer's books became less popular. The checks they brought in were smaller, and their lives became little by little less comfortable. The writer determined that she would at last turn her attention to this other book. She labored over it for a year and into the next winter, and slept little and ate less and grew unwell. At night while she worked her sister would hear her groaning and coughing, and then one morning, very early, the writer woke her sister and said, 'I have finished it at last. Now I must rest.'

"The sister put on a robe and lit a fire and sat down to read the manuscript at once, her needle in her pocket. But upon reading the very first sentence, she drew out her needle and pricked her finger to mark it. And the second sentence, too, she marked with her blood. And it went on like that as she read, until at last she had to go down to the kitchen to fetch a peeling knife. First she cut her palm and then she cut her arm and each line and every page was marked with the sister's blood as she read, such was the power and beauty of the narrative and the characters and the writer's language.

"Many days later, friends of the writer and her sister grew concerned because no one had heard from them in some time. Upon forcing their way into the house they found the sister exsanguinated in her chair, the manuscript in her lap all glued together with her blood. The body of the writer, too, was discovered in her bed. She'd died of an ague she'd caught from overwork and too little rest. As for the book she'd written, it was quite impossible to read even a single word."

"That was really interesting," Andy said, just as awake as he had been at the start, possibly more so. In a minute he would say so, get dressed, and go downstairs. "Thank you."

"You're welcome," Rose White said. "Now go to sleep."

He woke at the table downstairs, his laptop beside his head.

Rose White was on the couch. "I built a fire," she said. "Thought you might catch cold. Vermont weather is unpredictable, summer or not."

She'd done this, Andy realized, because he was entirely naked. His shoulders ached and his ass was unhygienically stuck to the rattan seat of the chair. "What time is it?" he asked her. "How long have I been here?"

"You were gone when I woke up," Rose White said. "Discovered you here when I came down this morning. It's past noon now."

"I must've been sleepwalking," Andy said. His laptop was open, and when he woke the screen, a prompt appeared. *Save changes?*

"Get dressed," Rose White said. "I'll make you a sandwich. Then you can get back to it."

He dressed and ate, reading over what he'd written the night before. It was rough, but it was also a reasonably solid foundation for revision. Moreover, there were four thousand words that had not been there the night before. This seemed like enough work for one day, and so, at Rose White's suggestion, they spent the day in bed and the evening drinking bourbon they procured from a locked liquor cabinet. Rose White knew where to find the key.

The next few days and nights were pleasant ones. Andy took leisurely naps in the afternoon. He shared his stash with Rose White. They took turns cooking, and let the dishes pile up. Rose White had very little interest in his life, and no interest at all in explaining anything about herself. If, after sex, she enjoyed telling him her strange little stories, at least they were mostly very short. Some of them hardly seemed to be stories at all. One went like this: "There once was a man possessed of a great estate who did not wish to marry. At last, beset by his financial advisors, he agreed to be married to the first suitable individual he encountered upon setting into town, and when he came home with his fiancée, his friends and advisors were dismayed to find that he had become engaged to a tortoise. Nevertheless, the man found a priest willing, for a goodly sum of money, to perform the ceremony. They lived together for several years and then the man died. At last a distant relative was found to inherit the estate, and on his first night in his fine new home, he had the tortoise killed and served up as a soup in its own shell. But this is not, by any means, the worst story about marriage that I know."

Another story began, "Once there was a blood sausage and a liver sausage and the blood sausage invited the liver sausage over for dinner." None of Rose White's stories were cheerful. In all of them, someone came to a bad end, but there was nothing to be learned from them. Nevertheless, each time she finished and said to Andy, "Go to sleep," he promptly fell asleep. And, too, each morning he woke up to find that he had, in some dream state, produced more of his dissertation, though after the second time this happened he moved his laptop and his notebooks up to the vanity in the red and white bedroom.

The groceries were left on the porch on the appointed day, and the dissertation progressed, and in the afternoons when it grew warm Rose White sunbathed topless on the patio while Andy did reps. Hannah called to check in, and to report her nieces would eat nothing but sugar cereal and mozzarella sticks, while her sister was camped out on a blow-up mattress in the dining room because she could not get up and down the stairs, and needed Hannah's help getting onto the toilet and off again.

"Everything's great here," Andy said.

"Any visitors?" Hannah asked.

"Yeah, some lady named Rose White. I don't know how long she's staying."

"Never met her," Hannah said. "So, what's she like?"

"She's okay," Andy said. He didn't really feel like getting into the details. "I've been really focused on the dissertation. We haven't really hung out or anything. But she's done some of the cooking."

"So, pretty normal, then," Hannah said. "Good. Sometimes the ones who show up are kind of strange."

"How so?" Andy said.

"Oh, you know," Hannah said. "Some of them can be a little strange. I'm gonna go make lunch now for the two small assholes. Call if you need anything. And I'll check in again later. As soon as I know when I can head back, I'll let you know."

"No rush," Andy said, looking out the window to where Rose White lay, splendid and rosy upon a beach towel. This was wonderful, yes, but what if she were developing feelings for him? Did he feel something for her? Yes, possibly. This was very inconvenient. They didn't really know each other at all, and she was, as Hannah had said, kind of strange.

The whole thing made him uncomfortable. Much to think about. He had a gummy and pretended to be working when Rose White came back in. But she'd only come into the house to use the bathroom and put her clothes back on. Then she was off for a hike, not even bothering to ask if he wanted to come along. She came back at dinnertime with a pocketful of mushrooms. "Psilocybe cubensis," she said. "I'll make us tea. The water here has some excellent properties of its own, but there's no such thing as too much fun."

"Isn't that dangerous?" Andy said. "I mean, what if you haven't identified the mushroom correctly?"

Rose White gave him a withering look. "Go teach your grandmother to suck eggs," she said. "Are you a man or a chicken, Andy?"

It was, again, the study of statistics that presented the problem. Nevertheless, Andy had some of the tea and in return shared his vape pen. It was the first time he'd ever tried mushrooms, and only pieces of the night that followed were accessible to him later on.

Rose White, sitting astride him, her hands on his biceps, the feeling that her fingers were sinking into his flesh as if either he or she are made of mist.

Rose White saying, "I think my sister must be quite near now." Andy tries to say that he didn't know she had a sister. He doesn't really know anything about her. "I'm Rose White but she is Rose Red." When he looks at her, her hair is full of blood. Rose Red!

The realization that Skinder's house has no walls, no roof, no foundation. The walls are trees, there is no ceiling, only sky. "It's all water underneath," he is explaining. Rose White: "Only the doors are real."

Later, he is seated in front of the vanity in the red and white bedroom. The bell on the wall is ringing. When he leaves one bedroom, Rose White is coming out of another. Andy has to sit down on the staircase and bump down, one step at a time. Rose White helps him stand up at the bottom. His head is floating several feet above his body and he has to walk slowly to make sure he doesn't leave it behind.

Two deer are arranged like statuary upon the flagstone patio. Are they real? Did these deer ring the doorbell? Do they want to come in? He finds this hysterically funny but when he opens the door, the deer approach solemnly on their attenuated, decorative legs. One and then the other comes into the kitchen, stretching their velvet necks out and down to fit through the door. Inside the velvet-lined jewel boxes of their nostrils the warmth of their breath is gold. It dazzles. Andy's head floats up higher, bumping against the ceiling. He stretches out his hand, strokes the flank of an actual fucking deer. A doorbell-ringing deer. A moth has flown into the kitchen, he's left the door open. It blunders through the air, brushing against his cheek, his ear. He opens his mouth to tell Rose White to close the door and the moth flies right in.

Rose White says, "Once upon a time there was a real estate agent who made arrangements to show a property. When she arrived at the property, she realized at once that her new client was none other than Death. Suspecting that he was there for her, she pretended she was not the agent at all, but rather another prospective buyer. Claiming she had been told to meet the listing agent around the back, she lured Death around the side of the house and told him to look through the French windows to see if anyone was there to let them in. When he did this, she picked up an ornamental planter and bashed in his head. Then she dragged the body of Death into the full bathroom and cut it into twelve pieces in the bathtub. These she wrapped in Hefty bags and, after cleaning the bathtub thoroughly, she parked her Lexus in the garage and placed these bags in the trunk. Over the next week, she buried each piece deep on the grounds of a different listing, and each of those houses sold quite quickly. Decades went by and the real estate agent began to regret what she had done. She was now in her nineties and weary of life, but Death did not come for her. And so she visited each of the properties where she had disposed of his corpse and dug him up, but perhaps her memory was faulty: she could not find the last two pieces. She is still, in fact, searching for Death's left forearm and his head. The rest of him, badly decomposed, is in a deep freezer in her garage. Some days she wonders if, in fact, it was really Death at all. And what if it really had been Death? What if he had only come to see a house? Isn't it likely that even Death himself must have a house in which to keep himself?"

Andy woke in his own bed with a dry mouth but no other discernable effects from the night before. In the red and white bedroom, his laptop was open. When he looked to see what he'd written, it was only this: *How to work? Deer in house. Not sanitary!!! WTF.* He deleted these.

When he went downstairs, though, there were no deer and no Rose White, either. She'd left a note on the kitchen table. "Headed out. Finished off bacon but did a big clean (badly needed!) so think we're even. Thanks for the hospitality. Left you the rest of the mushrooms. Use sensibly! Take care if I don't see you again. Fondly, Rose White."

"Fondly," Andy said. He wasn't really even sure what that meant. It was one of those signoffs like "kind regards" or "best wishes." A kiss-off, basically. Well. "Summer loving, had me a blast." Lester's acapella group liked to sing that one. He didn't even have her phone number.

While he was microwaving a bowl of oatmeal, he inspected the tile floor of the kitchen. He actually got down on his hands and knees. What was he looking for? Rose White? Some deer tracks? The rest of his dissertation?

He gave himself the rest of the day off. Texted Hannah: *There are a lot of deer around here, right? Do they ever come up to the house?*

She texted right back: *Lots of deer, yes. Bears too, sometimes.*

Well. He didn't feel like explaining that he'd had shrooms with a houseguest he'd also been having sex with, and that possibly he had let some deer into the house. Or else hallucinated this.

Without Rose White in his bed, he found he did not fall asleep easily. Neither did he work, in his sleep, on his dissertation. He made some progress during the days, but it was much like it had been in the apartment in Philadelphia, except here he had no excuse.

About a week after Rose White had gone, the servants' bell rang again. It wasn't midnight yet, and he was in bed, skipping to the end of a Harlan Coben novel because the middle was very long and all he really wanted was to see how it all came out.

He put a pair of pants on and went downstairs. At the back door was a wild turkey. After deliberating, Andy did as he was supposed to do and let it in. It did not seem at all wary of him, and why should it have been? It was an invited guest. Andy went into the living room and sat on the couch. The turkey investigated all the corners of the room, making little grunting noises, and then defecated neatly on the hearth of the fireplace. Its cheeks were violet, and its neck was bright red. It flew up on top of the cord of stacked wood and puffed out all the formidable armature of its feathers. Andy's phone was on the table: he took a picture. The turkey did not object. It seemed, in fact, to already be sleeping.

Andy, too, went up to bed. In the morning, the turkey was waiting by the back door and he let it out again. He cleaned up the shit on the hearth and two other places. This was when, no doubt, he should have called Hannah. But she was probably waiting for him to do exactly that, and really, she should have been up front with him. And also, he realized, he was having a good time. It was like being inside an enchantment. Why would he want to break the spell? The next night the bell rang again, though to Andy's disappointment it was neither a beautiful girl nor a creature at the back door. A grayish man of about sixty in Birkenstocks, a Rolling Stones T-shirt, and khaki shorts nodded but did not speak when Andy opened the door. He did not bother to introduce himself. He didn't speak at all. Instead, he went straight upstairs, took a long shower, using all the towels in the bathroom, and then slept for two days in the blue and green bedroom. Andy kept his bedroom door locked while the gray man was in the house. It was a relief, frankly, when he was gone again. After that, it was an opossum, and the night after the opossum, the mist was on the ground again. Skinder's Veil. When the bell began to ring, Andy went down to let his guest in, but no one was at the kitchen door. He went to the front door, but to his relief, no one was there either. The bell continued to ring, and so Andy went to the kitchen door again. When he opened the door, the mist came swiftly seeping in, covering the tile floor and the feet of the kitchen table and the kitchen chairs. Andy closed the door and at once the bell began to ring again. He opened the door and left it open. The guest was, perhaps, Skinder's Veil itself, or perhaps it was something which preferred to remain hidden inside the Veil. Andy, thinking of Bronwen's ghost, went up to his bedroom and shut the door and locked it. He rolled up his pants and wedged them against the bottom of the door. He left his lights on and did not sleep at all that night, but in the morning he was the only one in the house and the day was very sunny and bright. The door was shut tight again.

The last human guest while Andy was in Skinder's house was Rose White's sister, Rose Red.

When Andy opened the kitchen door, it was Rose White who stood there. Except, perhaps it was not. This person had the same features—eyes, nose, mouth—only their arrangement was somehow unfamiliar. Sharper, as if this version of Rose White would never think of anyone fondly. Now her hair was exuberantly, unnaturally purple-red, and there was a metal stud in one nostril.

"Rose Red," she said. "May I come in?"

This was the sister, then. Only, as she spoke Andy saw a familiar crooked tooth. This must be Rose White, hair colored and newly styled. And would he even have noticed her nose was pierced previously? Not if she'd not had her stud in. Well. He would play along.

"Come in," he said. "I'm Andy. Filling in for the original housesitter. Your sister was here about a week ago."

"My sister?" she said.

"Rose White," Andy said. It was like being in a play where you'd never seen the script. He had to give Rose White this: she wasn't boring.

"We don't even have the same last name," Rose Red said. She looked very prim as she said this. She was, it was true, a little taller than he remembered Rose White being, but then he saw her ankle boots had two-inch heels. Had she really come up the path wearing those? Mystery upon mystery.

He said, "My mistake. Sorry." After all, who was he to talk? He'd managed not even one complete paragraph in two days.

Maybe he'd do better now that she was here again.

Rose Red (or Rose White) went rummaging through the kitchen cabinets. "Help yourself," he said. "I was just about to make dinner."

Rose Red was regarding the plate beside the sink where Rose White's mushrooms were drying out. "Yours?" she said.

Andy said, "Happy to share. You going to make tea?"

"What if I made some risotto?" she said.

And so Andy set the table and poured them both a glass of wine, while Rose Red made dinner. The risotto was quite tasty and, Andy saw, she had used all of the mushrooms. Once again, he tried to discover more about the owner of the house, but like Rose White, Rose Red was an expert at deflection. Had he hiked any of the paths, she wanted to know. What did he think of the area?

"I've been kind of busy," Andy said. "Trying to finish my dissertation. It's why I'm here, actually. I needed to be able to focus."

"And when you're finished?" Rose Red said.

"Then I'll defend and go on the job market," Andy said. "And hopefully get a teaching job somewhere. Tenure track, ideally."

"That's what you'll do," Rose Red said. "But what do you want?"

"To do a good job," Andy said. "And then, I suppose, to be good at teaching."

Rose Red appeared satisfied by this. "Have you been on the trails at all? Gone hiking? So much to explore up here."

"Well," Andy said. "Like I said, I've been busy. And I don't actually like trees that much. But the Veil is pretty interesting. And people keep showing up. That's been interesting, too. Rose White, the one I mentioned before, she had all these weird stories." He wasn't sure whether or not he should bring up all the sex.

After dinner they had more wine and Rose Red found a

puzzle. Andy didn't much care for puzzles, but he sat down to help her with it. The longer they worked on it, the harder it grew to fit the pieces together. Eventually, he gave up and sat, watching how his fingers elongated, wriggling like narrow fish.

Upstairs, one of the bells began to ring again. "I'll get that," Andy said, excusing himself from the puzzle of the puzzle. In the kitchen he could perceive, once again, that it was not a kitchen at all. Really, it was all just part of the forest. All just trees. The puzzle, too, had been trees, chopped into little bits that needed arranging into a path. It was fine. It was fine, too, that a brown bear stood on its hind legs at the door, depressing the bell.

"Come in, good sir, come in," Andy said.

The bear dropped down onto all fours, squeezing its bulk into the kitchen. It brought with it a wild, loamy reek. Andy followed the bear back into the living space where Rose Whatever Her Name Was sat, finishing the puzzle. You could see the little fleas jumping in the bear's fur like sequins.

Rose Red jumped up and got the serving bowl with the remains of the pasta. She placed it before the bear, who stuck its whole snout in. Andy lay down on the floor and observed. When the bear was done, it leant back against the couch. Rose Red scratched its head, digging her fingers deep into its fur. They stayed like that for a while, Rose Red scratching, the bear drowsing, Andy content to lie on the floor and watch them and think about nothing.

"This one," Rose Red said to the bear. "He's going to be a great teacher."

"Well," Andy said. "First there's the dissertation. Defend. Then. Go on the job market. Be offered something somewhere. Get tenure. There's a whole path. You have to go along it. Through all the fucking trees. Like Little Red. Little Red Riding Hood. You know that story?"

"I don't care much for stories," Rose Red said.

"Oh, come on," Andy said. "Tell me one. Make it up. Tell me one about this place."

"Once upon a time there was a girl whose mother died when she was very young." It wasn't Rose Red, though, who was speaking. It was the bear. Andy was fairly sure that it was the bear, which he felt should have troubled him more than it did. Perhaps, though, it was all ventriloquism. Or the mushrooms. He closed his eyes and the bear, or Rose Red, went on with the story.

"Once there was a girl whose mother died when she was very young. They lived on a street where almost every house had a swimming pool in the backyard. Not the girl's house, but the house on either side did. There was an incident, the girl never knew exactly what, and the mother drowned in the swimming pool that belonged to the house on the left. It was a mystery why she was in it. It was late at night, and no one knew when or why she had come over. Everyone else had been asleep: her body wasn't discovered until morning.

"When she wasn't much older, the girl's father remarried a woman with a daughter of her own. Don't worry, though, this isn't a story about a wicked stepmother. The girl and her stepmother and the stepsister all got along quite well, much better, in fact, than the girl got along with her own father. But all through her adolescence, there were stories about the pool next door; that it was haunted. The family who had lived there when the mother drowned moved away—the new family loved their house and their pool, but it was said that they never went swimming after midnight. Anyone who went swimming after midnight ran the risk of seeing the ghost down in the deep end, long hair floating around her face, her bathing suit losing its elasticity, her mouth open and full of water.

"The girl sometimes swam in the neighbor's pool, hoping she would see her mother's ghost, and also afraid that she would see her mother's ghost. All the girls in the neighborhood liked to swim in that pool best. They would dare each other to swim after midnight, and the rest would take turns sitting on the edge of the pool, facing away, in case the ghost was too shy to appear in front of them all. Sometimes one of the girls even saw the ghost—a thrill, a ghost of their very own!—but the girl whose mother had drowned never saw anything at all.

"Eventually, she grew up and moved away and made a life of her own. She had a husband and two children and thought that she was quite happy on the whole. The path of her life seemed straightforward and she moved along it. Her father died, and she grieved, but her stepmother was the one who had been her true parent. Her mother she hardly remembered at all. Life went on, and if the path grew a little rockier, her prospects a little less rosy, what of it? Life can't always be easy. Then, one day, her stepsister called to say that her stepmother, too, was dead.

"The daughter left her children with her husband and flew down for the funeral. Afterward, she and her stepsister would sort out their childhood home so it could be put on the market. The economy was in a downturn, and the daughter was not sure she would have her job for much longer, so half the proceeds from the sale of the house seemed fortuitous. But the real estate market was not good, and she saw that over half of the houses on her old street were for sale, including both houses on either side. Several others were vacant, or seemed so. It seemed to her possible the house would not sell at all, but she and her stepsister gamely went on for three days, making piles for Goodwill, piles for the trash, and piles that were things they might sell or keep for themselves.

"They reminisced about their childhood, and looked through old photos, and confided in each other their fears about the future. They wept for the loss of the two mothers and drank three bottles of wine.

"Now, the house on the left was vacant, and so was the house on the right. The swimming pool of the house on the left had been emptied, and the swimming pool on the right had not. Twice, in the middle of the day, they climbed over the chain-link fence and went swimming when they needed a break from sorting. The last night, tipsy and wide awake, the daughter left the childhood house where her stepsister lay sleeping in the bottom bunk of their childhood room, putting on one of the old-fashioned bathing suits from the pile they were taking to Goodwill. But instead of climbing over the fence to the right, she climbed the fence to the left.

"She found that the pool, which should have been empty, was instead full of clear blue water. The lights along the edge of the pool had been turned on and she could smell the chlorine from where she stood as if it had just been freshly cleaned. Little bugs, drawn to the lights, flew just above the water. Some of them had already tipped in and struggled. They would drown unless someone scooped them out.

"The daughter walked down the steps at the shallow end of the pool until she was waist deep. The water was pleasantly cool. The elastic of the suit had long ago crumbled, and so the pleasant and impossible water came creeping up the skin of her thighs.

"For a while she floated on her back, looking up at the stars and trying not to think about the future or why the pool was full of water. One was uncertain and the other was a gift. She floated until she grew, at last, cool and tired enough that she thought she might be able to sleep. Then she turned on her front, to wet her face, and down at the bottom of the pool she saw her mother at last. Here was the face she barely remembered. So young! The long, waving hair. It even seemed to her that her mother wore the twin of the suit she was wearing now. It seemed to the daughter that she could stay here in the pool, that she could stay here and be happy. Step painlessly off the path as her mother had done. It seemed the woman in the pool wanted for her to stay. They would never grow old. They would have each other.

"She could have stayed. She was very tired and there was still so much of her life ahead of her. There were so many things she needed to do. But in this story, she got out of the pool. She went back to the house of her childhood and she woke up her stepsister and told her what she had seen. The stepsister, at first, did not believe her. Wasn't the pool empty? Perhaps, intoxicated as she was, she'd gone to the other pool, the one that was full, and hallucinated seeing her mother. The daughter argued with her. Her mother had been wearing the bathing suit that she'd drowned in, the very same one the daughter was wearing now. Couldn't the stepsister see how her bathing suit was wet? She was dripping on the tile floor.

"The daughter insisted she'd gone swimming in an empty pool. She had finally seen the ghost. Okay, her stepsister said, what if you did? But you didn't see your mother. There is no ghost. Your mother wasn't even wearing a bathing suit. She had a cocktail dress on. That's what my mother told me. And even if she had been wearing a bathing suit, it wouldn't be that one. No one would have kept the bathing suit your mother drowned in.

"No, the daughter said. I saw her. She was so young! She looked exactly like me!

"Come on, said the stepsister. She brought the daughter down to the room where they'd been sorting keepsakes. She spread out photographs until they found one of the mother. It was dated on the back, the date of the mother's death. Is that who you saw? said the stepsister. She doesn't look much like you at all.

"The daughter studied it. Tried to think what she had seen. The closer she looked, the less sure she was that she had seen her mother. Perhaps, then, all along she had been the one haunting the swimming pool. Why should hauntings happen in linear time, after all? Isn't time just another swimming pool?

"Now, Andy, it's time for you to go to sleep. But if you like, though I don't care for stories, I'll tell you one more."

Rose Red says, "Once upon a time there was a house that Death lived in. Even Death needs a house to keep himself in. It was indeed a very nice house and for much of the year Death was as happy there as it is possible for Death to be. But Death cannot stay comfortably at home all year long, and so once a year he found someone to come and keep it for him while he went out into the world and made sure everything was as it should be. While he was gone from his house, it was the one place that Death might not come in. He knows this, even though, at times he wants nothing more than to come home and rest. And while Death was gone from his house, all of those creatures who, by one means or another, had found a way so that Death might not take them yet, might come and pass a night or two or longer in Death's house and not worry he would find them there. In this way many may rest and find a bit of peace, though the one who follows them unceasingly will follow them once more when they put their foot onto the path again. But this isn't your story. As a matter of fact, those who come and stay owe a debt of gratitude to the one who keeps house for Death while he is away. Even Death will one day pay his debt to you as long as you keep your bond with him."

Andy sleeps. He sleeps long and wakes, again, before his laptop. Has he written what he reads there, or has someone else? Well. Bears can't type. It's morning and there is no one in the house but Andy. There's a pile of bear shit beside the farmhouse table, cold but still fragrant. The puzzle is back in its box.

And now the story is almost over. Andy continued to work in a desultory and haphazard way on his dissertation. No one else came to the kitchen door while he stayed in Skinder's house, but one night the bell woke him again. He went first to the kitchen, thinking he might see one Rose or the other, but truly this time there was no one there. It came to him that the bell he still heard ringing was not the same bell as before. He went, therefore, to the door at the front of the house, and there, on the porch, stood Skinder with his dog.

How did Andy know it was Skinder? Well, it was as Hannah had said. You would know Skinder, whether or not the dog—small, black, regarding Andy with a curious intensity—had been beside him. What did Skinder look like? He looked exactly like Andy. It was as if Andy stood inside the house, looking out at another, identical Andy, who was also Skinder and who must not be allowed inside.

There was a car in the driveway. A black Prius. There was a chain on the front door, and Andy kept it on when he opened the door a crack. Enough to speak to Skinder, but not enough for Skinder to come in, or his dog. "What do you want?" Andy said.

"To come into my house," Skinder said. He had Andy's voice as well. "My bags are in the car. Will you help me carry them in?"

"No," Andy said. "I'm sorry, but I can't let you in."

The black dog showed its teeth at this. Skinder, too, seemed disappointed. Andy recognized the look on his face, though it was a look that he knew the feel of, more than the look. "Are you sure you won't let me in?" he said.

"I'm sorry," Andy said again. "But I'm not allowed to do that."

Skinder said, "I understand. Come along." This to the dog. Andy in the house watched Skinder go down the steps and down the gravel driveway to the car. He opened the door and the dog jumped up onto the seat. Skinder got in the car at last too, and Andy watched as the car went down the driveway, the little white stones crunching under the tires, the car silent and the headlights never turned on. The car disappeared under the low, dragging hem of leaves and Andy went back upstairs. He didn't attempt to sleep again. Instead, he sat in the red and white bedroom, in a chair in front of the window, watching in case Skinder returned.

Hannah came back two days later. She sent a text before her overnight flight: *Margot's still in a cast, but we've agreed it's better if I go. No one happy and house is too small. Neighbor going to help out. See you tomorrow afternoon!*

He hadn't finished his dissertation, but Andy felt he was well on the way now. And he was going to see Hannah again. They'd catch up, he'd tell her a modified history of his time in the house, and maybe she'd ask him to stay. There were plenty of bedrooms, after all. She could even take a look at what he had so far, give him some feedback.

But when she arrived, it was clear that he wasn't welcome to stay, even to Andy, who wasn't always the quickest to pick up on cues. "I'm so grateful," she kept saying. Her hair was blue now, a deep rich sky-blue. "You were such a lifesaver to do this."

"I was happy to do it," Andy said. "It was fun, mostly. Weird, but fun. But I wanted to ask you about some aspects. Skinder, for example."

"You saw him?" Hannah said. All of her attention was on Andy, suddenly.

"No, it's fine," Andy said. "I didn't let him in. I did what you told me to do. But, when you saw him, I wanted to ask. Did he look familiar?"

"What do you mean, exactly?" Hannah said.

"I mean, did you think he looked like me at all?" Andy said.

Hannah shrugged. She looked away, then back at Andy. "No," she said. "Not really. Okay, so I've already paid the fare back on the Uber. It'll take you to Burlington and you can catch a Greyhound there back to Philly. But you have to go now, or you'll miss the last bus. I already checked the schedule—there's nothing if you miss that one until tomorrow morning. Don't worry about cleaning anything up or changing the sheets. I'll take care of it."

"I guess if you're sure," Andy said. "If you don't need me to stay."

She gave him an incredulous look at that. "Oh, Andy," she said. "That's so sweet. But no, I'll be fine. Come here."

She gave him a big hug. "Now go get your stuff. Do you need a hand?"

He left the ream of paper behind. He hadn't really needed to print out anything. That got rid of one of the canvas bags, and he lugged everything else out to the Uber. Hannah came down the steps to give him a sandwich. She took a look at his Klean Kanteen and said, "Is that tap water?"

"Yes," Andy said. "Why?"

"Ugh," Hannah said. She took the canteen from him and opened it, pouring the water out. "Here. Take this." This was bottled water. "It's from the fridge, so it'll be nice and cold. Bye, Andy. Text me when you get home so I know you're there."

She hugged him again. It wasn't much, but it was better than nothing. The way she smelled, the feeling of her hair on his cheek. "It's really nice to see you again," he said.

"Yes," she said. "I know. It's been such a long time. Isn't it weird, how time just keeps passing?"

And that was that. He turned to get one last look at the yellow house and at Hannah as the car went up the driveway, but she had already gone inside.

When he was at last back at the apartment in Philly, it was morning again. Andy was tired—he had not slept at all on the bus, or in any of the stations in between transfers—and he could not shake the idea that when he opened the door, Skinder would be waiting for him. But instead here was Lester on the futon couch in his boxer shorts, looking at his phone and slurping coffee. It was much hotter in Philly. The apartment had a smell, like something had gone off.

"You're home," Lester said without much enthusiasm. "How was Vermont?"

"Nice," Andy said. "Really, really nice." He didn't think he'd be able to explain what it had been like to Lester. "Where's Bronwen?"

Lester looked down at his phone again. "Not here," he said. "I don't really want to talk about it."

From this, Andy gathered they had broken up. It was a shame: he felt Bronwen might have been a good person to talk to about Vermont. "Sorry," he said to Lester.

"Not your fault, dude," Lester said. "She was not the most normal girl I've ever been with."

Occasionally over the next week Andy noticed how Lester sometimes looked as if he were listening for something, as if he were waiting for something. And after a while, Andy began to feel as if *he* were listening too. And then, sometimes, he thought that he could almost see something in the apartment when Lester was there. It crept after Lester, waited patiently, crouched on the floor beside him when he sat at the table. It was mostly formless, but it had a mouth and eyes. It reminded Andy of Skinder's dog. Sometimes he thought it saw him looking. He felt it looking back. But Lester, he thought, could not see it at all.

It wasn't entirely bad to have it in the house. It meant Andy worked, at last, very hard to finish his dissertation. Or perhaps it had been Vermont that had gotten him over the hump. All that had really been needed was for him to get out of his own way. When he was nearly done, Andy began looking for higher ed listings, and then, very soon, he was defending, and he was done, and he had graduated at last and had his first interview. He was very ready to leave the apartment, and Philly, and Lester, and Lester's ghost, behind.

The job interview did not go as well as he'd hoped. There were other candidates, and he was quite surprised when, in the end, the job was offered to him. But he took it gladly. Here was the path which led toward tenure and a career and all the rest of his future. Years later, one of the older faculty members who had been on the hiring committee got very drunk at a bar they all frequented, and told Andy that he had almost not gotten the offer, in fact. "The night before we met to discuss, Andy, I had the most peculiar dream. In the dream I was in the woods at night and lost, and there was a bear. I couldn't move I was so scared. The bear came right up and I knew that it was going to eat me, but instead it said, 'You should hire Andy. You'll be glad if you do and you'll regret it if you don't. Do you understand?' I said I did and then I woke up. And then at the meeting no one wanted to say much; there was a very weird feeling, and then someone, Dr. Carmichael, said, 'I had a dream last night that we should hire Andy Sims.' And then someone else said, 'I had the same dream. There was a bear and it said exactly that. That we should hire Andy Sims.' And it turned out we had all had the dream. So, we hired you! And, in the end, it turned out for the best, just like the bear said."

Andy said that this was extremely peculiar, but yes, it had all turned out all right. When, later, he went up for tenure and got it, he wondered if the committee had been given another dream. In any case, he was content to have what he had been given. He caught himself, once, at the end of a lecture, saying, "Much to think about." But there wasn't, really. His students gave him adequate ratings. It seemed to some of them that Professor Sims really looked at them, that he seemed to see something in them (or perhaps near them), none of their other teachers did. What exactly Professor Sims saw, though, he kept to himself. It was, no doubt, an unfortunate after-effect of the water he'd drunk so much of one summer.

There was this, too: although his children asked him over and over why they could not have a dog, Andy could not bear this idea. Instead, he got them guinea pigs, and then a rabbit.

As for Hannah, he ran into her once or twice at conferences. He went to both of her presentations and took notes so he could send her an email afterward with his thoughts. They had drinks with some of their colleagues, but he didn't ask her if she still housesat in the summer in Vermont. All of that seemed of another life, one that didn't belong to him.

Lester had dropped out of the program. He went and worked for a think tank in Indonesia. Andy didn't know if anyone had followed him there.

And then, years later, Andy found himself at a conference in Montpelier, Vermont. It was fall and very beautiful. He found trees quite restful, actually, now that he'd lived on the East Coast for so long. The last day of the conference, he began to think about the parts of his life that he hardly thought about at all, now. He'd given his panel, had heard the gossip, talked up his small college to fledgling Ph.D. candidates. Back in his hotel room, he looked at maps and car rentals and realized it would not be unrealistic to drive home instead of flying. It would be a very pretty drive. And so he canceled his plane ticket and picked up a rental car instead. He thought perhaps he might try to find the yellow house in the woods again, and see who lived there now.

But he didn't remember, as it turned out, exactly which highway the house had been on. He drove down little highway after little highway, all of them lovely but none the road he had meant to find. And, toward dusk, when a deer came onto the road, he swerved to miss it and went quite far down the embankment into a copse of trees.

He wasn't badly hurt, and the car didn't look too bad, either. But he thought it would require a tow truck to get it back up again, and his cell phone had no reception here. He went up to the road and waited some time, but no car ever came past and so he went back down to his rental, to see what he had to eat or drink. He saw, close to where the car had ended up, there was quite a well-trodden trail. Andy decided he would follow it in the direction he felt was the one most likely to lead toward St. Albans.

The trail meandered and grew more narrow. The light began to fade and he thought of turning back, but now the trail led him out to a place he recognized. Here was the patio and here was the Adirondack chair, grown even more decrepit and weatherworn. Here was the comfortable yellow house with all the lights on inside.

He went around to the front door. Well, why not? He wasn't a bear. He knocked and waited, and eventually someone came to the door and opened it.

The other Andy stood in the doorway and looked at him. Where was the little dog? Surely it was dead. But no, there it was in the hallway.

"Can I come in?" Andy said.

"No," Skinder said and shut the door. Andy waited a little longer, but all that happened was that the lights in the house went off. It was dark outside now and the wind was rattling all the leaves in the trees. There wasn't much he could think of to do, so after a while Andy went back to find the path again.

Acknowledgments

I'D like to thank Laurence Hyman for graciously giving his blessing when I approached him about my anthology in tribute to his mother.

Also, thanks to Elizabeth Hand, Merrilee Heifetz, and Shawna McCarthy; and George Sandison, Lydia Gittins, and the rest of the Titan crew for their support.

About the Authors

LAIRD BARRON spent his early years in Alaska. He is the author of several books, including *The Beautiful Thing That Awaits Us All*, *Swift to Chase*, and *Worse Angels*. His work has also appeared in many magazines and anthologies. Barron currently resides in the Rondout Valley writing stories about the evil that men do.

GEMMA FILES was born in England and raised in Toronto, Canada, and has been a journalist, teacher, film critic and an award-winning horror author for almost thirty years. She has published four novels, a story-cycle, three collections of short fiction, and three collections of speculative poetry; her most recent novel, *Experimental Film*, won both the 2015 Shirley Jackson Award for Best Novel and the 2016 Sunburst Award for Best Novel (Adult Category). She is currently working on her next book.

JEFFREY FORD is the author of the novels *The Physiognomy, Memoranda, The Beyond, The Portrait of Mrs. Charbuque, The Girl in the Glass, The Cosmology of the Wider World, The Shadow Year, Ahab's Return.* His short story collections are *The Fantasy Writer's Assistant, The Empire of Ice Cream, The Drowned Life, Crackpot Palace, A Natural History of Hell, The Best of Jeffrey Ford,* and a new collection out in July 2021, *Big Dark Hole* from Small Beer Press.

ELIZABETH HAND is the author of sixteen multiple-award-winning novels and collections of short fiction including *Curious Toys, Wylding Hall, Generation Loss,* and *The Book of Lamps and Banners,* her fourth noir featuring punk provocateur and photographer Cass Neary. Her stand-alone thriller, *Under the Big Black Sun,* will be out in 2022. Under non-pandemic conditions, she divides her time between the Maine coast and North London.

KAREN HEULER's stories have appeared in over one hundred literary and speculative magazines and anthologies, from *Conjunctions* to *Clarkesworld* to *Weird Tales,* as well as in a number of Best Of anthologies. She has received an O. Henry Award, been a finalist for the Iowa Short Fiction Award, the Bellwether Award, the Shirley Jackson Award for short fiction, and others. She has published four novels, four collections, and a novella.

STEPHEN GRAHAM JONES is the author of twenty-five or so novels and collections, and there's some novellas and comic books in there as well. Most recent are *The Only Good Indians* and *Night of the Mannequins.* Next is *My Heart is a Chainsaw.* Stephen lives and teaches in Boulder, Colorado.

RICHARD KADREY is the *New York Times* bestselling author of the Sandman Slim supernatural noir series. *Sandman Slim* was included in Amazon's "100 Science Fiction & Fantasy Books to Read in a Lifetime," and is in production as a feature film. Some of Kadrey's other books include *The Grand Dark*, *The Everything Box*, *Hollywood Dead*, and *Butcher Bird*. He's also written for *Heavy Metal* Magazine, and the comics *Lucifer* and *Hellblazer*.

CASSANDRA KHAW is an award-winning game writer, and former scriptwriter at Ubisoft Montreal. Her work can be found in places like *The Magazine of Fantasy & Science Fiction*, *Lightspeed*, and Tor.com. Her first original novella, *Hammers on Bone*, was a finalist for the British Fantasy Award and the Locus Award, and her forthcoming novella, *Nothing But Blackened Teeth*, will be published by Nightfire in September 2021.

JOHN LANGAN is the author of two novels and four collections of stories. For his work, he has received the Bram Stoker and This Is Horror awards. He is one of the founders of the Shirley Jackson Awards and continues to serve on its Board of Directors. He lives in New York's Mid-Hudson Valley with his wife, younger son, and certainly not too many books.

KELLY LINK is a MacArthur recipient and the author of four collections, most recently *Get in Trouble*. She is the owner of the bookstore Book Moon in Easthampton, Massachusetts, and the cofounder, with her husband Gavin J. Grant, of Small Beer Press. Together they publish the zine *Lady Churchill's Rosebud Wristlet*. You can find her on Twitter at @haszombiesinit.

CARMEN MARIA MACHADO is the author of the graphic novel *The Low, Low Woods*, the memoir *In the Dream House*, and the story collection *Her Body and Other Parties*. She has been a finalist for the National Book Award and the winner of the Lambda Literary Award for Lesbian Fiction, the Shirley Jackson Award, and many others. Her essays, fiction, and criticism have appeared in *The New Yorker*, *Granta*, *Tin House*, *Best American Science Fiction & Fantasy*, and elsewhere. She lives in Philadelphia.

JOSH MALERMAN is the *New York Times* bestselling author of *Bird Box*, *Malorie*, and *Unbury Carol*. He's also one of two singer-songwriters for the Detroit band the High Strung, whose song "The Luck You Got" can be heard as the theme song to the Showtime series *Shameless*. He lives in Michigan with the artist/musician Allison Laakko.

SEANAN MCGUIRE lives above a swamp in the Pacific Northwest, where the sunlight is *very* different (and often filtered through blackberry briars). She shares her home with four large cats, an axolotl, and a remarkably large assortment of books, dolls, and My Little Ponies. Seanan is the author of several dozen books across a variety of genres, under both her own name and the name "Mira Grant." She spends most of her time writing, which makes perfect sense, given the rest of the situation. Find her on Twitter at @seananmcguire, or at seananmcguire.com.

JOYCE CAROL OATES is the author most recently of the novel *A Book of American Martyrs* and the story collection *Night-Gaunts*. Her work has appeared in previous anthologies of Ellen Datlow's, including *The Doll Collection* and *Black Feathers: Dark Avian Tales.* She is a recipient of the Bram Stoker Award, the National Book Award, the PENAmerican Lifetime Achievement award, the President's Medal of Honor, and the A.J. Liebling Award for Outstanding Boxing Writing.

BENJAMIN PERCY's most recent novel, *The Ninth Metal*, releases in June 2021 with Houghton Mifflin Harcourt. He is the author of four other novels, three story collections, and a book of essays. He currently writes *Wolverine* and *X-Force* for Marvel Comics.

Before earning her MFA from Vermont College of Fine Arts, MARY RICKERT worked as kindergarten teacher, coffee shop barista, Disneyland balloon vendor, and personnel assistant in Sequoia National Park. She is the winner of the Locus Award, Crawford Award, World Fantasy Award, and Shirley Jackson Award. Her third short story collection, *You Have Never Been Here*, was published by Small Beer Press. Her novel, *The Shipbuilder of Bellfairie*, will be published by Undertow Press in the summer of 2021, and her novella, *Lucky Girl, How I Became a Horror Writer: A Krampus Story* will be published by Tor.com in the Fall of 2022.

PAUL TREMBLAY has won the Bram Stoker, British Fantasy, and Massachusetts Book awards and is the author of *Survivor Song, Growing Things, The Cabin at the End of the World, Disappearance at Devil's Rock, A Head Full of Ghosts*, and the crime novels *The Little Sleep* and *No Sleep Till Wonderland*. His essays and short fiction have appeared in the *Los Angeles*

Times, Entertainment Weekly online, and numerous year's-best anthologies. He has a master's degree in mathematics and lives outside Boston with his family.

GENEVIEVE VALENTINE is the author of *Mechanique: A Tale of the Circus Tresaulti*, *The Girls at the Kingfisher Club*, *Persona*, and *Icon*. She has written *Catwoman* for DC Comics. Her short stories have appeared in over a dozen Best of the Year anthologies, including *Best American Science Fiction and Fantasy*.

About the Editor

ELLEN DATLOW has been editing science fiction, fantasy, and horror short fiction for forty years as fiction editor of *OMNI Magazine* and editor of *Event Horizon* and SCIFICTION. She currently acquires short stories and novellas for Tor.com. In addition, she has edited about one hundred science fiction, fantasy, and horror anthologies, including the annual *The Best Horror of the Year* series, *The Doll Collection*, *Mad Hatters and March Hares*, *The Devil and the Deep: Horror Stories of the Sea*, *Echoes: The Saga Anthology of Ghost Stories*, *Edited By*, and *Final Cuts: New Tales of Hollywood Horror and Other Spectacles*.

She's won multiple World Fantasy Awards, Locus Awards, Hugo Awards, Bram Stoker Awards, International Horror Guild Awards, Shirley Jackson Awards, and the 2012 Il Posto Nero Black Spot Award for Excellence as Best Foreign Editor. Datlow was named recipient of the 2007 Karl Edward Wagner Award, given at the British Fantasy Convention for "outstanding contribution to the genre," was honored with the Life Achievement Award by the Horror Writers Association, in acknowledgment of superior achievement over an entire career, and was honored with the World Fantasy Life Achievement Award at the 2014 World Fantasy Convention.

She lives in New York and co-hosts the monthly Fantastic Fiction Reading Series at KGB Bar. More information can be found at datlow.com, on Facebook, and on twitter as @ EllenDatlow. She's owned by two cats.

ALSO EDITED BY ELLEN DATLOW